Vaudeville!

Gaétan Soucy

Vaudeville!

Translated by Sheila Fischman

ANANSI

First published as *Music-Hall!* in 2002 by Les Éditions du Boréal.
First published in English in hardcover in 2003 by House of Anansi Press Inc.
Published in paperback in 2004 by House of Anansi Press Inc.

This edition published in 2007 by House of Anansi Press Inc.
110 Spadina Avenue, Suite 801, Toronto, ON, M5V 2K4
Tel. 416-363-4343 Fax 416-363-1017 www.anansi.ca

Distributed in Canada by
HarperCollins Canada Ltd.
1995 Markham Road
Scarborough, ON, M1B 5M8
Toll free tel. 1-800-387-0117

Distributed in the United States by
Publishers Group West
1700 Fourth Street
Berkeley, CA 94710
Toll free tel. 1-800-788-3123

House of Anansi Press is committed to protecting our natural environment.
As part of our efforts, this book is printed on paper that contains 100%
post-consumer recycled fibres, is acid-free, and is processed chlorine-free.

11 10 09 08 07   1 2 3 4 5

LIBRARY AND ARCHIVES CANADA CATALOGUING IN PUBLICATION DATA

Soucy, Gaétan, 1958–
[Music-hall! English]
Vaudeville! / Gaétan Soucy ; translated by Sheila Fischman.
Translation of: Music-hall!
ISBN-13: 978-0-88784-782-0
ISBN-10: 0-88784-782-X
I. Fischman, Sheila II. Title. III. Title: Music-hall! English.
PS8587.O913M8713 2007   C843'.54   C2007-903453-5

Library of Congress Control Number: 2007927967

Cover design: Paul Hodgson
Cover illustration: Gérard DuBois
Text design and typesetting: Tannice Goddard

**Canada Council
for the Arts** **Conseil des Arts
du Canada**

ONTARIO ARTS COUNCIL
CONSEIL DES ARTS DE L'ONTARIO

*We acknowledge for their financial support of our publishing program the Canada Council for the Arts,
the Ontario Arts Council, and the Government of Canada through the Book Publishing Industry
Development Program (BPIDP). This book was made possible in part through the Canada Council's
Translation Grants Program.*

Printed and bound in Canada

for Denis Marleau

When I was finally alone, convinced of mediocrity, and when the least opponent was snickering nervously at my out-and-out defeat — when the keenest pain in my soul became something to laugh at — all alone, at the very back of a warehouse, I faced up to the impossible. Could anyone take that victory from me? For that which matters, which lasts, is the child of solitude. The rest is love.

— Rogatien Wondell
from JOURNAL FOR A RESURRECTION OF VINCENT

Joys and Mysteries
of Demolition

Part I

1

IT ALL BEGAN WITH A FALL. While he was crouching down to lace his boots, the young man took a knee between the shoulder-blades. He tumbled to the bottom of the ravine. The hole, some fifteen metres deep, filled three blocks' worth of space. The lad found himself in a mud puddle, rolled up like a carpet, the breath flattened out of him. The worker who had dealt the blow stood at the edge of the precipice. One of his workmates congratulated him, patting him on the back. Both were laughing. That was a good one, that fall. The lad wanted to send them a sign, tell them he thought it was a good one too. But he couldn't get back on his feet. We're in New York, late 1920s, on a demolition site. The lad was a brand-new immigrant. Or so he claimed. He went by the name Xavier X. Mortanse.

The work that day was being done under difficult conditions. The authorities had condemned a double fourplex, under the pretext of a threat to public safety. There was a whiff of speculation, though, and rumours were briskly making the rounds. The powerful Order of Demolishers was being accused of sabotage: building fronts had caved in, staircases collapsed, in what you might say was the nick of time. Lives had been lost. Resistance pamphlets were being surreptitiously circulated. "Hovels are being mowed down to make way for ornamented buildings to accommodate the rich, whose offices control the money in the four corners of the world." So forth. Former residents, now destitute, prowled the site in hostile little groups. Sometimes an insult would suddenly burst out, for no reason — like you hear in an insane asylum. The workers would go on whistling while they worked. Their hearts in the right place. They'd seen it before.

On the crew that had recently taken him on as apprentice, Xavier X. Mortanse sometimes wondered in what way the constant humiliations he suffered would contribute to his training as a demolisher. He had good reason to wonder. He was not from this country, but still: half the journeymen had first seen the light of day somewhere else. It might be because, with his bulk, that of a slender scallion, he was rejected instinctively by these massive men built like pianos. In any case, his youth, his candour, his comical accent and fanciful syntax, his face like a Pierrot fallen from the moon, seemed irresistible to their jibes and blows. They accused him of sins he hadn't committed. With no regard for his strength, they forced him to carry the heaviest tools. Two days earlier, some joker had poured into his bowl a sleeping concoction that had left him feeling so washed out that Xavier was surprised he was still alive, given that he'd nearly broken his bones he didn't know how many times that afternoon when he was completely limp. The apprentice accepted it all. "It's the know-how sinking in," he wrote to his sister. He tried to laugh along with the journeymen when they said that if ever they were short of provisions, they wouldn't have to draw lots to decide who'd be eaten.

The apprentice struggled to his feet. At the same moment, against the light and in fascinating slow motion, an eight-ton steel ball traced a sweeping parabola, then crashed into a five-storey façade that collapsed like a house of ash. A horde of pale birds, spinning, panicking, splashed up from the cornices that gave way, and the black mash of plaster and dust sank into the hole. It swept into Xavier's lungs. He coughed, spat a blackish gastrorrhea. Then, as the smoke dispersed, he spied the object that his head had struck. Had it not been for his hard hat (pink, as is customary for an apprentice, and bearing the effigy of an apple-green baby chick), he'd have cracked his head on it. That sort of thing forges ties, and he wanted to get acquainted. It was a polished wooden case, about the size of a shoebox. A sort of casket, a very pretty one, and touching and astonishing in the midst of all this rubble, with a tiny key inserted in its gilded lock. Xavier made sure that no one was watching him, then picked it up. That no one was watching him because the week before, meaning no harm, he had simply pocketed a rusty spoon, and then the foreman had butted him in the rear, because regulations were no laughing matter, if there was one thing he'd learned, it was that. Anything found on a destruction site belonged automatically to the Order of Demolishers, which was something not likely to leave his skull.

So he put the thing back where he'd found it, pronto. A series of panting, panicky thumps came from inside. Xavier felt sweat pouring around his neck. Someone buried by mistake would pound the walls of a coffin with the same frenzy. Not too sure what he was doing or to what it committed him, the apprentice concealed his discovery under some rubble, then ran to the ladder to exit the hole.

An hour later the noon siren whined and, as always, Xavier felt tears of joy spring to his eyes. He walked past the ravine again. He spied the pile of rubble concealing the casket just as he'd left it. He wore his usual smile, a ticklish puckering of the snout like you might see on a rabbit. Then picked up his lunch pail and joined his crew for a nibble.

The workers were gathered on a small vacant lot adjacent to the big hole. An old girder had been propped against some concrete blocks to make a footbridge. Some demolishers were sitting on it like hens on a perch, lunching. Xavier hesitated for a moment. The workers had stopped stuffing their faces and, while stuffing them, stopped babbling, and looked him up and down unkindly. "If you please . . ." Xavier said. The others exchanged questioning looks, then agreed to clear a space for him, two hands wide. Quite enough for his buttocks, as bulky as a slender scallion.

Xavier opened his lunch pail, actually a former cardboard shoebox transformed by his own devices. The cover was attached to the box by two strings threaded through four tiny holes punched with a nail, a matter of making a practical and convenient flap that opened like the lid of a coffin. First, Xavier extracted a checkered napkin from the box and spread it carefully over his knees, then he moistened each corner with saliva, a small ritual that intrigued more than one of the workers. After that came a blue napkin and, as he did every time, he wondered if it was indeed his sister — his sister whom he'd left behind, over there in his native land, and missed so much and wrote to every night — if it had been she who had embroidered the pretty pink and yellow sheep that adorned this napkin, or who. He tucked it neatly into the collar of his shirt as a bib. The journeymen, biting into oily sausages, pointed to the apprentice and nudged one another, laughing. Xavier merely sat and smiled. Sitting gingerly on his perch, legs seemingly sewn together, he ate his salad without oil or vinegar, without a fork, without anything. A fleshy petal of lettuce, a stick of celery with leaves, half a carrot for the health of his eyes, and a radish as fat as anyone could wish. His absolute rule was to chew every mouthful as many times as there are months in the year, thinking all the while about what he was doing, to keep his jaw from getting carried away. A vegetable is contemplative, not something to be swallowed in haste. One must respect food, which regenerates our flesh and bones, and try to understand its language. Vegetables talk too, in their way, he was firmly convinced. Therefore eating had implications for the mind as much as for the body, like a single solid line. To stuff oneself any old way — especially with meat, as he saw the journeymen do every day — was to risk ending up with bats in one's belfry, becoming a terror-stricken horse.

While he was chewing, he looked around. The scope of the work required half a dozen crews, some sixty workers in all, one of whom was him. The journeymen were scattered in groups across the vacant lot. Around the perimeter, unmoving, impassive, stood the demolished. They were considerably more numerous than the workers, whom they observed wordlessly, as steadily as wolves. A single gaze, dark and unanimous, was in all their eyes. Mounted policemen followed the line of the demolished, hoofs stamping; havoc was feared, on account of the expected funerals. Meanwhile the journeymen were singing songs in demolition jargon, swaggering, indulging in farting competitions. When he'd finished his sandwich, one of them flung the crust at the feet of a demolished, the way you might throw a chunk of fat at a dog. His companions laughed heartily at this insolence — all but the apprentice, who felt no contempt for these people. The demolished didn't deign to look at the remnant of bread at his feet. He stared at the worker without hatred, judging with his eyes. After this affront, however, the circle of the demolished had tightened around the groups of workers, and Xavier felt a contraction in the region around his epigastrium — it always bothered him when he felt anxious, and he had some trouble getting down the last bite. But the centaurs intervened, dispersed the demolished, and nothing more came of it.

And then someone spotted a floating buttock. It was clearing a path for itself through the heads of the demolished, finally emerging from the mass, and that buttock, baby-pink in hue, was actually the bald head of the elderly gentleman known as the Philosopher. The booming laughter, the bawdy songs, the vulgar dances came to a halt, replaced by a modest restraint, so impressive was the old man's mere presence. And Xavier's face lit up like a Chinese lantern.

The friendship that united Xavier and the Philosopher dated from the Affair of the Sneakers. When Xavier, who had just been taken on the day before, showed up at the destruction site his first morning, a foreman indicated that it was absolutely out of the question. Xavier asked, What? And the foreman replied, For the apprentice to work shod in sneakers. He had on a hard hat, didn't he? Well, he had to have the proper footwear too. To which Xavier retorted, Absolutely out of the question. The foreman slipped away, then came back one pair of boots later, hanging from his wrist by strings. He walked up to Xavier, who shrank back into a corner of a wall, completely hemmed in. He would leave, escape, give up his new job, rather than take off his sneakers. That was when the elderly gentleman known as the Philosopher interceded on his behalf for the first time. And negotiated a compromise. Namely, boots were found that were big enough for the apprentice to slip on over his sneakers. When lunchtime arrived, Xavier tore the leaden masses from his feet. He felt as if he were being lifted off the earth. He felt as light as a dragonfly.

Now the Philosopher lifted Xavier's pink hard hat and began to stroke his head with a fatherly hand. To everyone, "Tell me, boys, how are things going today?" and to Xavier alone, asked very quietly, "And you, my boy, are you pleased with how things are going?" He was the most senior man on the destruction site, and there was a good reason why he was called the Philosopher. He was incapable of demolishing until he'd thought it over, it was his obsession. Even so, he spoke very little. What was peculiar about his sentences was that he never finished them. They opened onto chasms. Such as, with a sigh: *weeks and months to build what it takes two days to destroy,* followed by a silence with vast horizons. The journeymen stood there stunned, tried to understand, feeling a vague concern, thinking about their old mothers. Yes, always saying things like that, incomplete and troubling, which disappeared into the sand. And so they called him the Philosopher. The Philosopher of the Sands of Silence.

When the meal was over, the old man took from his pocket a short plaster pipe that gave him a pensive air, in the way that wearing a sombrero will make a man look Mexican. The others would ask him then about his memories, about the Grand Era when demolitions were still done with hammers, and walls were smashed with fists. The journeymen were like children listening to their grandfather. While he spoke, the Philosopher continued to run his fingers through the fine hair of the apprentice. Xavier kept quiet, smiling, ecstatic at the friendship the old man was showing him. Until the Philosopher finally confessed that in spite of everything, he regretted having spent his life in demolition.

"Tell me then, journeyman, why did you persevere in the trade?" someone asked gravely.

The Sands replied that we don't change the way we are, and that, in any case, it was his trade, and that at his age you don't learn a new one.

"But my heart's not in it any more. It's out of my blood, you might say."

And the journeymen, measuring within themselves the extent of the passion that drove them, considered with superstitious respect the man who had been able to tame the fury inside him.

But no one is put on earth to produce unanimity! Take the arrival of Bernie Morlay, flanked by his two assistants. He was the dynamite expert, feared as much for his sarcasm as for the magical power of his sticks. Aware to the point of smugness that he represented the future of the Trade, that he belonged to the rising wing of the Order, he held in low esteem the golden age of handmade demolition, of barefisted hand-to-hand combat with brick — all the folklore about the Grand Era, the era of Barthakoste, Scafarlati, and their like, whom he called contemptuously "barn wreckers." He had made the Philosopher his whipping boy. He considered him to be a shirker and a drivelling old fool. With no other greeting, he addressed him directly:

"So, you pathetic old nut, I hear you're writing a book?"

There was, in fact, a rumour going around that, come evening, the Philosopher confided to paper the fruit of his long years of rumination. The old man neither confirmed nor denied. He kept the mystery alive.

Morlay's elbow was resting on the girder where the crew was perched. Casually he bit into a raw onion.

"If that's so, maybe you oughtta read one first!"

Making his two assistants guffaw. Everyone was waiting for a reply from the Philosopher that would shut him up. Instead they watched the old man submit, his eyes misting over. Xavier put one hand on his shoulder. The Philosopher gave him only a quick glance filled with emotion and guilt, like a child who has just been scolded. The journeymen scattered, embarrassed. The dynamite expert kept laughing. The sound of a tolling bell moved through the air, wearing seven-league boots.

2

THE STAIRCASE — WHOSE COLLAPSE, rumour had it, was due to sabotage by the Order of Demolishers — had taken as it fell a little girl of seven, child of the destitute. Which wasn't going to settle matters between the inhabitants and the New York authorities. The little girl had survived for a week and a half, suffering with all her broken bones. The demolition decree had been signed three days before her death, in a haste that was one more slap in the face to the future demolished. Who had decided, in silent protest and with a spurt of dignity, to hold the little girl's funeral in the chapel at the end of the street. And that the funeral cortège would make its way across the demolition site.

Most of the demolished were lined up on either side of the street as a guard of honour for the dead child. Others, younger, bolder, and more rebellious, were perched on rooftops, cornices, streetlamps, and posts. From there, they looked down on the group of workers who had gathered in the middle of the vacant lot. The workers were exposed. No roofs, no walls, nothing to give them shelter.

Meanwhile Xavier was still on the girder. He would have liked to join the other workers, to be one with them at this time of danger. But the Philosopher had told him gently, "Don't get mixed up in this, my boy," and then had gone away, seeming preoccupied. The only halfwit who stood near the apprentice, aloofly following the scene, was the dynamite expert, who went on munching his raw onion. For several minutes all that could be heard was the tolling bell, conscientious and haunting, accentuating the silence, and the thud of hoofs on cobblestones. Xavier was keeping an eye on the centaurs, who were making imperious gestures at the demolished perched here and there, but the young people only jeered at them and waved insolently. As for the other demolished lining the street, there was nothing the police could do. No law forbade citizens, even the demolished, to honour a funeral procession.

The procession finally started moving. It went slowly up the street towards the destruction site. Accompanying it was a makeshift band consisting of Breton bagpipes, tuba, Jewish violin, nail box, and bandoneon. A tune so slow and wheezy it made you want to hang yourself. Xavier came down from his girder and drew closer, fascinated. The demolished doffed their hats as the coffin went by, crossed themselves, genuflected, the usual. A priest had a cross in his hands and a beret on his head, Italian-style. The procession itself was thinly populated, made up of the child's immediate family. Two men in gaiters, clad in roughly matching rusty clothes, carried on their shoulders the small box of polished wood, perfectly simple and unadorned but attractive nonetheless, like a doll's shoe, intimidated, almost, at being the focus of everyone's attention.

Suddenly Xavier, who was present from afar, felt himself being grabbed from behind, then lifted off the ground. It was the dynamiter and his two acolytes, who, in their version of humour, intended to hoist him onto their shoulders and take a few steps in rhythm with the marching band of the dead. Extremely embarrassed, Xavier asked them to stop please, which eventually they did, snickering.

The cortège arrived at the demolishers. There was still a dense group of them in the middle of the vacant lot. A hail of gravel pelted down on them, flung from their perches by the demolished, whose pockets were full. Indignant boos rose from the workers, who dared not protest, however, and who were more and more overwhelmed by fear. A new deluge of pebbles. This time, one of the aspiring dynamiters picked up a clod of dried earth and aimed it at one of the young demolished, who was teasing the workers from the top of his post. The boy dodged the projectile and it crashed onto the coffin, spattering the priest behind it, who started to cough at the top of his lungs. The cortège came to a halt, the music stopped. There was a moment of consternation. No one knew from which side objects were going to fall. The centaurs were going in circles. A few journeymen started picking up stones, aiming some at the demolished on their perches, but the authoritarian Philosopher cried out, "No! Not that!" Finally a voice rose up from the cortège, a woman's voice, flinging a child's name into the sky: "Ariane! . . . ," and that helpless appeal, that cry of utter desolation, restored calm and silence and respect, all at once.

The demolished disappeared from their perches, slipped through the crowd, and vanished from sight. And the cortège started up again, with the heavy tread of a descent into a mine. The music started up as well, hesitantly, but the notes fell to the ground one by one, like asphyxiated sparrows, and at the end of the day only the bandoneon persisted, briefly, sounding like a harmonica in the mouth of a dying consumptive, and finally, it too fell silent. Then the cortège disappeared onto the side street, followed by a long trail of demolished. All that remained was the overheated midday summer air, shuddering like a sheet of tin.

But they did have to go back to work. The centaurs told the foremen, "Have no fear, we'll find them for you," implying wreakers of havoc and hurlers of stones. All these adventures had deprived the workers of their noonday naps, and no one was happy. Several had been scared to death and couldn't suppress the signs. There was a sense of discomfort among the crews. Some, to regain their courage, struck up the demolition hymn, all barking and throat-clearing; just hearing it, you could tell that it wasn't music to pick strawberries by. Here and there, bare-chested journeymen, knees to the ground, performed ablutions of dust while muttering formulas intended to chase the blues away.

Xavier was wandering across the destruction site. For the time being, he hadn't been assigned a task. He wasn't really shunning the foremen but neither did he run to meet them. The prevailing frustration and undigested shame on the site just then made him reluctant to draw too much attention to himself. And Morlay once again grabbed hold of his collar.

"Look down there!" said the dynamiter, his nose pressed against the apprentice's cheek, his breath reeking of onion. Across the site, near the crane, some journeymen had gathered and were valiantly clapping their hands.

"What is it? What are they doing?"

"Come here, I'll show you what kind of man your Philosopher really is, with his fine speeches about remorse."

Morlay put his arm around Xavier's shoulders in a move of apparent camaraderie, but actually he was contracting his biceps, and the apprentice felt his neck held tight in a vise. The explosives expert dragged the apprentice towards the crowd. The scene was unfolding near an old tenement building. It was held together by four planks and three screws, and preparations were underway to haul it down. A group of journeymen surrounded the Philosopher, teasing, scolding, mocking. Xavier wondered how they could treat a man that way, especially one for whom all the workers had such respect. Apparently it was to have a laugh. They told him, "Go, go!" they riled him, called him "old goat." If he tried to run away they caught him, surrounded him, and the old man, who thought there was nothing funny about it and who seemed to be getting tense, clenching and unclenching his fists like a man under threat, repeated: "Let me through, I'm not lending myself to this childishness any more! I told you, it's left my blood. Let me go!" But they pushed him back to the centre of the circle.

"What are they up to?" asked Xavier.

The dynamiter told him to wait a while, that he'd see what he would see.

The journeymen started a dance, which consisted of smacking yourself on the ankle, then clapping your neighbour's hand, moving faster and faster, letting out shriller and shriller cries. Xavier expected the foremen would want to put an end to this grotesque game, but they were playing too, slapping their ankles, hitting their neighbour's hand, all that (a strange sight). As the rhythm accelerated, the Sands of Silence underwent an odd transformation. Saliva filled his mouth and poured from his lips. He began making muffled grunts while something inside him still resisted, then shook his head, said no, desperately.

Soon, however, the rhythm grew frenzied, the cries unbearable, enough to make splinters of your head. And the Philosopher was nothing more than an amazing beast who aligned himself with a taurine instinct on the doorstep of the tenement building. And now, suddenly, he was leaping, rushing, running, so hard and so powerfully that it was like sledgehammer blows to the earth. He thrust his head inside the front door, which exploded off its hinges. Just then a panic-stricken woman was seen rushing out of the building, holding her baby with one hand and, with the other, pushing a carriage crammed full of sundry objects.

The Philosopher staggered back, wild-eyed, to the applause and laughter of his workmates. Half-stunned, he placed one knee on the ground. His forehead was covered with blood and he spat between his teeth like a man cursing himself. And, at once, the journeymen got to work with fierce joy.

"And that's not all," said Morlay, moving away. "This is the house where the staircase collapsed, with the little girl inside. In your opinion, young Xavier, did the Philosopher know or didn't he?"

The apprentice's heart was swollen with pity as he walked over to the Sands, who went on swearing between his teeth. But when Xavier tried to help him up, the old man sent him packing with one brutal movement of his arm.

3

FINALLY, XAVIER'S ASSIGNMENT FOR the whole afternoon was to haul salvageable hollow bricks to the bottom of the hole. In truth, it didn't matter that they were hollow. He must have transported at least sixty, sometimes over distances of a hundred and thirty paces in all. By the six-o'clock siren, he could have scratched his leg without bending over. He was coughing, dripping wet, his ribs and shoulders as if bludgeoned.

Tools were gathered up, the journeymen were beginning to desert the site, while Xavier was so limp that he pushed his slanting torso ahead of him as if there were a plumb line at the tip of his nose. When he returned his regulation boots to the foreman, half-stunned with fatigue and unable to do anything about it, his forehead slumped onto his superior's shoulder as if to sleep. The man didn't don kid gloves to send the lad packing. When Xavier got to his feet — the smack had been a hard one — the foreman advised him to screw off, and flung a total of one dollar and thirty-two cents at the apprentice's shoes. As wages for that afternoon's devotion to the cause of the hollow bricks.

Xavier sat in the midst of the piles, daughters of his deeds, and in order to breathe more easily he loosened the plankets of his devising, just this once wouldn't hurt. His head was empty, his body like a wet rag, but he had to stay alert so that he could react to the slightest noise, and hide if need be. He tried to keep sleep at bay by dozing spasmodically, one zzz at a time. For him, falling asleep was tantamount to putting one foot in the grave. To be walking and suddenly feel himself falling, engulfed by a trap he could never get out of. Even at night, he approached sleep only with apprehension and furrowed brow, and he had to make several attempts before he could sleep a natural death; on a number of earlier occasions he'd wakened with a start and frightened groans, his chest as if some big animal were about to sit on it.

But the day had been so rough from every point of view that, sitting in the midst of the bricks, he finally and inevitably foundered, and it was total eclipse. When he regained consciousness, the site was deserted and the sky was beginning to tilt. He was surprised that no journeyman had come during his nap to boot him in the ribs while ordering him to beat it, since being on the site after working hours was an infraction equivalent to attempted robbery.

Xavier got up, still exhausted, of course, but his head was back on the job. He mulled over the day's events and tried to sort through them, to determine what procedure to follow. First he tried to orient himself. Which wasn't easy, it was dusk, he was at the bottom of a hole, far from any streetlamp, and the buildings that could have helped him get his bearings had been demolished that morning. Only the ladders remained. He remembered concealing the casket under a pile of rubble a few metres from a ladder. He set out to look for it, walking warily in the faint light, over ground strewn with various kinds of debris. More than anything he feared rusty nails, which locked your jaws before the words were out of your mouth.

"Xavier? What are you doing there?"

A few steps away, Xavier could make out the Philosopher, who seemed as surprised, embarrassed, and uncomfortable as the apprentice at being caught in that place at that hour. The elder's bare skull was turbaned in gauze, like a hammered thumb. All that stuck out was the curtain of white hair that originated on the back of his head at ear-level, then fell halfway down his spine.

"I . . . You see, I fell asleep," said Xavier at last, glad to begin with a truth that was not entirely a lie. He paused, then, "What about you?"

"Me, I, well, um, not at all, I mean, um . . ."

Someone else was there. A squat silhouette, carrying a lamp and pulling a little wagon.

"Ah, that's my old lady," the Philosopher hastened to explain. "You see, my boy, we were in the neighbourhood and I said, I said to my wife and myself, 'What if someone's forgotten something on the site? Let's go and have a look.' You see, and then sometimes we go to make sure there aren't any dangerous objects, you see, glass, or rusty metal, you see, that a journeyman, or an apprentice like you, could get hurt on. I do that sometimes, my wife and I, when we've got the time."

The old man broke off, doubting that he'd convinced Xavier, but the apprentice accepted with unwavering faith what the Philosopher had told him. Of course he was only half-listening. The elder, a question of changing the subject, began again:

"I apologize for this afternoon." He pointed to his bandaged brow. "I don't know what happened, a relapse, I suppose. And then I was a little short with you, I mean when you tried to help me get up . . . I beg forgiveness."

Xavier gestured vaguely and distractedly, "No, really, it's nothing." And surreptitiously, anxiously, he eyed the ladders.

The silhouette with the lamp came closer. The woman must have been around sixty. Solid-looking, short legs, no ankles, hardly any feet, baby elephant model. From all her pores she exuded someone who'll live to one hundred and three. The Philosopher didn't seem thrilled when she joined them. He showed signs of irritation.

She looked at Xavier first, suspiciously. When her husband said, "He's Xavier, the apprentice I've talked about so much," no doubt hoping to steer the conversation in that direction, she merely gave a brief nod in the young man's direction. Then, moving on, as if the apprentice no longer existed, she said to her husband:

"Here, this is all I could find."

For a moment Xavier's epigastrium was in a knot, as he thought about his casket. But the object she took from her wagon looked nothing like it. It was twisted pipes that she called brass, a musical instrument, or something, and the Philosopher quickly stuffed the thing back in the wagon. He said, "We'll give it to the foreman tomorrow." His wife gave him a look. He gave her one too, as if to say, that's obvious, and once again said that they'd give it to the foreman tomorrow, as usual, for the benefit of the Order, while his wife, still not understanding, asked him why they should give it to the foreman tomorrow for the benefit of the Order, and the Sands finally became impatient.

"Go, go! I'll catch up with you! Go on, skedaddle!"

The woman went away, muttering that her old man was going off the rails.

"Pay no attention to her. Here, let's walk together for a while. We'll let her get ahead."

Xavier rummaged quickly in his head.

"It's just that I've lost my lunch pail."

There too he was able to lie while telling the truth; the funeral procession, the dynamiter's harassment, all that had made him lose his lunch pail and everything in it — checkered napkin, embroidered bib, radish and lettuce all that (and oh, heck).

"And you want to find it before you go home?"

Xavier wouldn't commit himself. The other man could think whatever he wanted about it. As for him, it was not, strictly speaking, a lie.

The Philosopher's wife had come to a halt some twenty paces ahead. She held the lamp above her head to ask her husband: now what?

"Coming!" cried the old man. Then to Xavier: "Watch out, my boy." The place wasn't very safe. At night, rats emerged from the broken pipes. Besides, the neighbourhood was infested with the demolished. If they landed on you in your demolisher's uniform, you see . . . It's just what those people want.

"Don't worry about me," said Xavier, who was becoming anxious for the old man to make himself scarce. He added that he had friends in the neighbourhood too, in case of trouble, just friends, that is, acquaintances actually, which was a bald-faced lie.

At these words the Philosopher thought he'd grasped the

reasons for the boy's ambiguous behaviour. His face darkened. He placed his hand on Xavier's shoulder and raised a paternal forefinger. The tip of that finger under his nose crossed the apprentice's eyes.

"Watch out for the ladies, my friend. Get into that and you end up in the gutter with rotten teeth, lips like sausages, and sickness in your lungs. I know whereof I speak, I was once your age too and I nearly stayed there. Promise you'll be careful?"

"I promise, Mister Leopold."

The Philosopher nodded slowly as he looked Xavier smack in the eyes.

"I promise," repeated Xavier, who wasn't entirely clear as to what the old man was talking about.

The elder hesitated again. Xavier shifted his weight from one foot to the other, impatiently.

"Another thing. No need to tell the journeymen tomorrow that I came by the site to clean up the objects that, you might say, could hurt somebody, you see. It's . . . It's better, you see, when good deeds stay in the shadows. You'll be able to keep the secret, won't you?"

"To the grave," Xavier reassured him.

Finally the man went to join his wife, and they began a lively discussion as they headed for the ladders, whispering mutual reproaches.

So. At this point, after making sure the old couple was out of sight, he had to be quick. With almost no daylight, it was Xavier's turn to hurry towards the ladders. Walking hastily, because all this business about rats and prowlers had knotted his epigastrium.

But at last he was there, with the little mound of rubble

at his feet, phew. He brushed it away, caused the casket to emerge. He blew off the excess dust, studying it, admiring it as much as he could in the dying light. He shook it — gently, out of concern for what might be inside, which could be fragile.

Or alive. Xavier remembered the pounding from inside. Could be that he'd been hearing things. Could be that a slight imbalance might have shifted what was in it, and falsely led the apprentice to think the pounding was being done by a living being. Possibly. And at that very moment, as if it were reading his mind, the thing inside started pounding on the walls.

Xavier quickly set the casket on the ground, as if it were suddenly blazing hot. Waited. Then brought a trembling hand to the key, which was still in the lock. But something occurred to him, made him stop. What if it was a rat? . . . The abandoned casket lies at the bottom of a wide-open hole, a rat gets inside, accidentally closes the lid, and the critter is imprisoned . . . And if that's the case, imagine its state of mind! Xavier sees himself being bitten on the throat, his jugular sliced open by an incisor while the rat polished off his cheek.

Unless he took the casket home with him, along with what was inside it, and took suitable measures when he got there, the most security-conscious possible, for instance, wrap an eiderdown around his neck, tie a pillow around his head, equip himself with a screwdriver, but that would be even worse because he could already see the rat escaping with one leap and edging its way into some nook or cranny of his cubicle, where Xavier would never again be allowed to live, because he'd be living with the constant fear and panic of seeing the critter loom from its hiding place! . . .

Xavier was about to leave, give up, too bad, it was too risky, when the pounding inside the casket started up again — but this time very softly, subtly, with an intelligent nuance.

The apprentice bit his lips, wrung his hands, and finally, with a snap, turned the key. Light shot out of the casket and Xavier was flung backwards as if he'd been shoved.

And he gawked, mouth open, eyes like slices of sausage. A frog was sitting there, legs elegantly crossed, tailcoat and opera hat askew, a cane with knob flung casually over a slender shoulder.

> *You'll*
> *know*
> *that*
> *I'm the girl of your dreams . . .*

It started singing, languorously, each phrase clearly standing out, and dancing too, staring at the apprentice with eyes that could light a fire in your pants. Xavier shook his head, no, no, gripped by a fear that was close to terror. The act went on for a good five minutes. Following which the frog took a bow, got back in the box, even pulled down the lid, clack.

After a long moment of stillness, Xavier took off his apprentice's hard hat, spat into it, put it back on his skull, well aware that doing so made no sense at all, but also that he couldn't help doing it either. He grabbed the box and sped towards the ladders, couldn't find them, too dark at the bottom of the hole, but was so distraught and panicky that he scaled the wall of the precipice and managed to hoist himself to street level. Once there, didn't know which way to turn. Didn't know where he was, whether he had a home or, if so, where. Had an urge to lift the casket above his head, hurl it to the bottom of the ravine and then run to the port, hop on a boat, any boat, stowaway if necessary, as long as the boat was going far, far away from this land of America, this hell capable of all manner of wonders.

He heard himself call out. Looked around him, crazed, thought of nothing but flight. But already the tumbrel was before him, barring the way.

4

IT WAS BEING PULLED BY A MAN bent double with the effort. Xavier was afraid it was a gang of raiders, demolition victims turned into hardened criminals. But a woman was following, a baby at her bosom and a little boy of six or seven clinging to her skirts. They didn't look particularly vicious. The tumbrel was overflowing like a garbage can. Chairs, mattresses, furniture held together with ropes, in precarious equilibrium. Xavier recognized the woman. She was the one who had noisily burst out of her dwelling when the Sands had butted the door in.

And said the man to his wife, jerking the tip of his nose in Xavier's direction:

"See, Maria, those people aren't satisfied with demolishing our houses, they have to come back and loot us."

Xavier made a motion of denial.

The man put down the shafts of his tumbrel and made his way to Xavier, who stepped back.

"What are you doing around here? Eh? Come on, talk!"

"Please, Giorgio, can't you see it's a child," said Maria, in a gentle voice that touched the boy's heart.

Giorgio studied Xavier from head to toe: skinny, long, shaking with fatigue and fear.

"So, you're a demolisher, are you?" asked the man, less abruptly than before. "You don't look like one."

"An apprentice, Mister. Just an apprentice."

The man seemed intrigued by something other than Xavier.

"How old would you be now? Seventeen, eighteen?"

Xavier did not reply. The man repeated his question, and again Xavier offered not one syllable. Finally he said:

"Apprentice, Mister. Not a full-fledged journeyman."

"Yes, I know. Your hard hat's pink."

Giorgio thought for a few moments.

"And that accent you've got . . . You been in America long?"

"I don't know, Mister. Two months and a half, maybe. Less. I don't know."

"You don't know?"

"I don't know."

"And you want to become a journeyman?"

The apprentice merely fluttered his eyelashes, which were long and curved, a fact that struck him whenever he encountered his face in a looking glass. He shifted his weight from his right foot to his left.

"And what have you got there, would you mind telling me?"

And Giorgio held out his hand. Xavier half-turned his back to protect the casket. He groped around in his box of lies, quick quick.

"It's a present from my sister, she stayed behind, it's to put my lunch in."

Then the toddler clinging to his mother's skirts asked if there was a rat in the box, because, according to a legend making the rounds of the children of the demolished, the journeymen of the Order fed themselves on bats and rats, and sometimes, when Xavier was on his way home after work, the children pestered him by repeating those horror stories.

Maria reassured her child.

"So what were you looking for in the hole at this time of day?" Giorgio went on, his inquisition not yet over.

But once again Xavier abstained from providing a response. He only assured the man that he hadn't stolen his casket, which did not, he swore, contain rats, and Giorgio realized that if this went on the boy was going to cry. The man seemed ill at ease and looked away. Maria asked the apprentice his name. And receiving no reply:

"You must have a name, what do people call you?"

Her voice was so solicitous that the apprentice spoke freely.

"Xavier, that's what they call me."

And saying that, he looked instinctively at his left wrist. Which Giorgio noticed. Without being rough, he grabbed hold of the boy's forearm. Asked why the devil the name XAVIER was inscribed on his left wrist in indelible ink. Again the young man made no reply. He withdrew his hand and hid it behind his back. He was beginning to sniffle, so Maria questioned him even more solicitously.

"What country are you from? Where did you live before you were here in America? You said you have a sister who stayed behind. Where is that?"

"I'm a Hungarian immigrant," said Xavier finally, hesitantly, like a pupil unsure of his answer.

Giorgio's eyebrows became circumflex accents. He looked questioningly at his wife, who shrugged, perplexed.

Giorgio cleared his throat.

"You say you're called Xavier, and you come from Hungary?"

Xavier fluttered his eyelashes again and, reflexively, looked at his wrist once more, immediately raising a blush, since it looked as if he wanted to make certain it was indeed his name. Then came the sound of a creaking wheel, and a man appeared, hunched over his bike, carrying on his back an old woman whose arms were tight around his neck, dressed in a multitude of shawls that floated in the wind. When it came level with them, the bicycle slowed down a little and the cyclist, teeth clenching a stogie, nodded briefly at Giorgio before continuing on his way. They watched him go, in silence, until the strangely hitched pair had disappeared at the end of the road.

Xavier started to panic; the toddler burrowed deeper into his mother's skirts, with cries of terror.

"What's going on there?" asked Giorgio, close to panic himself.

The frog was moving around in its casket with a frenzy that made you think of castanets.

"Are you or aren't you going to tell me what's in that box!"

And the child wailed, "It's a rat! He hid a rat in his box!" Xavier's skull was about to burst. He broke into a run.

"No! Wait!" shouted Giorgio. "We don't want to hurt you. There are lots of things I'd like to talk to you about! Xavier!"

But he was already far away, panting, aching, because running had given him a stitch in his heart and now he was trying to walk as fast as he could, despite his limping because of the stitch, actually. He got to the bottom of the street and felt even more trapped. That was where the chapel was, and the demolished had assembled there by the dozen, on the lawn, on the steps, inside. And here was Xavier, wearing his demolition duds! Three or four police cars were parked across the street. Some of the demolished were pointing to the steeple and crying, in voices filled with doom, "ASYLUM! . . . ASYLUM!" The officers answered them with disdainful sneers; they'd nab them eventually. With nightfall the heat of the day had dropped. It was even chilly, and there were campfires here and there, where beets and potatoes were cooking. People were grouped around them: men repairing shoes; women nursing infants; men with beards and spectacles, tattered and scrawny, waving sticks and talking politics, their fingers yellow from tobacco; old men so weak in the head that they waved to the policemen, smiling like babies; and the destitute of every sort, busy at the tasks of the poor — mending, tightening, joining, stitching; and all around were the sick and the sickly lying on hard-luck beds near tumbrels that looked like the twin sisters of Maria and Giorgio's.

Xavier hoped that he could stay incognito and cross the square without stopping, but he couldn't help himself, his legs stood still all by themselves when he came to the chapel. Inside, fires had been lit. Women were kneeling in prayer, curled up inside their pink shawls, they looked like the shrimp the Philosopher adored, which he shelled with his fat horny fingers at mealtime. Light from the embers filled the chapel with magnificent colours warm like blood, you'd have thought the disembowelled carcass of a horse hung by its forelegs from meathooks. Close to Xavier, a woman with hazel eyes was speaking to her child, her voice so gentle that Xavier wished he were that child. When she smiled you could see that she was missing some teeth, like a comb. Xavier couldn't take his eyes off her. Her blue surplice was pulled up over her hair, she had on a very loose and simple dress that conjured up for the apprentice a picture he'd seen in the Sands' illustrated Bible, which he liked so much the old man had cut it out and given it to him to pin on the wall of his cubicle.

But when she spied Xavier, the woman's face suddenly changed from ten to zero. She began to whistle between her teeth, indicating with broad pleading gestures that he should make tracks, on the double — he and his demolisher's duds. Which alerted others. And soon there were half a dozen hounding the young apprentice with their whistles, while he limped along because of the stitch still in his heart. They accompanied him to the alley, where Xavier, alone at last, eyes full of tears, slumped at the base of a wall and let out a cry to heaven, a cry that was a woman's name.

He stayed there, bewildered, eyelids flickering, stunned at himself. Because the name he'd just called out was the name Justine, and he realized that was his sister's name, his sister who'd stayed behind, to whom he wrote every night, whose name he had tried to recall for weeks, in vain.

5

XAVIER WALKED ALONG, glancing back like a hunted animal, protecting his phenomenal casket with both hands. When he crossed the main thoroughfares, he nearly caused disasters. A policeman called to him but, as it happened the light was turning green, and he disappeared into a stream of pedestrians. He bumped into them without realizing. He was taking such peculiar measures to go unnoticed — putting on airs, hugging the walls, drawing his head into his collar — that he achieved exactly the opposite.

But one thing was guaranteed: even on an unfamiliar street, he had only to lend an ear to the sound resonating inside his skull and he could find his way to his dwelling. Maybe the piece of magnet that he'd hung from string above his pillow was the reason. The sound was like a bell: when he went in the wrong direction it diminished, and it increased when he went in a direction that brought him near his cubicle. It was very practical, because the Philosopher had given him a map of the city and Xavier had nearly gone a little bit crazy trying to decipher just one corner of it. Once he'd reached his destination — namely, the building where he resided — the sound would disappear, mission accomplished. "I've got the brain of a bird," he said. "No need for a compass." Apart from this connection with his cubicle, the sound was of no help whatever. Disoriented everywhere else. No longer knew left or right. Not the sound of a bell, to tell the truth, but the echo that stays behind once the clapper has struck.

He turned onto the avenue where he lived, in the factory district. The trucks were parked, the sheds closed, the streetlamps gave off a glaucous light. All the same, Xavier detoured via the alley, to avoid walking past the Chess Club. It was a café, he'd been wrong to stop there one evening before on his way home from work. First he had lingered at the window, because the light emanating from it was yellow and warm. Two men were standing at the front window, as motionless as store dummies, over the sixty-four squares. Xavier didn't remember having ever learned the game, but it was obvious to him right away — the rules, the moves, castling, and the take en passant, it was as if this game had been flowing in his veins since the beginning of time. And to see the moves these players executed brought his epigastrium to his throat, because they so obviously shouldn't be made, in the interest of common sense. The bearded man in particular seemed to be making them deliberately. He strung together moves he must have thought up when he was first learning. It was the other man who won, by chance, so to speak — a horror, really. Spotting Xavier, the victor waved an invitation to come and play, if he was in the mood. Mortanse hesitated, finally went inside. He beat everyone there hands down, even the most experienced, and until past midnight his table was bathed in respect tinged with awe. He'd finally left, with an urge to vomit on the squares. All night long he kept playing in his head. If he tried closing his eyes it was worse, and a hundred and ten possible games scrolled before him, as if on a screen. By dawn he had fainted, and he got to work three-quarters of an hour late. He had written to his sister Justine, "Nothing is more dangerous to my mind than that game, if that's what it is. It's a thinking trap and once the soul is inside it, it's imprisoned, can't leave, panics in vain." He had promised himself that never again would he fall into that trap.

His detour through the alleys forced him to cross the yard behind the abattoir that provided meat for salting in the French way at Salaison Supreme, which lacked a circumflex. Fortunately, no animals' throats were slit there at night. A poster looked down on the carriage entrance, depicting a moustachioed man with knife in hand and crimson-stained apron; above him, on a ribbon carried by piglet-faced cherubs, the company motto, written in Latin, said "For Christians, extreme unction, for the devil's creatures, supreme salt." The asphalt in the yard was sticky with curdled blood and the soles of his sneakers squeaked when he walked in it. The background smell matched.

Xavier came at last to the tenement building. What time could it be? He headed for the elevator cage, which was, as usual, *sorry* to be *out of order*, as the placard said, and he had to go up on foot to his eighth-floor cubicle, arriving there half-dead. In the hallway only one night-light shone. He groped for his door but was no longer on sound footing, and had to support himself on the walls. All at once there was a presence at his side, a shadow, a climate, not even ten thumb-lengths from his heart. He recognized this presence from the coruscant blackness of the hair, from the woman-smell too. Later he would tremble when he wrote that name in letters to his sister. Miss Ohara. Peggy Sue Ohara.

She was twenty-two years old, and she impressed Xavier because of what she knew from having lived so much. And she could do incredible things with her hair. Every day it wasn't the same. She was a hairdresser, incidentally. Some evenings, to make a little extra and because she loved them, she sold books in a second-hand bookstore (so she said). She always wanted him to call her Peggy, just Peggy. But the apprentice simply couldn't.

She thought Xavier was getting home late and she kindly pointed it out to him. As usual in her presence, Xavier didn't know where to put his hands, his feet, his heart, his knees, his face, all that. "I worked some overtime," he said, which wasn't a very big lie, but he was beginning to think he'd done a lot of lying for one day, and touched his nose to check. Then recognizing the door to his dwelling, he stepped inside without a word. He hoped she would understand by that his wish to be alone. It was cramped, but at least you could be alone with yourself there.

"Hey! What are you doing in my place?" asked Peggy, laughing.

The apprentice squinted, studied the number on the door, then realized that yes. The error seemed to turn him upside down. It was as if exclamation marks were bursting from his skull. Peggy went up to him, and when she put her hand on his shoulder she found him alarmingly thin. His clavicle stretched the skin like a chicken's wishbone. Xavier felt his teeth chattering in his mouth. He was no longer really sure what he was saying, only heard himself speak. He witnessed himself with amazement, voice quavering as if he were being shaken by the shoulders. "He made the door explode by butting it with his skull — there was blood on his forehead — everyone applauded when she ran out — panic — it was in the house where the staircase had collapsed onto Ariane — a rain of steps with a little girl in the middle — and inside the chapel the colours — as if a disembowelled horse were hanging by his forelegs from meathooks."

Peggy Sue touched the young man's forehead, nearly burned her finger, and Xavier — exhausted, every nerve severed — took a nose-dive into her alluring hair, drawn there by the plumb line of his fatigue. Gently, Peggy set his head upright. Told him that she couldn't abandon him in such a state. The apprentice, docile and strained, put up no resistance.

Xavier's cubicle was hardly bigger than a grave, and nearly as empty. A bed, a chair, a table (a board actually, fastened to the wall with screws). A rubber hose emerged from the wall, from which a constant trickle of lifeless water flowed. The sink, tartared with rusty rings, was slightly to the left above the bed. That trickle of water, inexhaustible, tormented the apprentice all night long with an urge to leak. Miss Peggy flipped the switch; the bare bulb filled the room with greasy light.

Xavier advanced with forced little steps, as she guided him. He said things such as "I walked the whole weekend for fifteen days," not understanding what he meant himself, the talking happening inside his mouth, by itself, a regiment of words without head or tail jostling each other between his teeth. Peggy made him lie on a mattress of tired feathers packed into uneven little piles, through which, princess and pea, he could feel the metal of the bedspring. Delicately Peggy removed the casket from his hands. At first he didn't react. But when she started to put it on the table, he straightened up and grabbed it.

"I wasn't going to steal your box," she told him, in the patient and persuasive tone one uses to reason with a sick person. "It belongs to you, Xavier. I don't even care to know what's in it."

"A dead rat," Xavier heard himself say, as if his words were filtered through a dream.

She looked the boy in the eyes, then stared at his hands, which were long, slender, nervous, strong, like violins.

"Why are you looking at my hands?" said Xavier, embarrassed, hiding them behind his back.

"I'm looking at them and thinking, they're so beautiful, there can't be a dead rat in your box."

"I don't see the connection."

She said nothing for a few moments. Then tucked a playful lock of hair behind her tiny ear.

"You must understand, Xavier, you need to rest. You can't hold a box while you sleep. All I want is to put it down somewhere. Here, in the room. Here, where you live. I won't even open it."

Xavier thought it over, then he got up and set the box on the table (actually a board). He came back to the bed, lay down again, arms on either side of his chest. The fever had gone, but his lungs and his throat were glowing embers. He apologized to Miss Ohara. Reassured her, too, such sudden fevers were frequent with him. Nothing to worry about. These fevers could make him say or do things that weren't like him. He asked her forgiveness if he had been mean.

"No, no, Xavier dear, you weren't mean."

She sat on the edge of the bed. Her fingers played with the boy's smooth hair. She blew affectionately on his damp temples to cool them, the way you might blow on a cat's fur. She asked in a murmur why he wouldn't go to see a doctor. But already he was sitting up, ready to run. She calmed him, made him lie down again, gently. She hadn't meant right away, tonight, but some day soon . . . She knew one who was excellent, devoted, honest, Xavier wouldn't even have to budge, the doctor would come here to see him. The apprentice turned his face to the window. He was trying to assess the fall it would represent, if a doctor entered his cubicle by force some morning when he was still in bed; and whether or not he would have time to get to the window and jump . . . Told Peggy, "I'll go and see one myself," which he had no intention of doing.

She kept looking at him with her doe eyes. Xavier wondered if her face was so white because her hair was so black, or the opposite.

"Now, you're going to do me the pleasure of putting your peepers away for the night."

Xavier shook his head listlessly.

"I don't want to sleep right away, I have things to do first."

And over and over, "I don't want to go to sleep, I don't want to go to sleep," more and more feebly, until he was deep in a refreshing oblivion. Peggy tiptoed out. Just as she was about to close the door she turned to the casket, wondering what on earth was inside it. Not out of wanton curiosity but because the boy seemed to attach great significance to it, and because she realized she was sufficiently attached to him to be interested in whatever mattered to him. And that she could have opened the casket without his knowing, because Xavier was fast asleep (snoring softly, not at all vulgar, like a little girl who has played too long in the snow). But she had promised that she wouldn't open it. Life was too short to break promises.

Xavier lay with his left arm along his chest and his right fist over his heart, as if swearing an oath of allegiance. That long, bony, undernourished body, those delicate features, still those of a child, that gravity while he slept, as if what he was doing clashed with what he was. How badly this strange and touching boy rhymed with his life! She looked again at his hands. A pianist's hands, made for tenderness. Hands to bless and to absolve. Not to demolish.

She went out, closing the door soundlessly. Took the flower from her hair and placed it on the threshold, to protect the boy from bad dreams.

XAVIER WOKE UP an hour later, his eyes still filled with his dream. He had dreamed about a river, at night. The sky was the colour of smoke. Scattered limbs, legs and arms that had lost their torsos, were trying to climb up the banks, but journeymen demolishers were pushing them into the black water with shovels, shouting insults. Then he had toppled back to this side of the world, back to his cubicle. He looked around the room, where Miss Ohara no longer was. Then reviewed his dream, as we must do if we want to find its buried messages. But he couldn't take very much from it. He had dreamed about a river; maybe that meant Money . . .

As he sat up on his bed, he realized that he'd fallen asleep without loosening the plankets of his devising. Too bad. The clock in the harbour indicated past eleven. He sat for a moment with elbows on knees, forehead in hands. The memory of his day passed through his mind and he straightened up abruptly. The casket was still there. He went up to it, with a mixture of excitement and anxiety, and turned the key in the lock.

But in the end didn't open it. He felt that in his present state, witnessing a new wonder was liable to drive him around the bend (turn his brain inside out). First, regain calm, follow routine, as if no thread had been broken. So he sat at his table, picked up the basket from the floor and took from it the next day's lunch: three leaves of cabbage, half a carrot, and a square of chocolate the size of his thumb. Those squares of chocolate, incidentally, were a mystery. As well as his sin, for they ran counter to his nutritional principles. He had found about fifteen of them in his pocket on the day he'd suddenly realized that he was on the waterfront of New York, having disembarked from he knew not what ship. He often wondered if it was his sister, his sister, Justine, who'd stayed behind, who had secretly filled his pockets with those succulent and zero-nutrition squares of chocolate. It was just a detail but he thought everything had some importance, if you wanted to make head or tail of it. The slightest thing, and so on, to infinity.

Now it was time to write to his dear sister, who moreover, and strangely, hadn't answered any of his letters yet. He swung into motion, laboriously at first, but soon the words burst out, dazzling, unstoppable, and he wrote them down, as was his habit, on sheets of newspaper rescued from trash cans. Hours and hours. When the frenzy subsided, he saw flies where there were none. Stars, as if minute explosions were glittering around his eyes. The dawn of a new day.

He still had a lot to tell his sister, notably concerning his Plan to Reform the United States of America, which he'd barely had time to outline. What would it be like if one day he took over as head of this country! In the meantime, he had plenty of work to do: prepare his afternoon snack, race to the site, work for ten hours at a stretch, persist or perish, or both at once. Through the window he could see the dull sky. Nothing to stir him to put his heart in his work.

He thought about the day before him. Lazare, the foreman, the terrible Lazare, Lazare, Terror of the Walls, was supposed to be back. And suddenly the casket opened by itself and the top of the frog's head appeared, still wearing the opera hat. The frog winked at Xavier, whose face lit up, like a convalescent when the child he cherishes suddenly appears in his sickroom. Then sprang out of the casket, tracing an elegant parabola in the air, and landed gently on the apprentice's knees, like a snowflake touching down, thanks to the minuscule umbrella that cushioned its fall. "Frog in the morning," Xavier thought, "promise of joy." Now he was no longer alone in America. There was someone for him to love.

Part II

1

Lazare advanced towards the shore of the lake, where a child, shrouded in mist, was floating in a miniature boat, accompanied by a dog twice his size — a strange dog crowned with a sort of tiara, or maybe it was a dunce's cap, a child whose face was infinitely sad and who was gesturing to him, gesturing with his stump because one hand was cut off, and the peninsula resembled a dead animal, bristling with conifers under a smoky sky, losing its balance. Lazare was walking towards the shore with difficulty, his legs felt swaddled, and the child continued to call him silently. Lazare gestured back to the child, as though to say, "Wait! Wait for just a moment!" He unbuttoned his fly and started to relieve himself into the lake. The dog snickered scornfully. Lazare felt a gentle warmth spread to his crotch, his thighs, his buttocks, a warm and gentle sensation of swelling that at first was not unpleasant but before long became anxiety, a panicky anxiety, and realizing what was happening to him he held back with all his might, with his every fibre, but too late. He woke up in a warm, disgusting patch of wet sheets. And with his eyes barely open, a blinding pool of light landed on his face like a sopping rag. The first feeling of his day was an unspeakable horreur de vivre.

His landlady, who had just opened the curtains, was standing at the window lit by the implacable summer sun. Lazare promptly pulled his pillow over his groin. But perhaps the woman had had time to see the soiled sheets. With his hand, he shielded his eyes from the violence of the light.

"Close the curtains, my eyelids are burning!"

"You're the one who asked me to wake you at this hour. You pay before you go."

"Go?"

Lazare couldn't help taking a quick look at the sheets. (But no, nothing showed.)

"I mean before you go to work. Today is Thursday, rent day. I want you to pay this morning so I can do my week's grocery shopping. Don't worry, I'm not throwing you out."

The landlady's greasy jacket was buttoned inside out and backwards, as usual. Bending over to pick up the half-empty bottle of joyjuice that was lying in a messy pile of clothes, she moved her arm to stuff an enormous breast into her bra, the left one, always the left, always popping out of her bra unprovoked and uncontrollable. An ersatz gorilla, plump and beardless, shot into the chamber and onto Lazare's bed, laughing as he drowned him in drool, covered him with stunned and noisy kisses. His floppy ears lashed at Lazare's cheeks like a dog's tail. Lazare struggled, disgusted. Mrs. Ginsburg grabbed her son by the scruff of the neck, not violent but firm, and pulled him off the victim of his affection. The adolescent halfwit clapped his hands and said with remarkable bliss, "'azare, 'azare," while the latter, wiping his spit-wet cheeks, wondered helplessly, wondered for the thousandth time, what could have won him the bubble-head's passionate affection.

"We're waiting breakfast for you," said Mrs. Ginsburg, leading away her son, who was whimpering for "azare, azare," unwilling to leave him.

When Lazare was alone, he jumped out of bed. The room spun around for a few moments, result of the previous night's joyjuice, which once again he had abused. He had a lead cap on and a liver like vinegar jelly. (He had drunk to calm the crisis that he sensed was imminent, that was liable to send him to the Order's clinic again, for weeks.)

He kicked his demolition clothes into a pile to get them closer to the window, so they wouldn't be too near the bed. This hadn't happened for more than a month. Not in all the time he'd been rooming at Mrs. Ginsburg's. He'd thought he was, he'd nearly dared to believe that he was free of that disgrace. Was he going to be forced to move? Ten times in one year he'd had to change boarding houses, betrayed by his "leaky hose." He would depart without warning — at dawn, in the middle of the night — leaving the bed as it was, taking with him nothing but his lucky picture, abandoning clothes, knives, toilet case without further ado, cursing himself, heart swollen with hatred, leaving the sheets stagnating, stinking, wet.

Lazare took off his soaking pyjama bottom and tossed it into the ruined sheets. He pulled on his demolisher's pants but stood with his belly exposed to the air, feet bare, nipples like eyes. He stared at his lucky picture, the only one that adorned his walls, a photograph of the coasts of Baffin Island. Ice floes barely standing out against the grey sky, then a long strip of empty land, with no men, no vegetation, no shadow of anything at all: the only place in the world that he dreamed about, because there was *nothing*. It was the most beautiful image of nothing one could imagine. He'd been dragging it around with him everywhere since he was a child. One day he must go and live there. Set sail on a whaling ship, then desert and somehow manage to live in that emptiness. Since childhood, he had known that his life would end there, that those vast lands of nothingness were waiting for him, a kind of absolute destiny. He postponed his departure from one hunting season to the next. When would he finally make up his mind? He thought about the young woman. Won't leave without her.

He picked up the bottle of joyjuice, dithered over whether or not he was going to; finally took a first sip; then a second, much longer one, which he choked on and brought up nearly half of. The horrible liquid slid from side to side in his mouth. He got his breath back, his throat on fire. Poured what was left of the alcohol onto the bed, added a fair amount of lighter fluid, assured himself that his belongings were far enough away, then dropped a burning wad of newspaper onto the sheets. He went out the door that opened onto the inside courtyard. Nervously lit a cigarette, swaying his shoulders, working the muscles in his back, watchful, kicking his soccer ball against the wall. Eventually he heard a loud whooosshh and the fire had caught, with black smoke and wild flames. No more than five seconds later the terrified howls of Mrs. Ginsburg. Her older son, age fifteen, rushed up with a pan full of soapy water, the dishpan, and hurled the contents onto the mattress with a crashing and banging of broken plates and glasses. The younger son, equipped with a heavy blanket, rushed at the last flames to smother them. But the youngest had witnessed everything, all wailing and flapping ears. Stoically, Lazare went back to the little room.

They all caught their breath, relieved. Then the landlady blew up.

"You are completely out of your mind!"

"It wasn't me, I swear," said Lazare calmly.

The young demolisher gazed at his stricken bed. The result was satisfactory. No one could have known that someone had had an accident in these blackened sheets covered with burn-holes. Languidly, Lazare started getting into his work clothes.

"It didn't catch fire by itself!" the landlady went on, frightened and furious.

Lazare didn't get overly excited.

"I'll pay. It won't happen again."

The verb *to pay*, no matter how it was conjugated, always had a calming effect on Mrs. Ginsburg. And she knew that despite his flaws, despite his occasional eccentricities, this boy was a man of his word. She began to feel almost reassured.

"It won't happen again," Lazare repeated, diligently buttoning his checkered foreman's shirt.

He stationed himself briefly at the mirror. The wild ebony cowlick that jutted out from his forehead; the olive-yellow complexion and the deep circles under his eyes; the beautiful hard blue eyes that could bore holes in brick. "The face of an angel who's pissed off with Paradise," he thought.

"Instead of admiring yourself you'd be well advised to come to the kitchenette. I don't want the toast to burn too."

"I'm not admiring myself," said Lazare gloomily, without turning away from the mirror. "And don't worry about the mess, I'll clean it up myself."

"In that case." The mother urged her children to follow her, and the incident was closed.

Mrs. Ginsburg was filling tin cups with scalding hot chicory coffee.

"Have you noticed?" she asked her eldest. Then, in a hushed tone: "There's a floorboard that's come loose. Maybe that's where he hides it."

She went to the door to the kitchenette, pricked up her ear, checked that Lazare was still busy cleaning up, then came back to her sons at the table. While she was tying a bib around the neck of the retarded one, she went on, her voice still hushed:

"Anyway, as soon as he's gone you'll go and look. I think we can solve the mystery."

The mystery was what on earth Lazare Barthakoste did with his ducats. And though she had studied the question from every angle, the obscurity was intact. He must be as rich as Croesus! Of that she was convinced for two reasons. On the one hand, he was a foreman, and not just any foreman but a demolition foreman. And not only a demolition foreman but, as the son of the late Rudolph Barthakoste — who was known as The Great, about whom she'd obtained enough information to be not unaware that he was considered by his peers to be *the* demolisher of the past hundred years; and so as the son of Barthakoste the Great, and also because of his personal merits as a demolisher, which made him a virtuoso, a virtuoso of a calibre that might enable him to outclass his own father one day, and finally because of the kind of veneration his journeymen had for him, nicknaming him "The Terror of the Walls" no less, veneration that not long ago had made him, at the age of nineteen, the youngest foreman in American demolition history, Lazare was very close to the highest spheres of the Order, and consequently close as well to the impressive financial trafficking that was common there, which must bring him a substantial personal income, reasoned the landlady.

On the other hand — and this was the second reason that inclined her to think Lazare must be loaded — well, it was on the very day when the young foreman had shown up, answering a newspaper ad, to rent the little room where he'd now been living for nearly six weeks. She'd asked if the suggested rent was all right and he had replied that he'd have been prepared to pay twice that amount. The landlady had retorted, laughing, "Then I should have asked for three times as much." The boy had replied, "All right!" And agreed to pay her, every week, three times the rent originally requested! Wasn't that the behaviour of a rich man? A man so filthy rich he doesn't know which window to throw his money out of?

So there you go, what could he do with all that money? She'd had him tailed by her two functioning sons; he never went to the bank, and he was paid in cash. He must certainly go drinking in speakeasies frequently, but though her sons had tailed him, spied on him, he never spent colossal sums, at least not enough to eat into the fortune with which Mrs. Ginsburg credited him. He didn't have an automobile, bought practically no clothes aside from the bare essentials, and possessed, so to speak, nothing. As for cathouses and their tenants in petticoats and frills, as far as was known he'd never set foot in one.

Pondering this question, the landlady had finally come up with the stunning hypothesis that he kept his money on him. Maybe not on his person, maybe not in the pockets of his pants, but right here, in this little room where he lived. She held this conviction one long night, and waited impatiently for the young man to leave for work the next morning. Yet drawers upended, suitcases searched and searched again, all the seams of all his clothes explored yielded not a sign of any lovely large sum.

That morning, though, right after the young man had opened his eyes, as she was bending down to pick up the bottle of joyjuice, she'd noticed the loose floorboard near the window, and her heart was still thumping as a result. She was sure she'd finally found it.

But Mrs. Ginsburg had never asked herself what she would do if she discovered the young demolisher's spoils. Her intention was certainly not to steal it — the thought wouldn't have crossed her mind. She was crazy about money, so crazy that she dreamed about it at night or, rather, stayed awake and imagined herself with a huge fortune, greeted at the bank with respect, her sons dressed like English heirs, all that, but she was an honest woman and a good mother to the core. She wanted to know where the devil Lazare hid his money simply for the satisfaction of knowing where the devil Lazare hid his money.

"Careful, here he is."

Lazare went directly to the table, bit into his sausage, drained his still-scalding chicory coffee, without milk, without sugar, black as soot.

"All picked up," he said. "A bundle. In yard next to the garbage."

"You'll have to watch out for glass splinters."

"Swept up, nothing to worry."

And as Mrs. Ginsburg was complaining about her good dishes, now in crumbs, Lazare promised once again to reimburse her. His meal downed, he placed the rent money beside his plate and added a lovely wad of big bills that made eyes shine, all around the table, including the ones in the heavy head.

"This should cover it," said the foreman.

And went out, taking his leather ball, without saying goodbye. He preferred to hurl remarks like machine-gun bursts, because he stuttered.

2

Lazare turns left, heading for Astor Place. Already, ragamuffins have taken over the road. They are playing ball, running and shouting. Lazare makes his way through them, staring straight ahead, without seeing them. The ball lands in front of him; he catches it in mid-flight, an automatic movement of his arm, like a lizard sticking out its tongue to catch a fly. He stuffs the ball into his pocket. The youngsters ask for it back. He continues on his way, ignoring them. He forgot, no, he neglected, to go to the tobacconist's store yesterday and take possession of the envelope. He'll do so first thing this morning, before he goes to the site. The youngsters are still stamping their feet around him, demanding their ball, red-faced and outraged. At the corner of the street, Lazare boards a trolley. Takes a seat near the platform. A woman of indeterminate age holds a muzzled poodle on her lap. Across from him, a man with a thin moustache — the kind favoured by gypsies and movie stars — with slicked-down hair that soils his collar, is smoking a cigarette rolled from a dried corn husk. Lazare fiddles absent-mindedly with his leather ball, bounces it on his knees, plagued by a vague but vivid anxiety. The bus is amazingly underpopulated, you'd think you were in the suburbs, but suddenly there's a crowded station and a mass of people pile into compartments, pull down jump seats, all have to pull in knees, squeeze elbows. The trolley starts up again like a crate full of potatoes. Lazare looks away from the passengers, who fill him with incomprehensible contempt, their smell bothering him so much, his breathing is constrained. He rests his head against the glass. The sun, brutal, the streets, already jam-packed, the faces, the bodies all tremble in the scorching light and the smell of overheated asphalt. New York during morning rush hour, New York already an inferno.

He gets off at the next station, boards another trolley at random, soon disembarks, no need. He detours to avoid Central Park. He received a generous amount of greenbacks at the time of the Great Exodus when, fleeing New York justice with his father, he followed travelling circuses, putting up big tops and taking them down. Lazare would have been ten at the time. They made inquiries about country roads, he and his father, to find out if there was some wobbly old barn in the vicinity, some pigsty slated for demolition, and they sold tickets, a group of yokels gathered, and the little fellow, with practically no help from his father, hammer, screwdriver, sets of ropes, that was all, sometimes a draft horse too, the child brought down the building all by himself, as the dumbfounded bumpkins looked on. At the time, his father had started drinking heavily, and when he started drinking he never stopped. The Great Barthakoste believed that his son had exceptional gifts, and he was worried sick to see the talents of this child, over whose cradle the demolition fairy had bowed, who'd been born with a hammer in his hands so to speak, who'd demolished his first doghouse at the age of four, and whom Barthakoste had been taking to New York's destruction sites at the most tender age, conscientiously teaching him all the tricks of the trade early on, the way the priesthood is passed on, the Great Barthakoste was tormented by the sight of this angel's talent being wasted on woodsheds and chicken coops when it would have taken Detroit, New York, or Chicago for his gifts to be confirmed, to blossom, to come to fruition, for young Lazare, to become what he'd been for his father since birth — nothing less than the greatest demolisher of all time. But every police force in the land was looking for them, so they set off again along the dusty, dirty country roads, following circuses, travelling fairs, putting up with preachers and hostile villages, loathing forests, meadows, and mountains, you'd think there was nothing else in America, loathing them with all their pores, and constantly worried, hounded, wary of everything and everyone, sleeping and taking sustenance alone in their truck and, on nights when they were forced to stay awake, cursing the stars and the open air.

Lazare steps onto the street that goes to the tobacco shop. His skin is bothering him, itching again (like last time). He senses a vague threat, un-pin-down-able and undefined, taking on the strangest form. He thinks: "As if he won't be able to cope." He thinks about himself in the third person: "As if there were no way he could cope." A hunched old lady, mincing along with a shopping bag held tightly against her stomach; the display of unleavened bread in the baker's window; the configuration of a small heap of clouds; even the way the beard of a rabbi he runs into is trimmed — all of it, with no connection whatsoever to himself, as he knows, strikes him as morbid omens, dark warnings. And he thinks about the little boy in his dream the night before, the little boy in his little boat, waving his stump at him, movements in which he recognized the same warning, the shimmering of the same enigma, diffuse and tenacious.

To keep his queasiness at bay, he tries his best to look at things objectively, coldly professional. He assesses buildings, determines where to strike, so forth. He isn't known as The Terror of the Walls for nothing. The journeymen say he can knock down a house barehanded, by himself, and it's nearly true. He knows he's the best but he takes no pride in it. He says so if anyone asks him, in the same way that he'd say of a wedge of cheese, that's a wedge of cheese, if he was asked what it was. Ditto for his reputation as someone who has never smiled in his life. Which is simply true, though he doesn't work at it, and it's not an affectation. The bitter crease at the corner of his mouth is part of him, like the steel colour of his eyes, like his passionate loathing of the apprentice Xavier X. Mortanse. Impossible to change any of it.

Lazare walks past a church. Feels the same dark, visceral emotion every time. He saw it as a child. He was five years old, just recovering from the accident that nearly cost him his life. He saw a crew bringing down a church. His father had taken him there to admire the work. The bells had been removed from the steeple, the cross from the peak. It was a damp and icy November morning. Ten men were pulling on the rope wrapped around the belfry, and once it had been wrenched free of the metal and collapsed, maybe it was the after-effects of his still recent accident, but Lazare was so impressed that he went into convulsions. The Philosopher happened to be there. Seeing the child and the state he was in at the sight, Leopold asked to speak to the father. It wasn't good for a child to witness such a thing. It was liable to cause dreams of dizzying destruction too huge for him, which could cost him his health. The senior Barthakoste laughed bitterly, wouldn't hear another word.

"A mouse that wants to swallow a graveyard," the Sands, a.k.a. Mouth of Gold as well as Mot Juste, summed up.

Lazare is walking quickly, weaving through the mass of pedestrians. He senses an uncomfortable presence against his thigh, remembers the hidden ball, takes it out of his pocket, and then, when he meets a toddler of four or five, no more, his mother beside him, holding his hand, Lazare places the ball against the child's stomach, it's a ball in the colours of the French flag, places it there without stopping, without a word, automatically, the same way he'd drop a wad of gum into a garbage can, and continues unwaveringly along his way. Then abruptly turns right into an alley. The tobacco store.

"The boss is out on an errand, Mr. Lazare. He'll be back in a few minutes."

The young clerk has shifty, hangdog eyes, cheeks purple with acne. Lazare asks for two packages of Golden Bat. Immediately takes out a cigarette, and the overeager clerk gives him a light with his lighter. Lazare nods briefly, thanks. Wonders if it conforms with the rules for this clerk to know his first name. While he waits for the owner, Lazare goes to the window, looks out at the people walking along the quiet little street. He is racked by a violent itch, below his shoulder-blade, on his elbow, inside the auricle of his ear, but doesn't scratch. If he starts, he knows it will go on until it's a wound, until it bleeds. This virulent pruritis was one of the first symptoms, last fall. It had started at the same time as the peculiar anxiety he'd felt again the night before, that drove him to drink. The smallest, most insignificant object — a park bench, a coffee pot — all at once acquired a bizarre, a harrowing density. A kind of invisible blackness lurking deep inside things, addressing him with he knew not what signs. Next came insomnia, complicated by stomach pains that made him spend nights at a time twisting in his bed like a laundered sheet. Worse, he began to suffer an unbearable emotion that broke his heart whenever he saw the demolished on destruction sites. It was as if he were noticing them for the first time, and the keen moral pain their mere presence provoked was so new, and he could make out the source so faintly, that he was liable to hold the demolished themselves responsible for his suffering. He was angry with them for rousing his pity, hated them for it. He started to be absent from the destruction site more and more. He no longer left his house, tormented by an insurmountable sorrow. For days without end he did nothing but drink and play solitaire. Around Christmas, the Order took over. That marked the beginning of his calvary at the Clinic, which lasted for four months.

The tobacconist's low, greasy silhouette crosses the field of the window, makes the bell above the door ring, and without a greeting he says to Lazare, You're supposed to come on Wednesday, how many times do I have to tell you? He adds:

"I can't keep amounts like that here, it's unwise."

Lazare scowls, so what. The merchant takes the envelope from behind the counter. Always the same kind, with his code number on it. Lazare grabs it without checking the contents.

The merchant insists, as he does every time, every fortnight. With a sigh, Lazare opens the envelope, checks that it contains the usual twelve hundred dollars.

"And sign this receipt. I don't want problems with the Order like last month."

Lazare scrawls something quickly at the bottom of the sheet of paper.

"All right this once. But next time it's Wednesday, understand?"

Lazare leaves without replying. But hesitates on the doorstep. To decide if he'll go to the salon where she works, which is nearby, to see her, just see her, but time is flying, he has wasted enough as it is, and he goes in the opposite direction.

Yes, the same symptoms have returned, about a week ago, slyly. But he has sworn that he'll never go back to the Clinic. The inexhaustible afternoons on a chaise longue, under flannel sheets, motionless (don't move!), leafing through magazines, and the drugs that coursed through his veins, the leaden heaviness, the diet of hot milk, porridge, breaded fish, and fruit, all things he detested, for he ate nothing but sausages, even the stiff kindness of the chief doctor, a kindness he abhorred, considered hypocritical, that reminded him of his mother, and the alternating hot and cold showers; he'd rather jump into the Hudson than go through such ignominy again.

It's as if he couldn't get through it. He thinks about himself in the third person: it's as if there is no way for him to get through it. But ha, ha! He's getting married soon. He's getting married and he knows that will save him. Ha, ha, ha. It was last month — he was on his way home from a Wednesday evening at the tobacconist's store — that he came to a standstill. She was on her way out of her shop. He'd followed her, couldn't help it. Since that evening it has been decided. They'll marry, this fall at the latest. She'll agree to go to sea with him on a whaling ship, together they will settle in the vast emptiness of Baffin Island, where fate has been awaiting him forever. The last time he loved someone was twelve years ago. Twelve was also his age at the time. The little girl was nine or ten. Since then, nothing. Might as well call this the first time. But he's used to solutions that are short and simple. He'll learn how to do it. "You're the first and you'll be the last." Yes, those are the first words he will say to her, rehearsing properly so he won't stammer in her face on that someday soon when he finally approaches her. He'll have to get himself some civilian clothes. One mustn't frighten off a young woman with demolition togs. Dixit the Philosopher. The remark didn't fall on deaf ears. In the meantime, find out her name.

Lazare walks deeper into the alley. Smells of sewage and rotten fruit, of rancid oil. Sticky puddles that make soles squeak. Backsides of factories, warehouses, and garages, trucks with empty dumpers, rust, blemishes. He runs into a stable boy searching through the delectables. His horse stands patiently by his side; the tumbrel is filled with garbage. Rag-and-bone man. That was what he said last winter when the doctor at the Clinic asked for his earliest memory. Rag-and-bone man. The time he'd been run over by the rag-and-bone man's horse. He was five years old. There were red smudges of loosestrife across the road, calling out to him like a choir of angels. His mother had been distracted for a moment and little Lazare had rushed over to the flowers, laughing. The horse took off, thundering, filling the air. Lazare felt what a lark must feel when it crashes into a window. His collarbone shattered, legs broken. He fainted, experiencing an unusually intense sensation, as if he'd just been hit by happiness.

Lazare watches the rag-and-bone man for a moment, decides that he doesn't feel anything, then continues on his way. He stops at the end of the alley. Looks at the envelope, extracts the twelve hundred dollars, pockets three hundred or so. The shares he inherited from his father, which have been bearing fruit for thirty years under the nimble fingers of the Order. Lazare thinks about Mrs. Ginsburg. Suspects that she's fretting to know what he does with all his money (also, he has caught her sons following him). He shrugs, puts the surplus bills, hundreds, back in the envelope. Time to go to the destruction site. For a while now he has known that he's under surveillance. Every day, oral reports about him are submitted to the highest authorities of the Order, he's aware of that, he has his sources. His escapades, his high spirits, his refusals to obey instructions, his illness last winter, and his nocturnal hijinks on the worksites, where, high on joyjuice, he smashes as much as he can: all these elements render him suspect in the eyes of the leaders. The slightest wrong move and he's liable to find himself off the site, filing papers in the office — or even, to put it quite bluntly, forced to stay in the Clinic under duress. This would be a bad time to be late. Even so, before he sets out he lights up one last Golden Bat. As is his custom, he sets fire to the envelope full of banknotes with the lighter flame, then drops it nonchalantly down a manhole.

3

XAVIER X. MORTANSE WAS CERTAINLY not the very model of a demolisher, but he'd been sewn with good will. Only he was prone to cloud-walking. Sometimes, to coach him, they'd make him pound on a wall, and he would start to think about other things while he was pounding, and his pounding would subside, and he'd be on his cloud. Then Lazare would let out a shriek that would make you jump: "A baby hitting a cake with his rattle," so forth. And the foreman would pick up a tool and whack him in his floating ribs. Xavier would apologize, saying again that the know-how was sinking in, and apply himself with renewed good will. The journeymen sympathized with Lazare. Officially, the apprentice's training had been entrusted to him to avoid overtaxing him, since the foreman's nerves were still considered fragile, but most of the demolishers saw the Order's decision as a disciplinary measure, to punish him for his many acts of disobedience. This pairing would last quite a while. So they said. Either Lazare or Xavier. One of the two would go nuts.

When snacktime rolled around, Lazare was in the habit of devoting himself to the one passion he was known to have, aside from demolition: his leather ball. Sausage downed, he'd walk away from the crews and amuse himself by accomplishing feats with his leather sphere. Arms outstretched, as if to imitate an airplane, he sent it from the end of his right hand to the end of his left, balanced it on the nape of his neck, bounced it off his head, etc. It flew from his foot, faster than a speeding bullet.

This noon, though, on account of particularly violent stomach cramps, there was no ball time. Lazare remained sitting, looking gloomy, one hand on his belly while a workmate stroked him between the shoulder-blades by way of comfort.

Xavier had finished taking sustenance. And because he thought them pretty, he'd undertaken to erect a low wall of rose-coloured bricks — meaning no harm, the way you might put up a house of cards to ward off boredom while waiting for post-noon tasks. Lazare picked up a stone and flung it at his wall, which collapsed. Tears in Xavier's eyes. He saw it as malice pure and simple, from a gratuitously pernicious mind, and saw that it had nothing to do with the know-how sinking in. He made the effort to go tell his young foreman that he saw this as unjust. Lazare grinned as he approached, despite his cramps. The workmate who was pampering Lazare told Xavier they were there to demolish, not to build little walls, hi ho hi ho. To which Xavier (indignant) replied that that was no reason to commit injustices. And the apprentice began to vent his thoughts quite calmly, such that his listener would know that he was without rancour, or under the influence of bad advice, to wit, that eating meat and drinking joyjuice on weekends explained why Lazare experienced these jolts of quite bluntly noxious behaviour, and that it couldn't be good for his insides either, being prey to cramps. Lazare's grin went from ten to zero while Xavier was talking, he knew that, but it served The Terror of the Walls right, Lazare had done his best to let him vent his thoughts. Afterwards, to show that there was no grudge in his heart, Xavier went to fetch Lazare's ball and return it to him as a token of reconciliation. But here's what took the opportunity to happen. As soon as the apprentice's hand was on the ball it seemed to become alive or something and escaped from his hands, and as Xavier took a step to get it back, his foot inadvertently delivered the fatal blow and the ball took off, ending up in the middle of the road where a truck, such is life, decided to pass, and the noise it made and the breath that came out of it when the wheel of the truck squashed the ball made Xavier's hair spring to attention.

He was gazing, stunned, as if at some marvel. He turned in Lazare's direction. The Terror was walking up to him, very calm all in all, a calm that could make you shiver because of how he was glaring. The apprentice pulled in his head like a rabbit. Before he'd even started to mutter his apologies, he received the foreman's fist between his eyes, and it was as if a locomotive had landed in his face. Then came the hurricane. It took four of them to pull the foreman off his apprentice. Lazare went on beating the air, squirming like a cat in water, his workmates holding him back with great difficulty. Xavier was stretched out on the ground laughing like someone being tickled, giddy from all the punches he'd received, that's how badly it hurt. When he managed to stand up, the setting, the characters, all were waltzing around his head. He was so punch-drunk that he went on laughing idiotically, proffering thanks to those present, so forth, recognizing not a single face. He put his hand in front of his mouth and noted blood running from his nose as if from a tap. And his palm was grey, and his blood was black, and everything around him, even the bricks, even the bright colours of the journeymen's outfits, were nothing but black white grey, as in the movies. He could no longer make out colours.

And along came the head of the destruction site, telling him to hustle his behind. "Mortanse, who else? Mortanse, yet again!" A body approached. The apprentice recognized the Philosopher at his side, alarmed.

"Are you all right, my boy? Answer me, are you all right?"

Xavier gestured vaguely to show that he was. Not great, but all right. The old man was holding the apprentice by the shoulders, but Xavier freed himself to show that his legs could support him perfectly well on their own. No sooner did he try to take the smallest step than pain shot from his heel and all through his body up to his skull, in a dazzling shortcut, like at the fair when you make a bell ring by banging a base with a hammer.

Some journeymen held Lazare to their chests, murmuring tender words in his ear. Xavier thought Lazare was very lucky. To beat someone and then be treated as if he'd been beaten. The site boss grabbed Xavier by the collar.

"Scram, get a move on! You cause nothing but hassles. You want money, is that it?" Placing a small sum in his hands. "Now, vamoose, and make it snappy!"

Xavier held the few dozen pennies between his fingers and didn't vamoose. The boss ordered the others to keep working.

"You," he said to Lazare, jabbing the young foreman's chest with a threatening forefinger, "keep that up and it's the Clinic and forced rest, get the picture? Do we understand each other?"

The Philosopher suggested taking Xavier to see a doctor. The apprentice refused. The journeymen were slowly getting back to work; Xavier still couldn't distinguish colours. His ribs and left hand were causing him a lot of pain. Even so, he tried to pick up his hammer, question of doing his share, but a spasm jabbed his back, so sharp that he nearly lost the little bit of consciousness he still had. The Sands of Silence insisted on taking him to the Clinic, but once again the apprentice refused. The site boss ordered the old man to leave the apprentice alone and get back to work like the others. All the same, the Philosopher asked Xavier, "Why don't you go back to Hungary? From what you say, you've got a sister there who loves you, whom you love. Go back and join her."

Xavier managed to sputter, "See you tomorrow!" waggling feeble fingers.

He left the destruction site, still an apprentice, deflated. He ran into a group of demolished who dared not do anything for him. He'd intended to give them a smile, but his jaw hurt so much that he grimaced in pain instead. A youth flung a clod of earth that hit him in the eye. While under his shirt, the plankets of his devising were a wreck.

4

ONCE HE'S ARRIVED AT THE HARBOUR, his carcass
poled and billy-clubbed, Xavier X. Mortanse sits on a block
of wood. He's glad that now, after his long walk, he can
finally rest. His eyes can see far away and the sea is calm and
still, its belly offered up, mossy. Holding a phone book close
to her heart, the Statue of Liberty paints her ceiling; from her
look alone you can see that her mind's not on the task at hand.
Gulls fly around her, dropping guano (the aim of the game
being to lodge one in her eye). Others fly above the ocean
liners, making the sour cry of witches having nightmares; still
others spin from one grain silo to another, driven wild by the
aroma of rotten grain. A few metres from the apprentice,
around a crate holding nothing but citrus peels, some gulls are
squabbling, wings in an M. Groups of longshoremen walk by,
slowing down at the sight of Xavier, intrigued by his appearance and his turgescent face.

Walking here was no piece of cake. Sometimes he would
lean against a wall to ease the pain in his floating ribs. A
woman came to him, incidentally, while he was struggling
along his way. She had black skin, a handkerchief over her
hair, a thinker's eyes, deep as holes. She held out a glass of the

flavoured water that was her stock-in-trade. Refused the few coins he held out to her in exchange. He tried to tell her he'd think of her every time he drank water for the rest of his life. But he didn't speak clearly because of his swollen jaw. The ebony woman wished aloud for the boy to be in God's good books, and Xavier gestured too, faintly, priest-like, to show that he blessed her as well. And then he got back on the road.

Which has brought him here, to the waterfront, where he's gazing at the Statue who is painting her ceiling (or is she offering an ice-cream cone to someone on the floor above, he wonders). The block of wood he's sitting on happens to be the very one he'd chosen a few weeks earlier, on the day he arrived in New York. That is, on the day he assumes was the day he arrived in America. In absolute terms, what he knows by Jove is nothing. He'd become aware of himself again, as a body and mind all in one, sitting there, with no memory whatsoever of any crossing, as if he had been born, conceived, and created all at once, like an angel, speculating that he must have disembarked from one of those steamboats, only speculating, for how else could he explain the fact that he was sitting on this block of wood, thinking in a language that was foreign, nearly unknown, with no memory at all of the reasons that might have prompted him to leave Hungary, to leave his beloved sister, Justine (they must be lousy reasons)? No memory, really none, what's called zero. He'd ended up on the New York waterfront a few weeks earlier, without the faintest idea of why he was there, without papers, without anything save those squares of chocolate in his pocket, which he presumed had been put there by his sister, Justine, in secret, the day he left Hungary.

A few weeks, a month and a half at most. He awakened

on the New York waterfront, struck by a strange sense that he was being observed. When he turned to the left, he spied a young man who was watching him, who turned away abruptly as soon as their eyes met. Like him, the young man was sitting on a block of wood. He appeared to be as alone, as lost, as bereft as Xavier was. Perhaps they'd made the crossing together? Maybe then he could shed some light on Xavier, maybe they'd socialized on the ship, maybe Xavier had confided in him. Xavier had decided to approach him, and apparently the young man had had the same idea, for here he was, at this very moment, getting up off his block. He was walking towards Xavier, giving him a puzzled look. Xavier waved, the young man did the same, and then everything in his bones congealed. This young man was only his reflection in the big window of a warehouse. Xavier stood for a long time facing his own image, of which he had no memory either.

He had spent his first days on American soil wandering among the warehouses in the port. He was getting hungry, but dared not throw himself into the city. Since then, his across-the-landing neighbour, Peggy Sue, had told him about newcomers who speak not one word of American and spend years wandering around the city, not daring to enter it, carrying a single suitcase. Those people were not of the race of those who pocket their first million after five years. They were of the race of those whose lives make no sense whatsoever: living in unruly gangs, jabbering a mumbo-jumbo concocted out of Europe's old languages, more or less helping one another, more or less spying on one another, hiding in the merchandise sheds, watching out for a hint of a banana, quarrelling over a can of food, and searching through the delectables. Face hair and head hair grew on all of them at the same time, like a kind of vegetation, all in a block, creeping over all their faces, confusing them, making them doppelgängers of misery, the object of police pursuits, and the New York police ultimately, inevitably, nabbing them in their net like wild animals, then sending them off towards some very remote and thoroughly forgotten nowhere, still carrying their one suitcase, unopened after all those years, which contained nothing but two starched shirts, a clean pair of pants, a photograph showing faces from another world that they themselves no longer recognized, and Xavier shuddered whenever he recalled that story told him by Peggy, his across-the-landing neighbour.

But Xavier didn't care for searching in the delectables. (A Hungarian has his pride.) On the fifth day, hunger won out. He made his way on foot to the inside of the monster. He walked for hours, his hand held out. Into which no one dropped even one coin. He was amazingly dirty in both face and clothing, dirt that would repel even a kind heart. He'd ended up by chance on a demolition site, where the Philosopher took him under his wing. And there you go, he became an apprentice.

Which is why he comes back here — to the waterfront, on a kind of pilgrimage, to this port and this block of wood — when he's feeling low, or when he needs to take stock of his life a little. Comes here, too, with the vague hope that someone will introduce himself, will place his hand on his shoulder and explain to him gently the forgotten reasons for his departure from Hungary and his presence in America. Except that it never happens, he knows that, nor does a genie suddenly materialize before him as if from a magic lantern, and so he savours a comforting square of chocolate, which incidentally he has to cut smaller and smaller, for with each passing day there is less and less of it.

Today, though, his mouth hurts too much to chew, even to let the chocolate melt on his tattered tongue. So he gets up from his block of wood and sets off again, his wounds and his bumps even more painful after he's rested them for a while — it's always worse afterwards. Relieved all the same that his stay in the port should once again have been pointless, for he fears shedding any light on his own mystery, as much as he desires it. He cuts across the first alleys, relying as he walks on the sound that guides him from deep inside his bird's brain and directs him towards his abode. Soon he arrives at the long avenue that brings him, in less than twenty minutes, to the door to his building. Brings him as well to the abattoir that provided meat for salting in the French way for the Salaison Supreme without a circumflex. And from it comes the squealing of pigs. Normally, Xavier is at work at the hour their throats are slit. Another reason to be glad to have a job.

He turns back so he won't have to put up with that opera. Only, where to go? As a general rule he does this just on weekends. But this is an emergency. So he heads for the beauty salon where Miss Peggy works her dainty fingers to the bone. He stands at the window and looks at her with no one the wiser. Anyway, she's too busy to be aware of his presence. For him, it's enough to gaze at her. Whatever torment inhabits him, afterwards it is always diminished, eased.

Turning the corner, though, he stopped dead. She was sitting on the doorstep of the beauty salon, smoking a cigarette with the other girls. Xavier tried to vanish, but too late.

And Peggy ran to catch up with him before he was across the street.

"Come and meet my friends!" she said, laughing, to Xavier standing guiltily in the shade.

When she saw the state of his face, the extent of the damage, she held back a cry of horror. And right away the stream of questions, Who on earth had arranged his face like that, who had beaten him, had he seen a doctor?

"It's nobody's fault. An accident. They happen."

The hairdressers' cigarette break was coming to an end, Peggy had to get back to work. She swore she'd come and see him in his cubicle this very evening. She was still looking at him as she crossed the street. Between the buildings the sky was blue, a pure and painful blue.

Xavier resumed his roaming. He hadn't sworn, had he, that he would be there, tonight, in his abode. He was racked by a tremendous need for community. (But couldn't cope with the crowds on the main avenues. He felt even less like somebody there than he did anywhere else. He was always busy being ashamed of himself because of the demolition togs.) He spied a dog that had no more idea than he where it was going. They fraternized straightaway, the dog wagged its tail frenetically. Since I don't know if I'm coming or going, thought the apprentice, why not follow it?

The dog hadn't gone a hundred feet when he lifted his leg at the base of a statue that Lazare couldn't have noticed because he was miles away. In his mind and in his heart, though, he is very close to Xavier, because he is cursing him. Lazare walks steadily. Thrusts his hand into his pocket and takes out a black token, making it jump up and down in his hand like a coin. The token means that he's about to be assigned to a rat drop, something he loathes (demolishing is one thing, but he has a horror of sabotage). He is not unaware that such tasks are assigned when the upper ranks feel the need to keep a refractory bird away from the worksite. And what will happen after the rat drop? Confinement to an Order office, filing papers and licking envelopes? Lazare spits as if he could taste the glue in his mouth.

And it's obviously his outburst this morning, and the thrashing he gave the apprentice, that earned him this extravagant reaction from the higher-ups. His rancour and his hatred for Xavier were growing accordingly. A vagrant is singing and accompanying himself on the guitar. He stands near a bench where Lazare has his little routine (he often comes there when he has to think about something). Lazare goes up to the itinerant musician.

"How much d'you want for the guitar?"

"It ain't for sale, young fella."

"I'll give you a hundred," says Lazare, and takes a bill of that amount from his pocket.

The vagrant stares at him with something like dread. Lazare drops the bill in the hand of the dumbfounded musician, then grabs the guitar and calmly smashes it against a tree.

"Oh, why did you do that?" asks the vagrant, who meanwhile has taken care to pocket the hundred-dollar bill.

Lazare doesn't reply. He gazes at the tree for a long time.

"Music gets on my nerves," he says finally, without anger, without passion, without anything.

Ripping the bridge from the sound box, he detaches the main string, the E. "And this," he adds, wrapping the string around his hands and stretching it out to feel its resistance, "this can always come in handy."

The vagrant takes fright, takes off. On second thought, Lazare doesn't bother to sit on his bench and think. He gets back on the road, the words Salaison Supreme his North Star because that's near where Peggy lives. And where his apprentice, Mortanse (his fist clenches the guitar string with rage) also lives. He thinks too that he'll have to get himself a new ball.

The dog finally, inevitably, dragged Xavier very close to a vacant lot where a community of demolished had gathered. It was already dusk. Policemen were there, and Black Marias. An officer was deep in conversation with a delegate of the demolished. Xavier wrapped his fingers inside the links of the fence and watched some children who were playing tag, letting out cries of fear and panicky exuberance. One of them, carried away by his running, arrived at the fence, and his laughter froze when he spied Xavier. Only then did the apprentice remember that he was wearing his demolisher's outfit. He stepped back, agitated at frightening a child. He walked along the campground. Wobbly carts piled high with the most disparate objects, a jumble of furniture, linens, and lamps. Kettles where beets and potatoes were boiling, and the families grouped into clans, the clans into gangs. They had been swapping food and drink, fraternizing under the covers, warming their hands at the same fires, because for a week now, though it was still summer, after nightfall it had been cool. Mothers suckled children, some of them old enough to talk. Old women knelt in a circle and prayed, superstitiously. Had it not been for his work duds, the apprentice would have joined them. Even if it meant lying, even if it meant saying that, like them, he'd been demolished. They would have offered him water, lent him a blanket, and smiled as if he were one of them. A perfectly simple prospect, just not feasible. Xavier felt a pang.

Suddenly he recognized Giorgio and Maria, whom he'd met on the evening of his Discovery, when he emerged from the hole. They were drinking from steaming cups near their cluttered cart. The baby was asleep, wrapped in a checkered tablecloth. While the little boy wasn't joining in the other children's games, either from shyness or because he was a separate species, as suggested by the keen way he looked at them, at once detached and penetrating.

Giorgio got up and headed for the apprentice, who was already preparing to decamp. Giorgio started running to catch up with him. He shouted:

"Come back, child! Xavier, come back! I have to talk to you!"

But just as Giorgio emerged onto the street, two police-men intervened and drove him back inside the campground. The demolished looked at the apprentice, who walked away, sheepish, head down.

Now it was time to go home. (Xavier thought about his frog, who must be longing to put on the evening perform-ance.) Relying on the sound, the one etc., that he could barely hear, and from far away, he estimated the time he would need to get back to his abode at a good two hours at least. But along the way he let himself be tempted by the demon. He felt he deserved a consolation prize for the day he'd endured. And so he stopped at the café called the Chess Club, where his swollen jaw and his black eye provoked much whispering. There he wiped out a couple of opponents, while enthusiasts looked on admiringly, then left around midnight, filled with pride and disgust, swearing never to do that again.

But there was more. When he switched the light on at home, his frog was waiting for him in a dressing gown, holding a rolling pin. There followed a scene, such a scene, I tell you! . . .

5

To make the story short, Peggy had twice agreed to go out with the boy. Or let's say once and a half. She had noticed him in the neighbourhood often enough. He was decked out rather oddly. A too-tight jacket firmly buttoned, a stiff collar of the kind worn at the beginning of the century, a bowler hat. Something unbending and forced about his gait. She thought, He's poor. His manner was at once timid and tough, tight-lipped, bitter even, as if he were suffering a permanent humiliation. Or breathing a smell that he despised. She thought his eyes were beautiful. She ran into him so often, it had occurred to her that she was being followed. He didn't seem to pay her any attention. She ran into many others just as often, after all. He must work in the neighbourhood. She imagined he was a humble clerk, a pencil-pusher through circumstance. With very precise Dreams in the back of his head.

One afternoon, on the sidewalk in front of the beauty salon — it was break time and she was having a smoke with one of her girlfriends — she spotted him in the window of the drugstore across the street. She noticed that he was looking at her. Peggy thought, Normal, my face probably looks familiar and he's wondering where he's seen me. Very beautiful eyes though, proud and hard to please. She gave him a neutral smile. No reaction. At the end of her shift, though, around nine p.m., on her way out of the beauty salon, she saw that the boy hadn't moved, he was still visible in the window, and he raised his head as if she were the one he was waiting for. Fortunately, that evening she went home in a taxi with her boss.

The same scene was repeated four or five times over the following fortnight. To the point where her colleagues finally asked Peggy who that boy was sitting in front of the drug-store window, for it was obvious that he was interested only in her, had eyes only for her. The other young women teased her about it, as is customary. Peggy's reaction was testy and she butted a cigarette she'd barely started. Before going back inside the beauty salon she gave the boy a stern and insistent look. He didn't turn away. As if he were seeing without being seen. And often in the evening, when the day's work was done — you'd never guess, he would still be there. The boss finally suggested that she take Peggy home by taxi every evening, that would settle the matter. And now and then they might as well continue the evening in a little café, eh? Why not? It became their tradition. The boss listened to her with a peaceful smile, without condescension. Flattered to stir the interest of a person so distinguished, Peggy poured out her confidences. There were whispers that she was Madame's pet.

Finally, on a Friday night after a hard day's grind, she decided that she'd had it up to here. Told her boss, "Hang on a minute." She was going to set matters straight, once and for all. She walked purposefully to the drugstore. The young man saw her cross the street and he quivered like a dog. But by the time Peggy was through the doorway and had climbed the few steps, the place was empty. The young man had made his getaway through the emergency exit. Peggy went back to her boss. The taxi was waiting in front of the salon, Madame was about to open the door, but Peggy said no, not tonight, I'd rather walk. The boss's face changed, her disappointment obvious, even strange. But Madame got a grip on herself. "Are you sure?" she asked. "You aren't afraid of that doofus coming back?" Peggy ran a weary hand through her hair.

"I need the air. The walk home will do me good."

Madame put on a forced smile, then got into the car with no goodbye. Peggy set off immediately at a brisk pace. At this rate it would take her half an hour. It was windy, the folds of her raincoat kept flying in all directions, restricting her walk. She resigned herself to tying the belt, something she never did willingly. When her raincoat was fastened like that, it gave her a clumsy silhouette. She looked down angrily as she advanced. Finally pushed open the door to her building. And gasped in surprise. The young man was waiting for her with one hand behind his back. She looked around quick quick; people were walking by. She decided not to be afraid. The young man took a step towards her and murmured something inaudible. She asked him to repeat it but he looked at her, fluttering his eyelashes, motionless in his skimpy jacket, his stiff collar. All the same, he finally did repeat it, and this time she heard only the final words: " . . . and you'll be the last." And he extended the hand that had been behind his back. It was holding a bouquet. Peggy is a woman. An icicle melted inside her. Now he wasn't a pest who'd been spying on her for two weeks, ridiculous in a bowler hat that was too small for him. He was a poor and bashful young man who was offering flowers on which he must have spent his last pennies.

"I thought," he said, "that maybe we could," and didn't complete the sentence.

"Could what?" Peggy asked softly.

Courageously, Lazare poured out, I thought maybe we could talk.

He even went so far as to add, I've got something to ask you but not tonight. The young man smelled of alcohol. (To put some guts in his belly, she thought indulgently.) Peggy was surprised at her own emotion. He was so bashful. And his eyes were so beautiful. Yes, beautiful.

"Excuse me?" she said.

Daydreaming, she hadn't heard what he'd just said.

"I said: Baffin Island. Do you know it?"

"Umm, yes."

She thought she remembered it being in Africa.

"I thought," he said, "we could maybe," and his sentence stayed like that, one paw in the air.

"Maybe what?" asked Peggy softly.

Lazare poured out non-stop, "I thought maybe we could go to the movies I mean alone together the both of us."

"Why not?" she said, without taking her eyes off the boy's heart-meltingly beautiful face. "We could do that tomorrow, tomorrow evening."

"Yes. Tomorrow."

Then his hand trembled a little.

"My flowers," he said, "don't you want my flowers?"

"Oh sure of course I'm sorry I'm awfully sorry."

She took the bouquet and held it tenderly against her bosom. Smiled at him. She had a vague idea they were going to see an adventure movie set somewhere in Africa, on the Island of Baffin.

"See you tomorrow then?"

"Yes, tomorrow. Come and pick me up here at let's say seven o'clock, is that all right?"

A curt nod from the boy. By the way, what was his name?

"Call me Ishmael," said Lazare, thinking of himself in the third person: He'll have to be careful not to forget that he'd introduced himself by that name.

"Mine is Peggy."

"I know," he said, before suddenly turning and literally breaking away, practically at a run.

Past the corner of the street, when he was sure he was out of her sight, Lazare delivered a solid kick to a garbage can that hadn't done anything to him. The fabric was only a little bit darker at thigh level. The light was faint, luckily. For sure she hadn't seen. But a drop of anxiety persisted. He set off again, cursing between his teeth. You see, the effort he'd made not to stammer had made him forget himself a little in his pants.

6

So he shows up the next day as arranged, same bashfulness, same getup, same flowers, which this time she didn't know what to do with. She already had her bag, her umbrella, she didn't have three hands. And then, without being downright chic, she was dressed loyally: a little red, a little blue. For a first night out, all's fair in love and war. Whereas he, you'd have thought he'd slept in his clothes. It wasn't serious of course. But, well, it was starting off on the wrong note. She had the boy carry her umbrella.

The movie, though, thrilled her. First there was a medium-length Harold Lloyd, and she laughed herself silly. Then a heart-rending drama starring her favourite actress, her absolute star, Marie Peak-Forde, who brought tears to her eyes. They left. The boy hadn't laughed or cried or anything. Peggy wondered incidentally where the Island of Baffin fit in. There was a delicatessen across from the picture palace; they went there. Lazare still hadn't said anything, and he didn't say anything more once he was ensconced in the booth. Peggy was beginning to think that bashfulness, oh sure, it's touching, but still. She tried to discuss the film with him. He replied with monosyllables and shrugs. Hands crossed on the table, he didn't dare look at her. Now and then he lit himself a cigarette, without offering her one. Golden Bats, besides, which she hated, it was like smoking the hair from somebody's ass. She'd started to hold back yawns. Then said to him, By the way, yesterday you talked about something you wanted to ask me, what is it? The boy stood up.

"Can I walk you home?"

Peggy sighed, all right, if you want. And thought: "If you're looking for a lousy evening, this is it." She couldn't wait to be back in her own room, with her bum on her pillow, a good novel between her legs, and munching a green apple. Lazare was no more talkative on the way home. In the elevated streetcar he glared up and down, simultaneously troubled and furious, at any men who dared set eyes on his companion. Once they were at the door to the building, he reached under his jacket and took out an envelope. There was a picture inside it. A landscape such as you might imagine on a dead planet.

"What's this?"

Baffin Island, was what he said. It bore no resemblance to any idea of Africa that Peggy had ever had. He corrected her. Not Africa, the Far North. Well that's a topic of conversation, thought Peggy, scratching her nose. About time we came up with one, now that they were fence posts in front of her door. She was about to tell herself that she'd never see this boy again when he won a reprieve. Because he added, "That's where the great whaling ships berth, in the season when the ice melts. One day, I swear, I'll go whaling." He took back the photo, filed it inside his jacket. The little click hadn't gone off in Peggy's head before. Now, yes. She hadn't read Herman Melville but she knew enough to know that:

"Ishmael: you took that from *Moby Dick*. It's not your real name."

"Yes. My whole name is Ishmael Lazarus. People just call me Lazare. But you."

He interrupted himself in a bizarre way.

"But me what?"

"You, I'd like it if you'd call me Ishmael."

"I accept."

So that was it. She hadn't been mistaken. Beneath the appearance of a yokel freshly landed in town, this boy concealed a Grand Dream, something that has an effect on young women analogous to that of bouquets of flowers. She decided to give the boy a second chance. They'd go to the café next Sunday, is that all right with you? In the afternoon. And she made him promise to reveal then the nature of the request he wished to address to her. The young hero walked away with his strange gait, stiff and starchy. Peggy climbed the stairs to her place, repeating to herself, Ishmael, Ishmael . . .

The following Sunday then. First of all, the boy smelled of alcohol. This was the second time in no more than three encounters. Which struck her as a lot. Especially because it wasn't even two p.m. She was well aware of the havoc that joyjuice had wreaked on her childhood, she had no desire to relive that. And then there was the fact that Ishmael gave signs of a grumpy, contemptuous temperament. At the subway ticket booth an elderly lady took a long time going through the barrier after she'd bought her ticket, she had to pick up her packages one by one, and Lazare hissed between his teeth, "Come on, move it, I haven't got all day!" In front of a family of demolished, he remarked that those people could just get a job like everyone else. Finally, at the drugstore, once they'd been served, Lazare took a flask from his pocket and doctored his coffee with a finger of joyjuice. Peggy said, "Don't you think it's a little early?" To which he replied, that was the way it was with him, she'd have to get used to it. Which put a spring in Peggy's rear. Forty-five seconds later, she was already boarding a trolley. The boy had let her go without making a move. He sat there alone, stammering abuse.

Then Ishmael started following her to the beauty salon. Arrived in the morning, sat in the foyer. He did no harm, bothered no one. He leafed through magazines or looked glumly out the window. His clothes were more and more faded and worn, as if he really did sleep in them. It was no longer a figure of speech, it was what the boy really did seem to be doing. Peggy shampooed her clients some ten steps from him. She ignored him, toiling away as if nothing were amiss, struggling to maintain her perfect ease. Lazare would stay for twenty minutes, half an hour, and then, looking at his watch, he'd leave on the stroke of eleven. The fourth time it was a Tuesday morning, a light day, no clients. Peggy stared at him, her arms folded. He went on leafing through magazines, not reading or even looking at the pictures, turning pages for the sake of turning pages. She went over to him.

"Why do you keep coming here? What do you expect of me?"

"I thought we could maybe."

"Talk. Yes, I know. So talk."

"Here?"

"Here, there, what's the difference?"

And she abruptly let him know that it was important for

her never to see him again, not like this or any other way. He looked at her for a long time, with incredulity. So stunned that he let out a word of demolishers' lingo, without stammering: "Korekkiri dess'ka?" Peggy shrugged something like, go ahead, talk Martian if you want, it won't make any difference.

A week went by with no sign of the yokel. The atmosphere in the salon wasn't cheerful, though. It seemed to Peggy that the boss was cold-shouldering her. Since the evening when she'd turned down her invitation to the café, not once had Madame suggested seeing her home, as had been her habit. Without actually scolding, Madame kept pointing out tiny professional lapses on Peggy's part; she retouched her hairdos, so forth; indicated with the tip of her nose the hair-clippings Peggy had neglected to sweep up. The young woman felt that her nerves were fragile. She would arrive at the salon already weary, and constantly, for no reason, tears would spring to her eyes. Working nights at the morgue overtaxed her. She had no time for herself, etc. And then one morning Lazare turned up at the salon, reeking of joyjuice from thirty feet away, clothes covered with filth, belligerent. She had to threaten to call the police. Finally the boy ran away. Peggy had taken refuge in the staff room. Madame had just arrived. She was standing at the foot of the stairs. Now you can see what she looks like: a lady still beautiful, still dignified, with something Asiatic about her, and reassuringly in her forties. She held out a handkerchief to Peggy, who wiped her eyes with it. The handkerchief smelled of her. Peggy sniffed, smiled. "It's nothing." The lady leaned towards her cheek.

"You can tell me about your romance problems if you have any; you know you can tell me everything."

And as she whispered, maybe it wasn't intentional but her lip just brushed Peggy's ear, and the young girl promptly recoiled. Her instinctive shrinking disconcerted both women equally. Peggy looked at Madame with slightly frightened amazement. The older woman took back her handkerchief, though, and then, with a perfectly straightforward smile, "All right, back to work!" And Peggy would have forgotten the incident right away had she not noticed that, just as her boss set her high-heeled shoe on the bottom step, her ankle twisted — something that happens to women when an overly strong emotion lands at their feet.

7

FINALLY, XAVIER X. MORTANSE GOT used to Peggy, a person can get used to anything. In her presence he no longer experienced, as he used to, that sense of not knowing what to do with his fingers, his knees, his eyes, all that, and his soul and his lungs. She often came to visit in the evening. Sometimes she brought candy (or flowers). Xavier wasn't the type to accept. He sometimes forced her to go home with. "For dainty tidbits, you're all I need." Peggy had laughed. He hadn't said it to be polite. A gentle ray, playful, fresh, and amusing, to which he was sensitive and for which he was nostalgic once she was no longer there, emanated from her. He wondered too why she never did her hair the same way twice. Apparently just like that, for no reason.

There wasn't much to do when they were together. Peggy told him about her work at the salon. Things had been going better for two weeks now. Ishmael the yokel hadn't come back. Her relations with Madame were sunny and calm again; last Friday night the two of them had gone back to the pleasant little café for a chitchat. Etc. Or else she'd talk to Xavier about the books she liked, because reading was her addiction. One evening when the apprentice was dusting, she brought him a novel that had fascinated her. As the book was only about a hundred pages long, she'd told herself that Xavier, who admitted that he never read, might find the patience to finish this one. Leafing through the book, the apprentice went to the window, to take advantage of the daylight. A young Jewish lawyer was giving up everything to become a music composer. His ordeals. His courage in the face of adversity. So forth. At the end of the novel he was received by Queen Victoria.

Peggy had lit up a bold cigarillo, in imitation of the boss lady she admired, but she choked on it and ground it out at once, turning red. Xavier went to his friend and gave back the book.

"Interesting," he said (to be polite). "Those are made-up stories."

"Wait till you've read it at least."

Xavier wondered why she would say something so strange.

"But I did read it, just now, at the window."

He resumed his dusting. Someone who has just told a lie, thought Peggy, doesn't have a look like that on his face. She regarded him solemnly. What a strange boy.

The thing that was wrong between them was the frog. It can't be helped, between certain beings the electricity isn't there. Although Xavier encouraged the performer, leaned towards it with hands on knees, saying again and again, "Come on, you, sing! Sing and dance!" As soon as Peggy was in the room, the frog would start croaking with a stupidity that astonished the apprentice. Peggy felt uneasy when she saw her friend struggling. What exactly did he expect from the critter? Xavier resigned himself to filing the prodigy away in its casket. "It's shy," he offered by way of apology. And when he was trying to show his friend what the frog could do when in the mood, Peggy Sue listened without interrupting. "Even keeps me awake nights with all the singing! . . . " He finally fell silent. Peggy kept looking at him for a long moment, with the same grave and amazed expression. She ran her hand through the boy's hair, or stroked his cheek with the backs of her fingers. She gave him a sad smile, full of emotion.

Something else that Peggy often talked about was her favourite movie stars. When she talked she had a great need of her hands, moving them apart, then back together, bringing them to her hair all the time to tousle it, making them flutter like butterflies around her face. Xavier, who thought he had to follow their movements, felt slightly stunned. And then she went back to her cubicle, Xavier stayed alone in his, the weather turned a little greyer, and his worries got their punch back.

The apprentice still went to the site every day. He had pretty well recovered from his thrashing. The marks had gone from his face and he could recognize certain colours again — greens, for instance, blues also, if the day was really bright and sunny. It's just that the journeymen cared as little for him as they did for the first hammer they'd ever held. They left him alone in his corner, tapping away at his piece of wall. When the real work started they sent him packing, and Xavier would step aside, bashful and shamefaced, trying to put on a brave expression. It was no fun. There was also the fact that he was no longer receiving any dollars now and then, as he had in the past, so he could eat. He'd reached the point of dipping into his savings.

But all of this he hid from his friend Peggy, to save her

from torment. He even told her that things were better at work now, much better, that they were starting to accept him, that they'd stopped mistreating him, stopped playing rotten tricks on him. She was worried enough about his health as it was. (He always had to reassure her about everything; promise to eat properly, all that, to sleep eight hours a night.) Then, once Peggy had gone, the frog would go berserk, often for the whole night. When morning came, and with it puffy eyes, Xavier would say with a smile, "Nobody can say that *you're* good for my health."

One night when he was chewing his lettuce leaf, Peggy swooped in, all excited at the prospect of making him happy no matter what. Xavier was sitting at the table and looking out the window. The large framework of the elevated streetcar track traced its complicated curves against the light, and the sight of it — he didn't know why — made Xavier think of scaffolds. The setting sun cast its crimson glow into the windows, and the sight was soothing to the apprentice, whose morale was on the skimpy side. He stroked his frog with his finger (it squeezed its eyes with the pleasures of the flesh). He hardly turned around at Peggy's enthusiastic entrance.

Who had just been given a bonus at work, a windfall, a small sum actually, from which she wanted Xavier to profit. Before she suggested anything at all, Xavier refused. She insisted. Argued that he'd make her unhappy if he didn't accept. Was that what he wanted, to make his friend unhappy? . . . Xavier gave in, out of a sense of doing the right thing, overcome by the prospect of depriving her of the joy of thinking she could make him happy. Peggy sat at the foot of the bed and started explaining what she had in mind. She asked if he had plans for two days hence, which was a holiday. Xavier had entertained vague thoughts of using his Saturday off to write to his sister, Justine, who had stayed behind in Hungary. But that, he said, could wait.

"Good. Because on Saturday night I'm taking you to a vaudeville show! I'll bet anything that you've never set foot in one in your life. Am I right?"

Xavier put his frog back in the casket, then sat down next to Peggy. He turned to her, his expression serious.

"A vaudeville show?"

She nodded.

He thought it over.

"Will there be contortionists?"

This reaction amused Peggy.

"I don't know. Maybe. You're funny!"

She tucked away the lock of hair that had fallen onto her forehead. Xavier definitely didn't seem won over. He looked distracted, sombre, preoccupied. To entice him, Peggy set forth the programme for the evening. First there would be songs and dances, then circus acts, acrobats, etc. The highlight would be a pantomime show, with magic effects that she'd heard were spectacular, all the clients at the salon were talking about them. It was entitled *The Patched-Up Mandarin*. Not to mention the Grand Music, with Grand Orchestra.

"Why the long face? Don't you like music?"

"No long face," said Xavier.

"Yes there is."

One time, Xavier stops near a bandstand where there is a placard announcing an open-air concert. He sits down, all smiles and confidence, a little anxious too, because nothing assures him that he's entitled to see the show. There must be a good thirty people, many of them elderly gentlemen and a good many elderly ladies. The orchestra tunes up, a sort of oddball murmur that pleases his heart. When the instruments are tuned, the apprentice applauds and stands up, thinking it's over. But then, abruptly, with a cosmic roar, the real music erupts, and Xavier is blasted back into his seat as if by the breath of a bomb. He holds tight to his chair, bends double when the brasses join in, protecting his chest for fear it will be smashed in. At the sound of the little flutes he stretches his neck to drink in the air, like a drowning man etc. As for the strings, they get on his nerves with their phenomenal piercing sound, and for him it's like tin being ripped, along with a drop during a roller-coaster ride. It doesn't even take five minutes. The apprentice flees, beside himself with dread.

He shared none of that, however, with Peggy, who understood less and less why he was so suspicious. But the young woman had sworn that she wouldn't leave here until Xavier was on tenterhooks.

"And that's not all!" she said. "On Saturday I won't let you out of my sight. First of all, we're going to a department store to find you a suit, don't worry, I'll pay for everything. And after that . . ."

The apprentice protested briskly. Him, buy a suit? Him, a Hungarian immigrant? What a senseless way to spend money! . . . Peggy sighed. She made him understand and then admit that he couldn't after all go to the vaudeville show on a Saturday night dressed like an apprentice demolisher! . . . She went on expounding her plans. They would visit museums, like tourists rolling in dough; then they'd eat ice cream, and to wind up with a flourish, before they went to the vaudeville show, she was going to take him — now pay attention — take him to a restaurant for supper!

And the apprentice's suspicion intensifies. The quality of the food, the proliferation of germs, and what all else. On the contrary, Peggy maintains, there are excellent spots in New York where you could eat like in Paris. Besides, the place she thought of taking him, she'd eaten there several times, with her boss. With a wink, indicating her own appearance with a movement full of grace, like a swan spreading its wings, she let him judge the result. Xavier conceded that she was beautiful, maybe the most beautiful girl in New York. She let out a laugh of naive satisfaction.

She stood up, arranged her hair in a feminine way.

"But why do all that for me?"

"Heavenly days! Because I like you a lot, that's why," she said.

And dropped an impish kiss on the tip of his nose. The apprentice studied her, dumbfounded. Peggy went out, and her perfume continued to float in the room. The female odour of lilac flowers on a night in May, when they're hot.

8

When the great hollywood master D. W. Griffith, worn out from what seemed to him an endless train trip, arrived at the destruction site with his army of drudges, a half-empty flask of Scotch in each of his jacket pockets, handing out almighty slaps left and right to the boys carrying his bags, and staggering as if he had fourteen legs, that day was for the Philosopher — who'd been dreaming about it the way a young girl dreams about her first ball — a tall glass of bitterness and humiliation, marked in the end by an atrocious event.

It had been suggested that Griffith make a documentary film to the glory of the demolition industry, and after some negotiations that shillied and shallied back and then forth, the Master had finally decreed that the Homeric grandiosity of the theme was proportional to his own. He had dispatched photographers assigned to locate interesting faces to work as extras. And so the Sands of Silence had been booked. Although he'd first seen the light of day in Ireland, in the greenest of countrysides (he'd been four when his parents emigrated to America), he nonetheless had the features of an old Apache chief — the kind you see in movies, haughtily contemptuous of Paleface greed. None of this was his fault.

He had the looks of a Sage of Antiquity the way others are born with red hair or ears like barn doors, and the fear of not living up to what was heralded by his face was a secret source of torment. He'd been promised that he would appear in close-up many times. (They'd had to explain what a close-up was.) This cinematographic production would make him the very symbol of his industry (they explained what a symbol was). For eight days the Philosopher couldn't sleep.

Ida, his wife, spared no efforts to have her man appear on screen in his most convincing array. And so he signed in at the destruction site that morning in a getup that provoked a number of remarks behind his back. The Sands pretended to ignore them. He practised noble attitudes, hand on hip, tried to catch his silhouette reflected in glass, sometimes blushing, seeing himself as handsome.

The first source of sorrow that day was the poor treatment inflicted on his protégé, Mortanse. With Lazare banished from the site, delegated to God only knows what occult task, the apprentice had had a few days' respite. But now the idle crews, who were supposed to await the arrival of the cameras before they got down to work, were regaining an appetite for tormenting him, taking pains, with nasty gaiety, to make Xavier's morning a rhapsody of petty punishments.

First they pulled the Itinerant Sausage trick. The apprentice, who'd been given no orders, had dozed off on the remains of a sofa abandoned on the sidewalk, its springs piercing the fabric in places. They painted his bootlaces with glue and tied them together. Then someone let out a deathly cry, right in his ear; the apprentice leapt to his feet, looking lost, and before he could even notice that his feet were tied he started to stamp up and down like a tube. Later, they made him carry on his shoulder a beam so heavy that his knees buckled, and a journeyman shouted from the rooftops that he looked "like somebody trying to walk and empty his hole at the same time." The image was so accurate, so exactly right, that the phrase was repeated from one end of the site to the other, instantly becoming a classic. The apprentice did his best to laugh too. The Philosopher would have gladly consoled him. But he'd have had to sit beside the lad on bricks that would have soiled his clothes.

Early that afternoon, the film crew finally appeared. With curiosity and folded arms they observed the preparations, sometimes venturing to ask the technicians a naive question. When passing ladies lingered, so intrigued by the cameras' presence that they forgot the wind caught in their skirts, the workers levelled the usual bawdy remarks at them. To this nonsense the Philosopher added his own, but grudgingly, giving in to the herd reflex even though these young women reminded him of his daughters, the youngest of whom worked at the post office and was only seventeen. Soon a small crowd of onlookers surrounded the site. Policemen patrolled, ensuring that all was in order. Over everything, an implacable July sun spread its sizzling dust.

Without lifting a buttock from his folding chair, the Master, who'd more or less sobered up once the contents of a coffee pot were poured down his throat, was issuing orders in a voice that turned metallic as it burst from the megaphone. Wily, dutiful assistants bustled nervously about, scathing towards the underling, electrified by the threat of an ever-likely dismissal. Despite the constabulary presence, Griffith regularly pulled a flask from his pocket and offered himself a slug of Scotch, then wiped his mouth on his sleeve. With head in hands he moaned, "I've lost my genius! I've lost my genius!" then suddenly straightened up, ready to devour everything around him, with the brio of a lion. Relentlessly he ordered group movements to be repeated in a perfectly orderly way. Finally it was the Philosopher's turn to be summoned before the Master.

An assistant led the way, clutching him by the biceps. In his hands the Sands twisted his Presidential Rod, the insignia of the Order. Given the humility of his attitude, he resembled a repentant prisoner being led before his judge in handcuffs. He stood a few paces from Griffith for a good minute, during which the Master didn't bother to take in his presence. The old man was careful not to look at him improperly, though his gaze clung furtively to certain details: the filmmaker's moustache and fingers were yellow from nicotine, he was unshaven, his feet were bare inside his shoes, and his mid-thigh-length pants — think African safari — revealed thin legs seamed with varicose veins to the ankles. Eventually the Master deigned to turn his way. He took off his spectacles and then, very slowly, his eyebrows rose, as if propelled by growing stupefaction. The Philosopher didn't know where to go. He twisted the tail of his shirt like an intimidated child. He felt terribly *visible* with his scarlet velvet pants, his golden-tasselled beret, and, over his white silk shirt — the one he wore for Ceremony Evenings — his presidential sash, the pride of his chest. This outfit was his wife's handiwork. The Philosopher had repeated to her what he'd been told about the meaning of the word "symbol," and she had clothed her man according to what she'd understood of it.

Finally the Master let fall his verdict:

"What's the meaning of this comic opera getup?"

Which beelined right to the old man's heart.

Then began what seemed to him a slow and inexorable fall into the abyss. First he was stripped of his ornaments — sash, beret, medals — which were flung into a bag any which way, then his braids were untied. "To look credible," as one of the assistants informed him, they spattered his shirt with dust and mud. The old man offered no resistance, kept his head down like an officer being stripped of his rank. Then he was moved to the sidelines for a good while. He sat on a hollow brick, elbows on knees. Suddenly, a few inches in front of him, stood two sneakers. He looked up. The lanky silhouette of the apprentice was standing against the light, and the solar crown gave him a blinding halo.

"Why the devil were all the policemen in New York after them?" So forth.

The old man fluttered his eyelids like someone emerging from a dream who was being addressed in Chinese.

"Lazare," said Xavier, excited. "Yesterday you told me that when he was eight, Lazare drifted through the countryside with his father because they had all the police in America on their heels. You started telling me that yesterday. And then, pphttt. You took off. The foreman called you."

"Ah yes, I see."

The Philosopher was far removed from such matters. But he had scruples about never losing patience with this disarmed and innocent lad. And so he straightened up and began to explain how Lazare's mother had discovered the truth.

"The truth," repeated Xavier with greedy attention.

One morning, after asking little Lazare some trivial question, she panics as she realizes that her son, who has taken refuge in his room, doesn't even know the alphabet. She realizes then that instead of taking him to school, the Great Barthakoste has been taking his son to the destruction sites every day, to teach him the rudiments of that blasted profession. There followed a terrible scene, which Lazare witnessed. The poor woman was left for dead on the kitchen floor. And the father fled, taking to the roads and bringing along the eight-year-old child.

"And that's the story," said the Philosopher.

"For dead?" the apprentice inquires.

"Actually, no. Not a hundred percent. She'll survive. But messed up. Half-disfigured."

"Which means completely disfigured," said Xavier briskly.

"If you want. And she never recovers from her fractured hip. To the end of her life she would have one leg that marched to a different drummer than the other."

Xavier rolled this new information around in his head greedily, with lights in his eyes. He walked back and forth, fist to mouth, like a detective on the brink of a solution.

"Aha! So that's it. That explains everything," he repeated to himself.

The Philosopher made a vaguely weary gesture and walked away. Sunk in gloom, he observed the building that was about to be demolished, at which the cameramen had aimed their instruments. It was the theatre he'd watched going up when he was small, six years old maybe. A labourer toiling on the frieze had died after falling from his scaffold, a twenty-metre drop. The man, whom he'd known very well, had been a friend of his father's. Who sometimes brought him treats. The accident had hurt him deeply as a youngster. He was haunted by it for months. It was the first death of his life. And the building started to exert on him Satan only knew what unsettled apprehension, what dull and doomed attraction. He kept going there time and again, to the very spot where the man had come crashing down, where a tiny cross, a cross that he himself had drawn in invisible ink, marked the slab, and he stayed there for a long time, shocked and glum. The month before, when he'd found out that the Order had won the contract to destroy the building, he had come to visit it and he'd looked for the cross and found it, faded and nearly erased, but visible, in the image of his childhood memories. Those images of youth had been resurfacing for some time now, were superimposing themselves on his current existence like blurred photographs, and he mused that he was like a man who has examined his own life, who is beginning to walk in his own footprints again, and it was a sign that time was coming full circle.

And he mused again that within three days they would demolish something it had taken months to build. It seemed to him to summon vast developments, he sensed in it a kind of universal law, a secret wrested from the cosmic mystery. But his thinking never went beyond that. He was not *capable* of going any further. His silences were calculated so that he seemed to know more. For thirty years now, he'd been going in circles and ending up nowhere. A caveman in front of the femur of a mammoth, who has a premonition about some event that is heavy with future, who snorts, who scratches his scalp, who sniffs the bone, yet stays there, paralysed, mind limited by invisible boundaries, and incapable of inventing the Tool.

An impostor, yes, that's what I am, thought the old man (he was not without savouring this spell of melancholy). And all those people waiting for him to produce the Great Work! He would be the one to sum up, within the pages of a book, a life devoted to the joys and mysteries of demolition. And his own daughter, his eldest daughter, whose husband managed a Catholic print shop, brought him blank pages by the hundred to fill with his fruitful meditations, in preparation for the book that was perpetually to come, which he always claimed was just two fingers away from completion . . . Yes, Morlay the dynamiter was right to laugh at him. Yes, he was a man who was a living lie.

Near a sagging, bulging façade that had taken on the shape of an S, and was held together by who knows what internal fibrous and plant-like consistency — which the workers called in their slang "the hairs of the brick" and which seemed to develop inside the walls as they got older — a handful of journeymen, knees on the ground, were performing ablutions of crushed cement while mumbling requests to the wall. Farther away, they were pulverizing against their foreheads some rose-orange bricklets that looked like praline. These sturdy types were pounding each others' chests with sledgehammers. Habits and customs of demolishers.

An assistant of Griffith's beckoned to the old man, who humbly pointed a forefinger at his chest: "Me?" The assistant was a long, thin, ageless hank of human with olive-yellow skin. He had the embittered appearance of a man with no illusions about anything, and you could tell from his convex mouth that his most recent smile must date back to kindergarten. In the corner of his mouth, a cigarette, rooted there. His eyes, you might say, were on the point of popping out of their sockets. (The Philosopher recorded these details to take to his wife.) A death's head already broke through the waxen skin of his face.

The assistant hissed a few words in a strong Texas accent that the Sands could only half-puzzle out. Then he was positioned on a platform. The idea was to film him from a low angle to create the impression of power and domination. This was explained. The old man tried modestly to dominate the world with his chin, his shoulders, his eyebrows. To do so, he threw his head so far back that you'd have sworn he had a nosebleed. Which was pointed out, with no beating about the bush, and the old man blushed. More shots were taken. He could tell from the puzzled faces of the film crew that the results weren't considered convincing. The Philosopher was dripping from the armpits like a dishmop.

They started to line up another shot. This time they asked the Philosopher to look at the camera as if he were angry. He did his best. But he was so intimidated that his face suggested instead a little boy on the brink of tears because the big boys have just stolen his marbles. Along with which, at any moment his eyes might leave the camera lens to check that his performance was satisfactory to the assistant. Who, uprooting the cigarette from his lips, lashed out with an observation, his diction, if not perfect, at least intelligible.

"Show some conviction for fuck's sake."

He rerooted his cigarette in the corner of his mouth. The old man nodded his bonnet: okay, now he got it. He took a deep breath and launched into a series of angry grimaces, with abundant sniffing and salivation and the growling of a beast, a she-monkey whose baby has been snatched away from her, and the whole set burst out laughing. The Philosopher tottered on the platform, had to lean on the parapet to keep from losing his balance. And was told not to "act," to be "natural." Again, a new take. And then the old man did nothing more; not a hair of his lashes, not a nerve in his face moved, which is called not acting at all, from what he'd understood. The assistant heaved a sigh of resignation; one thing more going wrong, or one less. He declared that it would be all right, that they'd make do, and that it was time to move on to another shot.

"Bring on the jackass," he hissed.

Now they would launch into the allegorical sequence, "Experience Blessing Youth." The jackass alluded to earlier was brought on, presumably to depict the second figure in the allegory. Xavier still had lights in his eyes, his fist on his lips, the look of a detective on the brink, etc. He too was made to mount the platform. He knelt in front of the Philosopher, hands joined, while the old man placed a paternal palm on his skull to conform with the assistant's instructions. Who added:

"Look like you're talking. Say anything you want, whatever comes into your head."

The kneeling one could have asked for nothing more.

"It can all be explained," he said, and his face, raised up towards the Philosopher's, radiated naive pride. "The fact is, I've never seen someone swallow a sausage as fiercely as Lazare. He eats with a kind of anger, you'd think he was mad at his food. You see, when you eat you become what you're eating. And since we kill animals, Mr. Sands, because we murder them so we can devour them entirely, I mean their souls as much as their bodies, because we cut them into pieces and remove the bones, and because we eat them all the way to the organs, heart, guts, liver, kidneys, we have to expect — and this is my point — we have to expect all that foulness to get inside us, to become us when we swallow it, when we swallow this meat that's been killed. So Lazare's rage to eat was both mystery and company to me. But now I understand. I've seen that it came from his childhood, by gosh, and basically, by swallowing his never-ending sausages, what he was actually eating, what he was eating every time — *was his mother! . . .*"

Xavier had spoken those last words in a whisper, fingers hiding his mouth.

The stunned Philosopher took his hand away from Xavier's skull, out of an irrational fear of contagion. It had to come sooner or later. The lad was out of his mind.

"Put your hand back on his head!" shouted the assistant, this time with perfect clarity. "Look like you're blessing him, goddammit! Mutter whatever comes into your head!"

The Philosopher began to recite the *Our Father*, staring, dazed, at the apprentice, whose smile was radiant with the same candid triumph.

"Yes," he said. "It's all clear now. Next time I see Lazare, I'll explain. No more Clinic, no more anger, no more stomach cramps!"

"You poor child," the old man murmured.

But now it was time to move on to something else. They brought the Philosopher down from his platform, nearly shoving him in their haste. The old man obeyed, followed the movement, bad timing. New sequence, new allegory. This time, "Tradition Extending a Hand to the Future." The

Philosopher listened to the explanations, making a mental note of everything, tense and exuding good will.

And this was serious, because the scene would be directed by Maestro Griffith himself (the Sands's anxiety burned with brand-new zeal). And in his chair, which stagehands loaded onto their shoulders, the filmmaker was taken to the middle of the site. As for the Future, it would of course be played by Morlay, the sarcastic dynamiter. Cold sweat oozed onto the Philosopher's brow. He swelled up to the point of suggesting, "Why not another take?" The film-going public wouldn't see the difference. His request was passed on to the Director, who wasn't interested. What he wanted was Morlay's kisser, his unique demonic smile.

They lined up the shot. The Eye would see the about-to-be-demolished theatre in the background, and the dynamiter would walk up to Tradition, accompanied by his assistant, with three cameras aimed at him. So it was decided. Cowed by the Maestro's presence, but fired up with professional pride too, the Philosopher took deep breaths to overcome his stage fright and then, when Griffith called, "Action!" he shot towards Morlay, taking tremendous strides. Morlay was proceeding towards the old man, with his hand extended and a mocking look. Beside him, maybe two metres away, his assistant was unfurling the wire that would connect the detonator to the dynamite that had been planted in strategic parts of the building under destruction. The assistant held two more sticks of dynamite in his right fist. Morlay's fixed grin was a thumbing of the nose at the old man, who was coming nearer, teeth clenched. "Very good, excellent!" exclaimed Griffith into his megaphone. "Now, talk! Say anything at all, whatever comes into your head!"

"So we're all dolled up today, right, Mr. Symbol?" said the ironic dynamiter to the wounded old man.

The assistant laughed his approval. Morlay then slowed down a little so he could join the two sticks of dynamite the other man was holding out. No one ever knew why, or how, but suddenly the Philosopher felt an adverse pressure over his whole body, a kind of resistance to the air that was elastic and burning, while a buzzing oppressed his eardrums to the point of bursting. In the time of a blink, the assistant dynamiter became black and crimson smoke. A projectile landed on the old man's chest; he fell over backwards. For a moment he thought he was dead. When he stood up, half-stunned, ears filled with thunder, he spotted the projectile at his feet, the dynamiter. Who had his left arm and left leg torn off, half his face burned to a cinder, and who was moaning, help, help, the poor hand he still had holding onto the Philosopher's pants . . .

9

DUSK WAS SLOWLY COMPLETING its extinction, a dying
person with a pillow pressed onto his face. And despite the
huge plank fire and the big Xs of the beams put up as Signs to
mark the perimeter of the site, no one was in a festive mood.
Nevertheless, an evening of feasting and rejoicing had been
planned. The crews had gathered to entertain delegations
from the four corners of the biggest cities — Philadelphia,
Detroit, Chicago, so forth. Officials read solemn letters to the
foremen, who appreciated the tributes and offered thanks by
serving the delegates the Journeyman's drink, served in the
horn of a billy goat. But the accident that afternoon was
weighing on everyone's heart. Cameramen and stagehands had
mingled with the workers out of sympathy, conferring with
them with their arms crossed, without conviction, as in a
funeral parlour. Here and there, choruses of journeymen sang
pessimistic tunes. Moderate attempts were made to erect
human pyramids. Everyone had just one thought. Of the
young assistant dynamiter, all that had been found were a
few puddles of flesh, the visor of his cap, the heel of a shoe.
Morlay was suffering agonies in the intensive care unit of
some New York hospital. (The rumour was going around

that he would, alas, survive his burns.) As for Griffith, at the first opportunity he had dived into a taxi full of petticoats, languorous gazes, and sophisticated scents, and they never saw him again.

The Philosopher had withdrawn to the edge of the destrution site, away from the joyless festivities. His slack hands held the brown paper bag containing the pointless ornaments of his glory — sash, tasselled beret, ridiculous and pathetic medals (so they struck him just then). His shoulders felt as heavy as if he'd spent the day in demented demolition. Never, not even if he experienced twenty deaths and twenty other lives, would he forget that living wound pleading for help, for a lessening of his senseless suffering. Morlay's trembling hand clutching at his trousers. Like his gaze, the last vestige of the human in that bleeding piece of meat; his gaze, which had only one eye, the left one reduced to a pellet of coal hanging from its socket like a sleigh bell. Even when the ambulance arrived, even when the stretcher was slid under him with every precaution, Morlay's hand hadn't let go of Leopold's trousers, nor had his one-eyed gaze strayed from the face of the old man who was his whipping boy, his adversary, and the object of his contempt. There was an appeal in that gaze, and hatred in the appeal, an obstinate hatred that seemed mightier than pain, that told the Philosopher: Even when I'm suffering, even when I'm begging for your help, I still despise you, I still denounce you; and when the old man remembered that vindictive eye, he could distinctly hear Morlay's voice calling him a barn wrecker, and he stood up, neck sweating and heart pounding, like someone waking from a horrible dream.

To ease his turmoil, he observed the journeymen carrying

on in the deepest part of the site. By feigning the motions of a celebration, they were gradually getting caught up in the game. Laughter was heard now and then, somewhat forced, of course, but still heralding a thaw. Friendly competitions got underway between representatives of the different cities. Coals were stoked, lambs were shish kebabed.

How many of them used to be firemen, masons, plasterers, bakers, window installers, even lawyers, violinists, insurance salesmen, or wealthy young men? Few had actually started out, as Leopold had, in the profession of demolisher. They had known the satisfaction of work well done, the joy of seeing a job born, grow, fulfilled, each in his own domain. But one day or another they had all succumbed to the inexplicable fascination of demolition. You had to have experienced it from the inside to know what it was like. That feverish, subterranean, visceral excitement, quite literally diabolical. All knew to what dark, insidious, unspeakable region of themselves they owed the deep, insidious, unspeakable pleasure that came from mowing down slums, from devastating buildings. It revealed to them a bottomless hole in the heart of their being, something those who'd never held a smashing tool (except maybe slaughterhouse workers) could not imagine. They fed themselves on that, got drunk — guiltily, for sure, tormented too, but powerless to surrender such a heady feeling. To the point where sometimes it was the worker himself who collapsed. Victims of nervous breakdowns streamed into the Clinic, a genuine scourge in the profession.

Starting with me, thinks the Sands. Though he maintained that the rough-handled passion, the sensual pleasure it offered him, had "left his blood" for good, you never knew when it could re-emerge and mow you down, a shark surfacing without warning from an unruffled sea. Such as the other week, when before the very eyes of the expelled he'd bashed in the front door of the tenement building with his head (had he been able to see again the woman who escaped a moment later, pushing a baby carriage, the Philosopher wouldn't have hesitated to offer her half his salary for the month). Worse: not all that long ago he was sensibly at home, watching over the baby of his eldest, who'd gone out to do her errands, along with his wife, Ida. Tenderly he had bent over the cradle where the angel was sleeping like a baby. And all at once a terrible anxiety took hold of him. His fingers were wrapped around the bars of the cradle and it took a real effort of will to stifle the impulse in his muscles to break them. He raised his head, looked around this little girl's room, with its candy-pink furniture, its china ballerinas, and its music box, while a panicky fear welled up inside him, fear that an uncontrollable urge to demolish everything would be unleashed. He had of course no desire to do so, but what would he do if the urge did seize him? Fear of being tempted by that fear, tempted to give in to the fear that a temptation might sweep over him and strike him down: the anguish of an addict, of an alcoholic. He fled the house with the baby in his arms, terrified of himself.

A pale shadow arrived out of nowhere, that you might have taken for a ghost, gliding rather than walking, all at once there, in front of him, quick, made the blood rise to his temples. Xavier X. Mortanse pointed to the wooden crate the old man was sitting on.

"May I?" he asked, and sat down beside the Philosopher.

Who was still in a daze from his fright and said nothing. As for the apprentice, he dared not take up right away the thread of a conversation that had been interrupted a few hours ago. In silence, then, they turned their attention to the festivities. Which were now in full flight. The competitions (friendly) between the representatives of the various cities had been organized, multiplied, officialized, the bets were open to anyone. Songs rose up, wafted by a cheerful and fierce conviction. The main attraction was the Charge of the Moose. This entailed running a distance of twenty metres and crashing into one another, skull first. Again and again, until one of them fell (it was enough for one knee to touch the ground). The grand champion was a fierce Amerindian *Colossus horribilis* from Chicago, fast on his feet and bereft of a neck. A clamour greeted each of his victories. The huge board fire was spreading to the surrounding façades — ghostly, half-demolished, frenzied, capricious silhouettes. The lambs went on roasting under a bright sky that was convex like a magnifying glass.

Xavier had a question burning his lips, and he watched the Philosopher from the corner of his eye, trying to guess the auspicious moment. Finally he asked:

"In the end, did he see her again?"

"Did who see who?" asked the old man, with a hint of impatience that did not escape the apprentice.

But the boy was too eager to know.

"Lazare. His mother."

Leopold sighed through his nose: that again. It was a real obsession. But scruples, scruples; mustn't lose his composure with the lad. He began to scratch the calluses on his palm.

"After his father died, Lazare would have been twelve, the federal police sent him home to New York, to give him back to his mama."

Initially, that was all the Philosopher had intended to say. But Xavier asked, "Then what?" and he felt an unexpected interest in the story; he searched his memory and went on, gaze fixed, as if he were telling it just as much to himself.

"Meanwhile, his mother had made a new life for herself. She'd married an odd duck who was half-paralysed from poliomyelitis. (The Philosopher knew the word; one of his nephews had died from it.) The poor fellow, who felt himself pining away, was tormented at having no one to inherit his business; Lazare seemed like a gift from on high. Sadly, when you consider that the Demolition Fairy had bent over Lazare's cradle, you can imagine how blithely he picked up his adoptive father's trade. Because of all things, the fellow ran a watchmaker's shop. Think of it: learning to handle the little hooks, the tiny screws, the minute mechanisms, and all the rest. Lazare nearly went crazy. Only dreamed about smashing buildings. Actually, he had exorbitant ambitions for one so young, which is harmful, I swear; churches, for instance. It was his dream to demolish one; a church, I tell you; now, I'm not talking about dynamite and all those blasted inventions, you saw what happened this afternoon, didn't you? I'm talking about demolition the way we used to do it in the old days, when it was still a real profession. Well, demolishing a chapel, a church, with just the tools of the day — there was nothing more complicated or dangerous, because of the steeple, which you never know when it's going to collapse, I've known people who died that way! But that was all Lazare dreamed of at fourteen. A mouse that wanted to devour a graveyard. Though his mother shut him away in the basement padded cell, and cursed him and strapped him, the lad was stubborn as a jewel. He refused to learn the man's trade, and swore with gritted teeth that he was going to be a demolisher and that was that. The watchmaker began to shrivel up, to shrink, to wither away, in the end all that was left was a little heap, and then he died. The next year, cancer carried off the mother. I was there on the first morning Lazare, who was barely seventeen, showed up on a destruction site. Which wasn't far from here, on Twelfth Avenue. The commotion that greeted him, my oh my! Because he'd been a legend in those circles for a long time. Never saw the like before or since. They said at the time that he'd shrugged his shoulders over his mother's remains. And that's it. That's pretty well everything I know."

Silence. Then Xavier asked:

"But tell me, Mr. Sands, how can you know that such-and-such a mother is really the mother of such-and-such a child?"

The Philosopher frowned. Had he really heard what he'd just heard? He gazed at the apprentice, concerned and dismayed.

"What kind of question is that?" he whispered, nearly frightened by the apprentice's naivety.

"Oh, nothing," was Xavier's reply.

Then not another word. He looked straight ahead, pensive.

The Philosopher studied him with a kind of stupor, as if Xavier were something of a prodigy in his own domain. Where the deuce could this lad have come from? (A thousand times he asked himself that question.) His first meeting with Xavier. A tiny feeble voice had whispered behind his back, "Tell me, kind old man, would you have any dollars, dollars or some work to earn them?" Leopold had turned around. Filthy dirty, clothes — cruddy is the word, covered with dried blood and vomit, the lad's hand outstretched, a beggar's. The mere sight of him brought a pang of pity to the old man's heart. "Mister, I have supped on rummaging in the delectables." The Philosopher had pleaded in the starving lad's favour and they'd agreed to take him on as an apprentice, though he seemed so unsuited for that harsh trade. And just now, when the day's events led him to meditate on destiny, the old man wondered what aberration of fate had brought this walking lettuce leaf to demolition sites where walls were smashed with four-ton sledgehammers.

"You're a mystery to me, my boy," he couldn't help admitting.

Xavier turned to him a face that was smooth, naive, and open.

"I am?" he said.

"I can't figure out why you keep working at a trade that doesn't suit you at all. Wouldn't you be better off at school? Learning out of books?"

Xavier's face darkened.

"Books," he said. "They always damage your mind."

The old man's tone went up a notch.

"And what about demolition? Doesn't demolition damage your mind? . . . And your body too."

"The both of them together," the apprentice pointed out, forefinger in the air, but the Philosopher didn't follow up on that remark.

"It's all very well to have principles about nutrition, as you say, and about the meat we kill and the corpses we eat, but what can you do, we have to live the way the good Lord created us! Look at your build, and the breadth of your shoulders, you've got the makings of a colossus. But you eat like a sparrow. You're as weak as a man on his deathbed, just pick up a hammer and you break out in a sweat! Honestly, sometimes I take a look at you and I think, it can't be, he's going to faint away. Sometimes, my boy, you can barely stand up on your feet. Take a look at those fellows over there." He jerked his arm in the direction of the jubilant demolishers. "Lazare's father could chew bricks! What do you think you're doing around those people? What exactly do you want? You have to be one of them, understand? To be like them, the same race as them, otherwise they'll inflict the Tool on you too, like a wall."

Xavier's arms were folded on his chest, his expression dark and mulish.

"I was hired to do demolition and demolition is what I'll do" was all he said, and he said it unflinchingly.

He got up and started pacing restlessly, hands in the pockets of his trousers. The old man looked resigned. He knew that words would not overcome the kind of illusions this lad entertained. Sooner or later life would open his eyelids, and that, thought the Philosopher, was liable to be not a pretty sight.

Three journeymen were walking around the edge of the site. Leopold guessed that they were looking for him, for the needs of the Ceremony. They were still too far away for him to hail them. Xavier had come to a halt, still pondering.

"You said after his father died, Mr. Sands. And what was it he died of, Lazare, his father?"

The Philosopher hesitated briefly. Why confide that to the lad — and how would he use it? . . .

But why not tell him either?

"Murder. Lazare's father died of murder."

Xavier took his hands out of his pockets and slowly brought them to his face.

"Murdered how, murdered by whom?"

"Murdered murdered," said the old man testily, and slapping his thighs with his palms, he got up. "*Oï!* . . . *Kokoni iro-zô!* he said in the direction of his journeymen, which in the Order's argot meant "Hey, ho! . . . Here I am!"

One of the three men came up to him. Red brushcut hair, arms that could tie a knot in the legs of a stubborn horse. A former flautist from Carnegie Hall. He told the Philosopher:

"Come, Journeyman. The hour has come to Abash the wall."

Wearily, the Sands complied. As the eldest worker, he was obviously the one to play that role. He turned towards Xavier one last time, as if to tell him that he had no choice. The apprentice smiled to let him know that he didn't mind the Philosopher's leaving him, that he understood. There was nonetheless a watery element in his eyes. (For those who weren't full-fledged Journeymen were forbidden to take part in the Order's feastings.) The Philosopher gave him a sad little wave. He didn't know why, but he had the impression he was seeing the apprentice for the last time. He shook himself, shook off that depressing thought, and stepped onto the site. Xavier was then struck by an analogous premonition, so powerful that he began to move in his friend's direction. At once, though, the red-haired former flautist called him to order, pushing him violently six paces away. Xavier stepped farther back to show that he'd got the message. The man threw a stone at him, to make him step back even more.

Finally he produced a conspiratorial sign — forefinger and little finger raised — as if to drive away the evil eye.

Xavier picked up a hammer that was lying around. Slowly walked the length of the rope that demarcated the site, then stood still. He leaned heavily on one leg first and then the other, trying to put on a brave face, like the lone child who's excluded from the playground.

Once the Philosopher had joined his journeymen at the bottom of the hole, the hundred or so workers there formed a large circle, and four individuals lifted Leopold by his four limbs. The old man did not resist. He was carried like that, horizontally, to a low wall that was threatening ruination. Fitted into it, a paned window from which Xavier hoped with all his heart the glass had been removed (but he couldn't swear, the distance being fairly considerable). The limbs of the Sands were stretched, as if they had it in mind to tear him apart limb from, and then, swinging the old man at arms' length in an ever-widening semicircle, they finally bashed his skull into the window. The panes gave way at the first blow.

Now the Philosopher's head was sticking out the other side of the low wall. The journeymen kept him horizontal, and the window formed a kind of yoke for him. A man approached, arrayed in a woman's dress, coiffed in a woman's wig, made up and beringed and bejewelled like a woman, and unshaven. He planted a sober kiss on the Philosopher's brow. The circle of journeymen observed the customary silence. At last, with movements stamped with solemnity, codified down to the last comma, he began to wrap the Sands' long white hair around curlers . . .

The crews struck up a lugubriously gentle hymn. The

plank fire, which was no longer being fed, decreased in intensity, but rose up now and then with intense bursts of effort. The shadows were dying on the building rubble, fraying in long loose strands. "Someday I'll be one of them," thought Xavier, "and then they'll love me too," while the skewered lambs turned fragrantly above the embers, their hides blistering and wheezing.

The Patched-Up Mandarin

*For if we become attached to other beings, we must be
prepared for the attachment to be suddenly and abruptly
severed, life being a rope that spends most of its time breaking.*

— Xavier X. Mortanse
from LETTERS TO MY SISTER

Part I

1

Justine put down her cup of tea. It was twenty minutes past the scheduled appointment and now she was wondering if she'd been wrong to trust an individual she hardly knew. Luckily, the café was patronized by show people, it would stay open very late. She decided to wait till eleven o'clock. A few tables from her, a young woman was weeping: "After everything I've done for you, after everything I've been to you." She was addressing a young man with slicked-down hair who was ostentatiously paying no attention to her. He was looking out the window while he smoked a cigarette, his manner contemptuous and harsh. "Vain about the pain he's inflicting," thought Justine. "He probably slaps her when he demands money." Beside them, a fat oily man was shovelling in spaghetti, indifferent.

The man she was waiting for walked into the café. He had on a beige raincoat that was creased and dirty. He hadn't shaved. He was picking his teeth with a wooden match. He sat down without saying hello or doffing his hat.

"Good evening," said Justine.

"Mmm," he said, and flicked the brim of his hat.

He went on picking his teeth. Then:

"Why meet so late? I work early in the morning."

"I'm a pianist at the movie theatre next door. The show was over at nine-forty."

"Anyway, if it's news you want it's still way too soon."

"But it's been three weeks."

"So it has, young missy, so it has! But what can I do? With the speck of information you gave me. I started where you told me to: I checked out the port from top to bottom, questioned longshoremen, went to speakeasies. Incidentally, you'll have some expenses to cover. I have receipts, all that."

Justine thought about her savings, which were melting away. Never mind.

"I'll pay for everything, you know that."

"And then the young man, that . . ."

"Xavier."

". . . that Xavier. Who knows, maybe he boarded some steamship or other. They take on a lot of young people just like that, at a moment's notice. If that's the case he could be at the other end of the world by now."

"You mean I'd be wise to just drop it."

The man's greed was alerted.

"I mean it will be hard. And if there's one man who can find him for you, that man is me, Gary Hoobler."

He placed the match on the table and, with his tongue, noisily sucked his hollow tooth. Having to associate with such vulgar people. Justine felt tears of rage and despondency sting her eyes.

"Look, needless to say as soon as I've got any lead at all, I'll let you know. Do you still live in the same place?"

"No. That's one of the reasons I wanted to meet you. Here's my address as of this morning."

She handed Gary Hoobler a card.

> THE SANDS OF SILENCE
> ROOMING HOUSE
> OWNER: LEOPOLD O'DONAHUE
> ALL WELCOME!
> ETC.

The detective half-closed his eyes, burrowing into the small compartments in his brain.

"Hang on, wait. Leopold O'Donahue . . . Leopold O'Donahue. Right, now I remember."

As if it were a lesson, he rhymed off, "Elder of the New York Order of Demolishers, born in Ireland, nicknamed the Philosopher by his workmates —"

"Possibly," Justine interrupted, impressed even so.

"See, I know everything. So don't worry, I'll find your Xavier for you."

He placed his long, bony, damp, and hairy hand on Justine's forearm, trying to reassure. His smile revealed yellow teeth like a horse's.

"I don't believe I gave you permission to touch me."

Gary Hoobler took his hand away. His eyes said, "You're such a prude."

Calm and dignified, Justine sipped her tea.

"Actually," said the detective, "it's none of my business, of course, it's just curiosity. Once I've found your Xavier for you, what do you intend to do with him?"

"Kill him."

Gary Hoobler began to laugh softly. He picked up the wooden match and filed it away carefully in his wallet, which he then buried in the pocket of his raincoat.

"If that's the case, young missy, you'll have to go elsewhere. I don't play those kinds of fiddles."

"I'll do it myself."

Hoobler was getting ready to leave, but he stayed in his chair. Silence. The detective gazed at Justine with interest.

"Scared you, didn't I? Admit it," she said.

The detective snickered cynically.

"Oh, you know, I've seen it all. Nothing can surprise me any more."

Justine tightened her fox around her neck, pinned on her hat.

"Tell me though, no joke. Is that really what you intend to do?"

"I said that for a laugh," she said, standing up.

She dropped some change on the table and left.

Gary Hoobler had taken out his match. Dreamily, he was cleaning his teeth.

2

ON THE EVE OF HIS OUTING WITH Miss Peggy,
Xavier spent a very rough night. There'd been the day's events,
of course, the revelations about Lazare, all that, and then the
dynamite accident, which had stayed in his eyes like a bedaz-
zlement. He had, however, taken care to prepare for sleep.
He'd locked his frog's casket, then wrapped his belt around
it, buckled tight for extra security. He'd taken off the plankets of his devising. He'd stuffed his ears with a kilo of paper.

But the commotion from his new neighbours had kept
him awake till two a.m. The couple had come home around
eleven. From the man's slurred diction you could tell that he
hadn't deprived himself of joyjuice. The woman had loud,
phony laughter, as if being tickled, which grated on the
apprentice's nerves. Though he tossed this way and that on
his mattress, like an injured mouse under a cat's paw, it was
impossible for him not to hear, not to listen, not to multi-
ply his dejected sighs. He couldn't form a precise idea of the
activity the two were engaging in, which only annoyed him
more. The man made his demands in a plaintive voice,
while the woman acceded to them reluctantly and in return
for a promise of money. In the end, Xavier gave up (on both

comprehending and snoozing), and to kill time he paced, hoping that the grunts, the snickers, the moans of the couple — he was not about to forget that the woman was named Rosette — would stop before daybreak.

When he was finally able to sleep, it was only to waken twisted into ludicrous postures: the ostrich (face flattened into the pillow, bum in the air); or a dog scratching its ear (foot against cheek, like a telephone); or the hanged cat, most uncomfortable posture of all (standing on the back of his head, heels stuck to the wall). An hour of this and he was wide awake, with more aches than he'd had at bedtime. His face was hot, his eyelids on fire, and he was rolling the next day's events around in his head well in advance. And then all these trials that were putting his epigastrium in a knot. What? Visit museums and department stores? Eat ice cream? And then a restaurant, and after that the vaudeville show? Where would he find the strength? And what if he fainted in the middle of a street, all five senses leaving him at once? And what if he was suddenly overcome by suffocation in his chest? Surely Peggy would be annoyed, would dump him on the spot etc., wouldn't want to be his friend any more. And now the young woman's plans, which she'd hoped would bring joy and wonder, were turning into nightmares for the apprentice.

One thought, which made him suddenly jump out of bed, overshadowed all others. Miss Peggy had promised to buy him a suit, so be it. She'd also said that she would pick it out with him, and that he would wear the suit to the vaudeville show. Very well. But he was going to have to *take his clothes off in front of her*. He flung himself onto his mattress, using his body to muffle the horrified, muted beating of his heart, which was reverberating all the way to the walls.

The quiet growl of a dying dog escaped from his throat. With all his might, he called on memories of his native land. Straightened up, seemingly convinced. Bravely hung up his belt and hanged himself from it.

He took off by the seat of his pants, the hook was jerked out of the ceiling, and there he was, ass meeting floor, eyes astonished. He sat there for a long moment, saying over and over, "I nearly died." Finally, with all his nerves snapping at the same time, like ropes breaking, with his temple pressed to the wall, he sank into a sleep as deep as a blackout.

He slept late, and when he was finally able to get up he felt defeated, muscles heavy as if he'd spent the night fighting. He dressed apathetically and under protest, had to start over because he'd forgotten the plankets. He opened his frog's casket and stroked the creature's belly in a way she usually liked, but the diva was sullen. Unhappy at having spent a cloistered night, mademoiselle was sulking. "I'm sorry," he told her. "I'll never do that to you again." Miss Peggy knocked at his door as agreed around eleven o'clock.

He waited ten seconds before he opened the door, eyes closed, fist pressed into his chest. He was taking his life seriously.

And stepped back as if he'd been pushed. The first flower of the first morning of the world stood there before him in person. Peggy had painted her lips, whitened her face, shadowed her eyelids (just a touch), and two little blue feathers hung from the lobes of her ears. The red halo of her hat, the sailor suit with the pleated skirt, the flat-heeled shoes, and the ribbons tied around her black braids — "the only thing missing is the skipping rope," thought Xavier, with an emotion that seemed to go back to his childhood.

"You smell of the brook."

Said he to her, who seemed unsure that she'd really understood. Something in her gaze wavered like the flickering of a match. Xavier explained. Peggy was a spray of fresh water. In contrast, he himself felt as if he'd spent the night in a sewer. As far as he could remember, he'd never set foot in a forest, but he imagined that when you come near a brook you can guess it from its smell, and she had that particular fresh scent, or so he imagined, he told her. This connection didn't seem to make Peggy unhappy. The little light was back in her eyes.

Splendour of sky and sun in New York that morning, with the prevailing atmosphere of a holiday Saturday. Brightness of trees, grace of streets and bridges, extravagant magnificence of buildings. Even if it meant taking detours, Miss Peggy went along the most beautiful, the leafiest, most blossoming, and merriest avenues. As for Xavier, he walked along with his head down, as if plumb line at tip of nose. Miss Ohara wasn't overly concerned about his glumness. She was thinking about all the delights she had planned for him, which would win him over no matter what. She was sure that by wearing him down, she would accomplish Xavier's happiness.

"Besides," she said, "you'll feel better when you've changed your clothes."

Xavier turned off the street and went to a park bench, where he sat down, overcome.

"Now what is it?"

The apprentice made no reply. With elbows on knees, he was unconsciously watching the goings-on of some ants that were transporting blades of grass. A long moment passed. Peggy, sitting at his side, buttock to buttock, legs crossed; Peggy, turning her back to him while she studies her fingernails; Peggy, her shoulder resting on a tree behind; Peggy, finally sitting down again, this time at the other end of the bench, heaving great sighs up to heaven. All this to say that she was waiting. While Xavier, still and silent. For a quarter of an hour now he hadn't moved any more than a plane tree.

He finally reacted when he heard her sniff. Discreetly, she was wiping her eyes. Xavier said pathetically:

"I don't want somebody to buy me a suit."

With a tremor in her voice, Peggy asked why, and Xavier, categorical, said because.

"Surely you don't think you can go to the vaudeville show decked out like you are."

"These are my work clothes," he retorted, though not too convinced.

"And you think a person wears work clothes to the vaudeville show on Saturday night?"

She had spoken with conspicuous calm and modesty, so he'd be well aware that while she had every reason to lose her temper, she also had the magnanimity not to lose her temper. The apprentice was alert to that, he hated his own guts, but so what? That was really asking too much of him. With funereal gravity he assessed the consequences, the consequences for his own life and the sorrow he was about to inflict on the young woman. So it goes. He heard himself deliver these words:

"If that's so, I'd just as soon not go to your vaudeville show."

He saw Peggy's pretty fists drop onto her pretty thighs.

"All right, if that's it . . ." And she got up. Xavier, still hunched over, elbows on knees, kept looking up at her, resigned to himself as to a disease. Peggy was going to leave. Not before she assured herself that her purse strap was safely slung over her shoulder, a pretext for giving the boy one last chance to atone for what he'd said. Xavier was gazing glumly at his phalanges, the medial, the distal, the works. He regretted that he'd failed that morning, with the belt. The attempt had left some yellowish marks on his neck, which he tried to conceal by pulling up his collar.

Peggy exploded.

"Why, will you tell me? What the heck is so terrible about buying a suit?"

He replied that such things weren't meant for him. And added dully:

"Anyway I don't know how to do that, buy clothes . . ."

Peggy sniffled briefly.

"Good grief, it isn't complicated! You pick the one you want, you go to the fitting room, you look at yourself in the mirror, you pay, and then bye-bye. That's all."

She had made these remarks half for herself, practically in a murmur, to set her mind at rest; she had no illusion about their impact. All her fine hopes for the day were suddenly corroded, dissolved, vanished in twists of smoke. But now Xavier was sitting up straight! (His first movement in nearly half an hour.) It was the words "fitting room" that had hit the bull in the eye. She had to explain what that was. He wanted to be reassured all the way to underneath the plankets. He asked if he'd be able to go inside by himself.

"Why, of course," she said, taken aback.

Xavier's face lit up.

HIS FEARS DISPERSED, Xavier felt what he felt at the site every evening, when he took off his leaden boots: as if he had wings on his backside. Everything delighted him, amazed him, filled him with wonder. Often he burst out in great ingenuous laughter. At the department store, he let his long legs take him all over; he didn't understand the meaning of aisles, and was constantly ending up behind counters with salesgirls, which brought giggles from Peggy. It was all so new to him — the light fixtures, the Ali Baba abundance, the cheery tinkling of the cash registers, the pirouetting of dollars, the dazzling signs, the wealth, the floods of everything. At times his eyes hurt, as if he were staring at the sun.

Finally came the time to buy the suit. A two-piece suit, double-breasted if you please, hundred percent wool, and mouse-grey with blue pinstripes so fine that you had to put your nose right against the cloth to see them. And after that, watch out! Not one, not two, but *three* matching shirts with stiff collars, can you imagine! This disinterested, incomprehensible generosity, giving simply for the sake of giving, filled his eyes with water. Why do all this for him, Xavier? Miss Peggy herself chose the bow tie, a violet one no bigger than a thumb. Xavier gazed at himself in the mirror, incredulous, weighed down with doubts, wondering why these clothes didn't look as good on him as they did on the dummies he admired in the store windows. But Peggy assured him that everything looked ravishing. He whispered shyly in her ear, "Everyone's gawking at me! . . ." Laughing, she said, "That's right!" Her eyes were bright as she studied him from feet to head, biting the corner of her lower lip. The result was beyond her hopes, which had not however been slim. She asked permission to take his arm when they walked, to which "Of course, of course you can," Xavier replied, and they set off, the apprentice loping his long, lanky steps, and Peggy more than a little proud of the women's heads that turned as they went by.

Finally, at a hatmaker's window, the apprentice stopped short, mesmerized. "Would you like a hat too?" Xavier did not reply. His gaze seemed swallowed up by the display.

"Come on," said Peggy, pulling him away, "we're going to buy you a hat too."

Xavier tried on a good dozen. He displayed a temperamental, finicky inspiration, the last thing Peggy would have imagined. Finally, an exasperated salesman with a coat-hanger-shaped moustache gave them a peevish look. Xavier saw none of that. He was studying the hats, meditating on them, performing obscure checks on them. Treading on his own shyness, he tried to enlighten the salesman as to what it was he wanted. Unfortunately, his American wasn't up to expressing the desired subtleties.

He was on the verge of discouragement — Peggy thought he was actually going to cry — when all at once: a miracle. A lightning flash, love at first sight: a round hat with a narrow brim, the same grey as his suit, which the apprentice placed ecstatically on his skull, tipped back onto his occiput. Peggy produced an astonished oh! That hat had been meant for Xavier since the beginning of time. On the other hand, the salesman noted that it was also the least expensive of the items quibbled over, and without even bothering to put it in a box he stuffed it into a paper bag, from which Xavier removed it anyway, to put it on his head, apparently for good. They floated out of the shop. Peggy suggested that while they were at it, they buy him some shoes as well, but the apprentice swore that he felt just fine in his sneakers, and that he would never ever wear anything else on this earth.

3

AT THE ICE-CREAM PARLOUR, Peggy, who thought he looked funny, inquired as to what was wrong. With his spoon Xavier scraped the inside of his stemmed glass, crammed with bananas, ice cream, strawberries, and chocolate chips. He scratched the tip of his nose. Gently Peggy took hold of his chin and forced him to look at her, as Madame would have done (she was at the age for imitating the deeds of a person one admires and would like to be). She asked him why this sudden melancholy. But he was very happy, on the contrary; the happiest he'd been since coming to America.

"It's just, there's something bothering me . . ."

"Which is?"

He asked her then the meaning of a shriekingly vulgar American word. Nonplussed, Miss Peggy turned red and looked at the nearby tables. Xavier waited. Peggy made a microscopic adjustment to her collar, and cleared her throat. In a murmur, she brought to light the meaning of the term . . . The boy thought it over, nodding his noggin.

Then he started to rhyme off a hideous rosary of obscenities, asking the meaning of each one. She looked at him, dumbfounded. He obviously wasn't joking. She straightened the strap of her purse and agreed to reply, frankly and heroically. She put into it, though, a technical precision aimed at defusing any aspect of her explanations that might seem too blunt. Still, she was cautious, watching for the slightest reaction from the boy. This intensive course in the verbal facts of life ended with the apprentice in a kind of stupor that worried her, and that lasted. He blinked, his eyes like candles. All at once, hunching his shoulders, there was Xavier in the throes of infantile mirth. His laughter was contagious and Peggy caught it.

"What's so funny?"

"My new neighbours, the apartment next door." And the apprentice was still laughing. "I can't believe it! What is it about those people?"

He tried to communicate, though gestures, what he believed he understood they were doing, but his hands kept coming back to cover his mouth, whence laughter continued to emerge.

Just then Peggy, who was bringing a spoonful of ice cream to her lips, went numb. Two tables behind Xavier sat none other than Ishmael Lazarus. He was facing her and looking out at the street. He had on sunglasses. She looked away, unsettled.

Unsettled because, my Lord, he was handsome. He was no longer decked out ridiculously like a court jester. He was clad very simply — black shirt, linen trousers. Dishevelled, lips bitter, he looked like a wicked angel. Could he have followed Peggy here? . . . Again she sneaked a peek at him. This time he was facing her. He took off his dark glasses. Steely eyes, sharp as knives. Peggy jumped up, dropped a dollar on the table, and went out, dragging along Xavier, who suspected nothing and was still laughing.

All afternoon, whether it was in the shops where Peggy went to buy those little things women buy, or in the subway (with her, he wasn't afraid to take it), or on Broadway, Xavier was attacked by giggles that shook him by fits and starts like electrical charges. At times, overcome by straightforward hilarity, he offended people who thought they were the objects of it, and turned to look at him, blinking bulbous eyes. At the Metropolitan Museum, in front of a nude that was being interpreted by a guide with a billy-goat beard, the apprentice spattered the gallery with laughter so resounding that Peggy was forced to take him outside.

The restaurant where they were expected was downtown. Peggy had gone there with her boss often enough that she was recognized, which was flattering. They were seated at a table near the window, to show off the young woman's beauty. The interior design was in the art deco style that was all the rage. The banquettes were as soft as velvet; Xavier felt comfortable, he admired the marble columns wrapped in creamy brown scrolls.

Peggy started talking animatedly, and Xavier listened, blinking. About her part-time work as a bookseller and about her work as a hairdresser, which gave her pleasure even if it was a tough occupation. By amassing money, she hoped that in two years' time she'd be able to enrol in a highly respected school, that was her dream at any rate; she hoped to become an author.

"To write stories for Hollywood movies."

She went on to talk about the characters who came to the beauty salon. She took a hair curler from her purse and told him she'd been carrying it around for three days.

"Don't you want to know why?"

She was a little disappointed at the boy's feeble reaction.

"Umm, no," said Xavier, who saw nothing unusual about a young woman carrying a curler around in her purse.

"Well, I'll tell you anyway," declared Peggy, cheerfully gnashing her teeth. "Look, I've made a notch in it." She showed him a tiny scratch on the curler. "It's because, you see, the boss promised me that she'd use it to curl the hair of — guess who? . . . Go on . . . Guess! . . . " Her voice suddenly exploded, making the boy jump. "Well, I'll tell you: none other than *Marie Peak-Forde*, that's who!"

Xavier didn't know who that was, but didn't let it show. Peggy still did not understand why his reaction had been so lukewarm.

"Don't you understand? Ma-rie Peak-Forde! The movie star of stars! And my boss promised that I could shampoo her! Oh! My! I can't wait! I have to pray the Lord I won't die before Monday!"

The apprentice nodded and smiled absent-mindedly. He knit an anxious brow, eyes elsewhere, fluttering. And all at once Peggy had a terrible revelation. She felt like a stranger lost in the streets of an unknown city, where she doesn't speak the language and can't remember the name of her hotel. For weeks now, though she hadn't shown it, she'd been growing attached to this boy, she'd made headway, so to speak, in her feelings for him, to the point where now she didn't know where she was, or how to retrace her steps to where she'd started. And she thought about one possibility, one she hardly dared name or admit to herself, which struck her as catastrophic. Pink blotches burst onto her cheeks. Claiming heatstroke, she went to hide her embarrassment in the ladies' room.

She emerged just as Xavier was about to go to the kitchen — through the wrong door, what's more, and he nearly knocked over a waiter who was coming towards him with food-laden plates up and down both arms. Peggy led him back to their table. Explained that it was quite unnecessary for him to go to the kitchen to choose what they were going to eat, and presented him with the menu.

Xavier became absorbed in it. He wet his lips with a certain ill humour, as if the flavours were refusing to get inside the words that described the dishes. What kind of taste do they have? he asked, referring to the pretentious names. (How to answer such a question?) Peggy's trip to the ladies' room had been beneficial, as they usually are for women. Once again, she lavished on the boy the solicitude of an older sister.

"Nothing tempts you?"

"I don't know yet."

He finally closed the menu; just who were they trying to impress? He beckoned to the waiter, as he'd seen someone at the next table do. He was going to compose his own menu. Lettuce leaves with carrot peels, on the condition that no salt or pepper or salad dressing or anything. Cabbage cut into thin strips, soaked in boiling water, and that was that. Finally, a good-sized helping of milk, but served in a cup, not a glass, "a very opaque cup." (The waiter noted all of this with a hint of a smile.) Xavier explained to Peggy that good milk had to be hidden, otherwise germs and other walking disasters would be as crazy about it as he was, and that if his portion was brought in a transparent glass the germs would be the first to know, and they'd stream into his beverage in regiments. Before leaving them, the waiter suggested politely that the apprentice take off his hat, for reasons of decorum, and Peggy had a moment of strained anticipation. But Xavier complied with perfect willingness, as if not giving it a moment's thought. Then noted this peculiarity — even with his hat off, he still had the sensation of the hat on his head. How could all five senses be askew like that? With his eyes shut he'd have sworn that his hat still sat on his skull, but his eyes assured him that it was on the table in front of him.

"Just try to figure out the five senses," said he to Peggy, who didn't quite grasp what the young man was alluding to.

They were already finishing their food when Xavier decided to tell one of his dreams. He was back in Hungary, but a Hungary exactly like New York. People were jumping out of windows, and Xavier walked around bodies that were falling "like apples from a tree." The sidewalks were awash in legs, arms, "all kinds of torn-off limbs." Xavier was on his way to the priest's to recite his catechism. He was worried because he'd completely forgotten it. "I'll review my lesson on the way," he thought. But realized that instead of bringing his schoolbag, what he had under his arm was Strapitchacoudou's casket.

Peggy nearly choked on her coffee.

"Whose?"

"Strapitchacoudou's."

The other day, and for no apparent reason, the frog had repeated these enigmatic sounds twenty times in a row: Strapitchacoudou, Strapitchacoudou . . . He had jotted down the word. Spent part of the night trying to find a definition. What could the frog mean by that? In the end, he assumed that she just wanted him to know her name.

"So now I call her Strapitchacoudou."

Nervously, Miss Peggy butted her cigarette. She settled in her seat and crossed her arms over her firm and generous bosom. She gave Xavier a long, hard look.

"And by the way, she isn't my first frog."

When he was living with his sister, Justine, in Hungary, and they were children, they had tamed one; it slept with them at night, they took it in secret to the priest's school, they fed it deliberately deceased flies. Then one day, out of the blue, she was dead; his sister, Justine, had cried a lot. The frog had known a few tricks, such as ringing a little bell to get a fly, but it obviously wasn't Strapitchacoudou, no comparison. When he and his sister, Justine, were children, they were inseparable.

"Do you miss Justine badly?" asked Peggy after a silence.

Xavier smiled vacantly. Then said that he thought he'd been missing Justine all his life. That he sometimes had that impression. A little old lady came into the restaurant, dripping necklaces, fingers encircled with red stones, head topped with a tiara straight out of the mills of Lucifer. Xavier looked at her absent-mindedly, his mind elsewhere. Shaking, she took a seat at a table not far from them. A stuck-up poodle with a pink ribbon around its neck squirmed in her lap.

Xavier questioned Peggy in turn, to find out if she also had a country where she could store her childhood and her memories, the way he had the Hungarian countryside and his sister's image.

"A landscape that streams by, streams by, and streams by again."

"It's true," said Xavier, "I'd forgotten." She had confided to him that she'd spent her childhood in a travelling circus. And he'd noticed that she seemed none too keen at the thought of stirring up those memories.

He asked again:

"And your father? What did your father do? Was he an acrobat?"

"Ringmaster. Actually, he wasn't my real father, he'd adopted me. I mean, he was my father. The country of my childhood is my memory of him."

This said with a hint of sadness that didn't escape Xavier. He asked if it was because her own daddy was dead or something like that.

"It was a long time ago," she said.

And she could have added that he'd died in prison, of pneumonia. He had caught the little boy who'd climbed up to the window of the trailer and was looking at Peggy without her being aware, but maybe not totally unaware either, watching her undress, go to bed, fall asleep. Peggy was ten years old at the time. And her father, under the influence of alcohol, had beaten the little boy. Whose father had intervened, and a battle had ensued. Then a knife blade had sparkled in the sun. Peggy had witnessed everything. She'd never learned anything about the little boy, whom she'd only caught a glimpse of once or twice. She didn't even know his name.

"At ten, I became the responsibility of the state, as they say. I ended up in a boarding school run by nuns who were sticklers for discipline. And that's my story."

She could have added that it was there, two years later, that she had learned of her father's death. But she told Xavier nothing about that.

"I have a bit of a headache," she said. "I don't know, maybe the cigarettes . . ."

But Xavier barely heard these words. At the old lady's

table, the waiter was setting down a plate while naming the dish, and the name made the apprentice jump. He took one step over to the old lady. She stared at him, stunned. The dish in front of her looked like fried tarantula legs. He asked the lady if that was what they were. She seemed not to understand what he was saying. The poodle yelped as if it were being flayed. Xavier insisted, repeated his question, his voice louder, nearly threatening — you might have thought he was about to hit someone. The waiter arrived, prompt, discreet, efficient. Asked the young man to be so good as to go back to his seat and, to show that his request was equivalent to an order, grabbed hold of Xavier's elbow and led him back to his table.

He conceded that "Madame is eating frog's legs" to the apprentice, whose hands were shaking like leaves.

4

XAVIER HAD KNELT on his chair, forearms crossed on the back of it, he watched with unalloyed delight the spectators who were entering the hall, slipping into the rows of seats, getting comfortable. Showing affectionate cheer, he gazed at them in their evening suits, their sequined gowns — as if attending the same show forged family ties between them. He greeted them with lavish "welcome"s and "congratulations." People felt the same sense of nonchalant familiarity towards him, or so it seemed, for several returned his smiles, something that never happened when he spoke to passersby on the street, for instance. "Tell me, can we come back? Can we come back often? Can we? Can we?" Peggy nodded, kind and absent-minded.

Because two things worried her. As she had had demolishers as neighbours, she recognized the evening clothes they'd wear for comes the revolution. Always the same tailcoat, the same western-style tie, the same greased-back hair flattened on their heads like a tar slick, the same wide cuffs, so wide that they half-covered their hands, like clowns. Peggy spotted half a dozen in the house. Scattered, certainly, but still she thought she could see them now and then, exchanging signs from a distance. Maybe it was her imagination. In any case, a commando unit from the Order never augured well.

Her second source of concern was that one of those demolishers in party clothes was Ishmael, who had stared at her when he came in, stared unsurprised, as if expecting to find her there. (While Xavier — cheered up by the beautiful ladies in the balcony, who were having fun waving back at this great clumsy oaf — hadn't noticed a thing.)

Once the spectators were more or less settled and the lights were starting to dim, a powerful cry could be heard:

"This building is in danger of ruin!"

From the back of the house another echoed:

"It's a scandal! Look at the cracks in the ceiling! . . ."

Which provoked something of a ripple in the audience. Peggy looked in the direction of the voices. Wasn't surprised to see young men in tailcoats. There was a rush to start the show, with a goodly amount of orchestra.

And for an hour there was a tumble of extravagance, of wonders, of unexpected enchantments, of wild fantasies. Xavier was sure he would leave his reason there. He had trouble staying in his seat. The urge overcame him to howl with pain and delight. He ran his finger inside his collar, about to choke; cast looks at Peggy that were frightened with wonder. When a performer, the magician for instance, asked the audience a question, Xavier replied as if the question were meant for him. At the top of his lungs he shouted, "It's the two of spades! The two of spades!" then blushed at the laughter he provoked. It was all so different from anything he'd known till now. The brutality of the destruction sites, the hardness of the streets, the bruises and humiliations of every kind that were his daily lot — none of it had prepared him for this sudden explosion of paradise. So there was a place in New York for these islands of grace? Places existed, right here in this implacable city, where you could simply go and drink a big gulp of enchantment? When each act was over he clapped hard enough to burst his veinlets (he'll be left with a small bluish mark on the palm of his hand). Tears ran down his cheeks. Peggy stroked his knee reassuringly, gently, Easy now, you'll come out of all this jubilation alive.

At intermission, it took his friend several seconds to pull him out of his seat. It was as if he'd been sewn into it. He left the hall, supporting himself on the benches, stunned. And cries from agitators rose up in the crowd: "Scandal!" etc., "Danger of ruin!" Trickles of plaster drizzled from the ceiling by fits and starts. Commotion in the lobby, where drinks were being served in conformity with the laws (but if you knew what to say to the waiters, they'd add a swig of joyjuice under the counter). Some spectators were already decamping, because the fun and games were over now; the second part was actually devoted to *The Patched-Up Mandarin*, a musical mime-show, and you needed a head for culture to understand it. The ladies donned distinguished expressions, getting ready for art, while their escorts were already unwinding themselves with yawns, preparing for the same thing. (Luckily, the critics had extolled the "staggering scenic effects.") Xavier was garrulous, delirious. He described everything he'd seen as if Peggy hadn't been there too. He was bubbling with enthusiasm over Max the Rabbit Fireman, a tap-dance act starring a dancer helmeted in a carnival mask in the image of the happy rodent, who took leaps that made you think he was suspended in the air like a butterfly (the apprentice was unfamiliar with invisible wires). Peggy listened to him while she stroked his hands, which were like ice, his blood having collected half on his crimson face, half in his heart. There was nearly a small disaster. A gentleman went past her and his cigar almost burned an irreparable hole in Peggy's sailor suit, that's how close he came. (Especially because the salesgirl had warned Peggy that you could set fire to the fabric just looking at it.) Peggy gave the gentleman the big nasty look of a little girl who is very very angry. Then suddenly, over Xavier's shoulder, she spied Ishmael Lazarus again, his sunglasses working overtime. Mutely the young man's lips formed the syllables of her name, Peg-gy Sue O-ha-ra. Then he took a slug from his flask, wiped his mouth on the back of his sleeve.

Xavier turned around to see what was making Peggy look like that. He asked her. She said nothing; the show was about to begin again, it was time to go back to their seats.

And they found themselves in China. With its pagodas, its tapering beards that came down to the knees, its fingernails as long as penknives, its servants who were flat on their stomachs when they moved. A set that featured mountains, porcelain, nightingales, and rickety twisted gingko trees. Xavier was struck by the story from the very start. A young Mandarin, highly refined in appearance, was the pride of his mother, a princess, easing into her widowhood; he was all she possessed in the world. The princess led a secluded existence devoted entirely to the memory of her late husband, whose statue, adorned with flowers and venerated, occupied centre stage. Every evening, though, she shut herself away in a petite pagoda to which no one was granted admission. There she spent her nights amid the greatest mystery. One morning, after feeding her a potion, some witches took the young Mandarin into the petite pagoda. They unveiled before him a portrait painted on a screen. It showed the Mandarin's mother as a young girl, along with a man, a naval officer in a Western uniform, who had a patch over his eye like a pirate. The man, whom the Mandarin didn't recognize, had a baby doll in his arms. The witches then told the young noble — dancing, swirling, furies — that the child was himself and the unknown officer his true sire. Outraged that they should violate the memory of the man he'd always thought to be his father, that they should declare him, the young Mandarin, to be in fact a bastard by a foreign stranger to boot, the youth flies into a rage, goes on the warpath, tries to slay the bad fairies with his sword. They turn out to be too powerful, though, and tear him to shreds ("staggering scenic effect"). The first movement ends with the young Mandarin's scattered limbs. His hands open and close; his head sobs; the audience is spellbound.

"Are you all right, are you sure?" asked Peggy.

A feeble yes on the lips of Xavier, who was as white as linen.

Second movement: the princess of royal blood, despondent at having lost her only son, greets a messenger from an enigmatic Enchanter who lives in the eternally snow-clad mountains. He claims he can bring the young Mandarin back to life; all he needs is the decapitated head. In a scene that makes Xavier shudder, the princess pulls from a chest her son's head, which is still *alive* — it is the head from the first act pantomime; it flutters its eyelids, it silently weeps, and those in the audience exchange questioning looks, wondering, "How on earth can they do that?" This second movement ends with the appearance on stage of the young

Mandarin, who is now "patched-up." The Enchanter has brought him back to life by grafting onto him a tiger's body, two dog's paws by way of legs, a pelican's wings, a rat's tail. Only the head of the strange creature is still that of the young nobleman. Faced with this sight, the princess of royal blood bites her fist in horror. (Same action at the same time by Xavier.)

Third and final movement: confrontation with the Enchanter, whom the princess has had locked up. She has demanded that the monstrous Mandarin be covered with a veil so he won't offend anyone's eyes. Enter the Enchanter, feet shackled, masked as well. The princess orders him to give an account (eruption of strings and woodwinds). The Enchanter remains as haughty as a cello, and as his sole response approaches the monster and strips him of his veil (the princess hides her face in disgust). To show that this patched-up individual is well and truly and, in spite of everything, the princess's son, he places the Mandarin's headdress on his skull. Only now does the Enchanter tear off the mask he's been wearing. (Xavier, frightened, had covered his eyes with his hands, but now he spread his fingers to see.) Here, the musical tension swelled to the point of frenzy. The Enchanter had a patch over his eye! Was none other than the mysterious naval officer painted on the screen, who was, according to the witches' daring claim, the Mandarin's true father! At this revelation, the princess drops dead. And the Mandarin realizes that the witches spoke the truth, and as they come on stage now, dancing a round, he realizes too that from the outset they've been in cahoots with the cruel Enchanter. During the final tableau, sprawled out on the stage alone, the Mandarin dies of grief, deep in the dungeon to which he's been relegated —

this shameful bastard he has become in the minds of all the inhabitants of the kingdom. Feebly he flutters his pelican wings. A slave has secretly attached a dove to the tip of his rat tail. The bird tries to take flight but stays at ground level, a prisoner. The final spotlight, in decrescendo, goes out on this detail.

"Xavier? Xavier? Answer me. Say something."

The apprentice, staring blankly, was not applauding, not speaking, not breathing. He had fallen halfway out of his seat. Peggy shook his arm; this was starting to be not the least bit funny.

"And that powder . . . what is it, that powder on you . . ."

She brushed the boy's shoulder, which was covered with plaster dust. And suddenly she realized what was happening, had just enough time to look up; with a stormy crackling sound a chandelier dropped from the ceiling, heading for them, while Peggy screamed bloody murder. The chandelier stopped falling two metres above their heads, held up by its wires and with all its crystals clinking. A thick cloud of plaster dust had spread over them and over the spectators all around. From the big hole in the ceiling soon fell what seemed to be balls of fur, which pelted onto skulls, onto hair, onto bosoms — balls of fur that suddenly started running in every direction, and that proved to be rats. Next came howling, jostling, flooding towards the emergency exits, incredulity and horror, fainting. An agitator had climbed up on his seat, was waving his fist. "This is scandalous! These buildings have to be demolished! Fellow citizens, women and men alike! They're mocking us! They're endangering our lives! We must demolish this place, the sooner the better!"

And Peggy still shaking Xavier. His lips partly open, eyes

glued to the chandelier, as motionless as nails. His friend was coughing, bothered by the dust. Her fingers started to remove the clump of plaster that sealed the apprentice's mouth. Gripped by exasperation and panic, she gave him a slap. The boy came back to life.

"Come on, hurry up!"

Xavier let himself be swept along, crazed, no idea what was going on. Rats by the dozen ran over the seats, among the abandoned mink stoles and coats, fleeing in every direction, panicking too. The apprentice wondered in what dream he'd just lost his way this time. They arrived outside the building. The same commotion, the same confusion ruled the throng. Testily they shook their rubble-spattered clothes. Quarrelled over who would patronize the taxis. Some spectators were staying on, stupefied. The tailcoats, strategically positioned, kept saying the same things, calling for mobilization, circulating a petition, demanding the urgent destruction of the premises. In the crowd, no one was fooled. Decrepit or not, threatening ruin or sabotaged, it made no difference; the Order of Demolishers had taken a strong dislike to this building and that's all it took. They all knew they would never again set foot inside this vaudeville house.

Peggy Sue felt the onset of compassion. She was moaning over her beautiful ruined blouse. Over Xavier's new clothes, which suited him so well. Over this evening, which was ending in a nightmare. And she cursed the City, cursed the theatre, cursed the Order of Demolishers. Oh! She was going to start proceedings, you could count on her to do that! . . .

"Let's go," she said, taking it upon herself. "We mustn't miss the last subway on top of everything else. We're lucky it's nearby."

The apprentice followed, docile as a toy. He was looking down wide-eyed, still in the same state of anxious stupefaction.

"But still! What an adventure! It's horrible!"

"Terrible, yes," said Peggy, her voice streaked with tears.

But Xavier wasn't thinking about the chandelier that had nearly flattened him. He was thinking about the story of the patched-up Mandarin.

5

LAZARE WAS WAITING near the subway entrance, bringing the wineskin of joyjuice to his lips with increasing frequency. Soon it was flat and he squeezed it to sprinkle the last drops over his tongue. It was made of beaver skin. Casually, he tossed it in the gutter. The drink left an aftertaste of putrefaction, as if he'd been sucking on corpse juice, and the thought of it turned his stomach. He leaned on the wall, jaws agape, drooling onto his clothes, disgusted with living. Then took a small flask from his tailcoat and started all over again. "Sabotage and freeing rats, that's what I've come to." He chuckled, bitter and drunk. "This has to stop." The E-string he'd taken from the beggar's guitar the other day was in his inside pocket. A string like that could tolerate significant tension. He'd inquired. The answer he'd been given was a joke: "Strong enough to hang a sow." He fingered it now and then, with determination and just a touch of depraved affection.

He spotted them as they were crossing the avenue en route to the subway. He squeezed into the shadows. Yet once they were on the sidewalk, they came to a halt. They were much too far away — some sixty paces — for him to guess what they were talking about.

Xavier had slapped the side of his head with his palm.

"My uniform!" he said. "I forgot the bag with my demolisher's uniform!"

"Wait!" Peggy shouted, but the apprentice had already turned and bolted for the theatre.

Her skirt kept her from running after him. She waited on the corner, arms crossed, chewing at her lips. It was a place with little light and few people. She felt she was easy prey, a tender morsel of flesh offered to all the jaws of the night. She dared not turn around, afraid of being afraid, but she was all ears. The furtive appearance of a bird suddenly materializing from between two strips of latticework made her shiver. Lazare was slowly coming towards her, but she didn't see him.

Approached her.

"You're going to marry me, Peggy. We'll go to Baffin Island together and make a fresh start."

And Ishmael Lazarus held out a wad of several hundred dollars.

"And what was in this bag of yours?" asked the cloakroom attendant, who had plenty of fresher fish to fry, of Xavier. (The whole staff had been mobilized for the rodent hunt.)

"Clothes."

"What colour?"

"The clothes?"

"No, the bag."

"I don't know. I have trouble with colours. Next time I won't lose my ticket, I promise."

Testily, the attendant rooted around in the multitude of

bags that the frantic flight had left behind in the cloakroom.

"What kind of clothes, then, can you tell me that?"

Through the wide-open doors, Xavier was watching the beginning of a skirmish. A group of men, all tipsy, were taking the tailcoats to task, and already it was degenerating into blows. In the distance could be heard the siren of a police vehicle. The very impatient attendant repeated his question.

"A uniform," Xavier replied. "Work clothes, with a shirt, and it's checkered. Pink, I think I remember. Because, see, I'm a beginner in the trade."

"You're a demolisher?"

"Apprentice!" replied Xavier enthusiastically, holding up a correctifying finger.

The other man flung the bag at his chest, ordering him to screw off before he jumped over the cloakroom counter and smashed his teeth. Xavier swiftly tipped his hat and took a vanishing powder. He slipped through the shambles that was legal tender on the steps of the theatre, you'd have taken him for a rugby player who was walking around the fray, holding his bag under his arm the way one holds a football.

Peggy was paralysed. Lazare motioned insistently for her to take the money he was still holding out.

"On Baffin Island or elsewhere. In the Far North. Because it's so far away. And empty. Go in a whaling ship. Weeks and weeks of seeing nothing. Of not drinking joyju. Joyjuice."

She moved slightly in the direction of the subway, but he was blocking her way. She turned around. He was following close behind, calmly, determined as a sleepwalker. Anxiety made Peggy go to pieces. She realized that by trying to escape she was entering streets that were even darker, more deserted. Streets where there were factories shut down for the night.

Someone could slit her throat there, rape her, do whatever he wanted, leave her remains in the garbage, and no one would know. She felt an urge to sink to the ground and cry like a little girl. But she went on, with Lazare following her, seemingly indifferent and sure of getting what he wanted. He hummed in an odd way, tunes that he'd break off abruptly, remnants of his shattered childhood. Even at a two-metre distance she could smell his putrid joyjuice breath.

He caught up with her suddenly, broached her, planted himself in front of her, forced her to come to a halt.

"Let me go or I'll scream."

"Go ahead and scream, nobody will hear. Listen. Listen to what I have to say. I was afraid I'd lost you forever. But deep down I knew we'd meet again. You'll probably say there was no reason for me to run into you last spring when you were leaving your beauty salon. You're goi — You're probably going to tell me that life does things like that for no reason. I knew who you were right away. From the first look."

"But you're nothing to me, leave me alone. You scare me and I want to go home."

That he could frighten the young woman bewildered him. His stupor made him seem ever drunker.

"After all we've been through together."

"You aren't making any sense. We didn't even go out together twice!"

"What difference does that make?"

He was sincerely amazed at her objections, and almost glad they were such easy ones. Then, in a suddenly plaintive voice:

"I know you still love me. You can't not. After what the two of us have lived through. At the movies. Outside your door. Those unforgettable moments."

"Please, I beg you, let me go."

The young man's features hardened, his tone of voice as well, in one of those abrupt mood swings that drunks seem to specialize in. (He was groping his way inside a cave that kept getting darker, more disturbing, where he himself was starting to feel afraid.) He said again:

"I know you still love me. I know even if you don't. What gives you the right to make me suffer like this? *What right?*"

As his despair was reaching its height, Peggy experienced a vision of heaven, a gift from the gods: Xavier, nose in the air, stepping onto the avenue in the distance. With his long, lanky stride he was coming towards her and her persecutor. Through what miracle had he tracked her down? Tracked her down to save her! (Simple, though; he'd got lost when he left the theatre. Had taken whatever street.)

Again Lazare waved the wad of money under Peggy's nose.

"I love you," he said, shoving it so brutally into her arms, he nearly dealt her a blow.

She gave a nervous laugh, a grateful laugh, a happy laugh.

"Well, well, if it isn't Lazare!" exclaimed Xavier, delighted at the surprise. "So you two are acquainted, are you?"

Lazare pushed him aside mechanically, not even looking at him, his eyes locked with Peggy's.

"I'm asking you for the last time. Follow me. We'll go away together like we promised we would. We'll go away to the Far North."

"You're out of your mind," said Peggy, emboldened by the apprentice's presence.

And threw down the bills. The wind began to scatter them. None of them paid any attention.

Xavier placed a fraternal hand on his foreman's shoulder.

"Lazare, Lazare," he began, warmly. "All your troubles are solved! I've found out everything, I understand everything, now I'll turn on the light at the end of your tunnel!"

And once again, eyes still on Peggy, Lazare pushed the apprentice away, like a lion pushing away cubs that are trying to bite into its portion of meat. Xavier came back, weighing whether to put his hand on his shoulder again or not. Finally, yes.

"You have to stop eating sausages. There aren't that many solutions, and I'm telling you, that's the one. It's because your father was a wife beater, understand? And that's it: when you chew your sausage, it's as if your jaws are your father and your sausage is your mother. Now your mother, you loved her, kind of like how you love strong meat and joyjuice, and that's where it gets mixed up in your brain, like a danger. Otherwise it would mean nothing on this planet makes any sense, if boys stop loving their blessed mothers. So eating her like that, grinding her between your teeth every day, all year long, in the end it makes you feel as if it was you who beat your mother and left her for dead, and you punish yourself accordingly, with stomach cramps and drinking yourself to death. So reform your diet!" He tapped the foreman's collarbone, soothing and confident. "Abstain from meat, particularly sausages, and there you go, cured, absolutely free of charge, no need for Clinic, no need for moaning, no need for drowning sorrows with powerful recourse to joyjuice."

Lazare, who wasn't listening to this baloney, grabbed Peggy and backed her against the wall. The young woman was beginning to realize that the apprentice's presence wasn't really much help.

"You refuse? You're breaking our vows and preferring this moron? So it's no? Watch what you say."

"It's no now and it's no forever. You're sick. For the last time, let us go."

Lazare began to shake her by the shoulders. Anger aggravated his stammer and he spluttered abundantly.

"All we've been through together! And you dare refuse to follow me! All we've been through together!"

He raised a fist, threatening. But then she stabbed his face with her fingernails. (Xavier expressed his opinion with his head, apparently saying, See? That's what happens when you're stuffed with sausages!) Peggy's fear had turned to anger.

"Do you want me to tell you? I'm in love with someone else! And I'm going to marry him, soon! Do you hear that? Marry him!"

Lazare drew back, flabbergasted. He leaned against a lamppost, as if afraid of falling over backwards. Peggy's nails had left three lightning streaks of blood on his face. He collected some on his fingertips and licked them with an absent look. A dark stain appeared on his pants, at groin level, spread, finally ran down his thigh and dripped onto the sidewalk.

A car decided to pass; Peggy hurled herself in front, arms to heaven. The taxi braked just in time.

"Are you nuts, lady?" yelled the driver. "You want to kill yourself or what?"

She jumped into the vehicle, dragging Xavier by the elastic of his bow tie (he would have stayed; you don't abandon your foreman in a state like that). She instructed the driver to start, took a last look at Lazare. He was gazing at the brackish puddle that was growing foul between his shoes. Eyes devastated. Face in ruins.

"A dangerous lunatic," said Peggy, still trembling.

"Sausages," Xavier repeated in an expert's tone. "It's all the fault of the sausages! . . ."

And the taxi turned the corner, while the banknotes scattered in the wind like dead leaves.

Part II

1

IN THE APPRENTICE'S CUBICLE, all danger now pushed aside, Peggy was suffering the after-effects of her fright. Uncontrol-lable shuddering shook her to the very marrow of her bones. She felt nauseated, had an ache in her belly, and pain in her breasts. As for Xavier, the words he'd heard came back to him, and only now was he measuring their full impact. Of course it pinched him to ask her just like that, but, well, anyway:

"Is it really true? You're in love? You're in love and you'll marry soon?"

"What do you think? I just said it. To discourage him."

"I see. Because I was thinking that. Anyway."

He didn't push any further.

It was past midnight and Xavier used his penknife to make thin slices of his precious chocolate, melting it in hot milk and offering to his friend, for comfort. She had lain down on the mattress, and Xavier had brought the chair up to the bed, to be at her side, his heart an elbow-width from hers. He had covered her with his suit jacket and on top of it had placed the one blanket of which he was the happy owner. But Peggy kept shuddering.

"He'll come back," she said again. "He'll follow me wherever I go. He'll pester me all the way here."

"I don't think so. He seemed like somebody who understands. The ruined look of someone who finally understands. He won't come again."

"You think?" she asked.

Her voice was that of a little girl looking for reassurance.

Xavier probed his conscience to make sure he hadn't told an outright lie.

"Yes, I think so."

There was a moment of peaceful silence. The only sound was of the frog softly croaking away in her casket, a sign that she was asleep (and dreaming). The apprentice continued to work on his chocolate.

"Thank you, Xavier."

"No need," he said, still bending over his task.

"Thank you for what you are and for being unable to tell lies. It's so rare."

He gazed at her with little flashes of anxiety in his eyes. Then got up abruptly and started to pace the room.

"About that. This has been on my mind for a long time now."

Classic hesitation before going on. He took a deep breath.

"Remember, Peggy, the night I came home with a fever and you put me to bed yourself, all sensitive and kind, just like you? I told you I'd worked overtime. Not true. A lie. I'd waited for the site to shut down so I could go and get Strapitchacoudou's casket." Quickly adding, "Which I didn't steal, though, I swear! I so to speak found it. It didn't belong to anyone. I could have just told you. But my tongue lied all by itself."

Peggy smiled, moved and amused. It was just like him, all right.

"But it doesn't matter," she said. "That isn't telling lies."

"If a person starts lying, even just little things, there's no end to it. You climb up and up. And then you start to lie about the big things."

"So they say. In boarding school, the nuns were always drumming that into our ears. But it's not true. A person can lie so someone else won't get hurt. If they're little white lies. And if they're lies that you don't gain anything from, or that don't hide anything important. It's when you lie for profit that you're telling a serious lie. To profit or to deceive. As for the others . . ."

"You forgive me then?"

"Stop worrying about it."

Peggy was less cold inside now, was shuddering less, the pain in her breasts had calmed down. She was watching the boy with a smile of sisterly affection. He'd started stirring the flakes of chocolate into the cup of hot milk. (Scraps of cardboard, a ceramic ashtray, five or six matches, an old coat hanger, cleverly twisted, and the ingenious lad had concocted a homemade brazier.) At last she could explain to herself the precise nature of her feelings for him. She wasn't in love, not at all. She *cherished* him. No more tormenting herself. Her heart was now thoroughly cleansed.

"It's funny," said Xavier. "Wrapped up like that with the blanket up to your chin, you look like I don't know what, I couldn't really say, but I like it."

"Come and lie down beside me. No, never mind the hot chocolate, I'll drink it after. Come here first, let me make room for you."

The apprentice obeyed. His body responded with gratitude to the burst of beneficent warmth emanating from the young woman's body. You could do yourself good when you and another were together. Life was worth being put up with.

"You know," said Peggy, "I've also got a little lie to confess."

Classic hesitation before going on.

"Don't feel you have to. I haven't got the right to lie to you, that's very clear in my head. But you — you can lie to me if you want. Things don't always work in both directions. I eat my carrot, but my carrot doesn't have to eat me back."

They shared a long laugh. Then silence.

"But of course," said Xavier, "if you feel the need you can tell me your lie. If it will make you feel good."

"I've told you I sometimes work in a used bookstore, to make a little extra money. Not true. Lie. Actually, I sometimes work in, well, in the morgue."

They were lying side by side. Xavier rested his elbow in the one pillow of which he was the happy owner, and pressed his cheek against the palm of his hand.

"The morgue is a place like any other," he said. "A person can live there."

Peggy chewed at her thumbnail, like a little girl who dares not own up to some mischief.

"Well?" said Xavier, beginning to feel anxious.

Peggy turned to face the wall.

"What I do, you see, is, I put makeup on the dead."

LAZARE IS LYING on the grass in a park, hands joined behind his neck. He is observing, in the firmament up above, the slow swaying of the highest greenery. The unbearable pain of loving. One evening after his meal he'd come upon a little girl at the side of the road. Crouching behind a bush, with her skirt pulled up to her waist. He'd come back to put his tools away in the tumbrel and she hadn't noticed him. He stopped dead. He watched the clear trickle, barely gilded by the fires of the setting sun, and so bright and pure you'd have thought it was water flowing from a mirror. The earth drank up the foaming puddle between the little girl's feet, and some pale sparks clung to the blades of grass. The next evening, she started again. And for one whole week, the scene happened again every day. Lazare thought he was safe behind the wheel. But one evening, after she'd pulled down her skirt, she turned in his direction. Lazare flattened himself against the ground. Swore between his teeth. The little girl went back inside the trailer, letting out an impish giggle that reduced Lazare's heart to mush. He was twelve years old at the time.

After that, he went for weeks without seeing her. Some people said she was sick. She no longer left her trailer. When he missed her too much — missed her until it was as if he had an oppressive hole in his chest, a physical discomfort that was like hunger, like thirst, like an urge to die and an urge to cry — Lazare made sure his father was asleep, then stripped naked, offered up his body to the night, and climbed into the conifers. He got to the top of the pine tree, his flesh flayed, pricked with a thousand bruises, and his walnut-sized scrotum and the little teapot spout that was his penis some-times bled from having hurt themselves on the trunk, the boughs, the needles. He let himself be lulled, for half an hour, an hour, by the swaying of the crown, so close to the sky that his blazing flesh, trembling with fever, shuddered in the icy light of the stars.

And today, twelve years later — stretched out on the grass in the park, clothes soiled, heart beyond repair — he experiences similar relief, something like a blackout, as if after so much suffering all the nerves that were used for that function have snapped at once. He straightens up. His cheek is hot. Peggy scratched him like a panther. Did she really think he was going to beat her? He had raised his fist just like that, out of conviction, so she'd believe in the sincerity of his feelings. He would never hit her. He takes out his flask of alcohol, gets ready to drink from it, changes his mind. Instead, he shatters it against the trunk of a tree. He muses that he has never touched a woman in his life, touch in the sense of sleep with, not even a tender caress, not even a gentle fondling. He understands how pointless it has been, and he feels inside himself a powerful urge to destroy, which surges back into his veins. He knows now what he still has to do, knows where he has to go. He makes sure the E-string is still in his pocket. Then sets out, determined to resolve this matter, to resolve all matters, once and for all.

PEGGY HAD WEDGED her cheek against Xavier's shoulder-blade. The boy had fallen asleep. Now and then there were moans, like a puppy's. His heart was beating — she could hear it — in the oddest way. It was as if he were purring like a motor, then stuttering like a drum (no, she thought, like a sigh of thunder on certain summer nights); finally, it thumped like someone knocking on a door. She weighed whether or not to waken him. But you sleep so badly when you sleep in your city clothes.

She whispered in his ear, "Xavier, Xav . . . ," gently shaking his shoulder. The boy was sleeping like a plank. Oh well, too bad. She knelt on the bed. At least she could undo his bow tie. She unbuttoned his collar too, so he could breathe easily. Then started to unlace his sneakers.

The apprentice woke up at once, gasping, anxious. He felt his collar, realized it was open, saw Peggy at his feet undoing his shoes.

"What are you doing? What in the heck are you doing?"

And leaping out of bed, he quickly rebuttoned his collar. Peggy laughed.

"Heavenly days, there's nothing to be afraid of! I just wanted you to be comfortable."

But she stopped laughing. She'd never seen that look on Xavier.

"What's wrong with all you people in America? You're all crazy! You took advantage of the fact that I was in my dreams to strip me naked? To play with me and what else, you sow? Attach us together with my little tip, like those crackpot next-door neighbours of mine that are rotten with vice?"

"Honestly, Xavier, really, I just wanted —"

"I don't want you talking to me! I don't want you talking to me ever again! I don't want you touching me ever again! What did you want to see, mmmm? Mmm? What did you want to see? Are you going to tell me? No, I don't want to hear you ever again! You're a bad fairy, you wanted to wait till I was asleep and then tear me to shreds! Why did you take me to see that vaudeville show, will you tell me? You know something about my father and you've been hiding it from me ever since we met, and you took me there to see those so-called mimes so I'd understand? And then you undressed me, and you jumped at the fact that I was asleep so you could attach me to you by my little tip and then tear me to shreds, scattering all my limbs, till all I could do was get patched up? Mmm?"

"Xavier, I think you're dreaming, I think you're still in a dream, and you —"

"Get out, you goddamn bitch! Get out and stay out! Strapitchacoudou and me, we've got each other and we don't need anyone else!"

And with a smack he sent Peggy's untouched cup of hot chocolate flying to the floor. She made a move towards him, hands out as if to take him in her arms.

"Easy does it, Xavier dear, Xavier my friend. You're in no shape. Wake up, you're still dreaming."

"I'm not dreaming, I know what I'm saying! Get out! And don't touch me!"

She backed out of the room, appalled, annihilated.

Alone, Xavier again undid his collar, unbuttoned his shirt, and tore off and furiously flung to the ground the plankets of his devising. He went to his frog's casket.

"Strapitchacoudou! Strapitchacoudou!"

He shook the casket vehemently. The frog went on dreaming. He slammed the lid shut. Started flitting around the room bare-chested, closing and opening his fists like an autistic child. "Patched up, patched up," he said over and over, unable to calm his agitation. A seam had opened. There was a small drop of blood.

2

FOR A SHORTCUT, Lazare hopped over the fence at the slaughterhouse, while Peggy was sitting on her bed, weary, undone, the dial at zero, and three tablets in the palm of her hand. No matter which way she turned it over, the whole thing had no head or tail. The apprentice's words, their meaning, were still as impenetrable to her as if he'd spoken to her in Aramaic. Even though she was suffering. Why these dark, these horrible suspicions about her? Peggy tried to convince herself that the misunderstanding would blow over. "Tomorrow, Xavier's mind will be clear. I'm sure it was only a sleepwalking episode. That would be just like him. When he wakes up, he'll have forgotten, if that's possible."

And then Peggy swallowed the three tablets, which was a lot, since she was taking them for the first time and had no idea what effect they would have. (Madame had given them to her, Peggy having told her she sometimes had trouble getting to sleep.) She realized she still had on her skirt and blouse, they'd be all rumpled and creased tomorrow. Too bad, too weary. She lay down on her side, her head on the bolster. The oil lamp was still burning (it had come to her from her father). Peggy liked to go to sleep gazing at its familiar, sour flame, like a handful of night purloined from her childhood. The lamp was on the bedside table close to her face, and she felt its warm caress on her cheek. She thought, as if in jest, And what if I never wake up? Someone else would shampoo Marie Peak-Forde next Monday, that's all. She started counting sheep. Before the tenth had jumped over the gate, Peggy toppled into nothingness.

There are rungs from the top of the building to the bottom, riveted into the façade. Even if he makes it to the roof, Lazare won't be able to place his foot on the top one, which must be two metres from the cornice. So it's a question of climbing. Will he have the strength? Lazare estimates the ascent at around fifteen minutes, counting stops and vertigo. After that (but be careful not to pick the wrong floor), he just has to grasp the guardrail and he'll be able to step onto the narrow balcony. Risky, indeed. But with his pain killed, there is nothing still alive in him anyway. That pain, nearly constant, which has gone on for more than ten years now, which has been pulling him by the hair like a furious angel, dragging him so many times to this point where he felt his only choice was to shatter his skull with a rifle shot — now he's studying it indifferently, like a rotten tooth that has ravaged half your head and that, once extracted, no longer means anything to you. And so break his neck a hundred metres below when everything is already lost? To fall, when already there is nothing left inside the one who is falling? The fall of a hole into the void?

He walks through a scattering of garbage, of greasy paper bags with their bottoms torn, through a jumble of dense and rotten smells; finally, pushing away the last of the metal garbage cans, he embarks on the frightening climb. He spent his childhood climbing trees as high as steeples. Without fear, without anxiety, always feeling safe, protected on all sides, tucked away as if he were making his way through the thick, rough, abundant hair of a giantess, as if waiting for him at the top were the cold, harsh light of the stars. But to scale a building, to feel himself the plaything of the wind, to be sucked in on all sides by the mouths of the void, as easily dislodged as a fly. Lazare shuts his eyelids, tries to think about vast expanses of snow, about the bristly silence of the polar plains.

Once he reaches the seventh storey, however, something inside him jams, paralysed. The wind creeps in through the bottom of his pants, sends shivers from calf to buttock. He has reached the invisible limit that construction workers call the Cracking Point. On his left, no bigger than his fist and at once minute and terrifying, the mess of buildings like an overturned toy box. Their totemic mass rises into the russet mist of a city destroyed by fire, "the tousled concrete city of New York" (the Philosopher), while all around, in the distance down below, neon lights cast onto the damp pavement pools of colours that are those of freshly dismembered meat. And farther away, deeper still, like a face half-hidden in the shadows, the hole that marks invisible hovels — invisible but he can *sense* them, these surviving odds and ends and fragments of wood that cigarette butts are enough to kindle — and among them, like filaments of ectoplasm, clotheslines sag under the weight of clothes no sooner washed than soiled again because, as he knows so well, there is nothing to breathe in these places but dust and air made rancid by fuel oil, and despite himself he thinks about the misery of those ruined populations, now asleep, of raggedy hoboes down on their luck, of urban lice, and the mere thought of them stirs in him an atrocious mixture of disgust and pity, and Lazare is so tense on the rungs that all his muscles vibrate like strings while he sobs. His left hand suddenly leaves the iron rung for his inside jacket pocket. He has one flask left. His hand is shaking so much, however, that the flask drops, empties, travels far away in a straight line, like a streetlamp spotted from a moving train and then swallowed up by the night.

Lazare is suddenly shot through with an urge to open his fist, to let himself fall backwards and join the flask in the blue darkness of the hovels. But he resists with every fibre, and now a new strength fills him, and the ascent ends with lunatic ease, as if a fairy had picked him up by the collar, and carried him. Now he is on the balcony, and Peggy a scant three metres away.

Lazare has always hated the bedrooms of teenage girls. He knew the quintessence of them in the house of a landlady whose young daughter, age maybe sixteen, never got out of bed because she was dying of something. The mama pecked away at her daughter with tiny exasperations, which she saw as a thousand kinds of care, puffing up the patient's dying cheeks with kisses like pecks of a beak, and the girl endured her assaults of love with a touching firmness of soul, because she was a saint, her circle was convinced of this as firmly as wood. Her bedroom walls were covered in pink, and stuffed toys that had survived her childhood (and to which she spoke in "little girl" talk, thinking it was charming, the times when Lazare felt required by propriety to offer greetings) were lying in every corner, among a hundred and one useless and bulky thinglets — china ballerinas, music boxes, admirable pictures of Jesus, not to mention the frills and furbelows from the same recipe that decorated windows and canopy. She had her nurse deliver tender, thoughtful notes, obviously hoping that the young demolisher would grasp the frail allusions. One fine morning he'd had enough. He went into her bedroom at a strictly forbidden hour and, pulling the bedpan out from under the girl's back, poured its fresh contents onto her head and left, bumping into the tearful mama along the way.

And so Lazare feels a kind of gratitude for the fact that Peggy's bedroom bears no resemblance to that one. A shelf with some books, a writing desk, a simple dressing table with no ornaments, a chest of drawers with stockings hanging out. And Peggy herself, at whom he hasn't even dared glance, in the middle of the bed, illuminated by an oil lamp whose orange light shivers gently on her face, like water. Suddenly he hears the velvety chord of a guitar. Wonders where it can be coming from. Shuts his eyes, pricks up his ears. Distant at first, the sound of the guitar comes closer, gets clearer. At the same time Lazare feels a kind of light sweep over him, springing from within and escaping through all his pores, a light that oozes, and the impression comes to him that, just as one might try on a suit, he is now arraying himself in the body that will be his for eternity. Finally he opens his eyes to find that he's naked. Looks at his hands, their backs, their palms, discovers his legs, belly, feet, finally takes his diminutive dick in his fingers to accept calmly that he is standing inside his own twelve-year-old body. Lazare greets the thing for what it is, an event with no possible connection to the rest, coming from nowhere and passing for a moment through his life, a kind of peaceful wonder that it's pointless to torment himself trying to understand, at which it's not even worth taking the trouble to be surprised. *A passing miracle.*

And his twelve-year-old body, which he is rediscovering, inhabiting it as if he'd never left it, that body of light is himself — standing naked, leaning with the tips of his toes on the flower box bolted to the side of the trailer. This hazardous posture allows him to press his face against the bull's-eye window that opens onto the bedroom where the ten-year-old girl is, luminous and blonde as freshly cut wood. In theory she has no knowledge that he's there spying on her, but from the grace with which she undresses, from the calculated innocence of her motions, from the way that, before donning her nightgown, she puts away her day clothes with deliberate slowness even though she is completely naked, it's impossible that she is totally unaware of him either. It is their secret, a secret so secret they don't dare own up to it themselves. Lazare admires to the point of burning, to the point of suffering thirst and hunger, the clear, warm belly of the little girl, he has an obsessive foretaste of it in his mouth, he admires the pink buds on her chest, the gaze of a little newborn animal, finally the fold of her smooth sex, whose sweet intimate perfume he can guess at, and he closes his eyes for a long time, afraid of fainting.

When he opens them again, the moment of grace has passed. Lazare accepts it. He is there on the eighth-floor balcony of a New York tenement building, at the window of the bedroom where his only love sleeps motionless as death, the sole object in all the universe that has ever had any value for him, her face floating in the glow of an oil lamp. Lazare is naked, his clothes in a heap at his feet. In what dream, in what other world did he take them off? Now he's back in his twenty-four-year-old body, with his flat and knotty belly, his hairless white body, muscular and lean as a dancer's, and he still holds in his fingers the diminutive dick that hasn't grown, that has refused to grow, as if it wanted to be faithful to the only hours of grace ever bestowed on Lazare — the year when he was twelve, when he knew that little girl, in the erratic life of a travelling circus. He understands that if he has been allowed to relive that moment, it is a sign of what awaits him. This memory is the beginning of what will come in time, the absolute moment that will congeal in his eyes at the moment of death, towards which all other memories will converge, into which they will vanish as into a well. The image his blue eyes will gaze at for eternity.

It happened twelve years ago. Lazare lurking in the shadows, nose against the bull's-eye window, thinking he was safe. It was the sound of the guitar that told him the little girl's father was on the other side of the trailer. That evening, though, fascinated by the sight of the naked body, he hadn't heard the footsteps behind him. The ringmaster grabbed him by his hair and started vigorously slapping the boy, who all at once was ashamed of his nakedness. Barthakoste, Lazare's father, who was drinking in his truck, was alerted. He got there and before the ringmaster could even open his mouth, Barthakoste grabbed him by the collar and belt. Hoisted him over his head to the trunk of an oak tree. Methodically, and with the firm intention of breaking his spine, he started to hit the tree with the ringmaster. Who suddenly twirled his arm, something shone at the end, and Barthakoste dropped his victim and put his hand to his neck. He turned and faced the assembled troop. Between his fingers, blood was spurting from his neck at quiet intervals. He staggered, then dropped to his knees and fell over backwards. No one dared to step in. The little girl's father — out of breath, on hands and knees, knife planted in the grass in front of him — gazed at the dying man with a wild, guilty look. Blood hissed in the silence. Lazare saw a snake wriggle away from the spreading red slick. It went on for a terrible length of time. Then all at once the husky, gasping breath stopped. The body stilled, with no jolts or shudders. Barthakoste lay in his own blood, which was steaming calmly in the autumn dusk. Lazare sniffed, wiped his bloody nose with his fist.

But enough memories. Lazare presses his face against the window and studies the bedroom. Wants to be sure there's something to hang on to, a nail driven into the wall, anything. Yes. Right next to the bed, what's more. He doesn't put his clothes on, grabs the E-string in his pocket and then, opening the window carefully, waits. Peggy has been as motionless as a mummy. He steps into the room.

Gripped with remorse, Xavier made up his mind. He put back the planklets, checked his appearance in his little shard of looking-glass, thought he looked horrible, told himself, too bad, went out. On his friend's doorstep he hesitated. He heard a strange hissing, like a balloon being deflated, and was surprised: he could see from the glow under her door that there was a lot of light inside. Suddenly, behind him, the next-door neighbour.

"What's going on?" asked the man, tying the cord of his bathrobe.

"I don't know," said Xavier. "Why?"

The man came closer, looking concerned, while in the open doorway the worried silhouette of his wife appeared, and Xavier wasn't likely to forget that her name was Rosette.

"Something's not normal," said the man, putting his hand on the wall. "This heat. Do you know whoever lives there?"

The apprentice was about to reply with a careful lie when the bedroom door was flung violently open and an indescribable monster, something that looked like a blaze, a scarecrow, an octopus, a mad dog, charged directly at Xavier's chest, shrieking from all fifty of its flaming mouths.

3

IT WAS A STRUGGLE but Xavier managed to escape from under the monster's wriggling panic. He extinguished some tiny fire-starts on his shirt. Rosette quickly piled onto the blazing bed the blankets that horrified neighbours rushed to bring her. They were all coughing violently. Terrible smoke was rising from the mattress. And when Rosette's husband, who'd come running to smother the flames on the terror-beast, yelled, "Help, for Christ's sake, help!" Xavier realized what was happening, realized that the thing writhing in pain on the floor, skull covered with tar and blood, was what was left of his friend, Peggy Sue.

Xavier stood there paralysed, the only one idle in the agitation that was pressing against him on all sides. He didn't know until he saw Lazare hanging naked from the hook in the ceiling, feet swaying languidly above the over-turned bedside table. They had to pull him by the legs to prevent his corpse itself from catching fire. Windows were opened etc. to let the smoke out. Finally there was nothing left but to wait for the rescue-ambulance, which wouldn't find much to rescue. A helpless silence fell over the group, some seventeen in number, gravely surrounding Peggy. Nothing to hope for, except for her torture to be over soon. In the event that compassion required them to act, a very old man had gone to get his revolver. The young woman was drawing to an end with the panting of a dog, spasmodic and full of hatred, which she sometimes ripped with a scream. Her eyes were like bleeding marbles, one still moving, distraught in horror. The skin on her wrists was coiled in shrivelled, blackish garlands. Under the blanket, all her remains were shivering like someone soaking in a bath of ice. Lips and cheeks had melted. Her naked jaw was visible, clacking convulsively, grotesque and terrifying. Two women knelt, then three, then four. And finally the eye stopped moving, the blanket was still, Peggy was no longer screaming. "Life takes no time at all," whispered an elderly lady to her neighbour. Peggy had lived twenty-two years forever.

4

HAVING GOT NO ANSWER, the man opened the door a crack and stuck his head inside the room. He wore a broad-brimmed hat that smelled of cop. His face was that of a heavily bearded baby. He spied Xavier squatting in a corner, his fists under his chin, trembling, in the posture of a hunted rat. Embarrassed, the man studied the components of the decor: the makeshift brazier, the table screwed to the wall, the bed, why not call it a pallet, the plankets flung to the floor that made him wonder what earthly purpose they might serve, and finally the hook, torn out, forgotten on the floor, which had left a hole in the ceiling. There were hooks like that in every bedroom on the floor, similar to the one from which Ishmael Lazarus Barthakoste had hanged himself. The demolisher's uniform lay in a heap by the bed. The man rummaged nervously in his raincoat and took out a hand-kerchief to wipe his temples.

Xavier still hadn't moved from his corner. Shivering, gaze scattered.

"Inspector Monroe," said the man unsteadily, and produced his badge.

While Xavier, still nothing.

"I've been put in charge of the investigation . . . I mean . . . the . . . incident that took place next door, the other day before. May I?" he asked, indicating the chair.

He sat, took off his hat, wiped his forehead again, put on his hat.

"Listen. Don't think I'm looking for stories. I was told that you work in demolition?" He sneaked a look at Xavier's uniform. "Never fear, the matter will be dealt with swiftly. I've already reconstructed the whole thing. So, what do you think?"

The inspector was waiting, pleading and anxious, for a reaction from Xavier that didn't come.

"My very first investigation and it has to involve demolishers," he said as if to himself. "But I swear that. Listen. Let's say, shall we, that Mr. Ishmael Lazarus Barthakoste hanged himself for reasons that are his own business, of course, me, I don't judge anyone, that's not my way. That stool he climbed onto, when it fell down, it accidentally knocked over the bedside table, I don't know if you see what I'm getting at, and there was an oil lamp on the bedside table and it fell onto the bolster where the sleeping young woman's head was resting, and that way everything's clear, we don't have to look anywhere else or anybody."

As he spoke, Xavier came closer, with the cautious lateral gait of a crab. Finally sat on the bed. Said nothing, agreed to nothing, but seemed to be showing a little interest, which calmed the inspector somewhat.

"As for you, but you know how people have dirty mouths, somebody said he'd caught you outside Miss Ohara's door at the time of the tragedy. But here's what I suggest. You didn't know either one or the other and . . ."

"Peggy was my friend and Lazare was my foreman."

The inspector plugged his ears and said in a frenzy:

"I didn't hear a thing! I didn't hear a thing!"

He gazed at Xavier, made sure he wasn't saying anything more, finally removed his fists from his ears.

"Let's say you didn't know either one or the other — these things happen, don't they? To not know one person or another? . . . All right. You heard a noise," he mimicked the scene. "Or you smelled a weird smell," he sniffed, "you went out to see what was going on, and then" — broad theatrical motion of surprise — "and then you notice smoke. So that's how you happened to be there, with your hand on the doorknob. That's all. Let's confine ourselves to that version. Everybody will be happy, nobody will bother me, and we'll close the file."

"Peggy was my friend and Lazare was my foreman. We'd just spent the evening together."

The inspector burst into puppyish sobs.

"I don't want to hear these stories of yours. Please! Or I'll be obliged to pursue the investigation. I'll have to interrogate other demolishers. No, no! I beg you . . . I beseech you. Jews, Negroes, whatever their colour, my opinion on those matters is the same as yours. Deep in my heart I've got nothing but respect for demolition, believe me, one of my mother's cousins married the daughter of a member of the Order, I swear!"

The inspector wiped his eyelids with his handkerchief.

Slowly Xavier lay down on the bed, arms on either side of his torso, neck strained. He said again:

"She was my friend, he was my foreman. We'd spent the evening together."

Briskly and noisily the inspector left the room, plugging his ears.

Mortanse was now alone, facing the horror that had been tormenting him for two days. Impossible to think, impossible to breathe without having before his eyes those few seconds when his tortured friend had jumped at him, screaming. His mind was stuck in that crevice in time, he was suffocating, cheeks blue. A dread he couldn't get away from.

And that dazzling moment came back to his head time and again for over a week. For over a week his memory stammered that atrocious recollection. If all at once his attention was dismally, briefly monopolized by some pointless detail — "Better get rid of those banana peels before they smell" — he would be amazed that he'd been able to stop thinking about his pain for a moment, which was a way of coming back to it. When he'd stopped thinking about it, he would think about it again. Same thing when he made an effort to relax, and it's always a sign of great distress to have to make an effort to relax. He concentrated so he could fall asleep, sombrely, the way you get ready for a fight. With a great deal of will, by extracting logarithms for eight-digit numbers, by obliging his mind to get lost in calculations, he achieved a confused hesitation, with his head still operating on its own and he himself feeling nothing, when suddenly, inwardly, he exclaimed, "At last, I'm going to sleep! I won't think about it any more!" And at once Peggy in flames would assail him more violently still, waking him with a cry, grabbing him by the hair only to plunge him back into an even worse anguish.

Run away, go outside, anywhere, to no longer be where you are! But to cross the corridor, to smell the hideous smell of burned hide that still lingered there, that he inhaled as soon as he got near the door, to see again the site of the absurd, the impossible, the unbearable struggle, would make him blow his fuse. So he fled whatever way he could: fled the chair for the window three steps away, fled the window for the bed, tried to lie down and sleep a little, which his body was clamouring for with every fibre. He mashed the pillow onto his face, repeated the same vain attempts, got to the point of cursing his own existence, a prisoner in his own bones, grabbing hold of his temples, head full of sinister creaking. Finally, he stopped eating. It would have taken a pestle to force food down his throat. At times, seized by a greedy, frenzied appetite, he'd grab hold of anything at all, an onion, and sink his teeth into it without even taking off the skin. But no sooner chewed, the mouthful would turn his stomach and he'd spit it out again. His body and mind all in one block, henceforth torn apart. Henceforth torn between his panic-stricken mind, which raced around and around like a mouse in its wheel, and his exhausted body, which cried starvation, sleep, pity. The two parts that made him himself now as foreign to each other as an octopus to a step-ladder. And while he was experiencing these pangs, from her box every evening, rigorously, at the same time and until the trough of dawn, Strapitchacoudou sang in a way that would make anyone blow their gaskets.

He didn't write a single line to his sister, Justine, during that whole period.

It was not until dawn of the eighth day that the planets took a turn in a new direction. Something made a fissure in Xavier's pain, opened it, emerged from an egg. He was still thinking about the tragedy, but the images were no longer moving restlessly under his skull like so many cats in a boiling kettle. He could arrange them in front of him serenely. When the first soiled sunbeams came in the window, suddenly he was curled up; a great silence came into his head, where for eight days an incoherent din had prevailed. A fairy's fingernail, kindled at the level of his liver, had begun to spread its secret warmth. And he knew that healing was now possible. Life was asserting its rights, as they say, was calling him to the strange duty of going on. All he had left to do was to cross the long desert of grief. The three days following he spent taking care to take care of himself, eating properly, sleeping as much as possible, being nothing but considerate towards his damaged machine. To make every move slowly, diligently, meticulously, learning again, if not to cherish himself, then at least to respect himself, with the varying shades of sober tenderness that any convalescent requires. Finally, on the very last day, the very last night, he was able to experience his sorrow, and for two full hours, in order that she could depart this world deep in his flesh a second time, which is the once and for all, Xavier wept for the dead friend he had lost.

He rose on the twelfth morning and, proceeding calmly, his face smooth, fixed himself a lunch to take to work. He felt a pang as he donned his apprentice's outfit. How would they greet him after an absence of more than ten days? He went to the destruction site, in the chilly air. Never had the city seemed to him so grey, its verticality so oppressive. He stopped at some trees. The last time he'd seen them was in Peggy's company. A gentle sadness placed the warmth of a lantern in his chest. When he turned the corner he expected to find the cranes and the workers already busy. Instead, he saw the space of three blocks reduced to nothingness. A lake of rubble.

Xavier stood there, feet planted in the cement, plumb line pose.

"What are you doing here?" someone asked. "You've got no business here. Get out!"

The apprentice shook himself. The man who had spoken to him looked like one of the demolished. At any other time, Xavier would have run away in shame. But now.

"Where have they all gone?"

The man swept the air in a gesture filled with spite and contempt.

"They've gone, they've finished their filthy work. God knows where they're carrying on their infamy! Now get the hell out! Go to hell!"

Xavier took a few formal steps, the small steps of a dazed marionette. But he didn't know where to go, so he stopped. And now he had to look for his crew? Travel the city in every direction for that sole purpose? But how was he to find a crew of demolishers in the vastness of New York? How many days would it take, how many weeks? It was Needle and Haystack. You could never be at peace on this earth.

Disturbing Clauses

And when you put a mirror before another mirror, the image that results is not reflected infinitely, pay attention, because light has a speed, necessarily limited. And so when you gaze at yourself in a mirror, the face you see is already in the past.

— Xavier X. Mortanse
from LETTERS TO MY SISTER

Part I

1

SOMETIMES SHE IS CONTENT to sit on the chest of drawers by the window, not saying a word, not even looking at him. She can stay like that for a half-hour, an hour. She barely moves, just to scratch the tip of her nose, say. A fingernail of light at the end of a finger of light that scratches the tip of a nose that is also nothing but light. Her hair, light. Then she disappears again. Other times, though, he doesn't see her but she speaks to him, speaks directly into his head without going by way of his ear. Finally, there are the times when she sits at the foot of Tonio's bed and then he both sees her and hears her, and together they play some very amazing games she has taught him. Such as pretending they don't exist. She always wins that game. No sooner do they start than she disappears. He never calls her, for he knows that even if he did, she would not appear. She only comes into the world when she wants. She tells him that she doesn't exist, that it's as if she'd never been born, and Tonio is ready to believe it. His father, his mother, for instance, don't see her, don't hear her, don't sense her presence even though she is there. So for them, for Tonio's father and mother, Ariane doesn't exist. Ariane is the name she told him is hers. Like the little girl who went to the other side of the world, going along a staircase that collapsed.

Here is the place where they live — he, his father, Giorgio, his mother, Maria, and his little brother, who's nothing yet but a swaddled stump. It's a warehouse. A kind of roomette has been arranged for Tonio by putting walls around him that are no more than partitions. The only real wall in his room is the one that gives onto the outside, with a glass-covered hole that is the window through which Ariane sometimes comes into the world without saying anything to him or even looking at him. The Statue of Liberty can be seen through the window; that's what Ariane looks at, and the pier where the ships berth. In the warehouse Mr. Wondell — Rogatien Wondell — lives. It was he who suggested that Tonio's family move there. His father does whatever Mr. Wondell tells him to do. His mother doesn't like that very much, to see his father humbly obey, without discussion, everything Wondell says. In fact she doesn't really like Mr. Wondell, period. But you have to live somewhere once you've been demolished. That's what his father always says. And Maria replies, sighing, "I'm well aware of that." Giorgio admires old Rogatien. Feels affection for him the way you feel affection for a father. He tells Maria that Mr. Wondell is a genius. And with geniuses, well, all you can do is dedicate yourself to them. As for her, Maria, where geniuses are concerned, she honestly couldn't care less.

The warehouse is just a warehouse among others: a long row of them running the length of the port. The warehouse next door has a hole in the wall that lets you see what's inside. In this warehouse, coffins are stored. They come in every size. Some are just big enough to hold a swaddled stump.

Some have room for someone as tall as Rogatien Wondell. There are rich coffins, there are poor coffins. The first night, when they were moving in, Tonio asked his father if there were any dead people in them, and his father, laughing, said, "Don't worry, those coffins are empty." But Tonio wasn't worried. Even if there had been dead people inside them, he wouldn't have been afraid. In fact, he prefers to think that the wooden boxes are full. Full of those who'll be put there later on. Ariane teaches him these things that only a little girl who doesn't exist can know. In the same way, she knows the names of those who will one day fill these boxes with their bodies. She knows which coffins will contain someone some-day, and which ones will never fill holes. For instance, she points to a box saying, This one will become firewood, after it's taken back to the state of boards. There are also Tonio's favourite dead. His dead. He speaks to them often. He stands in front of the hole in the wall and stares at one coffin or another and talks to it very softly, hardly moving his lips, so his mother can't hear. He tells them secrets. Mind you, they don't answer the way Ariane does when she decides to come into the world in front of him, in his bedroom. They can't because they're dead. But Tonio likes to think they can hear him anyway.

Every day, without fail, men come to the warehouse next door, take measurements, then leave with some coffins, so Tonio understands that some of the dead have just died. Sometimes his favourite dead are among them. Tonio bids them a last farewell. Other times it's the opposite, men come to store new coffins in the warehouse. That makes new dead to meet, other corpses to love. Tonio often wonders whether one day he'll be in one of those boxes himself. Certainly he'll be shut inside a box, because he knows that sooner or later everyone is. But he wonders if his box is *already* there. Sometimes he thinks so. And supposing that it is already there, he wonders which one. And how big. Daydreaming, he gazes at the pile of poor coffins.

But this morning, he is looking instead at the port, the boats, the workers unloading them, the powerful winches that make chain noises. The sky is blue. The sun calm as an egg yolk. His mother is behind him, mending a pair of pants. His father is busy farther away. Helping Mr. Wondell get up. Tonio would rather not see that. Mr. Wondell spent the night pricking himself with tubes, which Maria thinks is vile and degrading, and that's why he fell to the ground and why Giorgio is busy getting him back on his feet.

And then all at once a very long, very luxurious automobile glides up to the warehouse window and a little man with a pointed moustache, dressed like a rich man, gets out. He has a cane with a knob, a coat over his shoulders. He makes his way to the warehouse door, followed by his chauffeur. Tonio has not seen these people before. When the man steps inside the warehouse, Maria half-rises from her seat, but the man, with a courteous gesture, advises her not to disturb herself. His chauffeur seems like a colossus to Tonio. He's as tall as Rogatien Wondell, but his shoulders are twice as broad, his chest three times as thick, and his skin black. The little man goes up to Tonio and, with a kindly smile, thrusts his hand into his pocket. Tonio thinks the man is going to give him a lollipop. But he holds out a small piece of cardboard. Tonio has only known the alphabet for a few months. It's a little hard for him to make it out.

> WILLIAM HOWARD CAGLIARI
> FINANCIER, INDUSTRIALIST, BANKER, IMPRESARIO
> INTERNATIONAL SPEAKER
> EXPERT IN PSYCHOANALYSIS
> ALAMAC HOTEL
> 71ST AND BROADWAY

Tonio doesn't really understand the meaning of the message on the cardboard. He guesses it's the gentleman's name. But Alamac Hotel, etc., he has no more understanding of this than of the series of numbers at the bottom of the card. Tonio doesn't know what an address is or what it is to have a telephone number. Cagliari pats his cheek. Finally, out comes the candy: he offers Tonio a lollipop. Then turns and asks Maria if Rogatien Wondell is there. He says "Madam" to Maria, respectfully. Maria points towards the other side of the partitions.

"Mr. Wondell is in a sorry state," she adds.

"I see. His perpetual bad back?"

"So he says. Anyway, he's got an odd way of looking after it."

"We'll see about that."

Cagliari goes in the direction indicated. The chauffeur carries his boss's hat and valise, his cane with the knob, his buttery soft gloves. Tonio wants to follow them. "Don't bother the gentlemen," says Maria softly. Tonio hesitates, then changes direction. He walks along the partitions, stops at a chink. From there, he can hear everything being said on the other side, see everything being done there. His father, Giorgio, is on his knees in front of Wondell, massaging his feet. The man is slumped in an easy chair upholstered in threadbare velvet, which he calls his Throne. The Throne is mounted on wooden crates that once held lobsters, if the pictures printed on them can be trusted. Wondell has covered his head with a brown paper bag with two holes punched in it for his eyes. He calls it the Mask of Shame. At his side, on a rickety pedestal table, some bent spoons, a candle, and two of those tubes that he plunges into his veins. Spying Cagliari, he says, "I say! Parsifal's back from Prussia!" Then shakes his leg impatiently; he's sick and tired of having someone fiddling with the soles of his feet. Giorgio gets up: "I'll go and make your tea, Master." Says Rogatien, "No, stay. Closer. Come here." Humbly, Giorgio sits on the floor with the lobster crates. Wondell places a heavy, tired hand on his skull, as if he wants to stroke his hair. Then Cagliari climbs onto the crates. Picks up a photograph from the pedestal table. Tonio knows which one. When he pricks himself with tubes, Mr. Wondell looks at it for minutes at a time. It's a picture of a young woman. Cagliari reads aloud the writing on it: "Your sister, Justine." Cagliari points to the picture. "And her? You haven't told her?"

"Indeed I have, my friend."

"And?"

"And the ungrateful woman wanted to tear my eyes out."

"I'd have been surprised if she hadn't. Is she still in New York?"

"I don't know. Don't think so. Though maybe yes."

Wondell yanks the Mask of Shame off his head and tosses it aside. His hair is white, silver rather, in a pageboy, like Joan of Arc. The colour of ice. His eyes are bloodshot, always, like a dog breathing its last. Apparently he was born that way. He also has a little beard, like a goat's. Laboriously, Wondell sinks deeper into his throne.

"So, how about the sparrow?" says Cagliari. "Where is he so I can have a look?"

"The sparrow? Gone. Flown away. Pffftt."

"Find something else, Albino. That's going a little too far."

"Ask Giorgio," says Wondell.

"Yes, Sir," says Giorgio. "He's gone."

Cagliari is wearing a smile. The Bad Little Boy smile that Tonio knew back when they were living in the houses that are now demolished. The smile the little boy wore when he'd caught a mouse he was getting ready to play with.

"So what you're saying is, you lost," says Cagliari.

"Not at all, my friend. I've won."

Rogatien Wondell gets up from his throne. He's not too steady on his feet so he has to lean on Giorgio's skull, who is still sitting submissively at his side. Wondell runs a caressing hand over the face of Cagliari, who looks tiny beside this stepladder. Tonio can tell that it's a caress to make fun of the rich man.

"You know, sugar pie, you're very cute dolled up like that. Tell me, how was Berlin? And what about your little cannon-fans?"

Cagliari doesn't answer, looking Rogatien right in the eyes.

"Don't be ridiculous, Wondell."

Wondell gets off the lobster crates and walks over to the colossal chauffeur. He stands as high as a door, is as long and grey as a femur. And thin! . . . His belt is undone, he's naked under his bathrobe, which is gaping like a well. The old apparatus hangs down, mauve-tipped flesh swinging from thigh to thigh, hanging almost to his knee, unused for centuries.

"And what about that brute, eh? Did you bring him to pug my nose?" he asks.

"I don't know. What do you think?"

Wondell shrugs, goes back to Cagliari.

"We'll find him, don't worry. Giorgio thinks he spotted him. Right, Giorgio? Apparently he's an apprentice demolisher, something like that. With your contacts in the Order of Demolishers, it shouldn't be too hard to track him down."

"That's not up to me," Cagliari says. "It's your business. But, well. Let's say I give you that good old benefit of the doubt. You can have a month. After that, you'll do what needs doing to pay me off. A bet's a bet."

Cagliari takes an envelope full of white powder off the pedestal table.

"If you had to reimburse me to the last cent," he says, "I don't know if you'd be able to keep amusing yourself with this."

Once again Cagliari displays his Bad Little Boy smile. Pretends to pocket the envelope. Wondell grabs his wrist, twists it. "Give that back! Now!" The chauffeur takes a threatening step in their direction, and Giorgio stands up, ready to defend his Master. Tonio is biting his fingers. He's afraid his father will get his face smashed in by the black-skinned colossus. But Cagliari, still smiling, eventually returns the envelope to the table and that's the end of it.

"One month, understand? I'm giving you one month. And don't you dare go into hiding. I could find you in Timbuktu."

Wondell replies simply, "Fuck you." The visitors leave the way they came. Then Wondell orders Giorgio to fix him an injection tube.

"Don't you think, Master, you've had quite enough as it is?"

Wondell brings up his hand to strike.

"All right. Half a dose then. Promise?"

Wondell goes back and sits on his throne.

"Now then, young Giorgio. We've got our work cut out for us."

"Yes, Master. We'll find him."

With his big, intense eyes, Tonio watches Cagliari leave the warehouse. The man attracts and at the same time frightens him. "Well, well, well!" says Ariane, directly into his head. She tells him that, as a matter of fact, just this morning the rich man's coffin arrived at the warehouse next door.

2

EVERY MORNING WHEN he got up, Xavier X. Mortanse wondered, while he was tightening the screws in his plankets, if it wouldn't be wiser to don his demolisher's outfit after all, reason being to come across as an enthusiastic apprentice. Invariably, though, he succumbed to the temptation of the clothes Peggy Suit bought him — the little-finger-size purple bow tie, the mouse-grey hat, which he wore tipped far back on the back of his head, so forth, and he was thus apparelled when he went out wandering in search of his crew. He took Strapitchacoudou along, for moments of respite. Only fair. Spending your life in a box, he mused, could make anyone blow his gasket. And his frog obviously liked to perform in the open air. While he got his dose of wonder in return. Fair's fair.

Xavier held the casket in both hands, wedged carefully between his ribs, because of a constant fear that someone would take it away. He looked up as he walked, because the skyscrapers never stopped amazing him. People in the neighbourhood were starting to recognize him. He left behind in the store windows a trail of amused faces that watched him cross the square. Sometimes he played with the children. Or rather the children played with him, always the same little gang, you'd think they didn't have school or anything, and they were enchanted by his hat, making it fly off his skull with a flick, and the apprentice, smiling, humiliated, had to run from one to the other, asking them to kindly stop, please. The hat flitted from one foot to the next like a fly. Till the kids got tired and left it to its owner, who donned it again presto, then got back on the road, so long, pals!

Mind you, these slight humiliations were nothing compared to what he'd already experienced. Because all things considered, and in spite of the idleness inflicted by his joblessness, this roving was giving him his finest days since he'd arrived in the United States. First of all, he wasn't getting punched any more, which was something. And then, except when he naively stumbled onto property that belonged to some hair-splitter who chased him away, his ears no longer suffered the shouted reprimands that had been his daily lot on the demolition sites. So all in all his spirits were good. Peaceful little houses — still peaceful, for there were still some here and there — made him stop now and then, and stirred in his heart sweet thoughts of home and safe sleep. He could spend a good half-hour dreaming about them, till curtains were parted and suspicious looks came his way.

But, well, those were no reasons to forget his duty. To demolish he'd been hired, to demolition had he pledged allegiance. He made inquiries as to where his crew might be, scrupulously, disregarding no clues, jotting them down, wetting the lead in his pencil with his tongue. He granted himself no weakness, so tempting when you're on your own. Infinite though New York's streets may be, he had vowed that he'd locate his demolishers. Patience, uprightness, and good will would triumph over adversity in the end. Xavier was in good spirits and he was determined to stay there forever.

After a week, though, the results were not encouraging. He'd been pointed once or twice in the direction of this site on that avenue. Xavier would rush there, muscles strained. And each time he'd see nothing but crews who boasted that they weren't his. "Make some inquiries at least." But think. Never mind questioning men and their dogs, never mind begging, sent smartly packing, no exception, and after a wait in standing position in the midst of unknown demolishers who treated him as if he were empty space, Xavier the jobless apprentice left, deflated. (Somewhat relieved all the same. "They didn't beat me.")

So he went here and there, there and here, hours on long, aimless roads. As for breaks, there was the one in mid-morning, there was the one at noon with the stick of celery, finally a snooze around three o'clock if he found himself an obliging public bench, where he would sometimes break carrot. Celery time was his favourite break. Xavier found the comfy little corner safe from gazes and, freeing Strapitcha-coudou from her casket, he treated himself to enchantment. Nothing but happy songs every time. "The Night the Bed Fell," "It's Winter at the Summer Camp," "Kiss My Dippidy-doo," "I'm My Own Grandpa," "My Paw Is Bleeding on Your Belly" — that sort of thing. Sometimes the frog would accompany herself on the banjo, sometimes on the accordion. Xavier smiled. God existed. It was good to be alive.

Then one noon, while he was looking for the secluded alleyway where he'd eat his vegetable, he bumped into a blind man. Walked past, actually. A blind man who wasn't wearing opaque glasses — useless anyway, Xavier had always thought, precisely because they can't see, like putting a diaper on a baby that doesn't have an ass, and the blind man, with no glasses or anything, was sitting with his back against what's called a wall, a hat in front of him, waiting for charity. The apprentice rummaged in his pocket, took out two pennies. Then, bending down to the hat — with a smile, for he was the kind of person who would smile at the blind — to deposit his pennies, he stopped, suddenly worried. In a tiny voice, he asked the blind man if he was a real blind man or an actor pretending, and the blind man said that if he could see the face of the person who'd ask such a question, he'd have already bashed it in, and Mortanse felt reassured. After words of apology, he dropped his two cents in the hat.

"If you want to be forgiven, you'll have to help me get home."

"Sure, Blind Sir," replied the apprentice, and right away, with eager dedication, slipped his hand under the beggar's elbow to help him to his feet. The blind man poured the small amount of money in the hat into his comically loose pants, not into the pocket on the left or the one on the right but actually inside the pants, below the belt, which was an old length of clothesline; then he worked the spring in his legs to make the money jingle inside his underwear. That's it. Ready to hit the road.

It was true that the blind man really was blind, because here's what happened and to prove it to Xavier, who still harboured doubts. The beggar charged into a ladder. And the man who was standing on the ladder felt the world give way beneath him like water and had to suspend himself in the nick of time from a streetlamp. Confusion and commotion ensued. Xavier tried, despite his nervousness, to rectify the situation, but because of panic was only able to deliver ladder-thrusts into the ribs of the hanging man, who really needed that. In the end, the apprentice knocked over a can of paint that a second worker had been using to paint the base of the streetlamp. Finally he packed it in and took off, with the beggar clutching his coattail.

When they were sure that they were out of reach, they leaned against one another to catch their breath. The beggar was huffing and puffing as if he'd lost his lungs. Then, finally calm, he exploded. What did this jackass think he was doing, and why in hell hadn't he said there was a ladder coming, what a thing to do to a blind man! Xavier had remorse at the tip of his nose like a plumb line. And unable to come up with anything to say except so wrapped up in what he was saying to Blind Sir, he'd totally forgotten that the man was blind and consequently to tell him there was a ladder coming up ahead. Jackass, said the beggar again. But Xavier insisted on continuing to be the man's eyes, and on taking him home, swearing on the head of Peggy Suit that henceforth he would pay absolute attention to details such as, Ladder, ahoy! The blind man went along with it, grumbling. Xavier smiled anyway. The beggar didn't seem like the wrong horse, and helping him gave the apprentice a few minutes' worth of good deed in what was otherwise an empty day.

And if earlier Xavier had been so absorbed in what he was telling his friend, it was because he was explaining lengthwise and widthwise his adventures as an apprentice in search of his crew of demolishers. The blind man listened, pensive. While telling Xavier the names of the streets he should take, he knit his big black bushy eyebrows and at times was powerfully surprised at the apprentice's story, notably with respect to some of the things the young man had done, or some of the ideas and opinions he held on the subject of America, the Order of Demolishers, his duties as an apprentice, all that.

They stepped into an alley, and Mortanse was surprised to note that it led to a cul-de-sac, no less. "The Blind Man's Cul-de-sac," declared the other man solemnly. His home was a pile of warped boards nailed to segments of post, with a plate of dead-man's-gums-coloured tin by way of a roof that didn't reach much higher than his chest, as well as one whole side with no wall at all, or boards or anything else, open air. In the middle of that, a pile of old cloth, old cardboard, old scandal sheets, where a large and verminous dog lay sleeping. Xavier stared, eyes like golf balls.

"What did you expect at a blind beggar's? Sardanapalus?" asked the blind beggar who was guessing at the other man's stupor. "I've seen good people, I've seen decent people, but I've never seen my hat filled with money. Seen — well, in a manner of speaking. But all right, find some space for yourself and sit yourself down. You seem like a youngster to me, so you do. How old might you be — sixteen, seventeen? And before that, what's your name?"

Xavier told him, laughing, that his name was Xavier. The blind man wanted to know if it was having the name Xavier that made him laugh. Xavier said no, he didn't know, he'd laughed just like that, no reason. And then the beggar said he'd thought jackasses like Xavier were smothered in the cradle, out of humanity and compassion, but the blind man said it nicely, as a joke, and Xavier knew it wasn't nasty. "Sit down though, won't you, I'm going to fix us a coin infusion: my own invention!"

The apprentice sat the edge of his butt on a stone, dusting

it beforehand with his hand. He set the frog-casket on another stone, stroked it tenderly. He smiled in silence at his blind companion. Who had also taken a seat, on the ground, with his legs crossed. Xavier went on tenderly stroking the casket. The beggar's eyes were the colour of blown fuses.

"Hey ho! Take a good look," said the man, who was handling the objects and reading them with his fingers. There were a scrofulous hot plate, a kind of saucepan, dented tin cups, what you will. "Once the water boils, we introduce coins, preferably those earned in the course of the day. After that, we have to add *this* coin." Which suddenly materialized between his thumb and forefinger, you'd have said like magic. It was a strange one-cent coin. It resembled the shadow of the moon when it cuts into the sun at the start of an eclipse, or a piece of nut a squirrel has bitten into. The beggar was as proud as the Philosopher had been when he told Xavier about his granddaughter's first violin concert.

"Can you see, you with the eyes? Have you ever seen a one-cent coin like this one? Eh? Have you? I found it in my hat one day. It's my grigri, my lucky charm, my shit-on-everything. Who knows where I'd be now without it?"

He dropped the coin into the boiling water. A few moments later, with a greedy expression, he poured some infusion into the cups, Watch out, it's hot. The blind man heard Xavier lapping from his cup. Well? What did he have to say about it? Xavier replied that it tasted a little like hot water, but he liked it, and he thanked the blind man, clasping his hand. The blind man seemed slightly hurt.

"It's good, it's good," Xavier reassured him.

Then, a stomach gurgle. He decided he was hungry. Broke a carrot and shared it with the beggar. Yahweh gives to His children, said the blind man mechanically, before taking a bite. They nibbled their vegetable morsel in silence. Xavier wanted to know if Blind Sir had always been blind or if it had happened just like that, and he settled himself more comfortably on his stone.

"First of all," said the man, "I'm going to tell you something. I haven't always begged. In my youth I worked in a slaughterhouse. It was called Salaison Supreme, I don't know if it still exists. They can say what they want, where slitting throats is concerned the worst isn't the sheep. It's the pigs! Ah la la, the pigs. Listen to one that's having its throat slit. But, see, that's not what I wanted to be. No, what I like, what I liked, what I wanted to become, was an opera singer."

And made a racket with his vocal cords to show Xavier.

"Anyway. You can hear what I mean. As for my eyes, well: only since the war. I went from one slaughterhouse to another. A defective rifle blew up in my face. And there I am; blind."

The beggar had started to whimper, convincingly pitiful.

Xavier had stopped chawing. He couldn't get over the man having been in a war.

"Don't tell me you've never met a veteran before?"

Xavier asked hesitantly if it had ever happened that he'd killed human beings. For a moment the blind man's black eyes gave the impression that they saw something, but the something was inside his head. Finally said, War is war, I tell you, and that's that.

Silence. Xavier feigned an interest in the lines of his palm.

"If you roam the streets," inquired the blind man, "how do you manage to get by?"

The apprentice admitted that this was something of a

problem because, though he stretched out his pennies and ate only the strict and the minimum, his nest egg was nonetheless nearly gone.

"If you need money, kid, you could show yourself in a circus. Because from the sound of you, I imagine the face on you isn't the man in the street."

The apprentice thought that was a good one, and his laugh made the beggar laugh back. However, Strapitchacoudou, who must have been wondering why she hadn't been allowed to do her noon-hour show, stirred impatiently in her box, and the weird sound worried the blind man, who asked, What is it?

Xavier had the casket on his knees. He hesitated, upper lip between teeth, tempted. Finally he said, "I've got a surprise for you," and with a wink at the blind man he opened the casket. Out leaped Strapitchacoudou. Who was in Mexican mode; maracas, sombrero, corazón, muchachas! The beggar's face went from ten to zero. An unexpected element in his invisible decor and it was the beginning of terror. The frog realized. Broke off right in the middle and discreetly got back in the box, closing the lid herself, clack.

"But? What is it?" The beggar's cheek suddenly sprang to life with a tic. "A portable phonograph?"

Xavier explained that it was a frog.

The blind man twitched his lips but nothing came out. Slowly stroked his jaw. Xavier waited anxiously. After asking him to repeat, and after he'd repeated, the beggar concluded that a blind man was being made fun of, and said so with muted rancour. But Xavier handed him the frog so he could check for himself. He could also feel the guitar, the tiny sombrero. A kind of black stupefaction still dominated his features. He had to accept it: the thing was a frog. A final jolt of skepticism.

"And what's to prove it was the frog that was singing?"

"I swear," said Xavier, putting his hand on his heart.

But he didn't have to swear, for on her own initiative Strapitchacoudou resumed her interrupted act. This time the beggar listened with enthusiasm and rapture.

The song over, Strapitchacoudou hopped out of the man's hands and onto Xavier's knee. And stood there, hand on hip, guitar over shoulder, her pose elegant and nonchalant. The beggar indicated noisily that he was convinced. Great was Yahweh! He punched his hand with the other fist, said Holy mackerel, then repeated words and gesture both. Xavier proudly stroked the head of his frog, whose eyelids were half-closed in sensual pleasure. Finally she got back in her box. Sounds of tidying up.

The blind man grabbed his empty tin cup and threw it in what he assumed was the direction of the big, flea-bitten, sleeping dog, and indeed the cup bounced off the animal's side.

"Hey ho! Hear that, Donkey-Pooh? See what you can do with a little exercise, you old drunk? Never could teach that dog any tricks!"

The dog merely growled, without opening an eyelid or moving from his pile of rotten rags.

Enthusiastically the beggar got up on his legs, talked excitedly.

"But the biggest jackass of all, young Xavier, is you! You're wondering how to earn a living when you've got a treasure like that in your pocket? Why, you could make a fortune with that frog. Think about it!"

And future prospects made the beggar splutter with optimism, and lay it on good and thick. As for him, he modestly offered his services as Xavier's impresario, so the gullible youngster wouldn't get taken for a ride, together, I mean you, me, and your frog, we'll conquer New York! And the Big Apple will be ours!

The apprentice listened, bewildered. But he'd never entertained the thought, and never would, of putting his frog in a show. What kind of idea was that? Besides, he himself had nothing to do with show business, he was an apprentice demolisher!

"And the hopes you've got with that demolition business? I listened to everything you said before. They're gone, they don't want you, I think that's perfectly clear! And even if you did find them, do you think they'd welcome you with open arms and songs of joy? And meanwhile you've got a fortune in your hands and you're letting it sleep."

The beggar rushed eagerly towards the apprentice — not brilliant, because between Xavier and him were the hot plate, the cups, all that, and the blind man's feet got trapped. He crawled to Xavier, clung to his trousers, groped for the casket. The apprentice was terrified.

"Come on, let me have that frog! Let me have that casket! You aren't worthy of that treasure! It's a crime to let such a fortune get away from you!"

Mortanse managed to shake off the beggar, grabbed his casket, about to run away. The beggar, still slumped on the ground, now raised a dramatic hand towards Xavier.

"No, stop! I beg you, stop! Don't worry, I won't steal your treasure! I won't."

He was trying to get his breath back, for the slightest

emotion, the slightest lively movement, made him lose it, because over time he'd developed a cardiac heart.

"In any case, it's too late for me," he said, choosing to be pitiful again. "Too late. Help me up."

Xavier moved his hand, cautiously. The blind man groped ahead of him, blindly, making moans like a small animal. When his hand finally met Xavier's, he straightened up perfidiously and flung himself at the apprentice; a frenzied battle for the casket was underway. Luckily there was the saucepan, and the beggar buried his foot in it, which set him off balance, and then Xavier was free.

The blind man straightened up, very ashamed of himself. He apologized, admitted he was bad. Nimbly thrust his hand inside his loose trousers and brought out the Good Luck Coin. He approached Xavier, groped for his hand, put the coin there.

"Here, this is yours. I don't have any hopes for anything any more. Besides, for all the good it's done me. Even though I swallowed it, defecated it, walked around for weeks with that coin in my boot, it never let me profit from its magical powers. I guess wonders don't rhyme with me. Maybe it'll be different with you. In any case, jackass, you need all the luck you can get. Take it."

Xavier absolutely did not dare accept. But the beggar insisted. "To earn your forgiveness. Please." The apprentice gave in to this final argument.

"Now go. I don't want you and that singing fortune around me any more. It pains me too much."

The blind man kicked his dog, hard, and the animal replied with a bark.

"Filthy beast! . . . You're like my sister, can't teach you anything."

Xavier withdrew slowly, unwillingly, fascinated by the beggar, who was delivering kicks to his own rear end.

. . . Back to the horror of the city, which he'd nearly forgotten. He no longer really knew where he was in New York, but relied on the pealing bell he could hear in his head to orient himself. He walked for an hour before he began to recognize the streets of his neighbourhood. He spotted a crowd of demolished. Slipped into it, thinking, after all, it isn't written on my face that I'm an apprentice demolisher. He tried to blend with the group, to quench his thirst for community. An old woman was talking and everyone was listening. She was saying, "I hear the Lafarmer youngsters spotted her too. She appears to children mainly. But they claim that her own grandmother, sick in bed had a conversation with her, and . . ." Suddenly aware that Xavier was there listening, she broke off. All the faces silently turned towards the apprentice. Xavier lowered his nose and left without a word.

At home, he meditated on the scrap of story he'd heard. Realized that it was little Ariane, whose funeral procession a few weeks ago had dangerously traversed the demolition site. For some time now a rumour about her had been going around, of which he'd only grasped puffs and pieces. She had appeared to some children, some even claimed to have spoken with her. She'd been seen dancing like a fairy on an electrical wire one night when there was a procession. Xavier, who saw nothing impossible about that, wondered all the same if such things were normal, and if anything at all of a person could be left behind when his mortal remains, devoured by the earth, were decomposing in a hole.

But he was torn from his daydream by the frog, who was making a din. He opened the casket to see what was going on. It wasn't to put on a show. The frog was snickering impishly, covering her mouth, and showing a ten-cent piece to the apprentice. Who realized, horrified, from her cruel imitation, that Strapitchacoudou had stolen the coin from the beggar.

3

THREE WEEKS HAD PASSED, Xavier had wandered, but too vast was the city, too numerous the demolition sites. Not so much from daring as from a kind of numbness that crept over him more and more often by the end of the afternoon, forcing him to move in a mechanical way, he'd pressed on as far as the Order's headquarters, but sent packing: naturally, no one was allowed inside without the badge of a certified journeyman. As for the demolition calendar — closed to the public, of course. So Xavier had to leave it to chance, and it was like hoping that if you threw fifty-two cards in the air, they'd form a castle as they fell.

There was also the fact that Xavier was travelling around New York with all the logic and consistency of a fly. Had his footsteps left a white trail behind them, his journeys would have looked, as the crow flies, something like a plate of noodles. Each day brought the same harsh experience of the city. Scenes spotted here and there pained him, spoiling his mood — a family's misery, cries coming from basements, sudden brawls featuring boot-kicks in an alley, and finally a squad of mounted policemen accompanied by even more disquieting plainclothesmen, who with blinding violence would expel a community of demolished who'd taken refuge in disused sheds (a woman running with one hand supporting a balloon-sized belly). And most of all, his health went flying. Temperature spikes would hit him in the middle of the street, dizzy spells, every so often his legs hurt so much you'd have said a subterranean demon was pounding his heels with a hammer at every step. And to crown everything, the less money he had, the more he was devoured by hunger. It had happened once that, at noon-hour alone, he'd devoured three leaves of cabbage, a slice of brown bread, a quarter of a turnip, and two carrots. Twenty minutes later this voracity led to his regurgitating his meal. Wiping his lips, he'd found spots of blood on his napkin. "I didn't know there was blood in turnips," he told his frog.

Until the morning when he checked the state of his savings only to discover that his worldly goods amounted to one dollar and forty-two cents. Fortunately the rent was paid. But he needed a dollar for food to carry on, while cutting down on everything, for one more week or less. Forty-two cents' leeway then, to handle unforeseen expenses. But after those seven days? . . .

Wild with anxiety, the tail of shirt outside his trousers, he set off on his weekly eight hours of roaming. Today, at least, he had a trail — well, a vague piece of information that had cost him six cents. A crew might have been spotted in the fish-plant neighbourhood. It was a good distance away, a three-hour walk, and he nearly wept when all he found there was a space that had been perfectly cleared, excavated, unplumbed, scraped clean, so forth. No one knew anything about the crew. Enough to put anybody's epigastrium in a knot.

Xavier went in circles for a couple of hours, a stranger to what was around him: to the setting, to the people who brought it to life, to their incomprehensible motivations. Finally he came to a halt near a newsstand. Tried to block the anxious thoughts streaming inside him. Told himself, you mustn't believe that the worst always happens. But he couldn't help it, he went back superstitiously to thinking of the worst, as if not thinking of the worst would lead to the worst happening by way of punishment. He read the headlines without thinking, too preoccupied for their meanings to work their way into his brain. One magazine among others, whose name he read several times before, all at once dazzled him. A publication devoted to demolition, published by the Order. (He'd heard of it, but had never seen a copy.) He assumed, heart pounding, that the demolition schedule would be printed there. He started to read it, upon which he was notified that it was forbidden to obtain information from magazines without having paid for them first. The magazine cost thirty-seven cents, which swallowed up practically all his cash. Yet he barely hesitated, paid. With Strapitchacoudou's casket under his arm he made his way to a bench, leafing feverishly through the magazine of his last hope.

He found himself in Times Square, overwhelmed by the Times Building and its angled chin. Long, low automobiles were driving around, scarcely inhabited, driven by greenish cadavers, and streetcars, trolleys you'd have thought were June bugs making their way through a colony of ants, while human masses moved in droning clusters, went in and out of buildings, revolved in the doors of department stores, agitated faces that shimmered at windows running up fifty storeys or more in the strident light. Xavier found it hard to concentrate, but he was too impatient to go to the trouble of unearthing a quiet spot for himself.

The magazine. First, pages without stories or captions, but with enigmatic illustrations. The mortal remains of a woman lying on her stomach on a bed of stones, skirts halfway up buttock, a dark rag rammed onto her head. Poor children with begging bowls waiting for soup-kitchen soup, their little hands handcuffed, some with faces sporting bruises. An old man, stark naked, one-armed, toothless, legless too, posed like a bust on an overturned trash can, surrounded by two men in journeymen's garb who smiled at the camera as if he were a hunting trophy. The martyred head of a horse, one eye blinded, whose nose had broken in the middle in such a way as to pull the end of its muzzle onto its forehead (here a mysterious word accompanied the illustration: *shinn'hat-soubaï!*). So forth. What could it all mean? Finally, in the centrefold, Xavier landed on the Calendar — at last! But only to learn that it had been written in journeyman's patois, of which the apprentice understood not a syllable.

His arms came unscrewed, the magazine dropped from his hands. Xavier looked straight ahead. Spending thirty-seven cents on that . . . A policeman was making his rounds, fingers crossed behind his back; he picked up the magazine and placed it on Xavier's knees. The apprentice could only murmur thanks. The policeman pinched the tip of his cap. "Glad to be of assistance."

At the corner of the street a village band appeared, huffing patriotic tunes into the brasses. Xavier didn't even notice. He had just touched bottom. And the bottom was muddy, verminous, full of temptations to sink deeper. He shook his head listlessly and said no to something, as if Misery in person were standing in front of him and he were imploring it to go away. In front of the band, a man dressed in multi-colours, ringmaster fashion, that sort of thing, was crying into a trumpet, "*Prepare yourselves, the Minute is coming. Prepare yourselves, the Minute is nigh!*" And when he was level with Xavier, by way of a joke — for the apprentice's stupor invited mischief — he brought the end of the trumpet closer to his ear and shouted his slogan into the apprentice's cranium. Xavier took off like a stone, with the panicky look of an alarm clock going off.

But calmed down. Looked around, at first amazed at being there, and then surprised at still being, despite the opposition of all those who opposed him, the person he was. Everything around him appeared incongruous and weird. It seemed as if the atmosphere was gaining in electrical shivers, as if on the threshold of a great collective release, the air vibrating in a way that suggested a sheet of tin. The apprentice noticed the magazine, which he'd likewise forgotten. And at once plunged into it again. For what right did he have to succumb to despondency? Who could say whether some piece of information, some detail liable to help him, to focus his research, to revive his strength, might not be found there? And so he landed on some pages, this time written in normal language. Intended for a very small public: *The Apprentice's Little Spot.*

He read, attentively even, but — not much to take from it, actually. Some edifying anecdotes, good-natured humour, drawings of teddy bears, a thousand leagues from the real atmosphere he'd known on the site. (In one illustration, for instance, little monks in cassocks were naively waving their hands by way of farewell. "A crew of missionary demolishers set to leave for Japan. Sayonara!") When he turned the page, a little imp sprang up: a portrait of Lazare. The mere sight of it made him shiver. The son of the Great Barthakoste was being held up as a model for young readers: "You too can become a Terror of the Walls! . . ." In the text that followed, as far as Xavier could tell, lies were piled onto untruths. He left those pages feeling more depressed than ever. And then, by chance, noticed the ad in a box.

The idea insinuated itself into him slowly — first in the form of a conjecture, abstract, so to speak, but that soon changed into precise temptations. The blind beggar's words came back to him, going around in his head like a hurdy-gurdy, "You could get rich with your frog." He consulted the depths of his pocket and removed the pathetic contents. Read the ad again.

He was distracted from his musings, though, because something decidedly strange was going on in the neighbour-hood. Carriages, automobiles, trolleys, so forth, had come to a halt, the passengers had disembarked, the crowd was now three times more packed than when he'd arrived half an hour earlier. In the distance, the leader of the band went on filling the space with his slogan, "*Prepare yourselves, the Minute is coming. Prepare yourselves, the Minute is nigh!*" which suggested that the end of time was imminent. Near the fascinated Xavier, a woman was pacing while murmuring like an actress rehearsing her lines before going on stage. An old man with a skipping rope over one shoulder was sniffling, telling his wife over and over, "I couldn't, I really couldn't." So forth. Everyone was waiting. Some with rowdy excitement, most gloomily concentrating, like someone gathering his strength for an ordeal that he fears will be beyond him. On the stroke of noon a siren whooped and, instantly, New York was transformed into a lunatic asylum.

Xavier didn't know which way to turn. A wire slanting down from the seventieth floor of the Times Building travelled across the avenue to the fifth floor of the building opposite. An individual holding onto this wire with his feet and head let himself slide down it at an insane speed, as if he were flying, but his feet came away accidentally, the wire-walker hit the highest branch of a tree with his belly, lost his breath, then waltzed on his wire like a paper lantern in the wind until, half-stunned by the shock, he couldn't engage the braking system and his head went smack into the wall of the building opposite. No one seemed to care. On the street, along the promenade, in the park, at the entrances to buildings and stores, each launched into his own song at the top of his lungs, dancing his own dance, each act feeding the dizzying cacophony of the group at large. Two very dignified old ladies, cautiously holding each other's hand, raised their legs in the air a little while warbling cancan tunes. The old man from a while before skipped rope with the means available, of which not much remained, while his wife egged him on by gasping into a harmonica. And the same vaudevillian madness was repeated by the thousand, on every floor of the buildings, as far as the eye could see. Some could be spotted hanging from cornices, displacing themselves in perilous fashion from one window to another, show-offs. Perched on the hoods of automobiles, young dandies were dancing and strutting their stuff. Some performed the cat hanging from tree branches. Others just did somersaults. None was inactive. All with no joy, no good humour, as if a chore had been imposed on them.

None except Xavier, who was dumbfounded, feet bolted to the ground. Which earned his floating ribs the head of a billy club swung by a policeman whose role was to deal with offenders. The same policeman who'd picked up his magazine a while ago now told him, like someone who isn't joking, "Hey, nitwit! Move it! Don't you know today's a holiday?" Xavier didn't even know what date it was. "It's the National Minute of Being Thrilled to Be Alive in the United States of America! Get moving, do something. Make it snappy, or I'll stick you with a fine!" And the policeman went into a little lateral hopping step, like a moose moving sideways. The apprentice made an effort. He lifted one thigh, put his hand on his hat, and applied himself as best he could to spinning like a music-box ballerina.

He had closed his eyes, spinning made him dizzy, when all at once someone yelled into his ears, Stop, imbecile, can't you see that the Minute is over? The apprentice opened his eyes, losing his balance a little. They'd already reached the stage of assessing the damage. Ambulance sirens whined. And firemen were taking down the wirewalker who had flattened himself against the wall a while ago, and was now as limp as a rag, unconscious. Several individuals, old ones in particular, dragged themselves along the ground, moaning. Sprains, dislocations, lumbago. Motors started up again. General atmosphere of anger and recriminations. One man pushed another, who was dressed as a majorette, and upbraided him for denting the hood of his car by pounding it repeatedly with his skull: "The dumbest act I've ever seen!" So forth, thousands of examples of madness. Xavier walked through the festive debris — confetti, streamers, splinters of glass, and shattered windows — not believing what he thought he was seeing. Here, there, traces of blood. Never mind. Twenty minutes later, people were going back to their offices, passersby going back to passing by, customers flocking once again into the stores, and the thunderous life of New York resumed its normal pace, its fierce and bustling course.

4

Jeff was wondering anxiously how come he was sitting on this sofa, bare-chested, next to this perfumed little man in a satin dressing gown. William H. Cagliari ran one hand, absent-mindedly and gently, through his hair, while the other hand was holding a book by Sigmund Freud about the interpretation of dreams. Jeff stared wide-eyed at the luxurious setting, didn't recall having ever set foot there.

"How am I, why am I here? And who are you supposed to be?"

"A friend," said Cagliari gently, dropping a kiss on the back of the boy's neck before going back to his reading.

"Who are you to be acting like this with me?"

It was a whisper full of panic and dread.

"Why, I'm a friend, you know that," Cagliari repeated calmly, and setting his book on the table, began to affectionately stroke the young chest. Jeff tensed up, wanted to extricate himself, and only then realized that his arms were bound to his chair. He squeezed his eyelids, again saying anxiously, "Where am I, what's happening to me?" suffering the little bites that Cagliari's lips were gently multiplying on his chest, like burns.

The telephone rang. Cagliari left the boy to his anxiety and went to the far end of the room. On the other end of the line, the wily voice of his associate.

"Master!" he said at once. "Master, you absolutely must come to the office. Ah la la, believe me, never in my blessed life have I seen! You must come!"

Cagliari didn't like to be told what he *must* do. He allowed his associate to grasp that notion. But the other man insisted.

"I swear, Master, it's absolutely necessary, you'll thank me! An act — you won't believe your eyes or ears. Never seen anything like it. A boy with a frog! . . . I'll say no more."

Cagliari's face lit up.

"A frog, you say?"

"True as I'm standing here!"

Cagliari hesitated for barely a second.

"I'll be there in an hour."

He hung up, unable to hold back an excited snicker. He returned to Jeff, leaned across to his mouth, tenderly nibbled his lips. The boy moaned, "What am I doing here? What makes you behave like that? Hey, I'm tied up!" And panted under the caresses like a dying dog.

Cagliari left the room, whistling. Advised his butler to look after Jeff, to take him back to the clinic. Then went to his sister's quarters. She was lying on her chaise-longue, pale, long, the colour of grey ointment. She had a compress on her brow, while a nurse was busy straightening the cushions for her comfort. Odour of matches and medicine.

Cagliari knelt, took his sister's emaciated hand and brought his lips to it, devoutly. Without opening her eyes, she told him that his moustache was tickling her and that it was unpleasant.

"Sister, I must leave you."

And with a sensitivity that was filled with veneration, he lifted the lock of hair that fell onto the woman's forehead.

"Again! But you promised! . . ." she moaned reproachfully.

"I know, forgive me, but that's life when you're an impresario. Look, I'll buy you that necklace. You know the one? From last Tuesday . . . But it's urgent, I have to go. I'll be back before this evening."

"And you're leaving me alone with this idiot?"

The nurse, used to such remarks, went on calmly preparing the syringe. Cagliari placed one last kiss on the fingers of his sister, who complained again that his moustache tickled her.

On the stairs he ran into Jeff, looking distraught and confused, being led by the arm by the butler; in passing, he pinched the boy's cheek in a familiar way. Then, as he pulled on his gloves, had his chauffeur summoned. And don't drag your feet. A frog, can't you just see it, he thought, snickering. He arrived at the exit with a:

"See you next Wednesday as usual, little Jeff dear!"

Who wondered, with a mixture of anxiety and stupor, who in heaven's name this man could be, this man he was seeing for the first time.

When Cagliari's car pulls up, the wrought-iron gate of the Alamac Hotel, where he has his suite, is opened. Actually the hotel belongs to him, as does a good part of the street. His sister and he live half the time there, half the time in the sumptuous villa adjacent to the garden of the clinic for lunatics. The Cagliari logo dominates the front of the hotel, dominates the wrought-iron gate, dominates the party room, is inscribed on the corner of every cloth on every table in every room. It was his father, Lester Cagliari, who acquired this palace. The Cagliari family had always had a fortune, but it was under Lester's reign that it became colossal. The young attorney with the handsome leonine head, a little like Schumann at twenty, had first of all contracted an extremely profitable marriage, connecting him to the Morgans, one of those great merchant families responsible for New York's nineteenth century. Two children were born, Belinda and William Howard, the chest-stroker. William was small and spindly, Belinda as long as a liquorice stick. Yet they'd been born on the same day, at the same time, in the same place. Their mother had suffered from hypersensitivity since that delivery. And throughout their childhood, her children saw her only in her lugubrious quarters, darkened by heavy curtains, for the slightest light burned her eyes, she said. Her forehead was constantly in her hands because of migraines, a tradition that her daughter would carry on when she reached adulthood. The mother played the piano too, when the pain in her head gave her some respite. She had an unhealthy passion for Schubert. For German culture in general, including her favourite musicians, her favourite authors, her favourite painting. And so the twins had a Teutonic governess who taught them to speak, fluently, the language of Goethe. They learned French as well. At Lester's insistence. For him, the word "civilization" meant France. He accepted more or less anything from that land. He was a speculator, a militant capitalist, he dipped into the public purse as much as he could, devoted himself flat out to collusion, put all his legal competence into performing perfectly legal deeds that were frauds, but nonetheless he worshipped Victor Hugo, whose *Les Misérables* had reduced him to sincere tears. He experienced his first depressive episode in 1886. For weeks he did nothing but cry, getting out of bed only to roam the streets, at loose ends, gripped by an unfounded melancholy. He suffered terrible grief though he didn't have the slightest idea what he'd lost. He had, moreover, developed a strange phobia about trees. When their foliage stirred, they seemed to be sending him signs. Lester wondered if he was actually losing his mind. "But," he reasoned, "if I were crazy, *truly* crazy, I'd have no doubt the trees really were speaking to me. And since I do have doubt, it means that I'm not crazy. And if I'm not crazy, then it's not a product of my imagination, and the trees are *really* treating me strangely." One June morning, he'd tried to drown himself in the Hudson River.

But, being a man with resources, he recovered fairly quickly. In legal matters, the New York Chamber of Commerce swore by him. He taught Constitutional and Contract Law in the most reputable schools. He was thought of as a member of a powerful secret society. So forth. In March 1888 an event occurred that transformed the destiny of New York City and, indirectly, of Lester as well. An unprecedented snowstorm brought the city to a standstill for two days. On some streets the snow was piled as much as three metres high. The paralysis was a godsend for Mayor Hewitt. It confirmed in spectacular fashion what was, in his opinion, the need for a modern transport system that would make the city safe from insults like this. And thus was born the massive project of building a subway system for New York.

Mayor Hewitt designed an original and brilliant "cooperation between public and private sectors." In some business circles, such state intervention in public affairs was seen as "unconstitutional": the government should no more be building transportation systems than putting up buildings, it was claimed. But the all-powerful Chamber of Commerce supported the "Hewitt formula." A prestigious attorney, widely regarded as an expert, was the ideal man to serve as ambassador to recalcitrant business circles. From that day, the Cagliarian fortune wore seven-league boots. Lester was one of those who could take part in the fabulous wheeling and dealing the project gave rise to. And from then on, the family's fate was linked to the American Order of Demolishers. For before you can build, you must destroy: dig, demolish, blow up — it's nature's way. Thanks to Lester, the Order had won the excavation contract. And the Order always remembered its friends. Which materialized in the form of various securities, properties, and banknotes.

But while his wealth was growing, Lester's family situation deteriorated. Being a potentate has never stopped feelings, and Lester was in love with his wife, who seemed less and less inclined to go on struggling to live. Bernice's lungs were no more than spiderwebs. He came home every night fearing that she had passed away. On the one hand. But there were also the children, who were a constant worry. The twins were then around fourteen. One day, young William had gone with his sister to her ballet lesson. He'd come out of it saying, "*That* is what I want to do." Laughter. "Master William wants to be a dancer?" "No, I want to be a *ballerina*." When this was reported to Lester, he didn't find it funny in the least. His son, his only son, wanted to be a ballerina? He undertook to make the boy more manly. Imposed a tough discipline to turn a poodle into a bulldog. Sessions of catch, cricket, boxing, fencing, French boxing, rowing, icy baths, and gymnastics. Introduced him to chess as well, deeming that nothing beat that game at forming a virile character. The two years during which he had to suffer that regimen were torture to young William, who was left with unwavering hostility towards his father. The only benefit was his fondness for chess, of which the youth very soon became a player of respectable talent. And he seized the first opportunity to free himself from his father's tyranny, which was to register in law at the University. Very soon he was neglecting his studies, playing hooky, certain that he'd just have to plunge into the codes on the eve of exams and he'd be successful. He spent his days at the Manhattan Chess Club. Where on several occasions, he met champions, Lasker, Marshall, even old Steinitz, who was destitute, half-crazy, suffering from gangrene in one leg, and whose cigars and coffee William paid for. It was there too that he met a young Canadian medical student who, like him had been bitten by the chess bug. Rogatien Wondell. An animadversion would spring up between them that would still endure some thirty years later.

At that time, his father's mental stability was already significantly affected. First, after the death of his wife, Lester began to suffer chronic insomnia. Then he was gnawed by a certainty that day by day grew more urgent, more obsessive — that "genuine" reality was being hidden from him. That his wife had only "apparently" departed this world. He began to believe in the occult, was initiated into spiritualism, consulted clairvoyants, read everything he could about theosophy and mediumship, finally spent a small fortune on ectoplasm and other "materializations" of the beyond. He travelled to England to meet a very old lady, skeletal, two metres tall, terrifying as a gargoyle but, noteworthy to him, wreathed in prestige from having conducted seances with Victor Hugo on the Isle of Jersey. Still, in his own way he'd held onto his senses and he was not a man who'd let himself be duped. Before long he had discovered the trickery involved. He went from disappointment to disappointment, which only intensified his desire to "know." He still felt that the veil of the Mystery was within an inch of being rent in twain before him, and that he would at last have access to Knowledge. This nose-dive into the World of the Paranormal went on for two years, at the end of which he was fished out of the Hudson River again. This time, it was impossible to bring him back feet on earth. He had to be locked up in the madhouse, in a padded cell, where he allowed himself to starve to death. When he breathed his last sigh the lion weighed only thirty-two kilos.

Those two years of mental illness had made a dent in the family fortune. And that was when young William, who was only nineteen years old, showed what he was made of. In just a few months the house of Cagliari had regained its prosperity and stability, and its wealth had actually increased. He had, moreover, acquired considerable power in the world of showbiz. By now he owns artists' agencies, music halls, theatres, nightclubs, and speakeasies. Thanks to carefully chosen notices of demolition, he has eaten up his competitors one by one. Showbiz is in fact just a pastime, the icing on his fortune's cake. It is above all to the Stock Exchange, which he plays like a piano, that he owes the millions that make him rich. For some years he has also been trying his hand in the arms industry. He has associates in Berne who, through complex manoeuvres thought up by him, launder his money and send it to Germany. He anticipates war in

Europe within five years, etc. And his ship sails on.

"A frog, can you imagine such a thing?" he asks his chauffeur as the car is wriggling through the quagmire of Manhattan.

"Yes, Sir," replies the black chauffeur.

"A frog! . . ."

"Yes, Sir!"

Cagliari emits a little laugh like that of a malicious mouse. He's cheerful but a little anxious too. Despite his lightheartedness, William Howard is secretly tormented by the fear of ending up like his father, totally nuts. Because of his knowledge of German, he was one of the first Americans to read the works of Freud, as a precaution. Furthermore, he's had a psychoanalyst brought over from Austria, whom he supports and who looks after no one but him. He is also an assiduous reader of Karl Marx. As for his fortune, so elegantly acquired by diddling with shares on the Stock Exchange, it will collapse like a house of cards before the year is out, with the Crash. But William Howard Cagliari won't care. He will already be decomposing in his grave.

5

CAGLIARI'S ASSOCIATE DISPLAYED a glum face, for it is a rule of the profession never to seem impressed but to give the impression that you've already seen everything, heard everything. Underneath the table, though, he was moving his legs and wringing his fingers restlessly. By cracky, if the Master didn't offer him a fat bonus for getting his hands on this! . . . With luck, because there were times when Cagliari could display a flamboyant generosity, he hoped — who knows? — to be able to bribe some influential members of the Order, thereby saving his old mother's house, over which the threat of demolition hung.

As for Xavier, he was waiting serenely on his seat, with his frog on his knee. Both of them aware of the effect created, they exchanged smiles of complicity. As soon as he'd spotted the full-page ad in the magazine — *William Howard Cagliari, official organizer of Demolition Celebrations. Shows and entertainments of all kinds, artists management, etc. Proprietor of numerous vaude-ville houses in New York and elsewhere* — Xavier had known that his life was about to experience a jumbo turning point. Oh, he'd dithered some at first, racked by what was left of his scruples, but now that he'd made the move, they went up in smoke.

Around him, on the tables, window ledges, mantelpiece: trophies everywhere. And artists' photographs, some already thirty years old, fervently dedicated to William H. Cagliari. Xavier and the man waited. Neither spoke. Now and then the apprentice dipped his lips into a cup of cold tea.

On the stroke of five p.m., Cagliari came in without knocking, putting a spring under the rear end of his associate, who immediately kowtowed. The impresario was accompanied by his watchdog-chauffeur. A certainty that he'd seen that face before crossed Xavier's mind, as fleeting as it was dazzling, however, for the next moment he told himself, no, I'm wrong, never laid eyes on the gent.

But wondering if it wasn't yes after all, because Cagliari also seemed surprised at meeting Xavier, as one is at the sight of an acquaintance one hasn't expected to be there.

"So *you're* the boy with the frog?"

"Umm, yes. Do we know each other, Sir?"

The impresario didn't answer, and it was hard to interpret his smile. Merely said, to himself, "How about that? This is even better than I thought."

And Cagliari sat in the associate's chair. Crossed his legs.

The associate shook Xavier's arm, he must comply at once, the Master was waiting.

Xavier stood Strapitchacoudou on her casket, and she burst into song. Almost right away Cagliari interrupted, and with a little motion so peremptory that the frog, quite on her own, hopped into the apprentice's jacket pocket.

"That's enough for me," said the impresario. "Name a figure. I'm waiting, kid. Set your price."

Xavier hunched his shoulders to say I haven't the foggiest, Sir.

"I suggest fifty dollars per show, at the rate of four shows a week, plus two unpaid matinees on weekends. An initial six-month trial run."

The apprentice, who'd been about to suggest seventy-five cents per session, nearly fainted. Then disbelief swept over him. Mister Cagliari must be pulling his leg?

"Not a-tall. I've got just one condition: you appear onstage with your frog. And dressed exactly like now. Hat, bow tie, sneakers — the works."

"Appear onstage too," Xavier repeated with automatic stupor.

"With your looks, you'll knock them out."

"Knock them out," Xavier repeated similarly.

Cagliari snapped his fingers and his chauffeur took a document from an alligator briefcase. Everything ready. Standard star's contract. It just needed his signature. He presented the document to the apprentice. Who bent his stupefied face over it. But the numbers were too big, the dollar signs seemed to stand out from the page, $ $ $ $ $ $ $ $ $ $ $ $, and whirl around till he was dizzy, till he couldn't understand a word. He grabbed the pen that Cagliari was waving under his nose, and signed, somnambulistically. The impresario took a wad of bills from the briefcase.

"Here's your advance."

The bills were of a colour that Xavier had never seen on dollars. Cagliari put ten of them into his hands. Two long tears ran down the cheeks of the apprentice, who couldn't even calculate what ten times a hundred dollars would be worth.

Cagliari gestured discreetly to his associate, who'd been

following the whole scene with dismay. Gesture that seemed to say, "Relax, I know what I'm doing."

"You'll start Friday night. Come to the Granada Vaudeville Theatre. Try to be there by six. Here's the address."

He instructed his chauffeur to drive Mr. Mortanse home. The chauffeur steered by the shoulder a Xavier who was taking distraught little steps, his eyes like candles: a mime who'd just been hit on the head by a rock dropped from the moon.

The puffing, sweating associate had inserted his fingertips into his jacket, the way Napoleon is depicted; he felt as if he was on the verge of a bilious attack. He rummaged in his pockets for his pills. Finally, he couldn't help it:

"What's got into you, Master, giving him such a sum? That dunderhead would've been happy with two bucks for his frog!"

Through some sense of cosmic equilibrium, it struck him that the amounts gained by the frog-artist constituted an equivalent loss to himself.

Cagliari sipped some tea and let enough seconds go by to remind the other man which of the two was a millionaire, and which had an old mother threatened with demolition. And went on to say:

"Actually, it's not so much the frog that interests me as the boy."

"Bah, he's a jackass," said the other man, whose liver was tearing itself to shreds.

"Maybe, maybe not. Anyway, it's even more fun when you put a big price on it. I'd have paid a lot more for this boy."

"But without his frog he isn't worth this." He clicked his index fingernail against his tooth. "So why?"

Cagliari gazed at his employee while his fingers twiddled the tips of his moustache, which were invented for just that.

"To piss off Rogatien Wondell, that's why. I'd pay any price to piss off Rogatien Wondell."

The associate slumped on the sofa, defeated. Cagliari looked at his watch.

"Say," he observed, "I didn't think it was so early. That means I've got some time."

He tipped up his employee's chin and gave him an angelically ironic smile.

"Come on, you'll be getting a little something too, you know."

Then to himself, with a hint of affectation:

"Mind you, it's not the day for my appointment. But with what I pay her, I really don't think my analyst will refuse to see me."

The contract lay on the table, filled with disturbing clauses.

6

AFTER YOU CAN IMAGINE what kind of night, Xavier X. Mortanse was itching to carry out the plans he'd hatched. It's no exaggeration to say that this sudden rise in fortune had driven him crazy, the first hours anyway. He just didn't know what you'd buy yourself with a thousand dollars. It was a terrible, an incomprehensible amount, a genuine bomb, and those bills, with their strange, nearly vicious colour, terrified him at first. They were worse in their abstract power than a sorcerer's wand, he just had to produce them and right away the impossible would happen, for they were signs that attracted the Powers, bent them to our desires, transformed that which was not into that which was, diabolically. The Luciferian archangel plaguing America had just entered his life, in the form of ten paper rectangles, and already he couldn't get them out of his mind, or burn them, or throw them in the trash, they had him by the throat. And this was just the start! Dollars were going to pile up in his hands, stuff his pockets, rain down on his shoulders like a beating.

But in the end he'd understood.

He'd finally understood that what was happening to him was a sign that the wind of things in America was beginning to change, and blow in the right direction. The scales were tipped a little more to the side than they should have been. He realized now, with his heart beating wildly, that having more money meant having more to give away. Many bank-notes were in the hands of penny-pinchers, but soon they would move into his, Xavier's, and from there, from his hands, they would radiate towards misery and various poverties. And so, towards dawn, he got four ideas, after which, calm at last, his fever had dropped. Four wonderful ideas.

As for the first, he'd signed a one-year lease — costlier, by the way, than if he'd continued to make monthly payments. So he couldn't think about moving before the following year. But he would certainly do so as soon as the lease was up: a low house with no storeys, as level as a cow pasture, where he would open his door to the destitute. That was his first idea. Which left three more, and he made them his programme for the day.

So there he was, going out into the street, his head singing, smiling at everything in spite of his fatigue (he hadn't rested his peepers for even a second). He laughed with the neighbourhood youngsters, who seemed to have no school or anything, who shouted pet names at him or delivered little torments to his hat, according to custom. His path brought him to a post office. He was the only customer. He eyed the wickets greedily, not knowing which one to choose. He went up to one, thought better of it, glided to another, finally aiming at a third, more enticing, so forth, until the young girl who was the only employee on duty at this time of day felt weary of following her customer from one end of the counter to the other. At last the gentleman made up his mind! He smiled at her and asked if she wanted to sell him some stamps, so he could send some bills to his sister. He had to repeat himself, as the girl didn't seem to understand. Eventually she produced a half-choked yes. While she was taking the stamps from the box, her eyes didn't leave the apprentice, as if glued. It bugged Xavier to know why young women always looked at him like that, their eyelids limp, pigeon's breast gently swelling. When she gave him the stamps, he asked for an envelope too, and once again he had to repeat himself, ah la la, what you have to do to get some service, he thought, sighing like someone who was a thousand dollars richer than he'd been the day before. She came back with the envelope, eyes still glued, it really was getting on his nerves. Xavier wrapped two hundred dollars in the twelve pages of his letter. On the envelope he wrote:

MY SISTER
IN THE COUNTRYSIDE
HUNGARY

and tamped down the stamp with a lady's finger. Then held out a hundred-dollar bill so the young employee would give him change from his purchase of the envelope and the stamp. As for her, eyes not glued now but moving with stupefied admiration from Xavier's face to the banknote he still held out.

"It's, well, I haven't got . . . I haven't got ninety-nine dollars and sixty-seven cents in here, Sir."

Xavier scratched the tip of his nose, fit to be tied. Then offered to come back tomorrow with the correct change, would My Lady of the Mail trust him for that?

"Why, of course, Sir."

Again, eyes glued. Xavier about to leave. She tried to keep him there.

"Have you thought about putting your address on the back of the envelope?" she asked (the only thing she could come up with).

Xavier slapped his forehead and rolled his eyes, to show that he often had to hunt around in his belfry like that. And on the back of the envelope he wrote:

This is from Xavier who lives in the red building with eight floors in New York in America on the avenue where the Salaison Supreme slaughterhouse is. AND I DON'T WANT THIS LETTER TO COME BACK TO ME!

He quite liked this last sentence, which seemed to him, in both form and content, to suit a person who's walking around with three hundred dollars in his pants. Then dropped the envelope into the mailbox himself. Tipped his hat goodbye. Said, pointing to his casket, "That's my frog," and would have been curious to know how the remark was interpreted by the girl, who watched him till he'd gone out, eyes glued.

Finally — meeting on the street a gentleman with no distinguishing features, ambling along with his briefcase under his arm — the apprentice was gripped by a thought at once disturbing and banal: why was he Xavier and not that man? And what happened miraculously at that very moment was that Xavier became the man and the man became Xavier, but as neither one had any memory of having been the person he no longer was, nor any other memories or characteristics than the memories or characteristics that belonged to the person he had become, in the end nothing was changed in the infinitesimal order of the universe, and each of them went on his way without noticing a thing.

7

XAVIER ASKED FOR THE ADDRESS of a bank, any bank, the closest, went there, received in exchange for two hundred-dollar bills two hundred one-dollar bills. He asked, Incidentally, aren't there any three- or seven- or eight-dollar bills in America, but the glum little old man behind the glass admitted that he had no idea, not being George Washington.

"I imagine it's simpler," he added apathetically.

The apprentice, forefinger beneath nostrils, meditated on that reply, which he deemed to be rich in prospects. In the end, he had to be told that he was wasting the other customers' time, standing in front of the wicket like that. Now, everyone knew that time was something no one in New York had too much of. So Xavier apologized, tipped his hat, turned around, and went smack into a glass door that he'd confused with the open air.

He got to a demolition site, any old site, the first one that came along, pockets full of sums of money. All he found were a few workers busy making a clean sweep, sorting, levelling, members of the category that the journeymen contemptuously called Housewives.

Around the hole, some thirty demolished. Including a

woman half lying down, her back against a remnant of furniture, holding a swaddled infant to her breast. Xavier went up to her and without a word tucked two dollars between her fingers. The amazed woman stared at him but he'd already approached another demolished, to whom he also gave two dollars. Then another. And another. The people looked, uncomprehending, at the banknotes lying in their palms. Mortanse held the casket under his arm, his left hand holding the fanned-out wad of bills, and while he walked he handed out bills with his right hand, all excited.

"Hey! Hold your horses! What's that?" shouted one of the demolished. "Stand still for a minute and tell us why you're doing this."

The Housewives had interrupted their tasks and they too regarded the apprentice with suspicion. Breathless, cheeks flushed, Xavier explained that it was a compensation for the demolished. The man who had spoken became even warier.

"What kind of wool are you trying to pull over our eyes? You people care about the demolished now? Since when?"

Xavier admitted that it wasn't an official initiative, but added that he wanted his action to encourage the Authorities to continue along the same path.

"It's an idea I got tonight."

"Where does it come from? Is it stolen?" The man didn't think Xavier looked like a man who earned millions.

"It's the money from my frog. Actually from Mr. Cagliari. Actually, it's my money. She doesn't eat anything. Me, just vegetables, and not many. She's a frog worth sums and sums. The blind man said so. She's all I've got left, ever since the other one with the black hair that smelled good, a genuine Indian from Canada — she's dead now."

"Easy does it, little guy, easy does it. Who's dead? Your frog? Is it a French frog from Canada?"

The apprentice, who was suffering from happiness, shook his head no. Set the casket on a stone and freed Strapitchacoudou. Placed the wad of bills in the frog's hands. He found it hard to contain himself, as if his body wanted to make all kinds of moves at the same time.

"All right, form lines," he said in a tormented voice. "Arrange yourselves in twos and step right up: Strapitchacoudou's going to hand out dollars! . . . Come on, move!"

He grabbed the stunned demolished by their sleeves and forced them into rows. He encouraged them with a slap on the back, ran from one to another, laughed like a wild man. Despite themselves, the demolished arranged themselves in twos and stepped right up to Strapitchacoudou, who with sparkling face had started to be lavish with the bills. Xavier had undone his bow tie, as his throat felt swollen with blood. He shouted at them again:

"Now sing, please, sing! Sing and dance!"

And so timidly, but with good will, the demolished swung into action. Two by two, holding onto each others' little fingers, they approached the frog in an unnatural kind of minuet, then received the dollars with a wobbly bow. Demolished could be seen springing up all over, drawn by the heaven-sent manna. They emerged from abandoned buildings, from water mains, from one-man cardboard cartons.

"Yes, it's true! Let's sing and dance to thank this nice boy," exclaimed a demolished with a Slavic accent who had just received his two dollars.

And flung his sheepskin hat in the air, then went into a

Russian dance. Some compatriots joined him, singing, stamping boots, tossing hats. Soon, they had pretty well all joined in however they could. One danced a languorous tango with an umbrella; another simply ran, slapping his thighs to imitate a gallop; one old man marked time by slapping his bald skull with his hands; a cripple played swing between his crutches, so forth. Xavier meanwhile was vaguely moving both torso and buttocks, elbows stitched to his body, like a four-year-old trying to dance. A hoary granny came up to him, stroked his face with a shaking hand, and dropped a fat kiss on his cheek, to unanimous applause. The Housewives emerged from their hole and one of them hailed Xavier, saying he had no right to do that.

Sure enough, along came some mounted constables, accompanied by Black Marias with sirens full blast. The demolished made haste to camouflage the bills they'd received. Xavier had shut Strapitchacoudou away again, and was now walking among the demolished. He offered words of love, tender compliments, thanks. As for the police, they scattered the crowd unceremoniously, claiming that open-air shows were forbidden, today wasn't the National Minute of Being Thrilled to Be Alive in the United States of America! The Black Marias zipped around the demolition site like Apaches, sirens screaming them on their way to sow panic. People fled, people ran, soon there was no one on the site but Xavier. Who was ordered to go home and never set foot. Proud of his deed, the apprentice gave them an angelic smile while telling them "bug off" with his inner voice.

Now he had just one thing to do and the day's programme would be complete. He returned to his neighbourhood and went to the police precinct. What could have happened to the body of his friend Peggy Suit, do you know, Officer Sir, the very beautiful young woman whose hair smelled so good and who was burned outside my door last month, Officer Sir? They wanted to know why he wanted to know, so the apprentice had to explain all the way down and all the way up, his friendship and all that, what bound him to his friend, etc., and they wanted to know what was in the casket, and examined Strapitchacoudou, who proved to be the froggiest of frogs in the usual sense of the term, which was all to the good because it would have complicated the explanations a lot if she'd lit up with all the fires of her talent, and eventually they told him that the manager of the beauty salon where Peggy had worked when she was alive had paid for a grave for the young woman, as well as for a tombstone with her name on it, which is very fortunate, given that otherwise she'd have been flung into a pauper's grave. Then gave the apprentice the name of the graveyard and the location of the hole therein. Xavier went to the flower shop next door. The young woman had a pigeon breast, etc., at the sight of him. He studied every bouquet with exacting and whimsical attention, like when he'd picked out his hat with Peggy. He apologized for hesitating, but the florist assured him warmly that he could take as much time as he wanted. He finally made his choice. What was left to determine was how many. He meditated for several minutes, weighed the pros, weighed the cons. Finally, with a heavy sigh — but he intended not to pour his heart into extravagant spending, no matter the size of the sum, and to limit himself to what was strictly necessary — he had sixty-three dozen wild carnations delivered to the grave of his friend.

Part II

1

His wife is fixing his lunch. She wipes her eyes on her apron. For the third day in a row her man isn't going to work on the destruction site. She thinks he's in the process of blowing a gasket. He has an obsession, and it would take a genius to extract it from his belfry. Her man had a dream in which that apprentice called Xavier appeared to him, calling for help. That's all. But ever since, Leopold has been sticking to his guns. He is sitting at the table, and while she fixes his lunch he knows she's thinking he's going around the bend. He muses that women always think their man is going around the bend at the very moment when he's finally beginning to see things clearly. To come up against the obstacles of life over a period of sixty years, encountering only bitterness, then die. Life is pointless.

Leopold gets up, takes his sandwich, stuffs it into the pocket of his trousers. As soon as he's outside his wife rushes to join her eldest daughter, going out the back door. Her daughter is in an automobile with her son-in-law, who is driving. Ida in turn gets into the car. They start up. They're going to tail Leopold all day. Her daughter asks Ida:

"Did he work on his book yesterday?"

Ida hesitates, shakes her head. For years, Leopold has been shutting himself up in the kitchen every evening, under the little cone of lamplight, to fondle books and scribble, darkening reams of paper. Hundreds and hundreds of sheets. The title (provisional) of the book is *Build or Demolish? Reflections in the Twilight of My Long Life*. Everyone in the house respects this work, including the half-dozen roomers. His fellow-journeymen are fervently awaiting this book that will sum up a life of solemn meditation. But since he had that dream, Leopold has stopped working on it and stopped shutting himself up in the kitchen. He sits in his rocking chair by the window and pouts. Staring ahead of him, sucking on his pipe. Sometimes he mutters, no one is sure what or to whom.

Ida tries to convince herself that this is merely a passing craze. It's not the first time Leopold has been in the grip of some whim. She just has to think back to the explosion of mysticism twenty years ago when he went bananas over the Blessed Virgin. He dedicated three months to a devotion to Mary that verged on debauchery. The walls of the boarding house were covered with images of her. You couldn't move without knocking down effigies. Rosaries hung all over, like sausages at the Portuguese delicatessen. Leopold had even persuaded himself that an icon of Mary he'd recovered from a demolished hovel oozed tears every Friday around three p.m. He went up and down the streets of the neighbourhood, displaying the miraculous icon, calling on infidels to repent. He had wanted to meet the bishop, submit the Venerable Object to his examination. The bishop had greeted him with a distrust that had considerably chilled the ardour of the Sands. And then overnight he'd got rid of all the knick-knacks, claiming it was all superstition. Ida — certainly a believer, observant even, but within reasonable limits — was very relieved.

Now their car is following the streetcar Leopold has boarded. He always goes to the same part of town. The one where the Sands of Silence assumes Xavier the apprentice lives. The apprentice always said he lived in the factory neighbourhood, but never mentioned the street. Though Leopold goes out of his way, applies to the civil registry and the immigration commission, inquires at police stations, even at the morgue (his heart trembling under his shirt), no trace of one Xavier X. Mortanse. On the first days when Xavier didn't show up for work, the Philosopher, who experienced a sorrow that surprised him, tried to console himself, saying that the boy had finally realized that he and the demolisher's trade weren't made for each other, that maybe he'd enrolled in a school, who knows? Or had even quite simply gone back to Hungary, to join his dear sister, Justine. But since his dream last week, his dream of Xavier's face calling to him for help, Leopold is convinced irrefutably that the young man is in distress right now, and that it is Leopold's duty to find and save him. So Leopold roams the streets, but has no doubt. He's certain that fate will bring them together one day.

And then what will happen? Nothing, except that he'll bring Xavier to the boarding house to live at his side. Leopold will treat him like the son he's never had. And that son will also serve as his guide. Only Xavier will be able to save him from the Deception that has been haunting him more and more since he began to sense the approach of death. He will learn the very plain, the very naked truth, by watching

Xavier live, by filling himself with the lad's candour, his purity, his gentle weirdness that may perhaps be quite straightforwardly — and this is what the Sands understood last week, in a kind of illumination — that may be saintliness pure and simple.

Leopold makes his way through the streets, crazed — overdoing it as usual, as Ida can't help thinking — as if he's imitating a man lost in the desert. He cries out at regular intervals. Cries out Xavier's name. Now and then from a window comes the terribly human reply "Shut your face." Leopold couldn't care less. He keeps calling the apprentice. Sometimes sinks to his knees, from despondency. Then his daughter gets out of the car and takes him something to drink. Tries to reason with him: "Come on, Daddy, let's go home, all right?" But with a theatrical gesture he pushes her away: "Don't try to divert me from my path!" His daughter gets back in the car. Leopold speaks to passersby, provides them with a description of Xavier: He may be walking around in an apprentice's outfit. And sneakers, he insists, that's right, sneakers! The people shrug as a sign of ignorance — or indifference.

A man starts to follow him, a black man dressed à la demolished, a butt between his lips, and Ida worries: what if the man is about to attack her Leo? But no, the man is laughing. The Philosopher's expressions and attitudes make him laugh. His expressions, his grand tragedian's airs, the way he's always hiding his face in his hands, as if struck down by misfortune. Finally the man says to him, "Hey, pops. What part are you rehearsing? Poor Mimi on her deathbed?"

And walks away, laughing with calm superiority.

Leopold freezes on the spot and stares down between his

feet. Stands like that for a long moment. Finally, swearing between his teeth, he strides resolutely in the direction of the car where Ida, his daughter, and his son-in-law are. He climbs in. "Home," is all he says. Ida gives little sniffs of joy. Leopold remains silent. Keeps his eyes glued to the window, watches the streets file by. The one he's angry with, is sulking at, is himself. He realizes that once again he's only made a spectacle of himself, put on a show. Still, his concern over Xavier, his desire to find him — the affection he feels for him, which nearly frightens him — hurt like a burn. But the Deception gets mixed up in everything. Follows like his shadow, taints everything he experiences, will leave nothing of him behind but some remains to be dropped into a coffin. Then, suddenly, his heart swells. And something happens that hasn't happened since the death of his "little mouse," his first daughter, who died of convulsions at the age of two. The Philosopher breaks down and sobs.

2

THE GRANADA WAS on Broadway, guaranteeing a fairly fierce audience, and Xavier, who just had to spin around three times to no longer know left from right, had had to ask passersby every fifteen steps, until finally there it was in front of him. An amazing building, with big, pompous, solid columns, making you wonder who on earth the people who put up buildings like this thought they were. Still, a sumptuous shiver tickled him as he was crossing the threshold. The wood floor gleamed like a skating rink.

Before he'd gone ten paces, he was hailed by a peremptory whistle. A tailcoated sexagenarian was coming towards him, hand ready to grab his collar, foot ready to boot his rear all the way to the exit.

"Where do you think you're going, young man?"

Xavier X. Mortanse said that he was Xavier X. Mortanse and, showing his casket, that this was Strapitchacoudou. He asked where he should go for his performance. The lackey studied his list with important eye and circumflex eyebrow.

"Ah, yes, I see. The frog show, right?"

Laughing, the apprentice said yes. The man asked what was so funny. Nothing, said Xavier. The lackey added that sneakers weren't allowed inside here and that one must have the decency to doff one's hat. The apprentice held it in his hand, for fear that they'd. And then, lifting his feet one after the other, he studied his soles, uncomprehending. He indicated to the lackey that *he* had *his* shoes on so why should Xavier be forced to take off his?

"And anyway, it's Mr. Cagliari that told me to dress like this for the performance, so . . . ," he explained with a shrug.

"In that case, follow me, I'll take you to the dressing rooms."

And the lackey turned around and sighed and rolled his eyes.

Xavier followed close behind, looking up, so impressed by the patterns on the ceiling that when the lackey stopped to make sure he was being followed, the apprentice, trotting along, walked smack into him. They went through some low doors, climbed some short staircases, crossed some corridors, arrived. Well, just about. For the lackey launched into explaining how to get from here to there, his dressing room. Xavier listened, nodding. Then, when he was alone, he was lost. He started wandering around backstage.

What he saw then was well worth living. A woman was sitting there, very elegant, very graceful, dressed like a swimmer, and she was reading the newspaper with a pipe in her mouth while she stroked her lumberjack's beard. Now and then she said yes or no to a man who was cleaning his nails while making amazing leaps, apparently perfectly calm. (A partition concealed from Xavier the trampoline the man was bouncing on.) There were bits of scenery such as broken landscapes, doors opening onto nothing or onto a wall, and Xavier's eyes followed the complicated rigging that soared high into the air, which caused his sneakers to trip over everything. Prop men came and went, period costumes were hanging at every chance they got, so forth. Xavier took out Strapitchacoudou and sat her on his shoulder so she could admire too. Suddenly, a cage, and inside the cage, with a leash around her neck, an ostrich. Who spied him too, and right away, pounding the floor with her long rubbery legs, in the grip of the foot-stamping tantrum of love. Her enormous false eyelashes went up and down like blinds, with the intention that the apprentice's tongue would hang out. He addressed a hello to her to laugh and make fun, which led the ostrich to drop droppings of emotion. "Easy does it, Leangreen, easy does it!" urged someone who was pulling on her leash. She swallowed an alarm clock to perk herself up. Xavier looked at her, laughing. But now, with a thrust of her powerful neck, she stuck her head between the bars and nearly snapped her beak around the frog, who was still crouching on the apprentice's shoulder, and now jumped back instinctively, which caused his sneakers to get caught in some rope, and now there was a pile of things falling to the floor. He tried to fix the damage by picking up these disparate objects, but while he was placing them on a console he set off he knew not what mechanism, and trapdoors gaped open, and panels fell, and the console freed a whole menagerie — rabbits, doves, hens, all the rest. Xavier ran to recapture them all, going from hare to bird, guinea pig to puppy. The little ballerinas fled, shouting, hands on their hair. In a panic, Strapitchacoudou had hidden in the apprentice's jacket pocket. Then came the prop men, each one swearing in his mother tongue. Xavier played he who does not exist, and vamoosed.

Suddenly, anxiously, he stopped in mid-flight. Asked a worker if there was a show with actors in it that night, because his fear of actors, who are lying devices, deceit machines, was boundless. The prop man said he had better things to do, with these critters swarming all over the place, and pointed to a man whom he called the stage manager, the apprentice was free to ask him.

Now this stage manager was a terribly busy man, who spoke to eighteen people at once. As soon as you were near him, you panicked. "And the subject is?" he said to Xavier, and he could have been barking. But whenever Xavier tried to get his question out, the stage manager was already tearing a strip off someone else, and the apprentice stood at the beginning of his query, forefinger in the air.

Then some doves escaped from the wings and flew across the stage, flaying the stage manager. "It's my skin you want? Is that it? My skin?" And he handed out whacks at random, at whatever or whoever passed his door, as well as to someone Xavier had not noticed in the general confusion, but whom he recognized at once: the blind beggar. With him was his mangy, alcoholic, rheumatic old dog. The blind man seized the unhoped-for opportunity of the slap to attract attention and tell his tales.

"Screw off, louse-face, you stink," the stage manager interjected. "I'm not interested in your pitiful act. I've told you fifteen times, haven't I? You, over there! C'mere. What's going on with those yellow spots, eh?"

The blind man was asking for another chance: "Come on, be nice, take a look, just this once." The beggar bent over and began to balance himself on the tripod formed by his skull and his hands. But his feet couldn't leave the ground, and his fat behind was sticking up in the air. He called his dog so the mutt would climb onto his rear end and sing. "He'll sing, you'll see! C'mon, Donkey-Pooh, climb!" The dog didn't. He lay on a coil of rope. The blind man fell to the ground, his cheek flattened under his own weight.

But back on his feet right away, as if all that: on purpose. He looked for the stage manager, who hadn't even glanced, beating the air with both arms, blindly. Grabbed hold of a passing hand and laid his lips on it, with passion. Thought it was the stage manager's, but it belonged to a tightrope walker, who yanked it away as if butter wouldn't melt.

"It's not his fault, he's drunk a lot in his life. We live near a factory where they make shoe-shine, you know, not the paste, the liquid, and that dog, Mister, I don't know how he does it, but every night he manages to sneak inside that building and get plastered on shoe-shine. But the factory's shut down now! And he won't drink any more! I swear! He'll go back to singing! C'mon, Donkey-Pooh, strut your stuff!"

And the blind man, who wanted to show how his dog sang, howled like the demented. The animal burped and walked away, disgusted.

"Hello, Blind Sir," said Xavier.

Expressive and silent stupor from the beggar. Who finally exclaimed, "My stars! It's the jackass!"

And literally threw himself on the apprentice. The four hands pressed to his heart, tears appeared in his eyes, which you'd have said were blown fuses. Xavier freed one of those hands and discreetly slipped some dollars into his companion's soiled pants. Effusions over, the blind man decides to occupy his full space. Again calls the stage manager: "Take a good look, it's the real thing! . . . " And to Xavier: "So you decided to show your frog? — Hey ho, Stage Manager, Sir!"

Realizing that drastic measures were needed to attract attention, Xavier placed his casket on a crate and then, handing out winks all round, reached into his jacket pocket and took out his favourite performer. Bowler, umbrella, British accent, "I was a dead and buried fucking old whore when I met you, Daisy," she said, so forth. Enthusiastic applause from the dancing girls, the acrobats, the lighting men, clowns, and morphine addicts.

A very young ballerina, pretty as a matchstick, made her way to the apprentice: "Isn't she sweet! Tell me, cutie, can I borrow her sometimes after the show?" And the blind man, proud as a papa, cried out from the rooftops that he was the one who'd discovered that talent!

Xavier, awed, smiled and thanked the people.

"Happy birthday," he said. "You're all wonderful too! I love you all! Bravo."

"So there you are," said the stage manager. "I was starting to think you'd never come. Anyway, if it was you who trained that frog, I take my hat off." Xavier protested modestly. "And your own costume, very fine, excellent idea."

And he explained to the apprentice that his act would come on after the intermission, after the commercial break and the news briefs. A wire had been set up on which his Strou . . . his Stra . . . his Strouc . . . in a word, his frog would sing, they'd train a spotlight on her and (eyeing the apprentice briefly) and another on him, from the bottom up.

"The suit, the hat, really, a hell of an idea."

The stage manager clapped his hands for attention, then got busy doling out instructions. A moment's silence. Then up struck the orchestra, up lit the sets, and as of that moment stage fright started to gnaw away at Xavier. Sensation so new to him, at first he confused it with an urge to empty his faucet. He bent over the casket.

"Listen up, are you going to give me a good show?" he asked in a tiny voice.

But the frog, arms crossed, with a sly expression, snickered inexplicably in her corner.

3

THEORETICALLY, OF COURSE, Strapitchacoudou belonged
to Mortanse, but on the whole it would be accurate to say
that Mortanse and his frog belonged to the blind beggar.
When someone told him, Screw off, when someone told
him, You stink, he claimed he was Xavier's impresario and
didn't intend to let them out of his sight.

A show seen from the wings is a beautiful woman with
one eye. Add to that Xavier having to explain everything to
the beggar, who liked to visualize inside his head — as, for
example, when the magician took a little box out of his hat,
which he spread out, showed off, stretched until it attained
the fabulous dimension of a piece of furniture — which
Xavier recognized as the console with the mechanism from
before, which he'd brought within an inch of disaster — and
then what should spring from it but two human heads that
bounced like springs, that stamped up and down from one
side of the stage to the other, shouting insults and spitting in
each other's face before they went back inside the console,
which swallowed up and folded back and rebent itself into
the little box that the magician placed inside his hat, and
bowed. The beggar refused to believe any of this, but Xavier

swore by all that was holy that it was indeed what he'd seen, what can I say, Blind Sir? After that, intermission, then the end of intermission, and anxiety grew in Xavier like a plant. A ventriloquist had taken a seat beside them, his dummy on his knees. The apprentice told him that it would soon be his turn, his and his frog's, and the ventriloquist replied, "Oh well," and that was that. While he was at it, Xavier took advantage of the moment to ask again if there was going to be a show with actors tonight, but the dummy reassured him, the whole evening would be vaudeville and nothing but.

"You're wise, youngster," said the blind man, "to be wary of comedians and actors. Ah! My rabbi knew what he was talking about. Music, that's all right. But he forbade us to attend theatrical performances. What he said, my rabbi, was that one can't spend twenty-five years of one's life making people believe every night that we are what we aren't, to people who know that we aren't what we are, but pretend to believe it, without it eventually shaking up our hat stands. They've been bitten by the bug of deceit, see, and other perversions of the reproductive sense."

Xavier wasn't listening to these rabbinical observations, distracted as he was by the arrival on stage of Moses, who'd just taken delivery of the Tablets of the Law. "If that isn't an actor will you tell me what it is?" asked Xavier, his epigastrium knotted. (He was addressing the ventriloquist's dummy.)

"But that's just advertising," came the reply.

And Moses took a bag of marshmallows from his robe, stabbed one with the tip of his patriarchal crook, and roasted it on the Burning Bush. "After a Revelation, nothing beats a luscious roasted marshmallow from Kraft," observed the MC. Applause. Then came news briefs.

There was a question on the blind man's lips, burning them.

"Tell me again, youngster. You must get large sums for your frog?"

Xavier didn't reply, his eyes glued to the screen. The first brief was some kind of report on New York slaughterhouses. Xavier recognized the storefront of Salaison Supreme. Horses, pigs, cattle were sledgehammered to the ground, then suspended from meathooks, legs wide apart. Spirited spectators imitated the cries of throat-cut creatures. There was talk of, among other matters, a union coalition with the Order of American Demolishers, and you saw slaughterers dancing and singing with journeymen at a feast . . . The second brief extolled a far-off country for reasons of tourism: its traditional costumes, its quaint festivities, its monuments, its monarchy. And Xavier was startled at the announcement that the country was Hungary.

"Ah! Hungary," said the dummy. "The Danube, Budapest, castles . . . We went there on tour long ago. I'd gladly go there to live."

"If I had the dough I'd end my days in Germany," said the blind man. "I saw it in the war, it was the last beautiful thing my eyes ever saw, Germany, that leaves a mark. My rabbi, who was from there, used to say that he knew nothing more beautiful than the Prussian countryside."

"But that's not Hungary!" the apprentice protested. "First of all, where are the beets? And the cross on the mountain? And the St. Lawrence River?"

The third and final news brief declared that there would never be another war, all that was finished, so forth, America watching over the world. Applause. Spectators stood at attention. Xavier felt the fateful moment drawing nigh.

But the blind man's question was still burning, to which Xavier had replied not much. He said again, salivating, that Xavier must rake in a pile of coins with that frog of his, and that, rich as he must be now, for sure and certain he'd given up looking for his goddamn crew. But the apprentice distressed him by replying, no, he hadn't given up his search, and added that in fact, while he was at it, he would distribute a portion of his tremendous salary to the demolished, hearing which, the blind man raised his hands above his head and subsequently flattened them on his hat, in an eloquent gesture that meant dismay.

"You say you give your money to the demolished?" he asked, and it was as if he had cramps in his stomach.

Still upset at what the screen had shown under the name of Hungary, Xavier replied absent-mindedly that he'd give some dollars to the blind man too, that he didn't have any just now, that he had so to speak given them all away, but that on his next payday he would stuff his pockets, the blind man's, that is, with them too, if he wanted, even a lot, a hundred dollars if such a thing exists. Expressive stupor on the beggar's part. Then tears of gratitude rolling into his beard. He began to murmur the names of the Prophets while swaying his torso.

An employee took hold of Xavier's elbow and told him, "You're on next, three minutes."

"You'll do whatever you want when your frog sings. Tap your foot, snap your fingers, whatever. Just one thing matters: *ALWAYS SMILE.* Aside from that . . ."

Xavier nodded, epigastrium in a state, arms and legs like soft butter. The blind man patted his shoulder.

"Don't worry, kid. With a pro like that, it's in the bag. And you — as of tonight you'll be a star."

That thought, which had never crossed Xavier's mind, chilled his nipples. He began to shiver.

But it was too late to retreat, turn around, clear out. In evening clothes, the stage manager announced to the audience the animal act of the century! And we'll say nothing more! Okay, said the spectators, going along. The stage went black suddenly, and inside the apprentice's head it was as if someone had uncapped a bottle of seltzer. His legs were frozen now, heart stuck in his throat. Someone gave him a push in the back, a voice told him, Go! but he couldn't take even one step. So he got another, stronger push.

And there he was in the footlights. Taking the spot full in the face, like a handful of salt, which blinded him as a result. Where the audience was, all he could see from the corner of his eye was an immense hole. He walked, tiny steps, hardly lifting his foot off the boards. His face was congealed in an icy smile like the one you'd see on an altar boy carrying the Baby Jesus in his hands. He went as far as the centre of the stage, where the wire was, above a pedestal table. With infinite precaution he brought his frog to the wire, hesitated again before setting her down . . .

"That's no frog, it's a turtle!" cried someone annoyed at how long it was taking.

Laughter.

But now there she was, on the wire. Xavier stepped back a little, to give the frog more room, then looked up at her with an expression like Joan of Arc getting her orders from heaven. During a long and silent minute, the audience gazed curiously at this frog in a tailcoat and top hat, crouched on a wire, being tenderly admired by a clown whose smile was wedged between his cheeks like a banana.

Okay, and then what?

Strapitchacoudou croaked, lengthily, slowly, deeply, like the froggiest of frogs, in the usual sense of the term. Some laughter. Then again, silence and expectation.

Strapitchacoudou croaked again. Again, laughter, more abundant.

And only then did the apprentice realize that his frog was going to perform nothing that anyone could call anything. He turned to the audience and doffed his hat by way of apology. Out of the corner of his mouth he tried to encourage his artist ("Move it, Strapitchacoudou, come on girl, move it!") Again, zero. Then, terribly embarrassed, he tried a few dance steps himself, if the term can be applied to a pathetic wriggling of shoulders and butt.

A very overripe tomato landed in his face. Which caused an ovation. Soon it began to rain galoshes. While Strapitchacoudou went on croaking . . .

The curtain came down and the stage manager raced onto the stage in a sweat.

"What happened? Tell me, somebody, what happened?" asked the blind man in full-blown panic.

Xavier recognized no one, heard nothing, walked straight ahead as if hypnotized. The stage manager went back to the wings, took one stride that brought him to the apprentice and delivered a punch to his face. Then gave orders to clear the floor of the beggar, who, though he howled Xavier's name, was led with his dog to the exit regardless, where a final kick in the rear sent him rolling into the garbage.

Xavier had collapsed onto a bench a good way from the

dressing rooms, off to the side, because nothing was too far from anything at this point. His face and his clothes were spattered with tomato, his mouth tasted of ashes and blood. At his side, straw boater in hand, Strapitchacoudou swayed and warbled tunes à la Maurice Chevalier. Then in stepped Leangreen, the hilarious ostrich, who'd been released from her cage. She came along with her gangly, gurgling stride. Her eyes sent out exclamation points when they spotted Xavier.

Who'd been so unaware of her arrival that he cried out in terror when all at once a fist-sized pointed head was two inches from his nose. All taken up with his interior flurry, he had barely noticed, on the fringes of his concern, a vague smell of boiled broccoli. Scooping up frog and casket, Xavier devoted himself to decamping. The ostrich went after him, and it was an awkward moment for Xavier, because she was now trying to sniff his rear end, now easing her neck over his shoulder and threatening to bite the frog, while Xavier tried to speed up while squeezing his cheeks, a most awkward undertaking, until finally, at wits end, he came to a standstill, contorted himself under the onslaught of the beak, and started shrieking in disgust and terror.

"Ah! There you are," said a prop man who with fine virtuosity lassoed the ostrich and pulled her over to him. While she went on stamping her feet, her eyes never left the young man who was speeding away, telling herself that she knew perfectly well, she had always known, that one day, for a second time, she would experience Love.

4

Over the following days, no improvement. And the public reaction was such that Xavier could have gone into business selling mismatched shoes. As soon as she faced the public, Strapitchacoudou was nothing but nothingness. After three nights, and as many flops, Xavier received an envelope summoning him to Cagliari's residence the following day.

Which happened to be a Sunday. And the rain it did fall. A fine, piercing rain that obliged Xavier to pull up his collar, with gusts that nearly made him lose his hat. Sinister, harrowing spasms ran through the trees. Of Cagliari's thousand-dollar advance he now had something like a hundred and fifty-two dollars and thirty-three cents. And if Strapitchacoudou didn't shake off her lethargy, how would he be able to pay it back? On his apprentice's salary, assuming that he ever found his crew, he'd have to toil for years, making no bones about anything, to amass such a bundle of sums.

And so, epigastrium in a knot etc. Still, he mustered all the courage in his two legs, and at six on the nose it was by means of a human foot that he set out to cross the city, because too dear the streetcar, too trying the subway. It took him a good three hours. The rain had even stopped. And there before him, at last, the refuge of a multimillionaire, planted in the middle of a vast garden delirious with flowers, big, red, unruly flowers, sensitive to the cold, etc., tousled willows weeping to the ground. Xavier jingled a bell and waited at the gate. A young man finally appeared, who didn't seem to have come because of the bell, because his features were marked with astonishment at the sight of the apprentice. The two boys observed one another on either side of the gate.

"Hello," said Xavier.

"Hello," said the boy.

Seeing the relationship off to such a fine start, the apprentice inquired as to whether this was indeed the residence of Mister Cagliari, here.

"Cagliari . . . Cagliari . . . ," repeated the other lad in a dreamy voice.

He looked around him, then:

"To tell the truth, and I really don't know why, or how, but at this moment, eh? Here and now, eh? You see, I'm not really too sure where I am . . ."

"Oh no?"

"But what could I be doing here anyway?"

All around him, the young man cast looks of surprise and amusement.

"Don't you live in this house?" asked Xavier.

"No, I don't think so. I've always lived in Oklahoma. In Kirkland, my town. But I know we're not in Kirkland . . . Oh my, well, well, well." A hollow laugh. "But what's happening to me? Have I been drinking?"

"No, I don't think so. You don't look as if you have."

"I don't think so too. Well, well, well."

The apprentice didn't know how brave a face to put on. He said that his name was Xavier X. Mortanse and the young man said that his was Jeff, pleased to meet you. They shook hands through the gate.

"My frog and I, because I possess a frog, and I have to tell you she's not an ordinary frog, we have an appointment with Mr. Cagliari. He's my impresario. I was given this address."

"Ah, you're an entertainer from the fair? . . . But, see, I don't know if he's really here. Come in though. Together, the two of us will find the answer."

He fumbled a little, in search of the motions to open the gate, as if experiencing the mechanism for the first time, then Xavier was inside the garden.

Jeff executed a few disoriented steps on the path. Then came to a standstill in front of a lovely stretch of mauve blossoms that absorbed him completely.

"Are you the gardener?" Xavier attempted, and those simple words made Jeff start.

"My goodness, you frightened me!" he said, laughing. "Well, good day anyway! What can I do for you?"

He looked amiably at Xavier, his physiognomy open.

"I simply asked whether you were the gardener of this pretty garden. It's a fine trade, gardener. There are worse, believe me."

"Me, a gardener? . . . Well, maybe . . . Actually, you'll laugh but I have no idea where I am. It's funny, though. What about you, do you live here?"

Xavier scratched the tip of his nose, thinking: "Mmm, yeah . . ."

Jeff began automatically to care for the flowers, and at

times he breathed one in with an expression of delight, or else broke off what he was doing as if he'd been struck by a sudden worry. Then, arms akimbo, he studied the sky, which was clearing.

"You have memory problems, I think."

"Oh, sorry, I hadn't noticed you. I don't know what's wrong with me this morning, but . . . But tell me, it is morning — isn't it? You . . ."

"No, I don't live here."

"By the way, you're really something, you answer questions before they're even asked."

"Well . . . But, I think, are members of your family in this house? Do you have a family?"

Jeff said of course, and named all the names, father, mother, sister, all living at the same address.

"In Kirkland, Oklahoma," said Xavier.

Jeff stared at him strangely. His eyes were asking, Who the devil are you? with awed amazement. Which was turning to dismay. Was about to become terror.

"Listen," said Xavier, taking his hand, "why not go and see the people who live in this house, maybe they could tell us."

"You don't know where we are either?"

"I do and I don't. I know where I am, but I don't know whether where I am is the Cagliari estate."

"Cagliari . . . Cagliari . . . No, I don't recognize that name."

"I had a hunch."

They turned onto the path that went to the villa. Now and then Jeff let his attention drift to a detail of a flower, then had to be reminded that they were on their way to the house and, perplexed, he'd get going again, then lose the thread of his thoughts once more.

"Do you live here?" Jeff asked politely.

Xavier put his hand on Jeff's shoulder and asked if it was a habit of his to lose his memory all the time, to this extent.

"Why, not at all. On the contrary, I have an excellent memory. But well, just now, I confess that I don't really understand . . ."

And there it was again, all of it, so forth, right up to my name is Jeff.

"But we met no more than five minutes ago," said Xavier, shaking the outstretched hand. "At the garden gate."

"Yes indeed, I have a vague feeling that I met someone at a gate. Is it the gate we can see over there?"

"I really like you," said Xavier.

The young amnesiac began to laugh.

"Me too, you know. I don't know why, I don't know you, but I'm fond of you, right from the start. Your looks are really priceless."

"Thanks."

Xavier brushed off a stump and grasped his friend's shoulders to seat him there. Took some lettuce from his pocket and gave Jeff the plumpest leaves.

"Careful you don't eat too fast. Lettuce, there's nothing better for what ails you, vegetables are contemplative. If you eat slowly, all the good things for memory that are in lettuce will go into your body and help your remembering."

Docile, the amnesiac agreed.

And Xavier launched into the saga of the apprentice looking for his demolition crew, telling about Lazare, victim of sausage sandwiches, telling about the smelly business of the Order, condemning houses, then about the danger represented by actors, who are lying machines, about his friend

Peggy, murdered by flames, and finally about his frog, lingering over some details. But all that was very hard to follow for someone who loses his memory twice a minute, which Xavier realized at the sight of his friend's features, reading anxiety. So he set out to put him straight on simple matters, for instance asking him the names of flowers, which the young amnesiac had at his fingertips, and of birds, trees, vegetables. Otherwise they were silent, and Jeff gazed at the sky.

"You look to me like someone who likes clouds."

"Yes, I like clouds that go away. Clouds that visit us and then come apart."

"Me too," said Xavier.

The house seemed to wake up all at once. Shutters were opened. Whistling teakettle, aromas of fried eggs, nurses; and dazed old men who appeared at the windows, wearing striped pyjamas, and gazed out at the garden with the look of not knowing where they were.

Jeff walked as if magnetized towards the smells of busy frying pans. He was greeted by a nun who was opening a curtain at a ground-floor window and waved to him as if she knew him. Xavier was about to follow behind his friend when a voice at his back asked:

"Looking for Cagliari? Why are you looking for Cagliari?"

Xavier turned and saw a man leaning against a tree by the path.

"Ah, at last!" said Xavier. "Do you know if it's here, Cagliari?"

The man wore a buttoned houpland that fell to his calves. His striped pyjama pants were visible. He had pale cheeks, mauve stains beneath his eyes, and in them the painful bitterness of those who know terrible things that no one wants to believe.

"If it's Cagliari here? But everything here belongs to Cagliari, the whole street, all the way to the hill. Everything there, everyone there too. Jeff, you, me. Once you step into this territory, you belong to Cagliari."

"But I didn't come here to belong to him, I came here to meet him."

And Xavier recounted in his own way his frog, his flops at the Granada, his advance, finally the summons from Cagliari. The man was still standing against the tree, stiff as a stick, his gaze hunted.

"Run away, my boy. Run away if you don't want something like what happened to Jeff to happen to you. You can't imagine what he's been through. He was made to do" — at this his voice broke in a whisper of terror — "*he was made to do vaudeville!* In a speakeasy, in front of filthy drinkers. Who were urged to ask him questions. Forced him to tell his story. Jeff wanted to run away, but he was chained to the stage, and his confusion grew, and his humiliation, and his anxiety, so that at every performance he ended up howling like the demented. Yes, the speakeasy that people in those circles call the Majestic. Which is owned by Cagliari!"

"And it was none other than Mr. Cagliari who, learning that a poor invalid was being treated that way, took the necessary measures so the young man would move here, to this private institution, at the expense of Mr. Cagliari himself."

A doctor (he wore a stethoscope around his neck) Xavier hadn't seen arrive had said that. The man in the houpland shot him a furious look before disappearing into the bushes with a conspiratorial skip. The doctor introduced himself to Xavier, explained that he took care of people who had problems with their heads.

Xavier, whose liver had started to quiver at the houplander's story, asked if he was eventually going to find out whether Mr. Cagliari lived here, does he or doesn't he? And the doctor said no, Mr. Cagliari lived on the estate just, just next door, which sometimes caused confusion, because the institute was number 77 and Cagliari was 77A.

"Ah la la, confusions, sometimes you could swear there's nothing else on this earth," said Xavier, to be philosophical.

Then nothing, intimidated, eyeing the toes of his sneakers.

"So you've made Jeff's acquaintance?"

"Yes, he's my friend," said Xavier. "I don't have many."

"Unfortunately, he's already forgotten you by now."

Xavier said he suspected that.

"But tell me, my boy, what brings you here to Cagliari's? Are you a vaudeville performer?"

"Oh no, not me, not at all, not a hint of a shadow of talent, no, no, never, not at all. My frog though, yes. Sings, dances, so forth."

"A frog."

"Yes, but, well, no. I mean, she refuses to sing, dance, so forth. Which is why Cagliari wants to meet us."

"I see."

The doctor scrutinized the boy with professional concern.

"And where is this frog of yours? Is that what you've got in the box?"

Xavier opened it. The frog was crouched inside, dull-eyed. And tickled her thighs, lifted them with fingertips — nothing.

"You see? She's always like that when I show her to people. Stage fright, who knows?"

"Don't you think that, on the contrary, she looks like the most normal of frogs?"

The apprentice shrugged a shoulder, why bother trying to explain. For a moment he felt tempted to look pitiful, oh, just a little, because the doctor's eyes contained an inspiring gentleness, but the apprentice stiffened just in time. Put the lettuce back in his pocket. Worked on breaking camp.

"You know, my boy, if you ever feel like talking to someone, or if you've got any problems, you're always welcome here."

Again the temptation, even keener perhaps, but again overcome. (Besides, wasn't it true that if the doctor, out of compassion, decided to listen to his chest, damnation and misery?) Xavier could not, however, stop himself from asking him a favour.

"Anything at all."

"Will you tell Jeff that he has a friend named Xavier?"

"Without fail. But look, he's just come out, you can tell him yourself."

"Oh, I wouldn't want to disturb him, he seems to be thinking about something. And please, tell him often! Maybe that way it will stay in his head, you never know."

"You never know."

For a moment the doctor watched the apprentice go away, then he too headed for the house. He walked close to Jeff, greeted him. Jeff did not reply. Arms akimbo, he was gazing at the sky, and the clouds that the enigmatic winds make and then take apart.

5

WHEN HE PRESSED the doorbell he was already past the hour by a twenty-minute length. He was given notice that Cagliari was not a man you made cool his heels, that accordingly the frog artist had no choice but to chomp at his fist hoping for the minute Cagliari might find to meet with him. "And how am I supposed to know if the minute has arrived?" He had only to come back every hour on the hour, to find out if Cagliari was in the mood, and then there you go, door slammed in face. He spent the day hovering at the gate, beating his biceps, his collar pulled up, wrestling with the drizzle and the chill, and counting the nails in the door. Finally he was shown in, coughing and sniffling, around seven p.m.

A butler of the stickler-for-etiquette school, purchased in London, led him through rooms and corridors into a grand salon where huge mirrors were hung, so high as to make you wonder who on earth would be able to see his reflection in them. Cagliari looked even smaller with all that. The impresario was concentrating on a chessboard, looking down at it haughtily. He paid no attention to the apprentice, who might as well have been a mosquito in a draft.

"I'll telegraph my move to him tomorrow," said Cagliari.

He was speaking to his sister, long and stretched out on a chaise-longue, back of hand to brow — the pose of a tragedienne at death's door. Her skin pale and bland as ointment.

"You pay him enough, he could let himself get beaten," she said.

Cagliari sighed disdainfully and moved a white rook from a1 to d1. The apprentice watched, his epigastrium in his liver lobes. He couldn't help it, the pieces moved in his head on their own. The lines of play came together, branched off, were deployed like a tree, with ramifications of variants. He had to turn away, as if at the sight of spurting blood.

Without taking his eyes off those damned sixty-four, Cagliari suddenly blurted:

"What's wrong with that frog?"

Instead of an answer, Xavier was gripped by a coughing fit. And so nervous that his stomach heaved at the same time. He managed not to vomit. The impresario waited as long as it lasted, imperturbably. Then:

"She's stopped singing? Stopped dancing? Plops onto the stage like a cow-pie?"

"Yes, Mister, that's right."

Eyes still glued to the chessboard, Cagliari abruptly stretched out his arm, hand extended as if to receive an offering.

"Reimburse, then."

Epigastrium, epigastrium.

"I paid you for your frog to sing and she doesn't sing. So reimburse me."

". . ."

"Very well, I get the picture."

And the impresario deigned to look up at Mortanse. Even

brought his face close. Inspected him, weighed him with his eyes, appreciated his form with a little mmm . . . inner, of course, while smoothing the tips of his moustache, which were invented for that.

"You're young, you're dissipated. You've already squandered your greenbacks on dancing girls. We know about that."

"All swine," the long, blasé sister let drop. (She hadn't even opened her eyes to see whom her brother was addressing.)

"If that's so," Cagliari went on, "I propose a deal."

Epigastrium, epigastrium . . .

Clause one: pointless for the frog artist to try his luck at the Granada Vaudeville show again. On the other hand, and secondly, he would henceforth work at the Majestic, "a small bar," he said, "a blind pig, if you will," where Xavier would wash dishes, wait tables, help prop men, mend banjos. Clause three: frogs sometimes have an impressionable sensibility, and maybe the Granada's great luxury had made her go blank. So she would be introduced, now and then, on trial, on the stage of the Majestic, for instance after the act by Leangreen the Psychoanalytic, Clock-Swallowing Ostrich. That way, maybe she'd gain the experience she needed for a new attempt in vaudeville's major leagues. As for the money, they'd see later on.

"The Majestic . . . ," murmured Xavier.

He asked if that was where his friend Jeff had worked, back when, as a laugh-writer, but Cagliari snapped:

"Jeff? Who's Jeff?"

"Nothing."

Cagliari walked over to his long sister and began to massage the soles of her feet. He looked up abruptly.

"You're still there?"

Xavier would have liked to say, to be polite and to be forgiven for not pleasing, that he shouldn't move his rook but take the pawn with the bishop, it was blindingly obvious to the most elementary eyes, but he lowered his nose, said nothing. He was shown out by the butler, this time a different way that took them down a new corridor, where Mortanse noticed a row of portraits by every category of artist, from every period, one of which struck him so hard that he froze there, feet bolted. The portrait of a very young man, without three hairs on his chin, squeezed tightly into a peasant's jacket, his gaze anxious, holding in his hands an open casket: *Pat Fitzgaben and His Singing Frog*. On the frame was a small brass plate where one could read:

Shawbridge, 1901 — New York, 1919.

6

XAVIER WALKED WITH HIS EYES to the ground, weaving through the New York throng. Sometimes — in the grip of a new uncertainty, surprised at not having thought of it sooner, as if there were no end to the sum of his miseries — his eyes searched, as if looking for his keys on the ground. Now and then he said words aloud, with motions of confused anxiety, inadvertently, intrigued the next moment that people saw him as out of the ordinary. Unconsciously he boarded a streetcar, rode for a while, disembarked any old where and then, imprisoned by the crowd, with no exit to port or to starboard, found himself in the subway, still soliloquizing. Xavier stood holding onto the post. Close to him, a young woman was putting on lipstick with the help of a small round mirror that gave off a perfume of powder. In a dinner jacket, over which a coat of dubious freshness, a moustachioed man dozed, holding a violin case. Two women, one with a child on her knees who was drooling into its fist, were talking about neighbourhood matters. A worker in a cap was reading the paper, a cold cigarette between his lips. All of reality was there, present in its smallest pieces, quiet and shimmering.

Unusual, though. A fly had just landed on the apprentice's knuckle. He looked at it, indifferently at first. Then abruptly, with startling obviousness, it struck him as monstrous. Not just the fly but everything around it — men, women, lipstick, violin case. "What's going to happen now, what's going to happen?" He brushed away the fly with a motion of fright. Had a very keen sense of imminent disaster. He started to have trouble breathing. Felt as if he were suffocating, as if his diaphragm were about to burst like the skin of a drum. His hands were sticky now, his forehead covered with slimy sweat. "I'm going to faint," he thought, panicking. "Faint in the middle of these people. What will become of me?" A terrible struggle began inside him: his body had become his enemy. He felt as though he had to concentrate to keep his heart beating, his lungs breathing, as if none of them could operate on their own. He felt *responsible* for the organs in his body, for their operation, which he had to *guarantee*. "I'm dying!" he thought, with a terrible inner cry, and felt his legs liquefy.

Nonetheless his legs carried him out of the subway car. But the stairs seemed to him an insurmountable ordeal. It took an infinitely long time to climb them. Then he was in the fresh air. Fortunately, he was just a few streets from home: he recognized his surroundings, heard in his head the echo that would guide him. Walking did him good, a little. The streets were clearing, passersby becoming scarce, the neighbourhood resembled an empty closet. "I am hideously alone," he mused suddenly, in a burst of self-pity that wet his eyes. "It must be my own fault." In a dimly lit alley he heard sounds that were muffled, deadened, like a rug being beaten: it was a man, and two hulks were finishing him off with their feet. He stopped moving, stopped crying, an inert mass tossed about by the blows. Xavier broke into a run.

Home at last! Where a poster had just been plastered on the front door of the building.

NOTICE OF DEMOLITION

THIS BUILDING WILL BE DEMOLISHED

WITH NO FURTHER DISCUSSION AS SOON

AS POSSIBLE, OK? THE STRUCTURE WILL BE PRESERVED,

THE DEMOLITION WILL BE LIMITED TO THE INSIDE.

HA HA HA HA HA HA HA HA HA!

INTERIOR DEMOLITION?

HA HA HA HA HA HA HA! THIS BUILDING WILL HENCEFORTH

HOUSE EITHER A SALAISON SUPREME SLAUGHTERHOUSE INC.

WAREHOUSE OR STUDIOS AND SETS FOR THE MARIE PEAK-FORDE

UNLIMITED FILM COMPANY. DECISION YET TO BE MADE.

WE ARE FEELING EACH OTHER OUT.

SO IT HAS BEEN DETERMINED!

THE DEMOLISHED WILL BE NOTIFIED IN THE COURSE OF TIME

ABOUT THE INSTRUCTIONS TO FOLLOW AS WELL

AS THE RIGHTS THAT THEY'LL LOSE.

THIS WAY AND NO OTHER!

DEMOLISH IS MY SHEPHERD!

HA HA HA HA HA HA HA!

No sooner had Xavier read this poster, his mouth an egg, than he took a horse bun smack in the face. The little boy jumped up and down, pointing with his arm.

"I got him, Daddy, I got him!"

The child's father, in a demolisher's outfit, was the man

who had just put up the poster; he was still holding his brush and pesky pot of glue. And just then Xavier seemed so alone and pitiful beneath the stars, with shit on his cheek, that a stray dog who was devoting himself to walking by stopped dead at his feet, gazed at him, then ventured a flick of the tongue along his sneaker, before continuing on his way, muzzle down, along his road of humiliation and misery.

Indifferent Ovations

And so it would appear that this creature often has a life and an intelligence distinct from those of man, and it is wrong for him to be ashamed of giving it a name or displaying it, by trying constantly to cover and conceal something that he ought to ornament and display with pomp and ceremony, like an officiant.

— Leonardo Da Vinci
NOTEBOOKS

Part I

1

ALONG CAME LEANGREEN with her rubbery gait. Her
foot made a sucking sound when it moved off the ground.
She had on false eyelashes, earrings, a wig as long as her neck,
and the effect of the apple-green lipstick smeared on her
beak was worthy of note. A dwarf in a clown costume followed close behind. He was pushing a wheelbarrow heaped
with around fifteen alarm clocks, in colours so bright and
varied you could have taken them for a dish of jujubes. The
dwarf teased the ostrich, pulling a feather from her rear end.
She hunted him down, charging into his skull with her beak.
The dwarf rolled onto his little legs, protecting his head with
both hands. And departed stage left.

Leangreen inclined her beak towards the wheelbarrow
and, in one gulp, swallowed the first clock. From the house,
a roar of malevolent merriment. She ingested a second, then
another, so forth. You could hear the clocks clink as they were
engulfed in her guts. Leangreen then made her way to the
footlights, and stared at the audience with her enormous eyes.

They scorned her, was that it? Very well, she scorned
them too, in return. Why were they rejecting her, why did
she turn their stomachs?

"A clock! A clock!" chanted the crowd.

Sobbing with rage, the ostrich strode upstage. Once again did as she was told, swallowed two clocks at once. Back to the footlights. Shook each long leg in turn, like a scale seeking balance. Her neck was ludicrously flexible and it was a marvel to see the clocks follow its curves. She ran stage left, ran stage right, in search of a compassionate soul. Then skidded to a halt over a distance of two metres, like a skater, when she thought she'd spotted such a one. The audience was cheerful.

She had left her native land, at the other end of the world, because, watch out! she'd been seduced. A young explorer with a tuft of blond hair, who answered to the gentle name of Tinwhistle. (The audience whistled.) She had been peacefully swallowing stones on the steppes when Tinwhistle came into sight, transfixed by love, his tonsils swollen. Oh! He'd sworn that marrying him would grant her human status! That his father was a wealthy oilman and that one day he would cover Leangreen's body with jewels and petroleum! Ah! Was there a heart here present that could share in the distress with which the young man's promises filled her soul? "Me!" said the dwarf, racing across the upstage area at top speed.

Leangreen raised her voice. Everyone here saw her as an animal, correct? But pay attention! She had a soul too. Wait just one little moment and she'd show them! The ostrich raced away feverishly to look for something in her wheelbarrow. She rummaged among the clocks . . . but came back all muddled. She must have left it behind in her cage, that's all, but she did have a soul, she swore!

"Big deal!" someone shouted.

Then came the day when Tinwhistle had to return to his country. He promised to come back in six months' time. A year went by and still no news. Oh! Only some mishap could have kept the boy from fulfilling his promises! So she decided to fly to his rescue. (The verb to *fly* was greeted with enthusiasm.)

The audience was more and more restless, while the ostrich was getting carried away like a powerful orator. She recounted her clandestine journey to the United States, then the zoos, the circuses — the hope, always thwarted, of finding her fiancé again. And then one day Tinwhistle walked past her cage. A small blonde was clutching his arm! The ostrich had cried out his name but all he had said was: "What's that animal carrying on about? I don't even know her!" (Prolonged applause.) And since then she has been treated as nothing more and nothing less than an animal. She was fed from a feeding dish, had to relieve herself in the sawdust in front of everyone! And why? Was she not in the land of Liberty? Wasn't someone who had abandoned everything, renounced everything — family, species, country — allowed to make a fresh start, with human dignity, in America?

The crowd's rhythmical chanting started up again, louder than ever: "A clock! A clock!" This time the ostrich refused, heroically intractable. And sailed into a panic, an idiotic agitation, again. Someone shouted, "Death to the unconscious!" Which was greeted with a burst of approving applause.

And then, enough's enough, Leangreen raised her head, dignified. She shook her wig, joined her pinions, took a breath. And struck up the melody of "La Paloma."

The stupefied spectators fell silent. It was a reedy voice,

exceptionally thin, higher than any human voice could be, and it seemed to filter through some hole in the sky, with a hissing sound, like a leaky pipe. The result was unbearable and fascinating. The ostrich sang, lashes lowered, wriggling her little rump.

Then, a burst of shrill ringing: the clocks began to jingle inside her stomach. Leangreen looked straight ahead, desperately. She shook her feet in a way that made you think she was trying to shake a mouse out of her pants. But the ringing went on and on. A very long cane in the shape of a hook suddenly materialized from the wings, and yanked her offstage so swiftly that for a few seconds, like those spots of light that persist under our eyelids, her tearful gaze went on glittering in space.

Half a minute and much applause later, the ostrich came back all smiles to take her bows. She craned her neck, blew kisses all around, from the tips of her pinions. "I am a psychoanalyst," she said again and again, with tears of gratitude clinging to her false lashes. Finally she picked up a bouquet of nettles that a young man had flung at her head, and then, wig pushed back immodestly, flowers wedged in her beak, withdrew for good. The dwarf came on, clothespin over nostrils, and mopped up the puddles of unconscious that she'd left behind.

Xavier Mortanse had bent over to pick up a jug that had been knocked down, and naturally a client took advantage of his posture to pinch his behind. "That's not very nice," the boy scolded him, and there was nothing the clients of the Majestic enjoyed more than being scolded by Xavier.

Those clients were called majesticians. The place was a former warehouse with a capacity of — what? — two or three hundred. Xavier had oft-times been tempted to estimate the number, but his tasks tugged at him from all sides: he had to wait on tables, empty ashtrays, pour sawdust over vomit, run for the banjos, and whenever he had enough free time to take up his calculations where he'd left off, the crowd had already changed, clients had arrived, others had left, tables and chairs had been moved, it was all changing constantly like clouds, and his calculations had to go back to square one with no great hope of success. About thirty tables occupied the centre of the room, called the Tooth Pit. On the periphery, in a troubling half-light, another fifty tables — or maybe sixty, or ninety, who could tell? — formed a belt that was called for good reason the Zones of Ferocity. Finally, along the wall on the right, behind a counter cluttered with silhouettes that were both scrawny and pot-bellied — a coyote in profile that looked as if it had swallowed a balloon, stroking his tum-tum the way pregnant women do — barmen were bustling, virtuoso beer-stein fillers. Here neither liqueurs nor feminine cocktails nor joyjuice was drunk. No, the Majestic stood out for the quantity, the paltriness, and the virility of its horsepiss. There would have been a revolution if the barrels had run dry. So they never did. Nor the paunches to pour them into.

Still, what the majesticians loved most of all were the shows, of which we've just had an example. Act followed act from eight p.m. till two a.m., practically uninterrupted. The girlie shows were certainly appreciated most. But there were also the Saint Vitus Dancers, natural contortionists, Clumzu the Blinker, of whom more later, some tottery old men blowing into kazoos, the apocalyptic grimacers, the banjo fiends. To which, of course, was added the act featuring Xavier and his lethargic frog.

Dark glasses on beak by way of incognito, the Clock Swallower was watching this act from the wings. Inside, she was raging. Such an adorable sailor, with such an adorable hat, and he only had eyes for that floozie! Who didn't do a damn thing on stage! A nobody of a frog, as useless as tits on a bull . . . The boy submitted to the crowd's sarcasm, and to the insults and the apple cores, with sad resignation, smiling regardless, because one must smile. The Psychoanalyst's heart flip-flopped at the thought that he was a misunderstood artist, and a potful of unconscious drizzled to the ground. Okay, so the adorable sailor was ignoring her, that was undeniable, was even running away from her. But she did not despair. One day his adorable eyes would open and the boy would realize that inside her and inside him there beat a single heart, like an egg sitting in two separate stomachs.

But for the waiter, hell was unquestionably the Zones of Ferocity, where the atmosphere was that of a brotherhood of buccaneers. Xavier never went there without shaking. Driven back to the circumference of the room like a belt of rubbish orbiting a planet — dark, stifling, antiquated, palpitating with a confusion of fever and electricity — you entered terrified you'd never leave, prisoner of the swarm of anonymous bodies, of the rumours and palpable threats, that grabbed Xavier by the throat as soon as he set foot on the short staircase that led to it. His only hope by way of a tip was an insult or a smack. A grimacing multitude snickered as he went by, caresses slid down his back, objects dropped furtively into his hands, purloined at once, so that he had no time to understand what was going on; all at once crutches were running, by themselves it seemed. Xavier had to fling himself from table to table, paws full of pitchers and a legless man underfoot, constantly having to pick up his pirouetting hat, a hackneyed joke that was the cross he had to bear on this earth.

"Will you stop! Please! Can't you see that you're hurting my body and my mind at the same time? And if you didn't drink so much devils' brew."

Which was met with a roaring belch followed by laughter as the apprentice made his way out, defeated, after he'd put his pitchers down any old where, that shadows carried sneakily away.

He also had to clear the diners' tables, then spend a good hour in the kitchens. He was allowed to feed himself for a few moments, on the vegetables left behind on the plates, congealed in a universal mud-brown sauce. Right after that came the great plunge into dishwater, a task for which he was theoretically, emphasis on theoretically, assisted by a teenager with a cylindrical skull, who was constantly startled, with overripe skin, with fleshy lips like blood sausages. His name was Clumzu. That was a detail Xavier wouldn't have learned from the boy himself, for after three nights' grind the youth had been unable to utter a total of one word; his head was a prison. The only sounds that emerged from his mouth were precisely these: "clum" and "zu," which had earned him his name. No one knew in what language those words might have something to say. For the youth, though, they obviously took the place of everything. In vain Xavier had shouted at him when he got there, "How's everything tonight, Clumzu my pal?" or, "Plenty to keep us busy tonight, eh Clumzu my pal?" Clumzu his pal gave no reply. He only understood very simple words — here, there, fast, me, you — which had to be accompanied by meaningful gestures. It wasn't till the third night, at the very end of the shift, when the imprisoned head went onto the stage, that Xavier learned it also had a perfect understanding of the meaning of the verb "to blink." That was what the majesticians at the last tables had shouted at him, and the youth started to spin, cheeks convulsive, tongue clicking like a coachman's, all that. Which was after all blinking. The apprentice didn't care for that act. Still, he congratulated Clumzu when he showed up in the kitchen, beside himself with joy. He went on spinning, all fires blinking, in the midst of the garbage bags, till closing time.

The last drinkers expelled, Xavier's final task was to repair the banjo fiends' instruments, a job that took him a good half-hour. He needed glue, he needed sticky tape, which his fingers got all tangled up in. In the end he had to administer slaps to his own face to keep from passing out, his nose on a table, pulled by a plumb line. He never left the place, though, without sharing with his colleague the meagre tip earned from his table service. Clumzu clutched the change in his palm, but if it had been a pebble he'd have clutched it the same way.

2

THE POSTER ANNOUNCING the imminent demolition was still plastered to the pediment of the building, but the work hadn't started yet. The tenants were awaiting instructions. People kept spinning their ball of wool, knowing they'd soon come to the end of it. Foam of the daze, daily grind of imminent disaster. Xavier went back to his abode around three a.m. As soon as his cheek hit the pillow it was as if a sledgehammer had conked his skull. He fell fast into the sleep of the dead. He hardly dreamed at all any more, he'd stopped doing that too. Or else he dreamed about that peaceful river, always the same, under a slate-grey sky, flowing with silent carcasses and scattered limbs of animals. A memory of Hungary, perhaps, that blood-dark river.

He woke up at first light, exhausted, his eyelids burning, as rested as if he'd spent the night hopping on one foot. He went on writing to his sister, to ease his mind and all else being equal, only to realize sometimes that sentences kept forming inside his head but his pencil was no longer following, was no longer tracing, and he sat there studying his apathetic hand in a hypnotic stupor. And that was when he wasn't under the spell of the chicken-and-egg problem.

There was something in it that looked like vice. For in order for there to be a chicken, there first had to be an egg, right? But wait. For there to be an egg, there had to have been a chicken beforehand. Xavier tended to believe that when all was said and done, the chicken came first. So it had to have been manufactured. But could living beings be produced without the egg stage? If not, the reasoning collapsed; you had to keep at it as if you were winding a watch: chicken, egg; egg, chicken. It plunged Xavier into the depths.

Past eight o'clock. Xavier set off again, fine weather or foul, looking for his crew. Doing that, he liked to be accompanied by the blind man. With whom tough negotiations were needed. Because Strapitchacoudou was getting back a hint of her old vigour by performing for an audience of demolished, though just the beginnings of songs, a few dance steps, executed wearing moth-eaten old slippers, a faded dressing gown tied with a mismatching belt, and hair curlers that she didn't give a damn whether people liked or not: the saw-tooth nutcase in decline. The apprentice was obviously no longer in a position to hand out money to the evicted, quite the contrary. Also, he'd given in to the blind man's entreaties on the matter of passing the hat. But he'd set his conditions. The total sums received from the demolished must not exceed twenty-five cents in all. Oh sure, the blind man had moaned. Xavier had stood firm. They would divide the sum collected into two equal parts, alternatively appropriating the remaining cent. Take it or leave it. The blind man took it.

It was at the end of one of those performances — when he was crossing the vacant lot and shaking with a feeble hand the feeble hands of some demolished, smiling at them likewise, agreeing with good grace to take a look at some pitiful act by a demolished who was looking for any chance to get out and speculated that the apprentice must have a lot of influence in vaudevillian circles — that a gap-toothed old lady, being piggybacked by a young man, wanted come hell or high water to speak to the frog artist. She was one of those who think that by talking very loudly and explaining a lot they'll be able to make someone who doesn't speak their language understand it. They tried to find an interpreter, but first they'd have had to know what language it was; it seemed to be a mixture of low Latin and machine gun. The old lady was despairing at not being understood, which had her in a state close to, because she seemed to be trying to warn the apprentice about some danger. She asked to be put down on the ground. There, she took a sheaf of pages from under her apron, and to universal stupefaction they turned out to be a copy of the *American Demolition Magazine*. How could it have ended up in the hands of a poor old woman? People began to gaze at her with a respect tinged with religious anxiety. She used her claw-like fingers to open the magazine and handed it to Mortanse. Who read: *SITUATION LIKELY TO BECOME INTOLERABLE. A seditious element is using delinquent performances to incite demolished populations to insubordination.* That was all he could understand, because the article itself was written in Stratakorek, the journeymen's secret language. However, a drawing illustrated the page, a rather crude daub, but one could recognize Xavier (his hat, his frog, his rabbit smile) flanked by an individual in a demolisher's outfit, who was staring at the apprentice with an expression of unparalleled rage — more precisely, the expression of someone who's just hammered his thumb. But Xavier wanted to reassure the lady: there was a mistake about his intentions, that was certain, someone must have spoken ill of him, but in truth everyone could see and testify to the fact that they weren't doing anything wrong, he and Strapitchacoudou, wasn't this a free country too? The lady shook her head, threw up her hands with the theatrical motions of the very old.

"Join us," said someone. "We'll protect you."

"I can't do that. And anyway it's nothing, I don't have danger on my back, I assure you."

No sooner had Xavier spoken than a police squad dawned on the horizon, and the street emptied like a holey basket. The police, arms akimbo, were keeping a strict and vigilant eye on the dispersal. The afternoon was nearing its end. Heavy drops of rain were starting to pelt down on the pavement, as fat as gobs of spit and sounding like slaps. The blind man and apprentice moved away in turn, innocently, hand in hand — like two schoolgirls, you'd have thought.

3

IT WAS A GIRLIE SHOW. The drinkers had come up to the stage, and now they were pounding it with their fists. Among the performers, a nervous girl and a beefy one who looked like a trucker. Naked, on their backs, they spread their legs in the direction of the spectators. A rubber doll was buried to the chin inside each of them. They were in the starting position for vaginal release. The idea was to expel the doll, as far as possible, without using their hands. Which they did: the little nervous one to a distance of over twelve metres, the trucker barely four, and her doll fell into the drinkers at the edge of the stage. But there was more; now the two women had to hurl themselves into the audience in order to get back their dolls, which the spectators flung from one table to the next like rugby players, and that was the part at which the trucker shone. It was the beginning of a monster shambles. In the end, the beefy one was the first to get back on the stage and drop her doll into the goal basket. She waved her arms in the air triumphantly, etc., to frenzied applause. She'd be, oh, sixty years old, around there.

With his napkin over his shoulder, Xavier observed it all with great earnestness, fists on hips. This show stirred in him all manner of thoughts, questions, calculations that led to dead ends. He had to be shaken out of his reverie.

"Yes, yes, coming!" he said to a majestician who was insistent about receiving his ration.

And following that, the apprentice started dashing through the confusion of the tables, mitts full of pitchers, jostled by the throng.

Finally there was a moment's respite. Xavier used it to sleep on his feet, forehead resting on the zinc bar. Someone grabbed him by the belt.

"You," he said, "I know you. Your name's Xavier and you work in demolition."

He had to pay close attention to what the man was saying, because he was in a very advanced state and his diction was pretty well stammering.

"Listen, you, don't you recognize me?"

Xavier studied the battered face with eyelids swollen as if stung by wasps. The man had trouble staying upright on his stool. He did indeed stir something like a memory in Xavier.

"Rosette. Next door to you. I'm her fiancé. Used to be anyway."

"I see."

"Hey, Larry, two more beers!"

"Haven't you had enough, Benjie?" replied the barman. "Remember, you gotta climb into the ring tonight."

A limp wave of Benjie's hand said no problem. He turned towards Xavier.

"Remember, I was there the night that poor young thing got burned" — belch — "to death."

"Peggy," said Xavier.

"Goes to show you. We don't amount to much."

"She was Peggy. Which isn't nothing."

"I suppose."

"Just because we die it doesn't mean we don't amount to much."

Benjie had exhausted what capital he had for thinking about such matters. With great difficulty he searched his brain. Now, why was it he was drinking again? Suddenly he remembered.

"Right, I 'used to be!' because she dumped me, can you believe it? And she dumped me you know who for? Eh? You know who for? For a demolition nabob, that's who! Now you're in demolition too, aren't you?"

And with a menacing look he grabbed Xavier by the collar. Then his face relaxed in a vacuous smile. Affectionately, he tapped Xavier's cheek.

"You I like though. Can't say why, but I like you."

"Congratulations."

The din became deafening again, because two new competitors had just come onstage. Benjie went on talking to the apprentice, but with the shouts from the crowd, hearing was impossible. This was the classic act of racing by mammary traction. Everyone had climbed onto the tables. By wagging his head, Xavier was trying to see the stage through all the legs. Once again, someone was pulling him by the pants.

"Why don't you answer me?" shouted Benjie into his ear. "I told you, my name is Benjamin Thurber!"

Absent-mindedly, Xavier shook the pudgy, callused hand held out to him. The drunk went on berating him in the auricle.

"See, I started by drinking five beers; then I drank three; and now, see, I just drank two and that's all. Funny, eh? The less I drink, the drunker I get."

He gave Xavier a laboured wink.

"Why aren't you laughing? That's one of my old man's old jokes. Don't you think my pa's gags are funny?" he added, his mood suddenly quarrelsome.

"Exc . . . me, but I . . . go ba . . . ser . . . ables!"

"What? I can't hear a thing!"

"I have to go back to serving tables!" Xavier shouted into the drunkard's eardrum.

And it was back into the majestician maelstrom for the apprentice.

Later, after the fiends' act, Xavier was in the wings fixing banjos again. He ran into Leangreen, dark glasses and leash around her neck, still fulminating at the girlie show, which she thought was so vulgar, and which incensed her. She wouldn't let the apprentice through. Every evening she waited in the wings for him like this, it had become the subject of smutty taunts among the staff. Head down, Xavier merely said: "'Scuse me, miss," and went around the Psycho-analyst. Being called "miss" was the bit of bone for her counter-transference to gnaw at, which kept her quiet. Her foot slapped the floor. Something freed itself from her hind end and went plop.

Xavier went back to the bar, a banjo in each hand. It was getting late, closing time soon, all that was left was Clumzu the Blinker's act. Benjie, on the other hand, was still on his stool, tilted slightly, like a mushroom.

"Rosette," he whimpered miserably. "My Rosette. And she dumped me for a demolition nabob!"

He sank into that thought as if into quicksand. Then he roared, proud as a rooster.

"I don't give a shit about them and their pussycats! Bring on the drink for crissake!"

The manager arrived, in a fury, and he looked like Willie Lamothe.

"There you are! Drunk as a skunk again, you little fucker! How the hell d'you expect to climb into the ring? You're already down for the count!"

The boxer waved a flabby hand, meaning okay, okay, no problema. For proof, he sniffed his last tears and got to his feet, leaning on Xavier's shoulder. With eyes shut tight, glass still in hand, he tried out a few nonchalant steps, then tumbled headfirst, diagonally, in the manner of a moose, finally collapsing into a chair and then flat on ass in sawdust, all consciousness wiped out.

"Why'd you make him drink like that, you goddamn battery-powered Mongol?"

"I didn't make him drink like that," Xavier defended himself, amazed that the blame was being placed on him. "I didn't even know he was supposed to be climbing into the ring. How do you do that, anyway, climb into a ring?"

"What are we going to do?" said the manager to the two bouncers picking up Benjie's amorphous meat. "We're three-quarters sold out."

"Bah, Benjie Thurber's a steak," said one bouncer philosophically. "He'd'a got torn apart anyway, as usual. Any old hambone'll do."

The manager turned to Xavier, eyes lit up and fierce.

"You don't know what climb into the ring is? Okay, you're about to find out."

"All right. What about the banjos?"

The two bouncers chortled.

"Never mind the banjos," said the manager, taking them out of his hands. "You're going to replace that palooka in the ring tonight!"

4

THE BATTLE WOULD take place in the sausage plant right near the Majestic, access through back alley. The air was damp and cool, with so much fog you couldn't see your own knees. The blind man was there, glad he could surprise his friend like this. He'd been guided here by a charitable soul who'd only cost twenty cents.

"If it isn't you!" said Xavier.

He explained that he couldn't go home right away because he was leaving.

"And where are you going, my love?"

"To be initiated into climbing into a ring."

Already the beggar was alarmed. What did he mean, "climbing into a ring"?

"I don't know yet, but I'm going to find out, so they told me."

He had no time to say any more, for he was grabbed by the collar and led away. The beggar was pushed aside unceremoniously. Xavier advanced, flanked by the bouncer and the manager. Only thing missing was handcuffs. He was holding Strapitchacoudou's casket against his riblets. Tiny rustling sounds dropped from the drainpipes, making Xavier shiver, and a greasy smell of delicatessen put oil in his nostrils. Staircases zigzagged downwards along the walls, stopping two metres above the ground. The apprentice wondered who would use staircases like that. Feet floundered in invisible puddles, redoubling his shivers. A cat appeared, making all three of them jump. Somewhere dogs were barking; they must have their reasons. Eventually a heavy metal door opened, a rectangle of wan light stood out in the dimness, and they stepped inside the sausage-trussing plant.

They went along corridors wainscoted with cement, then found themselves in the dressing rooms. A powerfully athletic smell mingled with the omnipresent one of meat being smoked. Along the walls, all in a row, barrels held salmon corpses cut into fillets, with a scent that made your head spin if you got near it, and they would be smoked as well. Two lightbulbs hung from the ceiling, frozen in the gelatinous air. What else was there to see? Metal lockers, two-thirds disembowelled, open like mouths; pensive socks, orphaned and mismatched; a sweater spattered with brownish blood; half of an upper plate; a rusty screwdriver, rags, a soft shoe without a lace whose tongue stuck out like a man who'd been strangled, so forth; and a Negro. With poxy skin and international calibre dentition, immaculate as piano keys. Teeth you couldn't miss, because he laughed all the time. The apprentice thought to himself: "There's one who was born on the bright side." The fact is that the Negro had injected himself with mescaline, and saw Xavier as very tiny, with arms so long he could scratch his heel without bending over, and a hammer-shaped, multicoloured penis where his nose should be, which ejaculated birds like a machine gun whenever Xavier opened his mouth.

Xavier thrashed about maniacally, defended himself with a chair and threatened to jump out the window. The bouncer had only suggested they undress him, then dress him in the boxer's singlet. Faced with such crazed pigheadedness, the manager — brain tuned to solutions — deemed that, all things considered, the effect would be even more striking if Xavier kept on his little striped suit, his little bottle-green shirt, his little bow tie, and if they attached an elastic to his hat, it wouldn't leave his skull under any pretext. For the rest, he was provided with two big black balls, heavy, I'll say they were heavy, that the Negro made him put his hands inside. Pointing to the boxing gloves, he said, "Balloon? Balloon?" and Xavier repeated, docilely, "Bubloon," to the hilarity of the mescaline addict. (The fact is, what he perceived at that moment was a penguin-Xavier, and found it irresistible to see that he could talk.)

Mortanse was sitting right there on the table, his legs were dangling, and he was swinging them the way little girls do. On his back had been draped a kind of dressing gown with sequins. The other man, laughing, finally wearied and got the gloves around his wrists. Now the penguin had to be shown how to use them. The Negro pointed to his own nose, then his own fist, as if donning the two black balls established a new relationship between these two parts of the anatomy. But even though the penguin sniffed the balls, bounced his snout on them gently, he wasn't struck by any particular conclusion. The Negro repeated again, "Balloon? Balloon?," merry as you might imagine. "Yes, yes, bubloons," replied Xavier, to show that, right, he got it. He kept gazing at the boxing gloves, which made him think of the breasts of a Negress. He was perplexed. Asked, by the way, what was he supposed to do with his frog box. The manager placed the casket in one of the lockers.

"You can get it back after your act."

Still flanked by the bouncer and the manager, Xavier was led to the auditorium, leaving the Negro to his philosophy. The apprentice, who wasn't expecting this, was considerably surprised. The makeshift bleachers, crammed with spectators, formed a U around the ring. Behind them, the warehouse was vast, empty, naked. Powerful floodlights threw a blazing pyramid of light onto the ring. A hubbub heavy with storms swelled the atmosphere, making everyone giddy. The three sat on a wooden bench located just below the ropes. The crowd was teeming like foliage.

The manager said to Xavier:

"There's still a trained wrestler act. You're on after that."

The apprentice nodded. And again, the bouncer's crude laughter.

A stocky mass came along, pointed to Xavier.

"Would you mind telling me what that lunk's supposed to be?"

The manager had to tell about Benjie Thurber's letdown, then he introduced the stocky mass to Xavier, saying, "This is your trainer."

"My trainer," Xavier echoed.

"You got a good right I hope?" inquired the mass.

The apprentice boxer scratched the tip of his nose by rubbing it against one of the Negress breasts. He was reflecting on the meaning of the question, of which he could make neither head nor tail. He shrugged, adding a smile to win forgiveness. The trainer turned to the manager.

"He really is a lunk."

The bouncer snickered and the manager, without replying, gave a hint of an enigmatic smile.

The lunk looked all around him. A jumble you might have thought was a hive covered with bees. People were talking, trading insults, spitting into one another's face. Brawls ensued, promptly defused by cops. Conspiratorial-looking individuals walked from one platform to another, holding lottery tickets. Near the entrance it was possible to obtain horse piss and hot dogs.

Then the apprentice's attention went back to the black balls that had been grafted to the ends of his arms. He wondered if that was what boxing was: to sit in the midst of a grimacing crowd, wearing Negress breasts for fists. But now the crowd was starting to yell, as the wrestlers had just come into the ring. In the left-hand corner was Pick, in the right, Pock.

Pock wore a cowl of orange leather that made him look like a cricket. As for Pick, who was already sticky with sweat, hair abounded on his chest, which could have been smeared with black seaweed. With edifying gestures, the referee solemnly instructed them on ethical considerations. Then the two athletes placed one knee on the mattress, clutched one another by the shoulders, and launched into a joust of skilled wrestling. The spectators threw themselves onto the rim of the arena like dogs set loose on a quarter of meat.

Some were for Pick, some were for Pock. And the supporters of Pick and the supporters of Pock were going at each other here and there. In the bleachers, with enthusiastic rage, people were squashing the hats of their neighbours in front. Unable to contain herself, a lady took off her smock, her blouse, and finally her brassiere. And flung it passionately towards the ring, where it came to rest on the referee's skull. Xavier craned his neck. He could only half-see what was going on between the wrestlers. When one part of the crowd cried Pick, he cried Pick; when the other cried Pock, he cried Pock. But he didn't really understand. Were the two men trying to dance? And couldn't coordinate their movements? A chair thrown from the bleachers nearly landed on his back.

After an indescribable lurch, Pock, finding himself underneath his opponent, very visibly bit his crotch. The crowd's protests were loud enough to turn the plaster ceiling into rubble. Unfortunately, at that very moment the referee, whose honesty couldn't be questioned, had bent down to check that the ends of both laces in his left boot were of equal length. The spectators exchanged incredulous looks. Never seen such a thing! Such bad faith! They were being treated like jackasses!

After that, the wrestlers engaged in mutual holds till you couldn't tell what was Pick's and what was Pock's. Moment of confusion when the crowd scratched their occiputs, trying to disentangle it all. The wrestlers came apart, disentangling, bounced up and down like popcorn, and Pock landed flat on his belly, with his opponent on his shoulders. He held the other man's head back and yanked thunderously at his chin. Pick's supporters were demanding, "One, two three! One, two three!" Now the referee had to act. But alas! He was bent over the ropes and scolding a spectator in the eighth row for picking his nose.

Pick howled, "Justice! Justice!" But there was no sign of that quality, as usual. And he couldn't take any more. Egged on by his fans, he pulled hard and tore Pock's head off. A kind of steaming ratatouille spurted from the vanquished wrestler's neck. It spread over the mattress, scarlet and brown. Pock's supporters joined forces with Pick's, all things considered. They were ecstatic. The victor held his opponent's masked head at arm's length. The man's beheaded body continued to jump around by itself, in the manner of chickens. Grudgingly, the referee had to admit that Pick had prevailed. He had him parade around the ring with his arm in the air. Pick boasted, "Justice! Justice! . . ." Some nine-year-old Boy Scouts, invited for the occasion, clapped their hands deafeningly.

Half a dozen Negroes took the ring away on the side where there weren't any bleachers. They had to push aside the fanatics who were trying to dip their hot dog buns in Pock's still-warm blood. People danced, flung chairs, at once furious and happy. And finally, to the centre of the U, was brought the trampoline.

5

THE BOUNCER, ASSISTED by the trainer, had laid Xavier on a bench, and they revived him from his blackout with a half-pint of beer and their four hands, all flung into his face. The apprentice stared wide-eyed, out of it for a few moments. Then, with concern close to panic, he brought the bubloons to his neck to check that his head was still attached. The manager was stricken with laughter.

"No need to worry. You'll be boxing, not wrestling."

With tremulous uvula, an announcer introduced a show featuring "trampoline boxing, ladies and gentlemen." The trainers climbed into the ring with their respective athletes. Xavier's legs were like jelly. Excuse me, What were they going to do to him? What were the bubloons for? . . . The floor of the ring surprised him when his feet sank into it. He lost his balance and ended up on the ropes, wrapped in his own limbs. The public, connoisseurs to a man, appreciated that first exploit. The trainer thought it had started well. Xavier was assisted in disentangling himself from the ropes.

"What is that treacherous surface?"

Someone had to explain that it was a trampoline.

"There's something wrong." The referee stepped in augustly.

And what was that?

"What he's wearing. It's not regulation. He's not allowed to box in that."

The bouncer chimed in with first-hand arguments. The referee owed a close friend of the manager five hundred dollars. Without saying a word, the manager nodded. The referee gave in.

"But not the belt, that I won't stand for. He has to take off the belt."

Xavier was stripped of his leather belt. Found that he was floating in his pants. Told the bouncer:

"Promise you'll give it back after the show?"

"Promise!" said the bouncer, who negotiated for the belt with a spectator as soon as he stepped off the trampoline, letting him have it for a dollar thirty-five.

The trainer grabbed Xavier by the fleshy part of his arm.

"Now listen carefully. I'm giving you just one piece of advice, that's all I can do, and you'll try to work something out, okay?"

The apprentice held onto his descending pants with one hand and lowered his head to listen.

He should watch out for the way his opponent used his feet. He's a virtuoso in that particular art. But if you pay too much attention to his amazing leg-work, he'll bash your face in with his right.

"Follow his fists and his face and nothing else, every second, or else! . . ."

"The way he uses his legs," repeated Xavier conscientiously.

To thundering applause, the announcer had just introduced the opponent in question. Clad in a striped leotard, he hopped up and down, clinging to the ropes. Then, like a champ, he saluted the crowd, bringing his Negress breasts together above his head. He had a narrow pointed moustache, Mandrake-style. His biceps looked like knots in a rope. The announcer reminded the crowd that the champion's name was Douglas Fairbrown.

"Pleased to make your acquaintance!" Xavier shouted, gloves framing his mouth like a megaphone.

With a quiver of a nostril, Fairbrown let him know what he deigned to think of him. Then, executing a triple backward leap, he rebounded on his head, finally ending up on his feet, legs together, arms a V. The crowd cheered and so did Xavier.

"Bravo!" he cried out.

And from the announcer, this rejoinder:

"And now! In the rrrrrright-hand corner! Weighing kilos and kilos! Please welcome Benjie! 'The Steak'! Thurrrrrberrrr!"

A segment of hot dog with mustard, lobbed by an indignant spectator, informed him of his error. The announcer went to Xavier's corner, beckoned there by the manager. The latter told him there'd been a substitution. He handed the announcer a scrap of paper. The announcer tottered back to the centre of the trampoline.

"Okay fine swell, anybody can make a mistake, ladies and gentlemen! So, as we were saying: In the rrrrrright-hand corner! His firrrrrst time in a rrrrrrrrring! Weighing as much as a stepladder! Xavier X. Mortanse and his little hat!"

Bursts of laughter and sarcastic applause. One of the

Majestic's regulars yelled, "The Frog Preacher! . . ." Tottering on the trampoline, Xavier offered the crowd a vague smile, hailed them with a wave of his bubloon. The dressing gown was lifted off his shoulders and a lemon rind flattened against his teeth.

"Protect yourself as much as you can," his trainer recommended. "If you see him give you an opening, deliver a good solid right."

The apprentice nodded, understood nothing. A bell rang, Xavier tried to figure out from where. He jumped; once again the audience had rushed up to the rim of the ring. Hands tried to grab him by the ankles. Xavier was pushed towards the centre of the trampoline.

The lemon's acidity made him shiver and screw up his face like a baby. Spellbound, he watched Doug Fairbrown's gymnastics. The guy had all kinds of legs, grew a new one with every dainty step. Fists curved towards his chin, arms rolling like a moving locomotive. He made a try at approaching the apprentice. So far, Mortanse just stood there, arms dangling, sucking at his lemon wedge. Occasionally he'd scratch his butt, or his nose, with his bubloon. Waiting for his turn to take dainty steps. He dared not do too much.

Fairbrown's whirling arm was astounding; he slugged the apprentice right in the face. For one brief moment the apprentice had a dazzling vision of the ceiling as horizon, then the trampoline did its stuff and he was vertical again, surprised, smiling, distraught. Already he had only a dull awareness of what was around him. He was in the ring and at the same time he was somewhere in the crowd, watching it all as in a dream. Everything was now running in slow motion: the faces and the buzz from the house, and Doug

Fairbrown still hopping and skipping around him like a kangaroo. Reeling delicately, the apprentice went back to his corner and bent over, to exit between the ropes.

"Where are you going?" the trainer yelled, to be heard over the boos.

"Wonhmmftrui."

The trainer extracted the lemon from his mouth.

"To Hungary," Xavier told him somnambulistically.

The manager came up to him.

"Listen to me, asshole. Walk out on this fight and you'll pay me back for every fucking ticket down to the last fucking cent!"

Xavier nodded in dazed compliance. The wedge of lemon went back to his gums. And he slipped between the ropes, and the crowd uproared. Xavier responded with a limp wave of his bubloon. A twenty-ton black steel ball charged between his eyes at eight hundred and fifty kilometres an hour. He took a congested stroll, elbows resting on the ropes, laughing vaguely at he knew not what. He spat out three little pebbles, which were his teeth. The lemon wedge was stuck between epigastrium and gizzard.

Vain as a bishop, Fairbrown pirouetted, executed counter-kielbasas that flabbergasted the crowd. Inadvertently, though, his feet got tangled in the ropes and the direction of his rotary movement was reversed. He went off at a tangent and splat into the front rows.

He climbed back into the ring immediately, lucky or plucky, putting on airs of I did it on purpose. The play of his feet started up again, prouder than ever.

The apprentice went over to ask if he was hurt, but his

face was greeted on six occasions by the opponent's bubloons. His own had become so heavy that he couldn't lift his arms. The blood stopped circulating in his wrists, where the laces of his gloves were garrotting his veins. And punches rained down on all sides. Overcome, Xavier's trainer mashed his face with both hands.

The referee had to step in. He pulled Fairbrown off his victim and forced him back to the ropes. Stamping feet, waving bubloons. The crowd went wild. From the top of a bleacher someone hurled a plucked duck onto the trampoline, and Xavier, laboriously getting back on all fours, could see the duck under his nose, as dazed as he was. The fowl was shaking its stumps and emitting distraught quack quacks. Xavier would have gladly done the same. As it happens, the duck was the last thing he remembered.

With his pants at mid-butt, the red polka dots on his briefs thrilled the crowd. His thinking was no longer inside his head but flying around him like swallows. The lemon rind was still stuck somewhere between larynx and stomach. The elastic on his hat had held fast. Now he had a vague idea about going back to Hungary on foot. Through a mist of blood he glimpsed a landscape, right there behind the bleachers, at the back of the house. Saw his sister, Justine, gesturing to him.

But Fairbrown facing him again, they were bowling balls now, he was taking punches directly in his floating ribs. Xavier pulled back into the ropes as far as he could. His opponent kept rattling his head with punches. One last uppercut lifted Xavier's feet off the floor and he was flipped into the air and outside the ring like a pancake, landing on a hot-dog stand, dead drunk from all the punches. The merchant completed the decoration by sticking a sausage between his inert lips.

The battle had gone on for twenty minutes. Strapitcha-coudou hadn't missed a thing, having taken advantage of the Negro's distraction to escape from the cloakroom. She was sitting, unnoticed, on a beam near the ceiling. Gazing avidly at Xavier's body spread out on the stand, unconscious, swollen, arms outstretched. A pitiful sight he was. But the sight of apprentice blood excited her more than she could bear, and she masturbated like a banjo fiend.

6

It was on the morning of the day after the day after his dazzling career as a boxer that the thing declared itself.

Xavier X. Mortanse hadn't left his bed for some thirty hours and hadn't really regained consciousness until dawn. Now it was nearly eleven a.m. He'd managed, with a struggle, to sit up in his chair. As there was no curtain on his window, he was prey to the sun, which hurt his eyes. The atmosphere in his abode was a steam bath. He tried to tidy up his thoughts but a weighty sloth, an inertia more powerful than the will, blocked their flow inside him. Not that he felt faint. Only a little feverish — just enough, so to speak — and feeling sick, therefore pamperable, without actually having to suffer.

He had to accept it: a significant part of his head didn't belong to him. It thought, felt, suffered, grew anxious — without his really having anything to do with it. He didn't tell himself, "Okay, now let's think," didn't tell himself, "Yes, the situation strikes me in a way that I regard it as judicious to hop on board the anxiety broom." Thoughts started moving by themselves, anguish swept over him, such is life, he had nothing to say in the matter. When he was thinking, it sometimes took him long minutes to realize this. He suddenly recognized that he was thinking when he recognized where he was and who he was. And he recognized that he was alone inside his head. In other words, to think was to forget that he was someone who was in the process of thinking, and when he again recognized that he was someone in the process of thinking, it was a sign that he was already no longer thinking. This struck him as being at once obvious and strange. He had more evidence of his solitude than of his existence. Maybe he didn't exist. But he was certain that he was alone.

And then look, something else. As recently as last week, said to his frog, "Guess what I've just done? Believe it or not, I've just solved a system of fifth degree equations. And I don't even know what it is!" Many such examples could be given.

He picked up his pencil stub, licked it, then noted on a page:

> If I say: "I know that my faucet is burning," it doesn't mean that my faucet stops burning, unless I am in a sense outside my faucet, which I observe, and that wee burn is something that is happening to me — but that wee burn is not me, I continue to be something other than that, and so I have a certain control over it. But if I say: "I am anguished," I'm not outside that anguish, my observation of it does not separate me from it, I am the thing that I observe, I am my anguish in the process of being observed.

He sucked on his pencil stub for a while then. If he was his anguish, he was also therefore the cause of it. But at the same time, that of which he was the cause was obviously something that he was experiencing. The same remark could be applied to sorrow, the sorrow of no longer having his sister, Justine, at his side, or of having lost his friend Peggy Suit. But who was the cause of what? Continuing down this slope, he slipped once again towards the abysses of the Chicken and the Egg.

A fly flew in the window, busy, quick-tempered, constantly changing its mind, making show-offy touchdowns on the table, on chair rungs, on the toes of shoes, obsessed by some monstrously pointless activity that was tormenting it like a troll. It landed just below the apprentice's weary gaze, and too bad for the fly as, with a nimble flick of the tongue, Strapitchacoudou made short work of putting an end to its troubled and inept existence. It was the kind of fly that frogs adore, its swollen belly ready to drop eggs. The disgusted apprentice turned his face away. And with a greedy smile, Strapitchacoudou carried the flavour to the privacy of her casket.

Xavier was still thinking about his page. He gave himself three more weeks. Three weeks to find his demolition crew. Past that, if he didn't reach his goal, he would manage somehow with the hundred dollars or so he had left and, come what might with whatever difficulties, he was determined to go back to Hungary.

He had reached this point, sadly, when he suddenly experienced a strange and completely original sensation. It was barely a tickle, a not unpleasant gooseflesh that spread across his chest. And then a lump formed in his throat, a lump that all at once seemed *alive*. He straightened up so suddenly that his chair fell over. A sticky spot had just appeared on the page before him. His heart started to beat very fast. He felt his face getting hot hot. A strange excitement took hold of him. Titillated and terrified, like a child about to take part in a forbidden game, he tried to ward off the tremors, to contain them, he paced the room with a kind of exaltation. But it spurted from his lips in spite of him, as if deep in his throat there was a little prankster, a pernicious goblin that was amusing itself by spitting pebbles from his mouth. After five minutes of this, the sheets, the floor, the table — might as well call it a board — were covered in blackish gobs of spit.

He started to panic. Sat down, stood up again. Lay down, then straightened up in the same motion, then paced again, his brain every which way. He wanted to run away from *that* — which was reality itself — the knowledge that he'd just spat out half a litre of lung. He ended up in the corridor, ready for anything. He closed his door behind him, locked it feverishly, as if trying to imprison what had just happened, as if leaving his abode would mean entering another Universe and Time. Alas, it was the same life still pursuing its course, and he remained, with no solution of continuity, the same living being who was in the process of regurgitating his blood.

Not too sure what he was doing, he pounded on his neighbours' door. He recalled vaguely what the drunken boxer had told him, and shouted the name Rosette! Rosette! . . . in the voice of a child who's afraid.

"All right, all right, I'm coming! My God, what's going on?"

Rosette rushed to pull on a dressing gown and make just one three-second stop at the mirror, but when she finally opened the door the apprentice was lying on the floor like a sack, unconscious.

7

FOUR OR FIVE INDIVIDUALS were in the waiting room. There was a shrivelled-up little old man who wore in the middle of his face, with an obviousness that didn't concern him, a purple and proliferating thing that was no longer a nasal appendage. A Negress whose mouth no longer shut, eyes open so wide you'd have said they were two golf balls stuck in a sugar pie. A little boy, finger deep in nose, was humming some loony tune and, unblocking his nostril now and then, or scratching his skin, which was covered with a chickenpoxy scab. Mortanse realized that he was lying on one of the benches, his head resting on Rosette's firm thighs. He tried to get up, couldn't.

"Take me home," he whispered.

"There, there, child, don't talk."

Xavier looked around him, filled with dread. And in comes the doctor.

"So, Rosette. I gather you're bringing me a new patient. He doesn't look at all well."

The two of them lifted the apprentice's limp body, dragged it into the doctor's office. Xavier moaned, he wanted to go home. They laid him on a pallet and the doctor bent over him.

"What happened, my lad? Vomiting blood? . . . You've been beaten, too, from what I can see. When? Was that the first time it happened?"

The doctor asked his questions slowly, his voice reassuring. The apprentice did not seem to understand his words. The doctor sighed.

"Look, don't be afraid of me. I'm a doctor, Dr. Stein. And I want to help you. It's just that if you don't answer my questions . . . "

"I spilled tomato juice on my shirt," said Xavier, but a deep cough seized that moment to tear his lungs apart; a black lump spewed from his mouth and splattered onto the floor.

His head fell back onto the pallet, exhausted.

Dr. Stein thought things over, unconsciously scratching underneath his very conspicuous stomach, like a pumpkin. Rosette sympathized, bringing her hands together. "Oh! The poor boy . . ." The doctor took out a stethoscope and was about to undo the apprentice's shirt. He curled up and turned to the wall, moaning.

"Please, be reasonable, it's essential that I listen to your chest. Come, come, why are you being so childish?"

But the apprentice stubbornly refused to take his clothes off, even his shirt, and Stein had no choice but to listen to his chest through the cloth. Then came a series of examinations that Xavier had finally agreed to, as long as they didn't force him to take off his clothes and didn't touch him below the belt or in the place where women have breasts. The boy's body gave the doctor a strange feeling. The effect of the pain that was eating at him, most likely.

Xavier had managed to sit on a chair in front of the

doctor's desk. He felt slightly better. Dr. Stein donned specs, started filling out papers. The apprentice waited, trying to read the thoughts on the doctor's face. Finally the man looked the boy in the eyes.

"I've got bad news for you. But I know that you'll be strong and face the music."

"The music," Xavier echoed with surprise and stupor.

"There's every reason to believe that you've contracted K's bacillus. Perhaps complicated by the beginning of I know not what. We'll have to investigate further, of course. But that's what it seems to be."

"I see."

Rosette had stayed behind, near the door, but a burst of compassion propelled her towards Xavier.

Dr. Stein went on:

"You're going to have to take very good care of yourself."

"Yes, Doctor."

"It's a very serious illness."

"Yes."

"What's most important is that you get a good rest. You may even, if need be, have to get out of the city air."

". . ."

The doctor explained that the bacillus was still in the early stages, despite the violence of this first attack, and that if he was careful the disease could be resorbed and he could get better. But if he neglected himself, it was liable to get worse, easily, and then.

"Then?" asked Rosette.

"And then you could die."

"Die," said Xavier.

"Yes."

Rosette took hold of the icy hands of the apprentice and he listlessly allowed her to.

As of today it was to be total rest, the doctor ordered. He would give Xavier some medicines, among them something to ease the violent coughing fits, but what he had to do most of all was rest.

"I'll make sure he does," Rosette promised.

"In any event, I'll drop in to see you the day after tomorrow, in the morning, around nine, Rosette told me you live next door to her? ... Very well. You must also beware of deceptive improvements in your health. There's a good reason why this disease is known as 'the tease.' It's a hypocrite. Sometimes you think it's completely resorbed, then it turns up again, five times more complicated. And finally, if you have mistresses, you mustn't do you know what with them, because, you see, this disease is catching. Promise?"

"Promise," said Mortanse.

And he thought, "I've got the tease. A disease that spreads death."

Rosette was up against him now, a melancholy Dr. Stein was wiping the lenses of his pince-nez, Xavier was crying. Sobbing till his shoulders ached, with his face pressed against Rosette's stomach.

8

XAVIER LET HIMSELF be taken home. In his hand he had a flask of restorative. There were two more in the pocket of his jacket. It was an ochre and odoriferous liquid that tasted like drugstore. It had taken a mouthful to give him the strength to make the return trip. It seemed to him that from now on his life would have that taste of medicine and death. Rosette was holding him up by his elbow, as we do with the very old. His legs were toothpicks, pathetic, as breakable as a heron's.

In the lobby of the building, he made his way unthinkingly towards the stairs, but Rosette dragged him to the elevator. It was fixed! She explained that the crews would soon be starting the inside demolition. Necessarily they'd start with the upper floors, and they certainly weren't going to walk up eight floors fifteen times a day. The apprentice listened to these explanations glumly. And by the way, what was he going to do when the work started? Had he even given it a thought? If he wanted to, he could live at her place for a while, in her new home, what did he think? Then he'd have all the time he needed to get better . . .

The apprentice said nothing.

The elevator did indeed work like a charm. It brought them to the eighth floor without mishap. Rosette offered to do some cleaning at his place, besides washing up the spilled blood, she wasn't afraid of infection, people fell sick when they lacked love, and love was something she had so much of that all she thought about was giving some away, but the apprentice said no thanks, not necessary. He promised that he'd rest, neither accepting nor refusing her offer to drop in every day, to see if he needed anything. She would bring food, fish, even beef — how long had it been since he'd had a good steak? . . . Xavier shrugged and went back to his place.

To find Strapitchacoudou bent over his sheets of paper, reading on the sly what Xavier was writing to his sister, Justine, so forth. He hastened to take away the paper. Panicking, the frog spat in his face, jumped up and hid under the bed, like a dog that's pissed on the carpet.

Xavier spent the next day in bed, doing strictly nothing. He gazed at the lead marble he'd hung above his bed, which he assumed to be the source of the sound he could hear in his head, that let him etc. At times he sank into a vague kind of sleep, the horrible deep-set kind in which the brain goes on working, haunted by formless and harrowing thoughts — the kind known only by the truly chosen. When he opened his eyes again, Strapitchacoudou was stationed on his pillow, observing him with disturbing steadiness, as if pondering some sort of attack. She forced herself to smile, though, executed some ballet steps, and Xavier, melting, stroked her head with his fingertips.

Early that evening he got up, took a few steps, surprised that he felt nearly fit. But soon experienced a severe drop in energy. He had sat down on the mattress when, without knocking, Rosette stepped into his cubicle. She had on a red dress, skin-tight, and her blonde hair was pulled into a twist, with a long ringlet hanging down on either side of her bosom, think torpedoes. With garrulous gestures and greedy giggles she set a still-steaming plate on the table next to the casket. She seemed to be in an extravagantly good mood, tittering over the slightest thing and humming tunes. As for Xavier, he gazed at her with glum and sickly stupor. She affected him like a draft, which gave him the shivers. She gushed to Xavier that she was going to take care of him, and that he was going to get better; that she'd made up her mind and was going to adopt him; that she'd treat him, if not like a mother, at least like a big sister; that all day long, yesterday and today, she'd thought about nothing else. Some weeks ago, she had finally found herself a rich protector, a prominent individual who respected her and wouldn't quibble over expenses. A demolition nabob, no less! Already he'd found her a lovely little house and Xavier would come and live there; she'd introduce him as her little brother who was convalescing. This man would give her everything — affection, protection, indulgence. She could even give up the daily grind for good and devote herself solely to Xavier's future, if he wished, and even bye-bye morphine!

This evening she'd taken a dose, oh, just a teeny tiny one, because she'd had a rough day: a former client, a boxer, had threatened to hit her because she had turned him down, and on top of that some children had laughed at her, etc. — But what was she thinking about? Here she was gabbing away while his steak was getting cold!

"I cooked it myself, I've got a hotplate in my room."

She moved the chair in front of Xavier and on it placed the overflowing plate. The slice of meat, as thick as a missal, was oozing pink blood into the fried potatoes and the mustard-glazed carrots. "Yum, that looks good!" And pretended to be hankering after it, to stimulate the boy's appetite. Xavier protested bashfully that he didn't eat those things. Rosette was undone.

"What're you talking about? You mean you don't want my steak?"

He said no and gave her a melancholy look.

"You were running a fever, you lost your appetite, that's normal, but it will come back, you'll see. Take one little bite, just to try."

Xavier scratched the tip of his nose. Without much conviction he began to explain what he thought about meat, that it was murderer's food, all that, we know the tune. To show his good will, however, and show that he appreciated her thoughtfulness, he snagged a shred of carrot and introduced it into his mouth. Chewed, chewed again, swallowed. Then said it was good, very good, really.

Rosette managed not to panic. She sat beside him on the bed and wrapped her arm around him. After some initial tenseness, Xavier discovered that Rosette's shoulder was comforting, her woman's perfume too, and he let himself be hugged more tightly. She wanted to make him understand that he had too many scruples, that eating meat wasn't a sin. From the dawn of time, human beings had killed animals to feed themselves, that was the way it was. Their bodies needed it to live. Refusing meat meant refusing to look after oneself. And the real sin would be to do his body harm. Did Xavier intend to let himself die? It would mean Xavier killing Xavier and that was truly how you became a murderer.

Rosette cut a tiny bite of meat, stabbed it with a fork, and brought it to Xavier's lips.

"Come on now, be reasonable."

Xavier squinted at the pink and grey wound. Fat had congealed on it. With eyelids closed, he let his jaw drop. Rosette placed the piece of steak in his mouth. His molars crushed one corner of the meat. Juice spread over his tongue. The appalling taste made him think of a dead horse, its eyes eaten by flies. There was a gurgling in his throat. The meat dropped from his lips. He drooled the putrid saliva into his hands. Walked over to the water pipe, washed his mouth, and then, grabbing the bottle of restorative, took two big swigs. He didn't know what to do next. Was he going to die because he was incapable of eating corpses? He collapsed in tears.

Rosette, horrified with pity, wanted to take him in her arms again, but this time he freed himself, grumpily. He asked to be left alone. Rosette was in a state.

"I'll come with Dr. Stein tomorrow. He promised he'd be here at nine. He'll help me reason with you. He'll listen to your chest, yes he will, and this time you have to let him. It's no sin to be naked in front of your doctor."

Epigastrium, epigastrium.

"Meanwhile, I'll leave you alone, since that's what you want. But I'm not taking the steak. I beg you, try to eat some. Look!"

And once again she moved the plate closer to the apprentice. Who picked it up and flung it violently at the wall. Then threw himself onto his bed, buried his head under the pillow.

Rosette gazed, disconcerted, at the scattered remains of

the meal. Another refusal. Always, whatever she wanted to give was refused, even when she was a child, that was the way it was. Sobbing, she left the room. The universe had been upside down ever since she'd been born with a penis.

9

THE NEXT DAY at dawn, his decision was made. He was going to take care of himself himself, according to his innermost convictions. Eat cabbage and carrots, sleep eight hours a night, do knee-bends. If worst came to worst, energy zero, a swig of restorative and adversity had better watch out! On its own, this decision gave him a new lease on life. He felt fantastically better now, rested and in fine fettle, and the crisis two days earlier seemed like a nightmare from which he'd awakened. He was healthy as a dragon-slayer.

They were very kind and all that, but really, he didn't need either the doctor or Rosette. Because how could a doctor who didn't know him from Adam understand after just one meeting, any better than Xavier himself, what was good for both his body and mind? Granted, Dr. Stein specialized in bodies; with his instruments he had examined, palpated, auscultated. But Xavier's body? Who could be a greater specialist than he himself? He himself who had inhabited that body for so many moons? Also, no need to poison your blood with meat, or strip naked in front of people. He'd do perfectly well on his own at completely ridding himself of the tease. In this context, to have spat up a lot of blood was a sign of health. A sick body was a body that kept inside it horrible things that could destroy it. As for Xavier's body, what had he done when he ejected all that bad blood but expel the undesirable amount of the tease that he was carrying inside him? His mind was made up. Another two or three good regurgitations and his health would be as good as new.

As Dr. Stein had promised to visit around nine o'clock, Xavier left his abode at half-past eight. He felt definitely perked up. He had washed his dirty shirt, taken care to restore a human shape to his hat, and the swelling in his face was going down. It was sweet to let himself go down eight floors in the repaired elevator, like lettuce being swallowed by a stomach that's in fine fettle. On the ground floor he took a slug of restorative to prepare himself for a fresh onslaught and then, full of energy, turned left onto the street, having in mind the dead-end where the blind man lived.

The beggar was sitting cross-legged, a squamous blanket over his shoulders. He was glumly fixing himself an infusion of coins. When he heard the apprentice's footsteps his face tensed up. He asked who goes there. Xavier replied simply, it's the jackass. And the blind man leaped to his feet. He flung his arms to the sky. He beseeched all the prophets. And finally said, Xaviééééééééééé! . . .

He made his way towards the young man, arms wide, and smashed his nose against the wall. Xavier tapped his finger against his shoulder-blade and the beggar turned, finally hugged him to his heart.

"Xavier, dear little Xavier . . . I thought you'd passed away! You were in such a state the other yesterday! . . . So those bastards made you box, eh? Ah, let me kiss you! Bless me!"

Xavier blessed Blind Sir, and how are you? And your dog, Donkey-Pooh?

The beggar mashed his hat onto his head with both hands, then began to whimper, Uhnnn, uhnnn, uhnnn . . . And explained as follows.

You see, there'd been a terrible misfortune! As recently as the morning of the day before yesterday! What it was, was, he'd wanted to ask about Xavier, being excruciatingly worried about him. He asked directions and found some people kind enough to take them, him and Donkey-Pooh, all the way to the Salaison Supreme, because he knew that Xavier lived nearby. Only, once he was there, how was he to find out exactly where Xavier lived, a mystery. So he'd called to his young friend at the top of his lungs. (Chest out, like a rooster about to sing, the blind man wanted Xavier to hear how he'd yelled out his name, and the apprentice had to plug his ears. Then the beggar went on.) And so on for many minutes. Till eventually his yelling attracted public condemnation. Though he fought and cast evil spells left and right, the crowd gathered around him finally got the better of him and Donkey-Pooh. And they were obliged to leave the neighbourhood. The tragedy had occurred some time later.

He broke off his tale.

"What tragedy?" asked Xavier.

The blind man bit his fist in pain.

The plate over a manhole had been removed. But listen to this! They'd neglected to put on a protective screen, as anyone would assume the law required! Donkey-Pooh, who hadn't sobered up for two days, had tumbled to the bottom of the hole, followed shortly, of course, by guess who? "Me!" bellowed the blind man. Who'd landed on his knees eight feet down, onto the back of his dog. From Donkey-Pooh came a muffled "Uhhhh!" Then he didn't get up. Dead, as they say.

"My dog is dead!" brayed the blind man.

"Oh, poor you!"

And Xavier delivered sympathetic little pats to his friend's shoulder.

"I yelled my head off for a good half-hour get me out! A policeman gave me to understand that there were rungs planted in the wall of the hole, practically touching my nose. How was I supposed to know? A blind man in a manhole? On my way out I told the policeman, 'Policeman, give me some money! You represent the city of New York and the city of New York neglected to protect me; I fell down the hole and Donkey-Pooh died. Give me some money!' The police-man told me, 'There was a sign.' I said, 'I'm blind.' He said, 'That's not my problem.' I followed him, call it harassment if you want, but I've got my rights and I know what they are. In the end he dragged me to the station. There, I kept a good grip on my end of the stick. I told them, 'Give me some money or give me another dog. A blind man has the right to have a dog. It's his eyes. Or give me money.' An officer pointed out that my dog was a poor pair of eyes since he'd fallen into the hole. And his colleagues all snickered. 'Then get me a better one!' I demanded. And look at what they gave me, the swine!"

The blind man went towards his old board roof. But between it and himself was the hotplate where his coins were simmering. Fall. Moans. And the beggar kneaded his scalded leg as if the pain made him want to tear it off.

Xavier said, "I'm here, I'm here," and helped him up.

"Ah! Xavier dear, is it true? You're really there? Ah, come here, let me give you a kiss."

The apprentice allowed that mouth with its powerful mustiness to kiss him.

"Now, take me to my hut, we'll come back later for the money."

And the blind man hobbled along, leaning on Mortanse's shoulder.

From beneath a jumble of trash he extricated a big plush doggie, covered with grime and lint.

"Here's what they gave me. And laughed! Can you imagine? It isn't even alive. It's a *counterfeit* dog!"

The boy said politely that it was a nice doggie all the same.

"You nitwit! I'll bust your nice doggie on your head."

Xavier conceded that it was obviously a little the worse for wear, but.

"A little the worse for wear! You call that a little the worse for wear? Here, take a whiff. He stinks of bedbugs, this piece of kitsch!"

"True, he doesn't smell like a rose," Xavier acknowledged.

And yet the tip of a tongue that stuck out of his mouth, and the ears that hung like bananas, gave him a certain something. With a hesitant hand, Xavier stroked the doggie's limp body. Some sticky moisture stayed on his palm.

The blind man held the doggie in his arms. He inquired about Xavier's physical condition. If he'd recovered from the boxing match. Whether he had any broken ribs. And his plans: what were they? And how did he intend to spend today?

Today, only look for his demolition crew. And if by chance he ran into a crowd of demolished, maybe he'd perform a frog-release followed by a hat-pass. He was determined, once he was cured, to go back to work on the sites, the project was still dear to his heart.

"Cured?" worried the blind man.

After that, Xavier was banking on going to the Majestic tonight to tender his resignation.

The blind man started to panic.

"Your resignation? . . . And your debt? Do you want to end up behind bars?"

The apprentice retorted that he had excellent reasons, maybe even vital ones, to lay off work for a while.

"See, I've come down with the tease, it was going around," he explained.

Eloquent stupor of the beggar. He asked him to repeat, not sure he'd heard right. Xavier repeated in his normal voice that he had the tease.

Another brief moment of stupefaction. Then the blind man started frantically spitting on the ground.

"And I've just kissed you on the kisser! The kisser!"

Xavier told the blind man he had nothing to fear, as he was not his mistress.

"You can be such a jackass, it's hard to credit," said the beggar.

And he spat on all sides, and rubbed his lips with his cuff hard enough to split them.

"All right, that'll do it, I think," he concluded, blowing two spell-preventing farts. "But you. Doesn't it bother you, coming down with K's bacillus?"

"Oh," said Xavier, with a confident smile, "you see, I'll be cured, don't worry about that."

"What makes you so sure? Did you dream that up inside your empty skull?"

The apprentice had a good laugh at that, because it was true, now and then, that his head was like a belfry with the wind blowing inside.

"I saw a doctor and he told me I'll be cured if I look after myself. I just have to rest, it's just the tiniest little beginning of the tease. A baby disease, you could say. Besides, I've already rejected a whole bunch from my body."

"That's a new one!" said the beggar sarcastically. "And just how did you go about doing that?"

"Instead of worrying, you'd be better off hurrying. It's nearly ten already."

The blind man rummaged deep inside his vast pants and took out a piece of clothesline. Then he tied that leash around the neck of his plush doggie, and dragged it along the ground three paces behind him once they were on their way. Hand in hand, as was fitting, both of them being people of habit.

Part II

1

THE CROWD HAD gathered around the child. Of the chapel, only the façade and steeple were still standing, like a theatre set. The little boy was talking with an eloquence of both word and gesture like that of Puss in Boots. His puffy trousers, tight at the ankle, his oriental slippers, his luminous face, and his tapering, spiritual hands, like the hands in pictures of saints — everything about him exuded the Arabian elegance, nimble and ethereal, of a little prince of the wind. "Women of courage," he said, "men of faith," and all listened to him with their souls at peace, with confidence and gratitude. He said, "Those eyes, which could not lie, those eyes have seen her, those ears have heard her." And voices rose up here and there and said, "Ariane!" in the way that Mohammedans pronounce the Holy Name and Spaniards say olé. The child brought his right hand up to his cheek, raised the other to Heaven. He looked as if he wanted to imitate a hunter with a rifle, but it was a movement full of grace to indicate the steeple. "Up there," he said. "There where the holy bells were. In that very chapel where her nuptials with the World which is not this world were celebrated. She appeared to me. She was dancing and her dancing was a balm for the soul, a honey of tenderness and generosity of spirit. And she said. She said that she was among us forever, always. That she no longer exists but she is all the more present among us, I swear to you on my very spirit she confided this to me. Women of courage, men of faith, she also said to me, the way exists, a way back exists. That the land of your fathers, the land of your mothers, one day, once again, will take you in. You will go back there to complete your days in the land of your beginning, have no fear, in the gardens that once grew beneath your feet, that you had to leave but whose dust and gold have stayed on the shoes of your exile. Fear not and do not lose hope. There will be a return. A way exists. As I swear on my spirit she told me. I was but a child of seven, bereft of all he could not name. But listen now. The extraordinary gift of words."

Once again voices rose up, litanical, speaking the name of Ariane. The boy's hand traced a slow semicircle, the wheel of the sun, to ask for silence. Something was happening. He pricked up his ear and his eyes seemed to be following the flight of a mosquito in space. "She is there," he said, and he brought his hand to his ear. "Speaking to me." And he closed his eyes in deep contemplation. Silence surrounded the group like a circle of fire. In the distance was the din created by the workers and the tools of demolition, on a cross street a dog barked relentlessly, but that was going on in a different world from the one where everyone, with bated breath, was waiting in silence for what would be revealed by the little prince of the wind. Who finally opened his eyes. "She has spoken," he said. "She told me: 'I have a brother here among you.'" Agitation in the gathering. "He is her brother because he is from a World that is not this world. He is still nearly a child. Where are you, brother of Ariane in the beyond? Speak, if you can hear. Come forward."

"Ariane's talking about you, Tonio!" said a man's voice, anonymous, ardent, stamped with adoration.

"No," said the little boy, "dear brothers in exile, women of good will and honey."

Tonio's gaze travelled from face to face, questioning. He said, "I am less than the rose that adorns your shoes. I am not worthy of the dust that flies from your slippers." The crowd murmured, moved, a rustling of leaves. A clucking of scorn could be heard. Faces turned towards Xavier. Halfway out of his jacket pocket, Strapitchacoudou was snickering, holding the flask of restorative, with which she was wetting her throat. The apprentice, terrified with shame, grabbed the flask, and in the time it took to recork it the frog was able to shout insults at the crowd, to deny the existence of the soul, to declare that all that was left of their Ariane was tiny remains in the process of decomposition. Xavier stuck his thumb in her mouth to shut her up; she bit it. The blind man was wondering what in hell was going on. He sensed the crowd's hostility growing around him, sensitive to it as to a draft. The child walked up to Xavier, who backed away, in the grip of an urge to decamp. Strapitchacoudou was still hanging from his thumb, sticking to her guns. People said, "Who are you? What do you want with us?" The blind man, realizing that things were about to go off in the wrong direction, started to run any which way, and Xavier took off in pursuit. "No," said the child. "Don't go, wait!" But they were already far away, and soon out of lungs. Xavier was afraid of spitting the tease, but finally no. It was a miracle that the beggar hadn't encountered a wall during his frenetic flight.

They got to the edge of the site where the demolishers were working. Xavier managed to pull the frog off his thumb, pop like a champagne cork. He stuffed her hastily into her casket, I'm locking you inside and I'll make very sure you don't get out, triple-locking in fact. The creature moved around inside restlessly and kept shouting insults. The blind man was furious, his lungs were on fire. What that frog was, was the devil! It had to be gotten rid of!

"She's not herself," said Xavier. "It's a disease that's been making her like that these past days. And I can't leave her in this state. After everything she's done for me."

The blind man thought that was far-fetched. Everything she'd done for him!

Xavier let himself drop to the edge of the sidewalk in a fit of despondency. He sipped some medicine, which snaked into his chest like ether. The demolishers got to work amid an apocalyptic hurly-burly. The blind man had to shout to be heard over the crashing and banging.

"That crew we can hear, could it by some miracle be yours?"

"What?"

Xavier had said that like a man who's just been wakened. The other man repeated his question. And then Xavier realized that they were at a demolition site. He stood up slowly, apprehensively, got closer. He walked around the site without taking his eyes off it. He saw faces that he could have named. Those who were working on the crane, those who were executing clearing manoeuvres at the bottom of the excavation, among whom he recognized right away the Philosopher of the Sands of Silence. Who happened to look up at that very moment, and spot Xavier. He waved broadly. The apprentice went back to the blind man.

"Well?"

Xavier hesitated, looking sombre.

"It's not my crew," he said finally. "Let's get out of here. Time to go to the Majestic."

He grasped the beggar by the biceps, but the blind man freed himself.

"This time, no. I'm quite fond of you, Xavier dear. But life with you has become too difficult, soon it will be dangerous. I want to go home."

"As you wish. Me, I'm leaving."

But the blind man grabbed hold of his sleeve, let himself be dragged along, unable to get by without the apprentice.

When he was at the top of the ladder and could finally climb out of the excavation hole, the Philosopher found the street empty. He called out Xavier's name without much hope. A passing journeyman asked him who the Sands was calling to like that.

"You know, the apprentice from last spring? The one called Xavier?"

And the journeyman rummaged through his memory and didn't know anyone by that name.

"But you do! Remember? The one who worked under Lazare!"

The journeyman walked away without a word, but his very silence was a reproach to the Philosopher, who already regretted it. The workers had agreed among themselves never to utter Lazare's name again. Ever since the lawyer had made public the young foreman's last will and testament, all knew that the traitor had bequeathed his entire fortune to a subversive organization that provided aid to the demolished.

2

ON THE SPEAKEASY door was posted a declaration of war.

OPEN! OPEN!

NEW YORK OPEN!

OUT WITH THE USUAL MAJESTICIANS!

MAKE WAY FOR THE SPIRIT OF DEMOLITION!

Xavier went inside, dazzled. He forgot about the blind man, who was getting lost in this throng of two hundred waiting in the cigar smoke and the hubbub. Money had been spent on the event. The place was unrecognizable, with its drap-eries, its frills and furbelows running along the frieze, its illuminated columns erected underneath the balconies, where notices were actually posted: "Do Not Touch. May Capsize," because they were made of cardboard. For anyone who had only seen the hall in a dim drunken light, now, in the lamplight, it was an impressive sight. The flooring in the Tooth Pit had been swept, washed, waxed, the tables arranged in a horseshoe, and on each had been placed a chessboard upon which young employees with slicked-back hair, reflecting the taste of the grand financier of the event, were distributing the chessmen, setting up the clocks. The stage had been transformed into a VIP stand, etc. And that was what had become of the Majestic, which only the day before had been home to Clumzu, the show girlies, and the banjo fiends.

Present was the usual mob that followed tournaments — analysts, journalists, onlookers, second-rate players — and polite greetings were exchanged. The leading competitors, keeping watch on one another from afar, darted eagles' eyes back and forth. Bumpley, the plump and famous Arthur H. Bumpley, organizer of the tournament, went nimbly back and forth, knowing everyone, starting conversations, wriggling his ass, convinced that he was liked.

The smell of fresh tobacco blended with the unsinkable perfume of stale beer that made up the Majestician's background aroma. Also detectable, though still indistinct, was the characteristic odour of the thinker: the musky fragrance exuded by a hundred overheated brains, gaining in strength as the matches progressed. For the time being, expectant and jittery, the chess nuts kept busy however they could. This one here, ashes on his jacket and a waxed-paper napkin on his knees, was placidly gobbling a sandwich, with mustard in his moustache, one for whom defeat wouldn't mean an urge to hang himself. That one there, in contrast, was sitting erect on his chair, back stiff, with the gaze of a hunted animal, afraid that if he moved his head, waves would escape from it, revealing to his opponents the variation on the Queen's gambit he'd been working on feverishly for weeks, shut away in his hovel. Yet another was swinging his foot, searching for saliva, impatient; he was confident that he could refute the Sicilian defence and he was burning to dazzle the world with it. As well as these gentle dreamers, there were some more sporting minds, lavish with handshakes oozing warmth. They liked to gamble. There were solitary megalomaniacs, financed by patrons to whom they'd already sold all the chickens that weren't yet hatched. They liked to kill. Finally, there were those who warranted suspicion, who seemed to belong to the sporting club but, once they were at the chessboard, showed themselves to be ogres, vipers, lions. In the midst of it all circulated caricaturists, two or three photographers, admirers as excited as hens, wielding autograph books, and very dignified gentlemen with the noggins of British lords, who wore women's lingerie under their three-piece suits.

As soon as a door could be heard slamming on one side of the stage, the hubbub dropped a notch, as if the volume had been turned down, and all faces turned towards the rostrum, lit up, in case Capablanca put in an appearance. But the honorary chairman wasn't living up to expectations. The name Capablanca reminded Xavier of something vague but profound. He asked around to find out what it was. He was seen as a moron. Hey, come on — Capablanca, former world champion. "I see," said Xavier. As for Cagliari, master financier of the event, someone had caught a glimpse but didn't know where he'd gone; even his associate was looking for him.

Xavier had to pinch himself to be sure the spectacle being offered to him was real. He'd come here to hand in his resignation, and look at what he'd found. It confirmed his impression that he was living in a universe under a spell, where, without warning, everything became its opposite,

Poverty became Fortune became Misery, all that. The Majestic was transformed overnight into a Chessian temple. Suddenly, a hullabaloo. An adherent of the hypermodern school had just twisted the nose of an adherent of neoclassicism, thereby inciting partisans of both camps. Xavier ended up as part of the crush despite himself. It would have swiftly become an official scuffle had representatives of the Order not intervened, implements in hand, for some bud-nipping. In vain did the troublemakers bawl and beg and get down on their knees and moan; they were expelled, banned from all competition for a year. This mishap reconciled the two men. They went off together to get pissed.

Xavier took a seat off to one side. He looked at the paper he'd been given at the entrance. *First prize, $2000. Second prize, $1000. Third prize, $500. The winner of the Beauty Prize for the Fiercest Attack will be awarded the sum of $400, courtesy of the American Order of Demolishers! Demolition is my shepherd! So it has been said! May the Powerful wipe out the Nonentities!* It would be an understatement to say that Xavier was tempted. He experienced a kind of light-headedness.

He stepped up to the counter. All the same, it cost three dollars to register. He obtained his card, a black token called 78. He wanted to know if he'd understood right. He would play his first match on the table bearing that number, correct? And he'd have to defend the ebony chessmen? "Whaddya think, jerk?" came the reply. Then, turning around, he received a putrid cloud smack in the face. A little man, goateed and well rounded, his expression radiant, stood next to him, clutching a cigar: Arthur H. Bumpley, the organizer.

"If it isn't Vincent Vilbroquais! I thought you'd gone back to Montreal a year ago, young man."

The stunned apprentice wondered who the man thought he was talking to.

"And how is dear Justine? I think I ran into her in Central Park a while ago."

Etc. But now a personality appeared, to whose side the organizer flew, abandoning Xavier in an abyss of perplexity.

It was twenty minutes past the hour foreseen for the start, and Cagliari was nowhere to be found. The hall was starting to smell of armpits, scalps, pipe-scented belches, and snapping nerves. Xavier's jitters hit him right in the faucet. But he wasn't alone: there was a long lineup at the door to the little boys' room. Xavier felt he couldn't wait. As he was acquainted with the premises, he remembered the toilet upstairs, in the management offices. He sneaked up, casket under his arm. He'd have gone unnoticed in any case, because just then applause welled, swelled, spread like a wave, finally was converted into a standing ovation. Capablanca had just appeared in the VIP stand. With him was old Master Marshall, U.S. champion for some twenty years now. After treating himself to a healthy dose of claque, Capablanca asked for silence. ". . . iends of N'York, 'ans of chess," and that was all the Cuban grandmaster had time to say because a cry rang out from one side of the house to the other that was no laughing matter. To wit: *Murder! Murder!*

The distraught man was pointing with one arm to an open door behind him. He repeated his cry. He also said, "*Police! Police!*" The hall was criss-crossed by various movements, incoherent and scattered. Some started hesitantly going to the stairs.

Pushing his way through the crowd, Arthur H. Bumpley rushed to the scene of the drama. The man who'd cried murder — Cagliari's principal associate, the man who was always on the verge of a bilious attack — had lost his voice. He went into the management office with Bumpley. Soon Marshall and Capablanca joined them, two or three bystanders as well. They all stood on the threshold, not daring to move a hair. Cagliari was glued to his seat, and in the most uncomfortable way, because a poker was stuck in his eye and through his skull, riveting him to the back of his chair. And yet at first glance he didn't appear dead. His left hand jerked spasmodically in front of him, as if he were frantically tapping a chord on the piano, while his intact eye was rolling in its socket, its expression one of extreme preoccupation. Those present gazed at the peculiar sight, asking themselves what the devil they should do about it. They stayed by the door, feet bolted. With a kind of heroic convulsion, Cagliari's hand managed to grip the poker. Arthur H. Bumpley took a step towards him. But just then, with an unforgettable sucking sound, the impresario himself wrenched the poker out of his eye. Straightaway, his head emptied like a wineskin, he writhed on his seat, and finally slumped, forehead on knees that were streaming with blood. Kaput.

"There!" said the man who had sounded the alarm. "The safe! . . ."

Which was gaping, empty.

"The tournament prizes were in it. In coin of the realm."

Bumpley sensed that now he had to take the initiative, for fear of seeing the situation turn to someone else's advantage.

"Actually, how come you're the one who found him? You were alone, as far as I can see."

Cagliari's assistant had brought his hand to his liver, which was being stabbed by a hundred icy needles.

"But I'd just got here, ten people saw me go into this office! I'm Mr. Cagliari's oldest associate, I depend on him for everything. Why would I kill him?"

And he sat down, overwhelmed as he thought of his old mother, who for sure was going to be demolished now, since they could no longer count on the protection of his boss and master. Big drops stood out on his forehead. Someone seized the phone, dialled the number of the police.

The gurgle of a flush could be heard, coming from the toilet just behind the seat where Cagliari's corpse was still quietly draining. The door opened. Xavier jumped.

"Whoops! Sorry," he said.

He'd started to close the door and go out the other one, the one he'd come in by, which opened directly onto the stairs. But a cry stopped him: "Whoa! Hang on, honeybee!"

Xavier took a step, came to a halt, intimidated by the gazes and the silence. He hadn't yet noticed Cagliari's remains, hidden as they were by the chair-back. A mixture of triumph and guile lit up the face of the dead man's principal associate, who had to have a name. Let's say MacFarlane, like the coat. Lorenzo MacFarlane.

"Gentlemen," shouted MacFarlane, "let us go on looking for he who profits from the crime!" (This surprising principle commanded the respect of the small gathering.) He added, "And he who profits most is that man!" With a dramatic arm he pointed to Xavier.

The apprentice put the tip of his forefinger on his nose: "Me?"

"Great Scott, Vincent Vilbroquais," said Bumpley with a delighted smile.

Matters were really taking a fascinating turn. To hell with

the tournament, for now. This scandal was too good. He was already picturing the local front page: "Young Canadian champion, missing for a year, murders vaudeville potentate."

"Step right up, child," he said to Xavier, "don't be afraid!"

Xavier approached, taking stiff little steps, holding the casket against his chest.

"I didn't do anything. What happened?"

Only then did the apprentice notice the wreck of the potentate. He was flabbergasted.

Bumpley took his time. He asked for a chair, climbed into it, lit up a butt. The small group stood around him, solicitous. Now Bumpley was savouring one of the great moments of his career. He'd always dreamed of being a detective, of surprising criminals, handcuffing them, taking pleasure from their defeat.

"Can you tell me," he began, "why you were hiding in Mr. Cagliari's toilet? Ehhh?"

Xavier's face went purple. He seemed to be embarrassed in the extreme, and that whipped up the circulation of the man facing him. From the corner of his eye, Bumpley was watching closely for signs of staggering recognition. The apprentice studied his fingers, as if he wanted to check how many there were.

"All right," he said (doffed his hat, replaced it, confused). "See, here it is, I had, you know, it happens to all of us, doesn't it, I had to go. That's all. To go. Maybe it was the restorative I drink. And then, when I got there. It was all occupied, I mean. I'm talking about the place. And, see, I didn't have the luxury of waiting. So I decided to do my relieving here, in back, in the toilet, because I knew about it. I've been working here for weeks. So that's it. It was urgent, so to speak."

Xavier had spoken in a tiny voice, like a child in the confessional who's taking it seriously. He fiddled nervously with his bow tie.

Bumpley had to admit that the alibi made sense, because he himself had been able to note that at such moments the toilets were always in use. But he wasn't a man to give back the marbles so quickly. Especially since Lorenzo MacFarlane whispered something in his ear. And at once Bumpley said:

"Apparently you owed Mr. Cagliari a lot of money?"

"Mr. Cagliari? True, he gave me a bunch of dollars. But then he didn't want them to belong to me. Except that I'd already spent a lot of them. He wanted me to reimburse him."

"And?"

"And I couldn't. A big debt, you could say."

"Ha!" said Bumpley, calling the others to witness.

He got out of his seat and slunk up to Xavier, catlike. Started pacing in front of him.

"And tell me, why did he give you all those bills? Eh? What have you got to say for yourself?"

"It was for my frog," Xavier finally conceded, and he clenched his fists and dropped his chin in shame.

"And you stabbed him in the eye with the poker and murdered him so you wouldn't have to pay him back!" said Bumpley, waving the cigar under his nose with fiery conviction.

"Murdered? Me?"

"Not you, him!"

"This is slander!" screamed the blind man, who had just appeared at the door, guided there by his Xavierian instinct.

Xavier shook his head, eyes bulging. What was the meaning of all this?

"If it wasn't you, how can you explain these traces of blood on your jacket?"

Xavier explained that it was for his health. That now and then he had to spit out the bad blood that was in him, etc., because of the tease, and that, sometimes, inevitably, a little fell onto shirt. The detective thought that was a good one.

"Gentlemen," he said to the others, who were following all this with unflagging attention, persuaded by Bumpley's composure. "This young man pokered his creditor, obsessed as he was with his inability to repay his debt."

"That's slander!" cried the blind man again. "This child is a saint! An innocent! You're accusing an innocent man!"

Bumpley waved his hand negligently, as if to say, let him bray.

"And he also robbed the safe that was in the office of our friend and patron." He turned towards Xavier. "And what was in that safe?"

Xavier shrugged.

"Dollars?" he ventured, full of good will.

"You see! And how come you know that?"

"I don't know. I'm assuming."

"Then I'll tell you. That safe contained the dollars to be given out as prizes for the tournament. And you stole them! And I tell you, gentlemen, he hid those dollars in that little box."

He pointed to Strapitchacoudou's casket.

The blind man bellowed with indignation, "Infamy! Infamy! We are about to condemn an innocent! Woe is us!

Woe and disgrace!" And with the plush doggie he struck out to the left and to the right, into the air.

Bumpley pounced on the casket and tried to tear it from Xavier's hands, but the apprentice defended it tooth and nail.

"You mustn't disturb her, she's sick!" Xavier insisted, his voice like a duck's because, in the heat of the battle, Bumpley had performed upon him a twisting of the nostrils.

So, there was a toilet in this office. But there was a closet too, which no one had thought of. From it suddenly loomed a man who spoke to the people gathered there, in a most courteous manner.

"Allow me, gentlemen. But I must inform you that you are committing a large-scale mistake."

"Rogatien Wondell," murmured MacFarlane between his teeth.

And Wondell had in his fist a very large six-shooter revolver. So in addition to Xavier and Rogatien Wondell there were: 1. Capablanca, 2. Marshall, 3. Bumpley, 4. Lorenzo MacFarlane, 5. the blind man, 6. some bystanders — nine persons in all. But with six bullets a man can do a fair amount of damage, all the same. Also, they only had to be told once.

"Gentlemen," said Rogatien, addressing Marshall and Capablanca in particular, "great artists like yourselves are not unaware of the price we bestow on our finest works. To attribute to this child the authorship of such an elegant act with a poker is an insult to my own creative genius. Is that not so, dear Grandmaster?"

"I share your point of view entirely, Sir," replied Capablanca courteously.

"In that case, gentlemen, you would oblige me if you

would allow me to leave with this hostage in order to protect my rear when I depart."

"Please go ahead, dear Master, go ahead," urged Capablanca.

"My thanks, gentlemen, and I apologize again for this contretemps."

Wondell had grabbed Xavier by the shoulders, placed the revolver against his temple. Dragged him to the washroom, of which the other door opened onto a hidden stairway etc.

"He isn't leaving with Xavier?" moaned the blind man. "He isn't taking Xavier?"

When they were outside, Wondell asked Xavier nicely if everything was all right. Xavier nodded. He was a little overtaken by the events. Wondell led him to a car that happened to be there. Tried to open the door. Nothing to be done: locked. He looked to the left, looked to the right, told Xavier, "Plug your ears, it's going to go boom." Then fired the revolver at the side window. And pushed a dazed Xavier onto the seat.

Wondell engaged the clutch, the car made an abrupt leap backwards. He concluded that he'd have to do something different with the throttle. The vehicle sprang forward, first in little jumps like a hare, then it began to roll along, to glide, with an ease that made Wondell laugh with contentment. It was the first time he'd driven an automobile.

"My car! Stop, thief!" cried a man coming out of his boutique, which sold assorted tricks.

3

"Don't worry, I know where you live. It wasn't easy, but I managed to find it."

The car was eating up the asphalt, the engine rumbling. Wondell drove without fear and pedestrians had better watch out. The car devoured half the sidewalk negotiating turns. But Wondell always managed to bring the vehicle back to the middle of the road, accompanied by a dark and sober "Olé!" When he spoke to Xavier he looked right at him, ignoring the road ahead.

"Know who I am?"

Xavier made no reply. He was cowering fearfully against the door. Gazed at Rogatien. Nose like a dagger, straight, brush-cut hair like silver threads. Eyes red like a rabbit's. Goatlike goatee, Uncle Sam-style. *Your country needs you!*

"Why don't you answer? Afraid I'll eat you?"

Scattered over the back seat were false noses with moustaches attached, envelopes of itching powder, sneezing powder, bloody hands made of soft rubber, etc., and a cane with a knob, which Xavier grabbed.

"If you whack me on the head I'll lose control and we'll both get wiped out."

The apprentice didn't whack, but held onto it anyway. Suddenly he heard himself say:

"I don't want to go back to live in the warehouse."

Then batted his eyelashes, stupefied, as if someone else had just used his mouth to speak.

"Don't worry, I didn't come here to take you back. You should be big enough to get by on your own. Besides, there's nothing I can do for you."

An old lady became alarmed, because the automobile was heading straight for her. A last-minute wrench of the wheel fixed that. Olé.

"Incidentally, how are you feeling? Your health, that sort of thing."

Xavier pondered the question. Finally answered:

"I've got my restorative."

Rogatien joined his eyebrows, intrigued. Then had to brake so abruptly that their foreheads banged into the windshield.

The vehicle started up again, unrepentant, valiant.

"Cagliari told me everything. That frog of yours, the washout of a show, the hell at the Majestic. Everything he put you through, that is."

They drove the wrong way down a one-way street. People and horns cried out. A policeman gave a loud blast of his whistle, noted the licence number.

Wondell tried to explain to the boy the nature of the ties between himself and Cagliari. That it was he, Cagliari, who financed his, Rogatien's, works.

"I have to say, the kind of research I was involved in had to be done, let's say, very discreetly. Obviously I couldn't ask the police to subsidize me. But after all those years, when my work was finally on the brink of success, Cagliari decided to tighten the purse strings. Under those conditions I had no choice, I had to play double or nothing. Either I showed up with unassailable proof of my success, or I paid back every cent he'd invested in me over the years. Cagliari agreed; this was a few months ago. Then you had to choose that moment to skedaddle. And while I was searching for you high and low, Cagliari knew where you were. It bothered me in a big way when I found that out this afternoon. So I gave him a little kiss with the poker . . . I must have every cop in New York on my ass. And the mob. And the Order of Demolishers. See what I mean?"

Xavier didn't reply. Too bad.

They finally arrived at the building where the apprentice lived. Night was beginning to fall. Rogatien was proud that he hadn't run anyone down. He could do anything, he felt like an Übermensch. He spotted the demolition notice.

"You'll have to find yourself an apartment. It won't be easy, the rate things are going."

They got out of the vehicle. Xavier took the lead, walking backwards so as not to let Wondell out of his sight, as if fearing an attack. He was still holding the cane. They entered the vestibule. Wondell sat on the bottom step. Xavier stayed on his feet, at a cautious distance.

"What about your wounds?" asked Rogatien, slightly ill at ease. "I mean, are they better, are they worse?"

Xavier didn't reply.

"And the faucet, still working?" The apprentice said even less.

"Tell me, what did it feel like when that man called you Vincent?"

The apprentice shrugged.

"I see," said Wondell.

There was a silence. Wondell was looking straight ahead, pensively. Xavier stayed on his guard.

"Look," said Rogatien finally. "I'd like . . . I mean, I'd like the two of us to go up to your room so I can examine you a little. That way I could . . ."

"Come up to my room and I jump out the window."

They stared at each other for a moment. Wondell realized that it wasn't worth insisting. Too bad. Too bad for him, too bad for the boy. Wondell mused that he was going to use his revolver for personal ends no later than that night. And he was agreeing to die without knowing.

"I'm sorry for what I did, Xavier. I sincerely regret it. But you see, it was all for Justine. It's not my fault if things went wrong."

He hesitated, teary-eyed.

"Do you forgive me?"

Xavier started to give him a whack, but when the cane touched Wondell's shoulder it was suddenly transformed into a bouquet of flowers. Xavier, dumbfounded, wondered by what miracle.

Wondell stood up, patted his shoulder compassionately.

"I think it's best if I leave. The car theft has probably been reported. If it were found outside your door you could have problems."

Xavier didn't take his eyes off the bouquet. Was it the cane that was bewitched? Or was this man some kind of Merlin?

"A rigged cane," said the wizard. "You can get one from Dwayne & Hoover for around $4.75." He took a package from inside his jacket. "Here, this is for you. You'll need it more than I will. Let's say it's a small loan extorted from

Cagliari. Inside you'll also find a letter I've written you. You'll learn a certain number of things about yourself. Anyway, you'll see. Now I have to leave you."

Wondell's tall silhouette moved away, got into the car, which set off at once, coughing and shaking. Xavier was now alone in the dim vestibule. Suddenly he threw the bouquet to the ground as if a demon were hidden inside.

And it turned back into a cane!

Xavier ran to the elevator, filled with dread.

Inside, darkness reigned. Xavier groped at the buttons, pressed one more or less at random, hoping it was for the eighth floor. But the contraption took him to its furthest limit, past the top floor even; when the doors opened, the apprentice was on the roof.

The evening was clear, with a scant band of flat clouds like breadsticks, orange in the last rays of sunset. For the first time, the apprentice was looking at New York from above. He could see all the way to the horizon. On the ocean side, the Statue stood out clearly against the sky. She faced the sea. It would have been better for her to look at what was going on behind her back; that would have shut her up, old Lady Liberty. She was pointing her ice-cream cone towards the sky, as if something up there was worth being pointed at.

Xavier opened his casket. Said softly:

"Strapitchacoudou? Strapitchacoudou?"

The frog was rubbing her eyes with her fists. The apprentice settled her in the hollow of his collarbone, then planted a dainty kiss on her head. Strapitchacoudou grumbled lethargically. A little girl being wakened.

"You're all I've got now," he murmured. "Always, I've only had you."

She shrugged her shoulders, not meanly. She felt like sleeping. Her eyelids dropped by themselves. Xavier smiled affectionately. You really love someone if you smile at her when her eyes are closed.

And the Statue was there, haughty and proud against the horizon. And Xavier dreamed about what would make for a good life. What the Statue could do if she had the slightest bit of justice in her head, instead of painting her ceiling. It would be good if some day she shook off her concrete bobby socks and went into the city for once. She would grow with every step, bumping her elbows on buildings, sowing panic among those who were rich for no reason. She'd bop the tops of rich people's buildings with her ice-cream cone, not to be mean, no, just to give them the willies. Then she would bend down, her fist on the ground, so that the wretched refugees, the huddled masses, the demolished, the homeless tempest-tost from every land, could climb like lines of ants onto her shoulders. Then she'd make her way back to the sea, taking them with her. She would head for Europe and she would keep growing, expanding with every step, and the deepest ocean would come up to her elbows, then to her buttocks, then halfway up her thighs, and she would reach Europe, she herself vaster than any continent. And one woman, one man at a time, she would take the wretched refugees, the huddled masses, the demolished, the grateful homeless, tempest-tost from every land, with the continent at her knees, and, moving like a general placing miniature cannons on a map of the world, she would set them down, each and every one, with infinite delicacy, in the countries of their birth, their never-forgotten homelands, down to the last inhabitant of the last barn in the last village.

A sudden siren drew Xavier from his half-sleep. He gazed at the Statue of Liberty. She hadn't budged. She still had her indifferent back to the city and its torments.

"Tomorrow, I've made up my mind, we're going back to Hungary," he told his frog, who had placed her head next to his, in a melancholy way.

4

Xavier ended up sleeping on the roof, under the stars, his forehead resting on the package bequeathed to him by Rogatien Wondell. All night he had held his frog's casket against his stomach. The dawn was cool. He woke up shivering. He didn't realize where he was right away. He stood up, explored the premises. There was an aviary that he hadn't noticed the night before, where pigeons were billing and cooing. New York was at his feet, blurred, at this time of day still flattened under heavy mist. The events of the previous evening suddenly sprang into his memory while he was walking along the parapet, and he realized that, yes, his mind was made up. He would go without delay to a boat, give a captain the entire small amount of money he had left, and set sail for Hungary, right across the sea. As of today he would leave this land of lunatics, this land of menaces and fears. He'd go back to his sister, Justine, to his village and his beets, even if it rained molten lead. Either that or hurl himself into the void. Right now he could feel the building trembling beneath his feet. He wondered if his head was playing tricks on him or what. But once again, sledgehammer blows were shaking the walls. A trap door opened and there stood a demolisher.

A cloud of grey powder rose from the trap door when the workman swept it with his arm, going, "Ugh!" He seemed surprised at the sight of Xavier X. Mortanse. Asked what he was doing there.

"I live here and I'd like to go home," said the apprentice.

The demolisher, of whom Xavier could see only the torso, bent down into the trap door and reported this remark to his workmates. They thought, that's a good one. And again sledgehammers pounded. The workman turned to the apprentice.

"You haven't got a home any more, dickhead. Tough luck, the Notice has been up for weeks. It's the streets for you now. Itinerate!"

The apprentice explained that he just wanted to get a few of his belongings before he left for Hungary. The workman retorted, don't bother, every object left in the buildings came into the immediate possession of the Order, for the demolition auction.

"Just let me go in for a minute. I'll give you some dollars."

The workman hesitated for two seconds, for appearances' sake. Then disappeared down the trap door to make room for Xavier. With his legs like rubber, the apprentice went down the ladder inside the trap door. A heavy smell of plaster grabbed him by the throat. Dust was sweeping into his cubicle, you'd have said snow, shimmering in the first rays of light coming in the window. Four workmen were there, interrupting their tasks to observe the strange new arrival. Xavier had no idea where he was. It didn't look at all the way it had the day before. The partitions that had separated his abode from those of his neighbours had been knocked down. A big notebook Peggy had given him, in which he transcribed his thoughts, was now covered with grey scabs; a bucket of the cement used to reinforce the framework sat on top of it. His table where he'd written, eaten, where he'd set up Strapitchacoudou to do her act, where he'd rested his forehead to cry, had been torn away from the wall and taken back to the state of boards. On a nail had been hung his last clean shirt, another gift from Peggy, which the workmen were using as a rag to wipe their hands on. Finally, there were destruction tools all over. The demolishers seemed like apparitions in the floating expanses of dust.

Suddenly a foreman, identifiable by his badge, appeared. On his head, by way of a hairnet, he wore a string bag Xavier had used for transporting his vegetables. Nothing to be said about any of it — it was the law.

But his money?

"Where are my dollars?" cried Xavier, on fire. "Give me back my dollars! I need them!"

The foreman went white.

"Dollars? What dollars? There weren't any dollars here."

"There were so! Underneath the table! In that string bag you've got on your hair! At least a hundred! And by the way, you ought to give me back the string bag too! It's a present! Are you going to take away my presents now?"

Xavier was quivering with indignation.

The workmen's eyes had turned suspiciously towards the foreman. One of them, moustachioed, observed:

"The thing I like about our chief is his sense of sharing."

"What are you making up now?" asked the foreman.

Then, to Xavier:

"Lying will get you nowhere, m'boy. And here, take this if you want."

Nervously he put the string bag back in the apprentice's hands. His eyes avoided his workmates'.

Just then Xavier gripped the foreman's arm so hard that he couldn't help grimacing in pain.

"I SAID, THERE WERE DOLLARS IN THIS STRING BAG!"

The demolition men had come closer and now formed an oppressive circle around the apprentice.

"My dollars, my Hungary . . . You can't do this."

"You heard, there weren't any dollars," said the man with the moustache. "Because if there were, we'd have divvied them up. Right, chief?"

"All right, enough hints," replied the foreman.

Xavier gazed at the powerful hands of these men, armed with menacing tools. He understood that he'd never see his money again. Everything had gone to the dogs.

But now, contrary to all expectations, the foreman piped up:

"Listen, men. How about showing that we're a little human. Couldn't we give the kid a chance? The storage room we fixed up yesterday, he could stay there for a couple of days, till he finds himself a new home?"

"Show that we're human," said the moustache ironically.

"Okay," said the foreman to Xavier, "I'll take you, it's up on the next floor."

Docile, Xavier let the man lead him. They came to a small cluttered room, fairly similar to the one where he'd lived these past months. There were bags of cement, gunnysacks hanging up everywhere, all sorts of tools. A table, might as well call it a board, was screwed to the wall, etc. A box spring without a mattress lay in a corner, buckled and bent.

"I want my dollars," said the apprentice.

"Okay, kid. I've got my flaws, but I'm not a bastard. We split it fifty-fifty, okay? There were ninety-nine dollars in all. I'll give you fifty, the bigger half. How about it? It's better than nothing, right? According to the law you aren't entitled to anything. But I feel pity for you. All I ask is, don't tell my journeymen."

Xavier said again, glum and obstinate, that they were his bills and he wanted them all. They were his. He needed them.

Briefly, the foreman contemplated the prospect of having the boy execute a seven-storey fall, via the window. But he was a softie and rejected the idea.

"Me too, I need money," he said.

The fact was, the foreman was Rosette's new lover, and he'd led her to believe he was a demolition nabob. And he did need a lot of dough to keep her enthralled, supply her with dresses, pay her Manhattan rent. All of which obliged the foreman to bend the rules somewhat. And he also had a wife to support, and three very young children.

"Take it or leave it," he said, and slapped the fifty dollars on the table.

Xavier wondered how far you could go on a boat for fifty dollars. And whether, at the end of a distance exactly equal to fifty dollars, they pitched the destitute traveller into the sea. He could swim the rest of the way.

Just as the foreman was starting to take back the bills, Xavier slammed his fist down on them. It was a done deal. The foreman started for the door. Then a thought stopped him. Theoretically, the contents of the mailboxes were supposed to be taken to the offices of the Order. But he still felt a kind of debt towards the apprentice.

"I'm going to do you another favour," he said.

He took a bundle of envelopes from the inside pocket of his overalls, started going through them.

"You lived in room 813 and your name's Xavier, right? Here."

Xavier looked at the envelope but didn't take it. A letter? A letter for him, Xavier?

"It was there in your pigeonhole. But if you don't want it."

Xavier took it. The foreman grabbed him by the collar.

"And don't forget! Not a word to the journeymen! Or else . . ."

He pressed his lips against Xavier's, tongue out, a juicy French kiss. The apprentice let him, impervious. The foreman pushed him away, his heart full of hatred, as if it were the boy who'd taken the initiative. The man owned a farm near New Ark. He went there, alone, every two weeks. His obsession was the twenty-nine dismembered Negresses. He smashed the femurs with stones, then sucked out the marrow, raw. And fell over backwards in ecstasy. Rosette was something else. He'd promised himself that, with her, he'd have healthy relations. He loved her.

Turned around. Exit.

Xavier stared at the envelope. There's a road between incredulity and dread and he was in the middle of it. Yet it was his address written on it, and his door number, and *his name*. He opened it slowly, shaking.

Above all, stay where you are. I'm in New York. I'll pay you a visit in the next few days. I've got something important to tell you.

Justine

Xavier lay down on the box spring, incapable of the slightest thought, eyes staring. On the floor above him, sledgehammer blows were shaking the walls all the way to deep inside his chest.

5

A CHECKUP SHOWED that his tease was doing quite well, getting stronger and stronger, spreading to his other lung. His sister, Justine, would most likely scold him for getting so sick. But was it his fault? Xavier was sitting on some bags full of cement powder. His room was a turmoil of tools. Material, ladders, disembowelled tin cans, broken boards, brick rubble and rubbish, rusty, twisted nails as long as tibias, two toothbrushes and a thimble — all strewn as untidily as if a bomb had gone off. The carpet consisted of fourteen million active dust mites, etc. Xavier stuck the tip of his nose out the window. The sky was pale and dull, whitewashed. The city was sweltering in the sickening heat. Down below, on the street, black dots were moving around, insignificant, incomprehensible, going in every direction, like ants that had lost their way. Xavier pulled his head back in, suffering dizzy spells that were growing more violent day by day. Besides, he was so weak, just sitting up was a strain. If he was absorbed in a thought, his torso would start bending imperceptibly; if he became aware of it he'd snap into an upright position, like a dog wakened by a blast. He was often overcome by a harsh cough, and some blood would leave a chalky taste in his mouth. A tiny lump he could feel in his throat would cause fits and starts of extremely sharp, stabbing pains. On the windowsill next to him, a notepad that had been a gift from Peggy, in which now and then, from time to time, he jotted his reflections. He'd just noted this one, which he pondered at length: *Baby comes out of female: I know. E.g. cow makes cowlet (piglet? calf?). But got in how?* Then, unsatisfied: *Sure not from mouth. Grows in body like grass? Egg?*

He dreamed about it, pupils blank. Then, as a rising wind gradually removes dead leaves, his thoughts broke away from him, scattered, moved into cushioned, smoky corridors, and soon he didn't even know what was being thought inside him, and his chest slowly began to bend, he was about to sink into a healing nothingness when the image of Peggy in flames suddenly flashed into his mind and he emerged from his drowsiness, letting out a deathly cry.

The door opened behind him. He didn't turn around, accustomed now, resigned to the fact that with no concern for him, the workmen would be coming into his room all the time to pick up a tool, toss in some piece of trash. But an unusual silence followed the sound of the door, which made him lift his chin. A bird sped across the field of the window.

"Is this where Xavier lives?"

The woman was standing near the door, not daring. Alarmed by the dimness, the absolute grime, the atmosphere of disease. Plaster and cement dust floated in the room, stuck to skin, got into clothes, hair, bronchial tubes.

"Are you the person known as Xavier?"

As he had his back to the window, the woman was seeing him against the light and had trouble making out his features. He had a detailed view of her. She wore a patched and rusty-coloured dress, criss-crossed with seams like a railway map, that buttoned up to her jaw. A stiff fox, plucked bare in patches and looking as if dogs had fought over it with their teeth, imprisoned her neck. And on her head, lopsided, a veiled hat that must have spent part of its career as a trivet. Never would Xavier have imagined her decked out like this. He wondered if the fever was making him see things that didn't exist. Finally she ventured to take a step towards him, circumspectly and reluctantly, and as she was lifting her veil, the apprentice saw her bare face. He brought his hand to his cheek in a movement of dismay and dread. What was going on? What did this mean? All at once it was as if the universe had just blown a gasket, and he couldn't understand a thing.

"Justine! . . . My little sister! . . . What happened to you? Were you sick? How could you change so much in such a short time? My God, I'm blowing a gasket."

Xavier bit his fist in anguish. Justine, who was standing in front of him, whom he'd left behind in Hungary just months before, his sister Justine who was barely twenty years old, had flabby cheeks and wrinkles and hair as grey as asphalt!

"I'm not your sister, Xavier."

A workman came in, grumbling, picked up a sledgehammer, went out, slamming the door. A brief argument in the corridor. Justine said nothing. She'd taken a seat on the edge of the chair. She gave the boy a sidelong glance that was stamped with curiosity, with indifference, with vague disgust and terror, like that of a child brought to a great-aunt's deathbed. Xavier was completely absorbed in his own anguish. So much for misery. So much for the tease, for the loss of Peggy, for his own imminent death: all that he could accept, at the end of the day, and if it made no sense at least it had consistency, you could string together disasters one after another, and in the end they made a life. But this Justine who'd been totally transformed into a little old woman! And claimed that she wasn't his sister! He closed his eyes for a moment, took hold of his forehead with both hands.

"Explain," he murmured. "Say what you want but explain."

Justine began cautiously.

"I've come to tell you who you are. What you are. I thought you had the right to know. And I don't think it will make you happy."

"But what do you want to tell me that I don't know already? I love you, what other truth do I need? I don't know what happened to you, but after all, isn't the important thing that you're here? That we're two again? Like in Hungary?"

"You've never been to Hungary, Xavier. What you call your memories aren't. I considered it my duty to come and tell you."

Xavier got up quickly, flight reflex. Flattened his hands against the window frame and stuck his head outside to inspect the sky, to take a deep breath of the void. He turned around, his expression incredulous.

"What are you talking about? Why are you saying things like that? You're making fun of me, aren't you? Watch out! I can make fun too!"

And wagged his finger mischievously. Tried for a childish look that would make her smile. The result was so pathetic that Justine, out of propriety and pity, turned her head away. The apprentice sat back down on his bags of cement. With his fingertip he nervously smoothed the brim of his hat. He decided to play the card of the happy, serene, relaxed reunion.

"So, little sister? Tell me things. What have you been doing these past months? Tell me about our dear village, what's its name, not far from Budapest, on the St. Lawrence River? How stupid to forget the name of your own village, I don't know what's wrong with me! And our fellow citizens and friends, tell me? And the priest? And his fourteen children? How are they? I miss them all so much."

He put on a face that he hoped was a nice expression. Justine fell silent. Xavier swallowed. You're standing on a rickety stool, hands bound behind your back, a rope around your neck: how do you feel? Like Xavier at that moment. Whence the need to come up with something, anything, to say.

"Did you get my letters, little sister? I wrote you every day, or just about, every line that I invented, that I scratched onto paper, every single one was for you. I didn't stop thinking about you for twenty-eight weeks! And hoping! Even when I was wrapped up in something else, even when I was with my friend Peggy, deep in my heart, like a mooring line, you held on there, and I knew that in spite of everything we'd be reunited one day. And now, today, you're here. Oh my sister, my little fairy with her little wings, my little girl, my little zaza . . ."

He started to take Justine's hands in his, but she jerked hers away. Out of words, he took his last square of chocolate from his pocket, offered it. She didn't take it. Still said nothing.

Panicking, Xavier turned towards the window. He had a tremendous thirst for emptiness. He wished for some space, some horizon, some as-far-as-the-eye-can-see. But everywhere, buildings blocked the view, blurred angles, confinement, and the white sky itself, standing like a wall. He closed his eyelids: blackness and evanescent mauve dots, with something like a hair that went up, down . . .

"We're going back to Hungary together. That's why you came here, isn't it? I'm forgiven, aren't I? I don't know, I can't remember why I was forced to leave you, to run away to America, which has been my prison for close to more than twenty-eight weeks, but I suppose they thought I was guilty of something, and it had to be something serious, you don't send children of the fatherland into exile just like that, for the fun of it. But I'm forgiven now, and that's what you've come to tell me, isn't it? I had an idea the other day: the two of us, when we're back in our country, we could raise chickens. Because there has to be a chicken for there to be eggs! I've solved that famous riddle all by myself! It's very clear in my brain now! We'd give their eggs to the Hungarians and in exchange the Hungarians would give us bills. Life could finally begin again, and you and I, you and I —"

He broke off, epigastrium knotted. There was the din of hammers, the cries of workmen, their laughter and squabbling, and the harrowing cracking sound when boards were pulled up, like breaking bones. But that was in another world. Here in this room there was nothing but a heavy, deep, pensive silence that nothing spoiled, the silence of a dead star, and they were cooped up inside it. Finally, the woman spoke:

"Look at me." Xavier kept his eyes obstinately lowered.

"No, look at me closely and answer: do I look like someone who could be your sister? At my age?"

"I don't understand what you're talking about. I don't want to hear any more bad things like that."

"But I have to tell you anyway. You're the one who asked for an explanation."

Xavier hesitated briefly. Then, eyelids closed, he expressed himself gravely, painfully, ready to hear.

"Do you know who Rogatien Wondell is?" asked Justine. "Do you remember him?"

Xavier's features contracted. Then expressed himself slowly again, with an air of resignation. A voice that wasn't him, that knew more about him than he did himself, was repeating inside his head, "I don't want to go back to the warehouses. I won't spend the rest of my life there."

"I never agreed with what he did, I would have refused if he'd asked me. It seems that it was Cagliari, you remember Cagliari? Apparently he's the one who financed Rogatien's work. Obviously, we couldn't expect" — she hesitated, looking for the proper word — "these results."

The apprentice stood up on his legs and despite his weakness, his exhaustion, started pacing the room, his expression intractable.

"I don't believe you, none of this is true. Do you hear me? Me, Xavier, your brother? I don't believe you. You expect me to believe that those 'results' are me? Enough! Why are you telling me these lies, why are you telling me such horrible things? What have I ever done to you? This is going to turn my brain sideways."

"What you've just said proves that deep down you know the truth, that you already know what I've come here to tell you. Part of it anyway. Never mind, I've got something here that will convince you."

She pulled from her bag a notebook bound in leatherette.

"This is Rogatien's journal about you."

Xavier sat on the bed, hands between his thighs, as if he wanted to stop them from grabbing the notebook in spite of himself.

"Read the first page at least. If you don't know how, I'll read it for you."

Xavier finally stretched out a trembling hand. Then, as if carried away, grabbed the notebook, opened it, rushed through the first pages. While he was reading he repeated, with a scornful and painful snicker,

"That's impossible. Come on. That's impossible."

"I was against it. I've always been against it. The whole thing is too monstrous."

"Quiet. Keep quiet," he moaned.

He fired the notebook at the wall. Pressed his fists against his temples.

The day was already fading. The grey light seemed to be asleep in the room, immobile. Objects lost clarity, then disappeared completely if you looked at them closely. Drifts of dust floated in the room. Xavier stared straight ahead, absently, lips slightly parted.

"It's not true," he said finally. "You're lying. This notebook is false. Like the gospels! Why and how have you turned so mean? Why don't you even care about hurting me?"

Xavier shook his head, eyes glued to the floor as if he were speaking to the carpet, to one of the twenty-three million active dust mites that lived there. He rushed to the window again, so energetically that Justine made a move towards him, afraid he was going to jump. But he held onto the window frame with both hands.

"I've never read or heard anything like this since. Since I stopped being in a woman's body. Do people think I'm crazy? Do they want me to be not me? Do they want my life to be not my life, and for me to believe it? That's a good one!"

He pretended to laugh. His heart was thudding, his legs were making him suffer. He felt a burning pain in the groin.

"If you don't believe any of it, why does hearing it cause you so much pain?"

Xavier brought his thumb and forefinger to the root of his nose. He stayed like that for a while, head bowed, eyelids closed, brows knit. Then flew to the bed, to Justine's side.

"Remember, little sister! I was very sick, horribly sick, a month of fever, when they decided to separate us, to send you to boarding school far away, where there were only other little girls. Remember how we cried! And that time when you wanted to teach me how to swim, and I couldn't. And your little bud that I tickled like a mad dog! That wasn't twenty-eight weeks ago! Twenty-nine! We loved to walk along our beautiful river. The St. Lawrence River!"

"You think that's all like Hungary?"

"It's like what life was for me! I had only you, remember, I beg you!"

Strapitchacoudou had got out of her box and snuck up to Justine. Unbeknownst to her, the frog was just a few fingers from her face. Soon the performer struck up:

> O say can you see
> By the dawn's early light
> What so proudly we hail'd

Justine let out a horrified cry and the frog went back to her casket in three panicky leaps.

"What in heaven's name was that?" asked Justine, breathless with fear.

Not hearing, Xavier had started flitting around the room again, now and then stumbling into the garbage that was strewn everywhere.

"Memories, memories! I've got more than if I were a thousand years old, and you're going to find out, you meanie! I remember everything exactly. The beets! The . . . The . . . The time the Prince of Hungary, we were at his parade! And when I rubbed the soles of your feet, because we'd been climbing trees too much! Everything, every single thing!"

Xavier picked up his shopping bag in his clenched fist, waved it under Justine's nose.

"And that, you cruel girl! Do you mean to tell me this doesn't come from home in Hungary?"

Justine avoided his furious gaze. Replied, Come on now, bags like that, you can find in any vegetable market in New York. Xavier flung his to the floor. Choking with rage, he let himself collapse onto the bed. Justine threw herself at him and struggled to pull off one of his sneakers. The boy fought back, moaning, but weakened as he was, she got the better of him. She tore the shoe from his foot. It gave off a foul musty smell. She took the boy's leg in her hand. In a red-hot voice, and pointing to the sole of his foot:

"And what about that? Doesn't that prove what I'm saying?"

Xavier turned his head away, refused to see. Suddenly she dropped the boy's leg.

"There's nothing more for me to do here," she said, and headed for the door.

Xavier staggered over to her, seized her in his arms.

"Don't touch me!" she screamed, but he held her even tighter.

"Love me! I beg you. Love me the way I love you! Or ten times, a hundred times less, if you want! But don't leave, don't go away, don't leave me alone in this darkness that's coming so close to me. I can't live without you, for twenty-eight weeks now I haven't been living. I exist, terribly. You are all my memories! All the ones that matter! Oh my Justine, oh my zaza! The whole universe doesn't have room for my love for you. If you leave I'll have nothing, it will be death, my corpse from one end of all things to the other. There won't be any more world! Oh, my sister. Beings are irreplaceable, understand? Am I the only one on earth who understands that? I don't want to know what is true, whether I'm right or wrong or what, I want you to be there, I want someone who loves me and someone to love! And I want it to be you!"

The apprentice's arms dropped, heavy and limp as dying snakes. Justine freed herself, shuddering. Xavier got down on his knees again, buttocks on heels, chin on chest, all his nerves severed. Justine stared at him, calmly, harshly. Without trembling or anger, she took a revolver out of her purse and pointed it at the apprentice's still-bowed head. That was why she'd come here: to lodge a bullet in the back of his neck. Saying nothing, explaining nothing: to annihilate him. If she had found him asleep when she'd arrived, that was most likely what she'd have done. But she had seen his eyes, his face, heard that voice, and all at once — Though she knew what she knew, though she'd reconciled herself to the fact that this boy was not her son. Before those eyes, before that face, it had been impossible for her to silently pick up the weapon and fire it. She couldn't distinguish clearly what had made her decide to speak at the last moment. If it was pity or a secret urge for revenge towards this thing that had usurped Vincent's face, a desire to make it suffer by revealing what it was before she exterminated him. And even now, now that she was pointing the gun at his head, Justine knew nothing more.

Xavier raised his face to her, spied the revolver, was barely affected by the sight, only slightly surprised. He looked her in the eye without fear, without anxiety. But there was a demand, a fossil of hope, a staggering appeal. He wasn't asking to be spared, that was clear, she could press the trigger, that was of no importance. His gaze was begging for something else. And those eyes were Vincent's eyes, that thing was beseeching her with the face of her son, Vincent! . . . Justine's hand began to tremble. She put the gun on the table. Then, overcoming a profound reluctance, she bent over him.

"I'd like to sympathize with you, I wish I could do that, but I can't. This mixture . . . this fricassee . . . There are too many people in you, there's no one."

Without thinking too much about what she was doing, she took out a few dollars and placed them under the revolver. Then left. Without a farewell, without turning around, abandoning Xavier to his solitude, to his unshod foot, to his final night.

6

Justine stepped onto the staircase, having called for
the elevator in vain. Before she had climbed down twenty
steps, though, she came to a halt. She couldn't abandon him
like this. In a strange and frightening way that, if she thought
about it too much, opened up chasms, Vincent was in there,
part of the thing that had beseeched her not to leave was
Vincent, was taking part in what her son Vincent had been.
She leaned on the banister. Now the debate was going to
start up again, was going to cast her once more into her hell.
But she threw her shoulders back. The question, a thousand
times, in her head, had been decided. Xavier was not Vincent,
period. To feel compassion for him, to go so far as to accept
the illusion of the face and voice, to give in to a surge of
nostalgia about him would be to betray Vincent, to associate
with a creature who had plundered the soul and the face of
Vincent to live out its own wretched existence. She had done
the right thing, all in all, not shooting. Forget this Xavier, act
as if he no longer existed — that was the best thing to do.

Justine set out on some dark and squalid streets. A family,
bashful and furtive, crossed her path: mice along a base-
board. The little troop slipped away along a path that crossed

hers, hurrying as if there were a curfew. On all sides, shacks with roofs sagging as if a giant had sat on them, with rusty tin façades, their windows blinded by slices of cardboard, and with chimneys askew, threatening to collapse at any moment, held up by two boards and three nails. And everywhere, penetrating, aggressive, acrid, the smell of turnip soup, of a mixture of lye and kerosene. She finally came to the open avenues. The window of a café stopped her. A chess club. Too bad. Her entrance into this world of men created a slight commotion, temporary of course, because here she was among lunatics who couldn't be distracted from the tarantulas in their bonnets for long. Justine inquired about the washroom. Then, nature's call answered, she asked if she could use the phone. She wanted to advise her landlords that she'd be coming home later than usual. While she was waiting to be connected, she examined the place, which was fraught with an atmosphere all too familiar. Beards and shirtsleeves, dead cigars between lips, young men, sallow and haunted, wasted eyes, Eastern Europeans, half down-and-out, half-genius, rabbis shokelling and bustling while they sucked on pawns taken from their opponents, uniformed postmen, a soldier with stripes. Learned gathering of addicts, the same all over, indulging unimpeded in their vice amid a muffled rumbling of shifting chairs, of tinkling coffee spoons, of contemplative coughing, of throat-burning pipes being lit. Finally, at the other end of the line, it wasn't her landlady but her landlady's husband, Leopold O'Donahue, the Philosopher, who answered. Justine told him that she'd been delayed but would be back within half an hour. The Philosopher said, "No problema." Justine thought he was speaking strangely, sounding evasive and preoccupied. She hung up, thanks, crossed the room again, finally back on the road, memories putting a lump in her throat. Vincent was well and truly dead. Some shreds of him might be clinging to that Xavier, but they were shreds that actually should have been set free, and Justine mused that she should have fired after all, but what? The harm, the good, all of it was done.

Yes, dead. The newspaper headline: "Young Canadian Dies Accidentally." The ups and downs of postal flow being what they were, the last missive from her son didn't reach Justine till some weeks later. The contents of the letter would set the record straight for anyone. At seventeen, Vincent had left Montreal for New York, taking along a bursary awarded him by Cagliari so he could devote himself to the sole passion that had been consuming him for ten years: chess. Cagliari had conveyed the news: "Dear Justine, that child is a genius. At his age, Capablanca was no better. Send him to me as soon as possible, so I can make him into the future world champion. It won't cost you a penny. I'm a slut, as much as you want, indeed I pride myself on it. But you know that my spine has always bowed to talent." Genius, sure; why not? But a constitution so frail, despondent over the slightest thing, depressive, defenceless before the judgement of others, carting around the weight of his existence like a ball and chain of wretchedness. When Vincent felt that he lacked the strength to live, he would take refuge in gardening. Justine saw him somewhat at peace only when he was hoeing, seeding, transplanting, orchestrating with taste that was very intricate, very sure. She remembered the beautiful garden he'd designed in the backyard of their house at Sainte-Agathe-des-Monts, on the shore of Sand Lake.

And so Vincent had gone to New York, out of duty more

than anything else. At the first important tournament he'd collapsed, winning the first three matches, then was massacred in the other ten — by opponents who didn't come up to his ankle. In his final letter to Justine he had written, "This passion of mine for chess is giving me a rough time and it's going to kill me. I've never said this to anyone, never even admitted it to myself. But I detest playing. With all my soul." He had jumped out a fifth-floor window.

The day when she'd had to identify her son. She had spent the night on a train, shivering in pain. Alone, with no support. Having also to endure, for eight hours, a rowdy group of medical students whose vulgarity was beyond comprehension. New York appeared to her at dawn, and affected her like a machine for crushing lives. She went to the morgue, had trouble walking, they had to put her in a wheelchair, literally paralysed with grief. Vincent's body had been taken from its refrigerated container. The skeleton had shattered under the impact of the fall. His head, though, and his face, had been strangely spared. "The way he fell," explained a young man assigned to the cold room. "His head landed in a bush." Then added in all seriousness, "He was lucky." It was such a stupid remark that Justine couldn't hold back a sardonic snicker. To see this healthy boy, his face covered with spots, the same age as Vincent who was lying in his drawer in bits and pieces — this employee who existed instead of her son, by usurpation — made Justine think the universe was definitely haywire.

And there were still forms to sign. There would be a waiting period to get through before the burial, she was told. She had replied, "No. He'll be cremated." She was also obliged to meet the medical examiner, it was the law. She didn't recognize him right away; after all, a quarter of a century dims memories. He said, with a note of painful surprise, "Don't you know who I am?" The medical examiner was Rogatien Wondell.

Two days later she went again to the New York City morgue. She expected some ceremony, not religious but something resembling a last farewell, some formality; she was given an urn, told that her son was inside. The fatigue, the grief that had made her distraught, even the trouble she had speaking English in this city that she hadn't visited for over twenty years, these factors affected her in such a way that her indignation, instead of exploding, turned her to ice. She signed a *receipt*. From then on New York washed its mitts of her. She brought the ashes back to Montreal, then to Sainte-Agathe-des-Monts, where she scattered them in Sand Lake. But what did she know? It could have been the ashes of a dog.

She comes to the brightly lit main thoroughfares, and in front of a grand hotel she gets a taxi. Crosses this part of the city where she lived for ten years, where she now doesn't recognize a thing. Sometimes, though, a street corner, a square, a café that's now a launderette, brings a flood of unexpected memories. The car stops at an intersection, waits for the light. Through the window Justine spies the boarding house where, thirty years ago, she lived with Rogatien Wondell. They had known one another since childhood, lived in the same building, eaten the same pistachios, the same pork and beans, they were in a sense brother and sister. On the side wall of that building from their childhood, Rogatien had one day (how old could he have been? Eight, nine?) written this barbed oath: *I beelong to Justine Vilbroquais fore evver.* On the day they arrived in New York, the first thing Rogatien did, once the suitcases were unpacked and the furniture was in place, was to write out that oath again, with the same spelling, on the wall of the hotel where they were staying. Justine wonders if the inscription is still legible. The taxi starts up again.

Ten years of her life spent here, and nothing left of it. Ten years that ended grotesquely and trivially — that is to say, one day she found out that Rogatien had been unfaithful to her, etc. "Once! Just once!" he yelled, while she was gathering up her worldly goods. And she'd left. Made a new life for herself, gave birth to her son, Vincent, whose papa had died during her pregnancy, so forth, had half her left breast cut off because of cancer, things happen, then they scatter. So that New York life was far away, old stories that didn't even hurt any more. But now, nearly twenty years later, following their meeting at the morgue, Rogatien is sending her inflamed and delirious letters. 1. He'd never forgotten her. 2. They could start again. 3. "After everything we lived through together." This last argument has never bothered any woman. Justine read it without really looking at it. In fact, she'd thrown most of them away. Until that day last April, when she received from him these simple words: "Come to New York. Very serious matters. About your son, Vincent. You may not have lost him as much as you think!" She'd only agreed to meet Rogatien once. He explained it all calmly, pedagogically, from the lofty position of his frontal lobes — those of a scientist. And so the nightmare began. As of that day, it had been impossible for her to leave New York. She paced restlessly, as if she were in a cell two metres square. What to do about Vincent? What to do about this Xavier?

The taxi stopped in front of the rooming house where she'd been staying for weeks. When she was paying the driver, Justine was surprised to remember that today was her fifty-ninth birthday; she'd thought about it this morning and then it had slipped her mind. The house was fast asleep. Only the Philosopher was still up, under a small cone of light in the kitchen. They were linked through Xavier, but since an opportunity to talk about him had never come up, neither of them knew it. Justine thought it would be polite to say hello to the man.

"Still working this late at night?"

"Eh? What's that?"

The impression she'd had earlier on the telephone was not refuted. The old man had an insomniac's red eyes, his shirt was half-unbuttoned, and he was badly shaven, with forgotten tufts of whiskers on his neck. Sheets of paper were spread out in front of him, covered with drawings, circles, strikeouts, a muddle. Open books, with illegible annotations in the margins, the kind made by very small children.

"I said, You're still working this late at night?"

"Uhh, no," said the old man, getting out of his chair self-consciously. "Shall I pour you a coffee? There's some still hot. The real thing, not chicory."

"No thank you. I want to sleep."

"Ah, that, sleep . . ."

She waited for more but it didn't come. They stayed there in silence. Justine decided they had nothing to say to each other.

"All right, well . . ."

The Philosopher started to move, as if he hoped she wouldn't go up to her room right away. She asked if anything was wrong. Blinking, he said not at all.

"I'll go up to bed then."

He followed her to the stairs. When she put her hand on the banister, he grabbed it eagerly.

"I've got something to confess to you!"

Good grief! He's not going to say he's in love with me! thought Justine wearily. In the past few days, Leopold had aged by ten years. His lips quivered, his left eyelid fluttered. His complexion was ashen, with prominent red and blue veinlets. She thought, That man is going to die soon.

"There's something . . . I've never said this to anyone. Only my wife knows."

Classic reluctance to go on. In his eyes, senile terror.

"Well?"

"I. Pffff. I've never learned to read or write. In school, I tried. But it never got into this noggin of mine."

"But that's not serious," she said mechanically.

She didn't understand why this confidence was so poignant. Then, click. His book! That famous book of his! That his daughters, his workmates, his tenants made such a fuss about! The old man looked like one of the demolished. Justine repeated her remark, gently this time, while she stroked his fingers.

"There, there, it really isn't serious."

"All my life, I've lied," he said with tears in his throat. "To myself first of all, Madam, to myself first of all, that may be the most serious. I've put on an act for my fellow workers too, for everybody. I misled people into thinking I knew when I didn't. And I understood when I didn't! And that I could see when I couldn't see a thing!"

"What is it you're talking about?"

Leopold looked at her, in a daze. He was trying desperately to get back the thread of some very old meditations.

"I don't know. About everything, about life. I'm going to die and I won't have understood anything."

"But it's the same for everyone, really. And maybe there's nothing to understand anyway."

He closed his eyes, put his fist on his forehead as if to drive it in.

"And yet in there, in *there*, it seemed to me there was something! How many times have I told myself, 'That's it, it's going to unblock!' But it was no good, it stayed stuck inside. And I played along, I put on airs. I acted mysterious, acted the part of someone who lets it be known that 'one day he'll talk.' I pretended I could read, often I went to work carrying a book. My fellow workers looked at me with respect. An educated woman like you, you must think I'm a scoundrel."

"Why on earth would you think such a thing?"

"My life is a lie. All of it. But it's over now. I don't want to lie any more."

"Don't turn yourself inside out like that. Why say that you've made a mess of your life? You're a grandpa, your three daughters love you, you've got your health and some fine years to look forward to."

But the old man didn't listen to these facile consolations. He spoke with a crazed exultation.

"Tomorrow. Yes, tomorrow. I'll bring everyone together. My daughters, my oldest colleagues, the roomers, everyone! And I'll talk. Finally they'll see me as the wicked man I am."

"You mustn't humiliate yourself like that. Anyway, everyone who loves you, when they find out the truth they'll forgive you."

"You think so?"

The same appeal as in Xavier's eyes tonight.

"I'm sure of it."

"You're just saying that to reassure me."

Midnight. They heard the twelve strokes without batting an eyelash. Suddenly, Justine had had it up to here. She felt sympathy for him, but. To be stuck halfway up a staircase consoling a distraught old man.

"Go to sleep now, you'll see about all that tomorrow morning."

"No, stay!" said Leopold, his voice choked with fear.

"I'm tired, I want to sleep."

She did her best to smile at him, took her hand away from his as tactfully as she could.

"We'll talk about it tomorrow, if you want. Good night. You ought to go to bed too."

She started up the stairs, disappeared into the shadows upstairs. Leopold stayed there alone, staring into space, quivering, his lip tremulous, and always, in his eyes, the dread of an old man thinking about death.

Justine sat at the little yellow desk under the only window in her room. Neon signs lit the streets as if it were daytime, dropped flowers of light onto the slippery sidewalks. She could write without even switching on the lamp. She pushed some music scores off the blotter and with her hand voluptuously smoothed the big, soft, textured sheet of paper. Along with a pair of silk gloves, this letterhead with her name on it was the final luxury she was allowing herself. She wrote in one go, without haste and without having to search for words. In French, but too bad. The New York City police would just have to find a translator. Finally she placed the envelope prominently on the blotter. She would mail it tomorrow.

From her skirt pocket she took a small bottle of pills. Started to undress. She felt empty, yet at peace. She had acted in harmony with herself from start to finish. She had no regrets, no missteps to feel guilty about. As had been true all her life, which she had lived in a straight line, like an arrow, always her own mistress, despite the hard knocks, despite the betrayals. It was no small thing to be able to say that. She picked up the bottle and popped a sleeping pill into her mouth. And all at once it was obvious.

The thing had come about on its own, slowly, the way a plant grows, in the most deeply hidden part of herself. She realized that the decision had been made long ago, though she was only now aware of it. It would be not a sudden impulse but, on the contrary, an act carefully pondered, in that deep place where our various forms of strangeness become inter-twined. She took a second tablet, then a third. Finally gulped as many as she could. Not even hard to swallow. Little sips of water and down the hatch. She stretched out on the bed, caressing her arms, filled with tenderness towards herself.

There, now she just had to let the mental music play. To fill her heart with the sweetest memories. The weekends she'd spent with Vincent at Sand Lake, for instance, in the house she'd inherited from her family. At fourteen, too, when she had triumphed at the piano during a school con-cert. All that. It felt sweet to let herself sail on. Sweet as well to think about the letter that would be found tomorrow, in which she informed the police of Rogatien's activities — the theft and defilement of bodies, the works, quite a programme. Yes, it was sweet to die so much in harmony with herself, caressing her arms and her belly. To reach that point, she mused, feeling absolutely in tune with your heart and conscience, was a sign that it was time to go before some little thing came along and ruined everything. The smut, the treacherous remarks, the betrayals — she had forgotten nothing. But she was going to die upright, on her own two feet, so to speak.

Abruptly, the whole perspective was overturned. A sickening queasiness crept into her body. She opened her eyes. The ceiling was spinning like a lottery wheel. Some vile beast was making itself comfortable in her belly. Then came a terrible revelation, as indisputable as death. *She'd been wrong! Xavier was Vincent all the same! And she had abandoned him just when he most needed to be loved!* The image of her son, tonight, when he begged her with his eyes, an image that imposed itself with absolute force, wrenched the first agonized cry from her. She wanted to get up, to run and join him, but she was feeling bottomless pain, as if her stomach were bursting, and a kind of soap began to foam at her lips. The convulsions started, she fell out of the bed. Her feet, her fists pounded the floor, her whole body jolted, and it made such a racket that the Philosopher came running. But at the sight of the foam, of the torn mouth, of the tongue swelling like a penis, he grabbed hold of his head, unable to call out, unable to act, able only to run away to escape the horror. He wasn't found until the following day, curled up, shivering, under the front porch of a small house fourteen blocks away. Still twitching between his lips was the tail of the mouse he was eating alive.

7

STRUCK BY A BURST of patriotism, Strapitchacoudou launched into "The Star-Spangled Banner" with no solution of continuity, striking up the first couplet again once she'd come to the end. She was perched at the top of a ladder, right fist over her heart as she sang. As well as her opera hat in the colours of the flag, she was decked out with an immaculate goatee à la Rogatien Wondell. Xavier could no longer hear her. The lightbulb shed its greasy light. The leatherette notebook he'd thrown at the wall lay in a pile of dust next to a toolbox, and he couldn't stop looking at it. Once again he was sitting on the bags of cement, and with his remaining strength he was struggling against himself, against the temptation to read that manuscript, when he'd resolved to tear it up and chuck the pieces out the window. Anyway, what would he gain by poisoning himself on that tissue of absurdities, of lies that were outright fabrications by who knows whom who knows why, whose sole purpose was to make him suffer? The frog finally broke off her singing and, following Xavier's gaze with her eyes, she spotted the notebook. Three leaps and she was there. The apprentice began a movement to stop her. But Strapitchacoudou started to read, with meaningful expressions, miming surprise and keen interest, snickering in places, opening her eyes even wider than usual. Xavier couldn't take any more.

"Stop! I forbid you!"

And he walked towards her and she scampered away. Xavier picked up the notebook. Held it in his hands for a long time. He knew he'd succumb in the end. *Journal for a Resurrection of Vincent.* He sat on his bed and slowly turned the pages. On those on the right, calculations, graphs, results of blood tests, temperature, etc. The comments were on the left-hand pages, helter-skelter, overlapping, anarchical, and written by a raging hand. Xavier tried to convince himself that he was only *looking* at the pages, looking but not reading. But certain words grabbed his attention anyway, and curiosity won the day.

> *That's it, I've got what I wanted. He is alive. Breathing, anyway, though still comatose. Good for me! Delightful dosette of adorable morphine to celebrate quietly all by my lonesome. Only hope he'll survive, at least till Justine gets here, currently in Montreal. Also of course till Cagliari returns, at this point still in Germany. Can't wait to see the look on his face.*

> *Since day before yesterday gets up, takes a few steps, but still very weak, collapses after three metres. So far I've had to spoon-feed him myself, like a baby (gruel). I'll have to go on, I'm afraid, or so the little experiment I tried this afternoon leads me to believe. He has a very pronounced liking for chocolate, so I put a bar of it in his hand, to see what he'd do with it. In his*

effort to get it into his mouth he only managed to mash it into
his eye. Little problem of coordination then. Let's hope it will
resolve itself, because —

Xavier felt the wing of shame pass over him. He skipped
a good many pages and when he came to these words: . . .
and on account of the hormones I'm obliged to inject, he has
developed a kind of bosom, oh, not much, a little thirteen-year-
old at most, but if it continues . . . he skipped some more.

> *Something rather upsetting has happened. First, that acci-*
dent on the wharf, a crate full of a thousand books broke away
from the crane and killed the rag-and-bone man's horse. The
only thing to do was take him to the slaughterhouse, but as it
was Sunday, the truck couldn't come till the next day, and there
was no question of leaving the cadaver out in the sun. So the
horse had to be taken to one of those sheds in the warehouse,
exactly adjacent to ours. We have easy access to it through a kind
of fake window, I mean a square-shaped hole in the wall, with
no glass or screen. It didn't occur to me to worry about it, but
after this meeting with Justine, this meeting which was prickly,
sometimes rough and marked by unbearably violent feelings,
when she scratched my cheeks, spat in my face, out of gratitude
I imagine, like the good Christian she claims to be, I couldn't
find a trace of Vincent when I came back, and for a moment my
heart stopped beating. I'd reached the point of wondering
despondently what I was going to be able to do, when I heard
strange noises, as if someone were kneading flabby, slimy things,
followed by sounds of suffocation. Coming from the shed next
door. I went in and what I saw —

Xavier stopped reading. Angst-ridden sweat was making his temples sticky and he was struck by a violent coughing fit. He flung the notebook far away, swore he wouldn't read another line. But he couldn't help it.

> . . . what I saw then turned my stomach, though it wasn't the first time. I found Vincent up to his waist inside the horse's belly, which he'd torn open with his own hands and whose viscera he was devouring, raw. I had to pull him out by the legs, because he was about to suffocate. A most unsavoury sight. His mouth was full, overflowing, he was sticky with blood all the way to his belt, he was moaning and groaning like the demented. He spent the next hour in a state of agitation such as I'd never seen. Normally, when he's restless, I soothe him with chocolate. This time though it didn't work. I had to knock him out with a massive injection of morphine. All night afraid his heart would pack it in, that he wouldn't survive. Next day, luckily —

> My surprise when he started to talk, because language had come back, which makes me laugh. And in the language of Molière, if you please! No sentiment, I promised myself. But I'm growing attached to him all the same.

> . . . in that respect. And since he bears within him nearly equal portions of individuals called (I was careful to note the given names) Xenon, Albert, Vincent, Isabella (whence the need for hormones), Ernest, Reinfeld, I thought that to call the former Vincent "X.A.V.I.E.R." wouldn't be a bad idea at all, given my childish liking of anagrams. (So that he wouldn't forget his name I marked it on his wrist in indelible ink.) I'm amazed

myself that he can stay in one piece. Thanks to him, I've recently become convinced that not all our memories are lodged exclusively in our brains. "Xavier," for instance, seems to carry within him, in disorderly fashion, granted, bits of memories belonging to the life of Albert, while all he possesses of him is liver and lungs. So forth. Fascinating prospect for future investigation.

> How does he perceive himself? How does he adapt to living like this? Where does he think he comes from, what notion does he have of his own origins? He is of course still too incoherent (Will that be corrected over time? Certain signs allow me to hope so) to answer such questions, should I dare to ask them, but I wouldn't let myself ask at this stage (fear of regression, fear of collapse). Still, something has happened that opens a breach in this darkness. I was looking for something in my papers when I realized I was missing the photographs I've had in the pocket of my satchel for decades. Photos of Justine when we were twenty. Not that I spend my days gazing at them, but their sudden disappearance struck me as odd, as I was sure I hadn't taken them out myself. Shortly afterwards I discovered that "Xavier" had concealed the photographs under his pillow. (So he went through my papers when I wasn't there? Meaning that he was capable of doing such a thing?) Two days later, during the night, I heard something coming from his corner. I tiptoed over and watched without his knowing. Xavier had switched on his bed-side light, was sitting on his bed, and with a steadiness that disturbed me he was studying one of the photos. Even at this distance I could see which one it was. It was a portrait of her that she'd signed: "Your sister, Justine." He was studying it fervently and sadly, the way you would study the face of a close relative who had died. (Was it the portion of Vincent in

him that was so moved by this sight?) I soon could see that tears were rolling down his cheeks. With which I would associate the following: on the shelves in the shed, on the day when I arrived, there was a colour brochure, like a tourist leaflet, extolling the beauties of Budapest, "the jewel of Hungary." I don't know how it could have got there. The fact remains that Xavier seems to have a kind of fascination with that brochure. The other day he was studying it with an affection and fervour reminiscent of the way, a few days earlier, I'd seen him looking at the photo of Justine. And when he became aware of my presence he quickly made the brochure disappear under his bed, as if I'd caught him doing something indecent.

> I note that for some days now Xavier has been fabricating. He says that his name is Mortanse (where the hell did he come up with that?), that he has a sister called Justine, whom he had to leave behind because of his forced departure from Hungary! To elaborate a fiction around that, to invent a life for himself. It's both fascinating and appalling.

> . . . and I had seen that this life of seclusion was becoming a strain on him. He kept tirelessly walking along the walls, going in circles, delivering kicks to the door of the shed. But there was no question of his leaving the warehouse. Not right away. Too frail, first of all, as well as being dysfunctional. And then we had to wait for Cagliari's return from Germany, which had been delayed. So as I was coming in that afternoon, I saw that Xavier had freed himself from his bonds (his agitation often forces me to tie him up), that he'd wrecked everything — my surgical instruments, my furniture, my flask — and I found him stretched out on the floor, unconscious, like a mop. He had

certainly taken something, his clothes were covered with vomit. There was a dried verdigris foam at the corners of his mouth. I dragged his inert weight to the bed. I had nothing left to use as a remedy. Xavier had broken everything, as I said, and I had to run to the apothecary to stock up again. I didn't think to padlock the door to the shed. When I came back, there was no sign of him. Xavier had run away. God knows where he might be now. It bothers me all the more because a few days ago, on some very precise parts of his anatomy, there appeared some signs of tissue degeneration and I'm afraid it's irreversible —

Xavier watched the pages of the notebook blacken and curl as he burned it on his makeshift brazier leaf by leaf. "None of that is true," he kept saying, his eyes vacant. But when he tried to put back the shoe that Justine had torn off him, he had to concede that he was well and truly *signed*. On the sole of his foot there appeared, in scarified letters:

Rog. Wond., April 1929.

8

JOLT OF SCORCHING heat, belated. Six days of steam room before the icy rain and pneumonia of autumn. The sun was beating down, a scream of light. In his room, the apprentice was sizzling hot. Without water, without food, prisoner of a lethargy that had nothing to do with rest. He was thinking about Jeff, about Peggy Supine Underground, about the black woman who'd given him a drink of her flavoured beverage one day when he was bruised all over. For hours he couldn't move a leg, lift a hand. An inert, foreign mass was pressing down on his pallet with all its weight. He had wakened with a corpse in his bed, and that breathless windbag, that sack of remains and humours, was his own body, insistent on enduring. His body, which had become as little him as were, for example, the walls of his room, the plankets, the makeshift brazier. That strange thing was in the process of dying and as he was the one who lived inside it, who still, incomprehensibly, continued to live there, it was in the process of killing him too. It was sweeping him slowly into a dissolution that had no face and no answers. In ruins, like the world.

At times the thing coughed up blood, which Xavier now

lacked the strength to spit out. He kept in his mouth this smooth, acrid mucus, which he soon found himself forced to swallow. And so the tease wouldn't leave his flesh. "I'm done for." At the same time, so what? Because what good would it do? He desired nothing, least of all to go on. He mused that ending it all wouldn't explain much. Knowledge of death taught nothing. The shame of existing solely for the feeling of existing, finally. All the apprentice asked for was a little peace, a little quiet, before it was all over, returned to the stupor of nothingness, which he could glimpse.

Peace and quiet, why not? On Saturdays and Sundays, you wouldn't have found a single hammer on the job in the whole building. But there you are. Strapitchacoudou was out of control. (The bipolar loony-tunes in her up phase.) She lost herself in a veritable marathon of vaudeville acts. Everything went into it, her pranks, her acrobatics, etc. She was insolently radiant, with a vigour of which the apprentice didn't have even a drop. Life was exploding, exuberant, aggressive, throwing off a thousand sparkles, around a bed of pain.

When night fell, Xavier's torment went on. Putting on horn-rimmed glasses and wielding a pointer à la Herr Doctor, the frog gave an interminable lecture on General Relativity, arguing in the greatest detail that, in consideration of a few ad hoc reforms, of course, Einstein's thesis was not metaphysically incompatible with the transcendental principles of Kantian criticism. When she had said everything she had to say, she was content to crank out, for as long as she could come up with them, the decimals following pi, which she claimed were periodic in the long run. Finally, in the morning, with akimbo arms and Mussolinian chin, she ran through the room with a satisfied look. She eyed the decor up and down — the wanton destruction, the desolation — with all the vanity of a conqueror before a massacre of his own devising.

But she was startled. For here, standing like a collapsed marionette whose strings have just been activated, was the silhouette of Xavier, tall as a turret. The frog backed up, ready to flee. The apprentice's legs were rigid, he could no longer flex his knees. He walked towards her with the gait of a jumping jack. Strapitchacoudou saw the towering shadow coming closer. But Mortanse came to a halt, wobbling, dazed, and closed his eyelids. The frog waited, on the alert (will he fall? won't he? . . .) The boy hiccupped. A thread of blood appeared at the corners of his lips.

He opened his eyes again, resumed his walk, staggering but determined, borne along by his idée fixe. His cheeks became coloured with mauve spots. He wanted to pick up his frog, but the pointer she was carrying was actually a needle-stick and she pierced his skin between forefinger and thumb. Then ran to safety on the windowsill. As a kind of game, sparring like a toreador, she avoided the gigantic hands trying to swoop down on her. She stuck her tongue out at him. Finally, letting go of the needle-stick, her tiny arms flapped like the wings of a dragonfly and she began to buzz around the apprentice, chirring like an outsized insect. Xavier protected his face. He was beating the air with broad movements of terror. Then half the world gave way beneath him, his left knee collapsed, and with a moan he subsided. That unexpected movement disconcerted the frog. She didn't have time to change her trajectory. She went crashing into the boy's shoulder. Then flew off again, straight into his mouth.

The apprentice got back on his feet. Returned to his bed,

leaning on the strewn scrap metal. The frog's feet were kicking, with all the energy of rage, between the boy's lips. Xavier didn't unclench his jaws. His face was radiant with voluptuous revenge. He grabbed hold of the casket and, in a manner of speaking, spat Strapitchacoudou inside it. Then came the closing of the lid, double-quick, on the squirming panic. He took the length of rope that held his pants up and firmly tied the box with it. From inside, the railing of the extravagant one could be heard. She was throwing herself hysterically against the walls, screaming threats and imprecations. Xavier was savouring his victory with the smile of a dying man who at least will be reconciled with the universe when he goes.

He left the casket on a heap of tools, in the grip of a sudden, glum disgust. He went to the window, which was daubed with the blue of the sky. Looking at the azure was painful, like sticking your finger in your eye. He stared at it, though, and then at the sun, defiantly, without fear, indifferent to the pain in his retina. When he looked down at the street he was blind. Stayed blind for a good minute. For a good minute thought he would never see again. Then his right eye started to make out vague shapes, swarms of them that little by little became clear: there was a crowd in the street. With his left eye, though, he was taking in nothing at all. Eye burned to death. "Like Peggy," he thought.

A long banner crossed the street from one building to another.

> *WELCOME MARIE PEAK-FORDE*
> *AMERICA'S SWEETHEART!*

The apprentice recalled, without being affected by it, a conversation he'd caught between two demolishers about a parade in which the movie star would travel the neighbourhood streets by limousine to greet the New York crowds. So today was the day? And Marie Peak-Forde would be going by here, under his window? . . . Xavier gave a brief laugh, piqued and bitter.

He was about to pick up the casket when his eye fell on the package given him by Rogatien Wondell. Initially, too worried about what he was liable to find inside, he'd refused to unwrap it. Later, he had quite simply forgotten. Over all those days the package had lain under the leaky sink; it was soaked right through. Xavier picked it up. The paper it was wrapped in tore like the flesh of a cooked fish. The contents appeared. Thousands of dollars. On the top bills something was written, a word, washed out by the water from the sink, Xavier couldn't easily read what it was, the word "sorry" maybe. He thrust both hands into the soggy mass of bills. They decomposed in his fingers as soon as he tried to pick one up. Rot by absorption. Mortanse went back to the window, carrying the package. He flung the wadded banknotes as high as he could, hoping that the wind would grab them, scatter them, turn them into a swarm of green butterflies. But the sodden bills stayed stuck together. A single dense pile that went crashing into the middle of the alley. Where the garbage was put out.

When he was putting on his hat he felt something strange, a kind of burning, on his scalp. He ran his hand through his hair. Realized that it stayed in his fingers, falling in long locks, as resilient as a spider's web. Xavier brought his hair to his nostrils, smelled it. Then put his hat back on, perfectly indifferent.

Walking past the remains of his notebook, though, he had a moment's hesitation. He opened it at random. Things he'd written weeks ago. He read only this fraction of a sentence: " . . . and once I'm President of this country," hastened to turn the page, gripped by shame. He read again: "Beings are irreplaceable." He picked up a pencil, pondered for a moment, then wrote: "I would simply have liked . . . " but went no further, thought it wasn't worth the trouble of going on, and flung his pencil out the window too. He went to the door with the casket under his arm. Strapitchacoudou called to him in her most enticing voice: "Xavier! . . . Pssst! . . . Xavier! . . ." It was the first time she'd spoken his name. For a few moments, the apprentice stood there motionless. Then shook his head and went out. The corridor still smelled of burnt flesh.

9

THE HUNCHBACKED DWARF, eyes bulging, whip in
hand, walked through the one-armed bandits pouting and
muttering, quite shamelessly displaying his contempt for the
clientele. The best-patronized of his machines was called
Mary Had a Little Lamb. Only adult males were allowed to
play there. Daddies who still had the souls of children
inserted three pennies into the slit between little Mary's
buttocks. There was a clinking sound as bulbs lit up. Using
the lever, the daddies then tried to control the steel wire at
the end of which hung a lead marble. In a bin, some sixty
mice were milling about, magnets attached to their pink
tails. With skill, with luck too, the daddy could magnetize
a mouse and, by virtue of the wire, move the rodent over a
funnel. From there — and this was the highlight of the game
— either he let the mouse escape into the pit, where a
grinder awaited and its tiny life would end with a brief sound
of scarlet suction, or else it dropped into the mouth of the
funnel. The tube of the funnel was stuck into the lamb,
whose legs were firmly tied. Two times out of three, the
daddy couldn't even magnetize a mouse. And of those that
were magnetized, there wasn't a chance in ten that one would

drop into the funnel, hurl itself, panicking and clawing, into the sheep's vagina. But it did happen. And the ewe would bleat and her muzzle would twitch. The jolt would be transmitted to a tray heaped with delicacies, by means of a rope connected to the ovine's jaw, and the candies would tumble via a downward-sloping footbridge into the hands of toddlers whose only assignment was to enjoy the treat.

Xavier continued on his way. He followed the congested avenue, where the atmosphere was one of impatience and overheated expectation. Souvenir dealers had put up their stalls. At the entrances to alleyways, small carousels went merrily around for the pipsqueaks. There were acts with strongmen, with jugglers and clowns, with spiritualists who frisked the breeches of your thoughts, and confetti-sellers and hot-dog stands. Mortals assembled, whole families, acquaintances greeted each other, creating a pile so dense that for a moment Xavier had to come to a halt. He paid no attention to the gazes turned his way, reproachful or bewildered. Light jumped between the faces, trembled in bodies, like the hands of a feverish patient. Xavier walked through the crowd, distressed by these faint touches, these slight collisions, this minuscule jostling. He had the impression that he was being torn by nails, like cloth. There was just one moment and it filled the Universe entirely. And no one was anyone any more.

The windows of buildings were filled with faces, with bodies that had climbed onto one another, resembling crates stuffed with onions, while on the street scruffy urchins, ragged and scrawny, wove between legs, making sure they'd be in the front row for the parade. Xavier stopped to observe them. With commando-style discipline they hailed one another, exchanged agreed-upon signs; all had lollipops stuck in the corners of their mouths, and caps covered with badges, all swiped from merchants' stalls. Yes, all of these, even a dog charged by the multitude, who went from hand to hand, and from one pants-seat to another, sniffing and shocked, even the bums whose bewilderment travelled against the crowd, up to and including the demolished all were starving, all thirsting to admire the appearance in the Eucharistic Species, the Real Presence, of America's sweetheart.

A throng of policemen joined hands to form a chain. They cleared the centre of the avenue by pushing the crowd back to the sidewalks. Their armbands were adorned with a pink heart that had a portrait of Marie Peak-Forde inside it. The crowd was so dense that it was getting hard to set one foot in front of the other. Smell of sweat, hot dogs, roasted corn, and pressurized pavement. Now and then Xavier came to a halt, adjusted the casket between his legs, then plugged his ears to give them a rest from the hubbub: the shouts of peddlers, the annoying safety suggestions that came through the bullhorns of the guardians of the peace, the advertising slogans repeated to the point of rage, of disgust, that were fired mercilessly from the loudspeakers:

> *Deceased at the hands of Fu Manchu*
> *in her last film,*
> *Marie Peak-Forde*
> *is resurrected!*

Xavier found himself near a group of girlfriends. They were secretly laughing and standing away from one of them they were a little ashamed of, while at the same time they admired her audacity and the power of her passion. She was extremely fat. She wore a mantle with the actress's name on it. Across her bosom, you'd have said watermelons, was spread an impressive collection of miniatures bearing the image of the sweetheart. Likewise her hat and the floating balloons, attached to her shoulders by a wire, that kept aloft the venerated name. She jumped up and down, smothered in fat, carrot-red. She waved little bells tied to her wrists, chanting at the top of her lungs all the while, "Marie Peak-Forde is resurrected! Marie Peak-Forde is resurrected!"

And because of her foot-stamping she eventually bumped into Xavier. Her considerable bulk threw him off balance. He got up, smiling at the lady to let her know that no offence was taken. She looked him up and down, shocked and amazed. The hat of the boy, who no longer had human form, his shirt spattered with dried blood, his feet — of which only the right was shod, the other being bare, no sock or anything — it was all an insult to the sacred moment she'd been preparing to live for three weeks now. She shot the apprentice a look that was spit in his face. She moved away, still waving her arms in a frenzy. Mortanse picked up his hat. "She is part of life too," he thought.

He took refuge in the first alley he came to. After all the hurly-burly he felt almost happy. Some warehousemen were unloading crates from a truck. Xavier stopped walking to observe some children playing marbles. In the shadow of the buildings, the marbles looked beautiful and fresh. Beams of light clung to them and drew out bursts of colour. Xavier would have liked to play with these little boys. To kneel down with them and make clever use of his thumbs.

There was also a comical puppy, his feet still too big for

him, his ears and tongue hanging to the ground. At each round of the game he made nervous, exuberant little leaps, barking at the orange and red and green marbles, which he thought were eyes. Without realizing it, Xavier smiled at the puppy. Near the children, and without quarrelling, pigeons pecked at the seeds that leaked from the crates being shifted by the warehousemen. A quiet breeze streamed between the walls, bringing a little coolness and the smell of lilacs from who knows where. From the alley, the sky looked calm, comforting, and as gay as the marbles in which it was reflected.

A profound and horrible emotion wrenched the apprentice's heart. God, how he wanted to live, to love this life! God, how talented he'd have been at simply appreciating the gift of existence, its warm colours, the morning wakening of birds and streets! To have friends and love them! He would have asked for nothing more — only to be accepted, expected and greeted, and to be able now and then to rest his forehead on a friendly bosom, a woman who would gently play with his hair. A dark justice had decreed that he would never be entitled to that. And this image of happiness was driven into his heart like a stake.

"Hey, guys! Look what's standing there," shouted a boy, and his friends stopped playing at once.

"Haven't seen that one for ages. Holy mackerel, take a gander, he's bawling!"

The children formed a mocking circle around Xavier. He'd arrived at just the right time, because they were starting to twiddle their thumbs, to push marbles. Have some fun at the sight of a walking ruin: there were worse ways to kill time while they waited for the Sweetheart's arrival. One child tried to get the casket away from the apprentice; asked what was inside. So forth. And they wondered where the heck he was going like that, with just one sneaker! A little laughter never hurt anybody. Xavier leaned against the wall, then took off. He passed through the circle filled with threats. His eyes were very small, misted with confusion. He walked, giving himself airs of paying no attention to the children, who were following close behind him. On his back, between his shoulder-blades, he could feel their little words — harsh, innocent, cruel. The leader of the gang must be about fourteen. He barely came up to Mortanse's elbow. He'd caught up with Xavier now, was walking level with him. He was smacking him on the back, ironic good-buddy style, and the force of the smacks kept increasing, as if to test how far he could go. With every blow, Xavier nodded acceptance with humility, with a slight bend of the torso.

"In this heat wouldn't it be smarter to lose your hat than to cool off your left foot? Here, let me try it!"

Mortanse kept his hand on his hat, moved forward, eyes ashamed and staring.

"At least take off your shirt!" the young leader went on. "Come on, it'll cool you off."

The others echoed, "Yes, yes! Off with his shirt!" And got worked up over this idea for no reason. The apprentice continued his puffing and panting walk, while the kids could think of nothing but his shirt. It had become the most irresistible joke in the world. Suddenly the apprentice stopped. The kids did the same, to keep a cautious distance, because after all the boy was a tall one. They were delighted: "How about that! He's really going to take it off!" And everyone was quivering with excitement.

The apprentice looked them in the eyes, one after the

other, which didn't impress them. Insolently they held his gaze. And the smallest ones writhing with giggles. Xavier wedged the casket between his thighs and slowly dropped his shirt. The children fell silent instantly, and drew back. Wincing, the little leader murmured, "Holy Mary Mother of God . . . " The chest of Xavier X. Mortanse was no more than a repulsive wound. His belly and back were covered with graffiti, written on his flesh with quicklime. Including this, under the shoulder-blades: *Christopher Columbus was put in irons for having offered a world!* And on his belly, the most legible, in bigger letters:

I beelong to Justine Vilbroquais fore evver.

Finally, Xavier removed the plankets of his devising, designed to flatten his breasts. Which appeared in their splendour. One resembled an eggplant in colour and form; the other, oblong, teat-shaped, a kind of limp sausage dotted with mauve pimples. Xavier gazed at the kids. His silence was angling for he did not know himself what help, what unlikely explanation. He lowered his nose, from shame and regret, from fatigue too, and walked away without a word. No child followed him. The alley disappeared into another and Xavier continued to follow it. Stitches ran around the base of his neck; ditto at armpits, where there was no hair or anything. He met a donkey whose sick snout was oozing. The animal was alone and unable to move forward. Its left rear leg was wrapped in a grimy, decomposing bandage. Xavier took off his hat and placed it on the donkey's head, to protect it from the sun.

"Do you know where people come from? I've finally

figured it out. They come from the night. One night — she's sleeping — and some night enters a woman. And life is caught, like a fish in the sea. Myself, I've never been inside a woman's body. The pieces I'm made of, maybe. Because as it happens I'm a little community all on my own. Myself though, never. Never been inside my mother, who besides wasn't even my sister. As for my father. A father: I'd like someone to explain to me what that means. I mean, do you understand?"

The animal replied with the full wideness of its gentle eyes. The apprentice nodded, stroked the donkey's rump, then abandoned it too to its fate — life being only that, encounters, ruptures, he mused.

Xavier was approaching his destination. To do so he had to walk back towards the crowd. According to the official schedule, Marie Peak-Forde would soon appear in her limousine, and all faces were turned towards the pavement. A brass band marched by, with a sound like scrap metal and thuds from a drum that were hollow and stupid and narrow, as if they were trying to cram an idea into your head with a hammer, and the spectators loved it, clapping in unison, asking for more. No one was paying attention to Xavier, who went along hugging the walls, bearing the cross of existence. At the sight of him one woman covered her child's eyes. The apprentice kept moving. Bare-headed, the casket against his ribs, tits in the air. His hair was missing in patches, puddles of sand on a lawn.

A painted portrait of Marie Peak-Forde stood three storeys high. A throng had gathered beneath this effigy, exclaiming hurrahs and she-is-resurrecteds, while confetti flew, a sigh of feathers eructed by a wolf after dining on fowl. A boy who looked like a demolished had perched on a cornice to get an uninterrupted view of the parade, but who knows, his foot slipped, he collapsed ten metres down with the sound of something bursting. Other demolished came running. But the police made quick work of scattering these fine folk, pushing them back with barking dogs and long-range bludgeons. The corpse was evacuated from the premises on the double.

Xavier X. Mortanse finally came to the demolition site. Now it was merely a ravine. It was surrounded by heavy steel cables that were supposed to prevent extreme behaviour by the crowd. The apprentice slipped between the cables. The muffled rumbling of the crowd pushed heavily at his back. He skidded, tumbled, straightened up, fell again, then rolled. In that way he got to the bottom of the ravine. Sitting in the dust, he tried to regain his strength, what was left of it. He got back on his legs. Limped to the pyramids of sand and plaster, over there.

He knelt and then, with his fingers, his nails, he dug, till he'd made a deep enough hole. Inside the casket, furious kicking. Xavier set it down in the hole. Started to pile earth on top of it, the heaviest he could find.

"What exactly are you doing there?" asked Ariane.

"Putting an end to it," was his reply, without interrupting his toil.

The Philosopher was wandering through the crowd. He had escaped from the Clinic. Walking with head down, fists in pockets, even his hair grimy. Muttering to himself, bits and pieces. Without thinking he looked over towards the site, which reminded him of something. He spotted Xavier very clearly and recognized him as such. But as he'd been convinced that he was no longer right in the head, he thought, "The Sands of Shame sees things that don't exist." And so he went on wandering, not knowing what to do with his hands, a wreck, indifferent.

The apprentice, concentrating on his task, moved away to collect some compact earth.

"I am a little girl. My name is Ariane."

"I know who you are."

The sky, a vast, aggressive, triumphant blue, without a cloud, was burning, wide open. Its law ripened the moment, exhausted the trees, pushed every living being a little closer to its death.

"Basically, you have one admirable virtue," said Ariane. "Which is courage."

Xavier took the remark seriously. He stopped what he was doing, meditated. And finally said, "Courage? I'm afraid of everything, I've shed tears non-stop, I've never understood anything about how things are done. Courage, me?"

"You're the most courageous friend I've ever had."

"Farewell to you too," he replied, as he finished erecting the tumulus of sand.

And gazed upon it, very absorbed, as if anxious to make an important decision. With a kind of paroxysmal detachment, a frenzy of rejection, he also took off his pants, his undershorts, and tossed them onto Strapitchacoudou's grave. He stared with glum astonishment, as at a mystery that is weary of being mulled over, at the sutures that striped his skin at groin level, as well as at the big ball of flesh in the middle of his thigh, which over the last few weeks had doubled in volume and tripled in weight, had become hard as stone. On it, swollen, violet letters that read: *Flower of meat*.

In his crotch, where there was neither hair nor prick nor balls, a tiny faucet six centimetres long jutted out — one vertebra too many, perhaps — operated manually and daubed with red paint.

The apprentice dropped to his knees. Sweat, dust, plaster, all of these had settled on his eyelashes. Now there was nothing but a mist that streamed with light in front of his right eye.

"Look all the same," said Ariane. "It doesn't cost anything, and you can tell me what it is."

With the back of his hand, Xavier rubbed his eyelids. A tuft of dried dandelions, stems broken by the sun, bent, withering, towards the ground.

"Those are flowers," he said.

"Do you think they're thirsty? Maybe we could give them something to drink."

Xavier had trouble straightening up. With a glance he took in the expanse of the site. There was room for how many flowers inside, how many trees? Here, a stream could be added; there, houses for birds could be hung from the branches. On June nights people would come here in twos to look at the stars. "Peggy, Lazare!" he prayed. "Help me realize this Garden!"

"I'll go and find water," he said. "I'll ask the guys up there."

"Yes, and meanwhile I'll give them some shade," said the light, while Xavier moved away, dazed, sometimes falling, a camel in the desert whose eyes have been put out.

It was a struggle but he got to the escarpment of the ravine. Above him, the tumult of the crowd was growing. The great moment must be nigh. But surely someone would give him a little water. Now it was a question of climbing up there. Xavier gathered his last strength, made a run. Managed to go up a few metres, harshly gained. Then fell back heavily to the bottom of the slope. Dust flew around him. Stretched out on the ground, he coughed for an endless minute.

He got up. Stuck his feet back in the sand and plaster, and started his climb once again. With the help of his hands, his knees, his teeth, he pushed, pulled, held firm. He was very close now. He was beginning to catch sight of the public, who had their backs to him. He tried to crawl, to hoist himself for one last forward move: "Water! Water! . . ." But it was as if everything under him collapsed. He landed on his back, his stomach, banged his head on a stone, found himself in the middle of the escarpment, out of joint, in a heap, vomiting black liquid. And then, in a shower of garlands and confetti, greeted by a fierce clamour, Marie Peak-Forde's limousine came around the corner of the street. And with one last cramp in his heart, the apprentice gardener came to an end under an indifferent ovation.

Nagasaki, summer 1988
Longueuil and Sainte-Agathe-des-Monts,
March 2001–May 2002

Anansi offers complimentary reading guides that can be used with this novel and others.

Ideal for people who love talking about books as much as they love reading them, each reading guide contains in-depth questions about the book that you can use to stimulate interesting discussion at your reading group gathering.

Visit www.anansi.ca to download guides for the following titles:

Vaudeville!
Gaétan Soucy
978-0-88784-782-0
0-88784-782-x

The Immaculate Conception
Gaétan Soucy
978-0-88784-783-7
0-88784-783-8

Atonement
Gaétan Soucy
978-0-88784-780-6
0-88784-780-3

The Little Girl Who Was Too Fond of Matches
Gaétan Soucy
978-0-88784-781-3
0-88784-781-1

Gargoyles
Bill Gaston
978-0-88784-776-9
0-88784-776-5

The Law of Dreams
Peter Behrens
978-0-88784-774-5
0-88784-774-9

The Tracey Fragments
Maureen Medved
978-0-88784-768-4
0-88784-768-4

Returning to Earth
Jim Harrison
978-0-88784-786-8
0-88784-786-2

True North
Jim Harrison
978-0-88784-729-5
0-88784-729-3

Paradise
A. L. Kennedy
978-0-88784-738-7
0-88784-738-2

The Big Why
Michael Winter
978-0-88784-734-9
0-88784-734-x